THE CRANBORNE CHASE

THE CRANBORNE CHASE

A Novel

David Burnett

HAMISH HAMILTON
LONDON

First published in Great Britain 1981
by Hamish Hamilton Ltd
Garden House 57–59 Long Acre London WC2E 9JZ

British Library Cataloguing in Publication Data

Burnett, David, *b. 1946*
   The Cranborne chase.
   I. Title
   823'.9'1F   PR6052.U655/

ISBN 0–241–10418–1

Photoset, printed and bound
in Great Britain by
REDWOOD BURN LIMITED
Trowbridge & Esher

To my mother and father.

'For an outlawe this is the lawe, that men hym
take and binde.
Without pytee, hanged to bee, and waver with the wynde.'

The Ballad of the Nut Brown Maid

Part One

THE CHASE

CHAPTER ONE

The herds of deer that roam Cranborne Chase were already moving in search of grazing when dawn broke and the sun began its climb into a cloudless sky. Deep in the woods that border the open downland, sunlight spilled amongst the branches as the deer browsed and the rabbits left their warrens to crop the glades. A lone wolf rose from its lair and padded across a small clearing. Suddenly it sunk to its belly. The curtain of ivy that hid the entrance to an abandoned badger's set on the edge of the clearing had stirred, lifting slightly. The wolf sniffed the air. Catching scent, it loped silently into the shadows as behind it the curtain parted and a man's face, unwashed and sand-stained, appeared at the mouth of the set.

The man glanced round, cautiously quartering the surrounding coppice for signs of movement before tossing a longbow out of the set. He pulled himself clear of its entrance, climbed to his feet, shouldered the bow and hurried into the wood.

His left arm hung limp at his side. His bare legs were scratched and scarred and filth caked his uncured roe-skin jerkin. His hair, kept short by a knife blade, hung hacked and lop-sided round hollow cheeks and a fledgeling beard. After crossing a ride he paused to rest at the foot of a beech tree. He pressed his face to its trunk, tiredness and despair momentarily merging into self-pity. Once he had been a woodman, content cutting hazel for sheep hurdles and thatching spars. He sighed wearily as memory flooded back. Ten months had passed since the morning Prior Audley came to the cottage with soldiers and the king's warrant, but even now he could not forget the half-smile that had edged Audley's lips as he ordered his men to blind him in one eye and

3

sever one of father's hands for poaching his pigeons. Even now he could remember the heat of the iron, the panic that had made him reach for his bow. Even now he could hear his arrow slam into the wattle behind Audley's head as mother screamed 'Run!' and the soldiers drew their swords. And now, in the August of 1345, he was a fugitive and outlaw, worth no more than a wolf, someone to be hunted down by the Chase verderers and strung from the nearest tree.

He smiled grimly as he ran on towards the Salisbury track. There was no blood on his hands yet, but there soon would be. For once he was certain what had to be done. If Audley was dying, as Matilda thought, it was vital he prevent the physician from reaching him. How else could he strike back at the prior for turning him into a condemned criminal who skulked in a hole in the ground and snatched pence from peasants and tinkers? But it was foolish of Matilda to risk her own neck. There was a reward for his capture. What if she had been followed or it be proved to be a trap?

*   *   *

She had arrived last night at dusk, quietly calling his name as she slid between the trees. He had been sitting outside the set sharpening stakes for snares when he heard a twig snap under-foot. He quickly lifted his bow.

'Thomas?' A woman's voice.

The rustle in the undergrowth drew closer. Matilda entered the clearing, stumbling as she floundered through the deep bracken that hid the set. At eighteen she was a year younger than her brother; yet they shared an apparent frailty, the same sense of brittleness and fragility – long limbs, fine bones, eyes of the palest blue. Briars studded her waist-length hair and her cheeks were flushed after the five mile journey from Cranborne. She grinned and flung out her arms.

Thomas dropped his bow and ran into her embrace. Neither spoke, each of them determined to keep reality at bay a moment longer. A faint smell of wood smoke mingled with those of brine and damp rushes in her hair; the familiar scents of the home Thomas dare not return to. He breathed them in, thinking back to their last meeting – that May morning she had found him lying outside the set, his face bruised and swollen, his left arm twisted behind his back after it had been broken by another of the outlaws in hiding on the Chase with one blow of a quarterstaff. Since then it had been too weak to risk another ambush and he had spoken to no one. Questions bubbled up inside him as Matilda slumped into the bracken. She seemed tense and on edge and when she spoke it was in quick, short gasps.

'I met two o' the priory foresters. They thought I was courtin'. Then became suspicious. Bastards!' she added, remembering their laughter as one stroked her thighs with the butt of his whip.

'You should have turned for home,' said Thomas angrily. ''Tis too dangerous. Father needs you.'

'He needs us both.'

'But if Audley learns where you've been?'

Matilda's face lost its delicacy, becoming cold and hard and impassive. ''Tis only a matter of time 'afore he finds you. You know that, don't you?'

'Stop it!'

Matilda swallowed her anger. First soothe, then goad. Rising to her knees, she unwrapped a small linen bundle and said calmly: 'I've brought food, a boiling fowl, curds, a loaf, ale.'

Thomas tore a leg from the chicken and thrust it into his mouth. As she watched him eat, Matilda began to question his chances of survival. The last four months had sapped his will to live. His finger nails were torn to the quick, his gums were raw and the warm reek of decay hung on his breath. His nerves had worsened, for at every motion or sound, however slight, his eyes widened with panic: even here, outside his only refuge, the fear still lingered.

'Can you lift a bow again?' she asked finally.

Thomas nodded. 'I burnt the splint on the night of the quarter moon. The break's still weak, but I could hit a hind at eighty paces.' He glanced at his sister. 'Why?'

Matilda drew in her breath. 'Audley's dying.'

For a moment Thomas was too stunned to respond. He gazed up at the now reddening sky, seeing in its emptiness the sallow corpse of the prior.

'I think it's true,' she added.

The image shattered, turned from triumph to rage. 'You only think! For God's sake say what you mean or keep silent!'

5

'Listen to me, Thomas!' cried Matilda. 'Yesterday I was pluckin' fowl at the priory. Audley was lying in the refectory wrapped in quilts. He looked feverish, as pale as goose down. I overheard him order Brother Peter to take a letter to a Sarum physician called Buckle. 'Tis thought in the scullery that he's the wealthiest physician in Salisbury and is coming to Cranborne to bleed Audley. Don't you understand? The prior must be real poorly to call on such a man.'

'It means nothing. All monks are bled.'

'Listen! Brother Peter offered to draw up his charts. He refused, said the stars always lied to a man on his death-bed. Then he saw me and said, "Goose girl, go tell your mother that only devils dance on a dead man's grave." He must be dying. Why else would he say such a thing?'

'It don't make sense,' said Thomas slowly. 'Why can't Brother Gilbert cup him?'

'I don't know, nor does it matter,' snapped Matilda tersely. 'If Audley lives both you an' mother'll die; that's fact.' She paused, kneading a fist into the soft sand excavated by the badgers. 'He's doubled the reward for your capture.'

Thomas turned to her: she looked away. 'So now I'm worth twenty shillings.'

'Dead. Only half that alive.'

There was silence. Matilda glanced at her brother. One side of his face lay in shadow, sunlight played on the other. It was almost as if one half of him was already dead. His whole body started trembling, then seemed to collapse inward on itself.

'Audley'll only be content when you an' mother are cut from the gallows an' fed to carrion,' she said harshly.

'I know that.'

She sneered. 'An' what else do you know settin' snares an' suckin' eggs to fill your belly? Nothing! I'm the one who has to feed an' clothe the rest of the family, who has to dress father's wrist an' do your labour in the fields, who has to try an' keep the peace 'tween mother an' Audley . . .'

'No more!'

Matilda wrenched Thomas's hands from his ears. 'But there is more, an' you must hear it. Father's certain Audley intends having mother tried and burnt as a witch. Twice he's preached against her on Sabbath.'

6

Thomas shook his head in bewilderment. 'Oh God,' he whispered, 'why can't he leave us Woodwards alone?'

''Tis no use calling on Our Lord,' said Matilda contemptuously. 'I've seen him watching her in the market place, waiting for her to put the rope round her own neck. Prayer'll be no help when the soldiers come callin' for her.'

'But she means no harm.'

''Tis not what she means, 'tis what she does.' Matilda sighed. 'Jack the cowherd's been saying he saw a hedgehog suckling one of his cattle in their byre. He says it were chatterin' as it drank and that it sounded like Alice Woodward. Audley got to hear of it. Last Sabbath at Mass he accused her of being possessed by devils.'

'He's mad!'

'Or she is.' Matilda smiled. 'On midsummer morn she bartered two of the swine for a parchment covered with Latin words. It don't matter that she couldn't read 'em. The travelling hawker who sold it swore blind it had been scribed by a royal physician and that the words were charms to make the barren bear. Mother pulped an' boiled it, giving a sip of the potion to every wedded woman in the village. Some are now with child, mother amongst 'em. Old Mistress Morrow, who must be a hundred if she's a day an' whose Ned's been under turf since 'fore I was born, thinks she'll soon be in child-bed. 'Tis no use talkin' to mother. She won't listen. But if she keeps on like this Audley'll charge her with witchery.'

Again the silence. Matilda waited in the hope that Thomas would realize what was expected of him. Instead he sat staring into the gloom, distant and remote, as if deaf to what she had been saying.

'We're doomed, Matilda. All of us,' he said finally.

'God, you're worse than mother!' cried Matilda angrily. 'You'd as soon swing as see sense. The physician must be killed. You must do it. You've already been condemned to the gibbet for firing at Audley an' not even he can hang a man twice. But if he dies because the physician doesn't reach him, mother'll be safe and you'll have a chance to flee the Chase.'

Thomas buried his face in his hands as she added: 'You've no other choice. How long can you go on living in the greenwood like a cornered rat? A week, a month, another year?'

7

'I don't know any more.'

Matilda gripped his arm. 'Thomas, here in the forest it makes no odds who lives or dies. I came by chance in May. If I hadn't you'd have long been picked clean. That'll happen if you bide here much longer.' She paused. 'Will you do it?'

Thomas lifted his head and stared into the blue of her eyes. They were expressionless, bereft of pity. He felt his heart beat quicken and the sweat of fear on his face as the answer formed on his lips. Yet he could not say it.

'For God's sake, Thomas! It only needs one arrow. I'd kill him myself if I could.'

'I'll do it.'

Disgusted at her own harshness, the way she had goaded him into an acceptance of what had to be done, Matilda threw herself back into the bracken. There was nothing else to be said. She glanced up at the darkening sky. 'I must go.'

'Stay,' said Thomas quickly.

'For a moment, no longer.'

The two of them sat silently in the twilight; Thomas grim-faced and withdrawn, Matilda steeling herself for the return journey. It was she who broke the silence. 'Buckle will be coming tomorrow or the day after. When you've done it, go to Salisbury. I'll get word to you as soon as it's safe.'

'And if I fail?'

'You won't. You're the best archer in Cranborne.' Matilda bent forward to kiss him. 'I must go.' Their eyes met for an instant. Then she was gone, lifting the hem of her skirt as she vanished into the dusk.

Thomas did not move. For nearly a year this clearing had been his home. Here he had known hunger, boredom, loneliness. Of recent there had been days when he could not bring himself to crawl from the set, choosing instead to stay underground, curled up as if still in the womb, till day gave way to night. The thought of leaving frightened him. But first he must cold-bloodedly murder a man he had never met. He forced the physician from his mind. Matilda was right, it had to be done. Anything was better than having to endure another winter like the last; the clawing his way through the snow in the mornings for fear of being buried alive by the overnight drifts heaped round the set. For six weeks, dressed only in rags and animal skins, the bitterly cold wind searing his throat as he tramped the waist deep snow, he had lived on stray deer, hacking at their carcasses with his knife and then struggling to build a fire. Three times during those weeks he had been trapped by the wolf packs roaming the Chase, once remaining underground for two days with the corpse of one who had tracked him to the set sprawled across his legs whilst its companions snarled at the entrance. And then, in May, he had been attacked and left for dead by the felon who had broken his arm and taken the pittance he had stolen from the victims of his own ambushes. Again Matilda was right, that too would one day happen again.

*   *   *

Thomas shuddered slightly as he rose from the beech tree and hurried on through the woods. There was to be no next time. Just one arrow, two deaths – then flight. His fingers looped tight round the shaft of his bow as he approached the track linking Cranborne with Salisbury. High above him the sun shimmered in the haze of its own heat. He could feel its warmth on his back. When it next set he would have killed. He walked out on to the track and looked up at the trees that bordered it. In some places their sprawling branches towered overhead, almost bridging it, in others banks of briar and bramble smothered its route. After glancing along it in the direction from which the physician would approach, he forced his way through the undergrowth to an oak tree. Its limbs hung low over the ground. He hesitated, then swung upwards into the air. A moment later he was crawling along a broad spreading branch that overlooked the track. He unslung his bow, took a cluster of arrows from inside his jerkin and lay face downward, straddling the branch with his knees. And waited.

CHAPTER TWO

Few of the peasants flocking into Salisbury for market even noticed the figure standing in the doorway of a stone-built house just inside the Castle Street Gate. But those who did, and recognized him, cursed as they passed the gilded sign hanging above his head. Little love was lost between 'NATHANIEL BUCKLE, Apothecary & Doctor of Physik, Purveyor of Fresh Live Leeches to the Court of Tuscany' and those he had once, many years ago, sold worthless purges or a pair of well used worms. Then their curses gave way to smiles. Cupping blue blood and peddling eternal life to the wives of merchants and barons may have made him wealthy, but he still seemed as sour-faced and snappish as ever, standing there in a heavy fur-trimmed cloak in the bright August sunshine.

And today, strangely enough, it was the past that Buckle was contemplating. He stood in his doorway a moment longer, his mind dead to the waggons rumbling over the cobbles, the shouts of the tollmen at the Gate, the incessant clatter of hooves and clogs. After glancing at the letter clenched in his fist, he watched the tonsured head of the monk who had delivered it vanish behind a line of wool-laden pack horses. Then, as if waking from a trance, he turned and slammed the door behind him. He patted his face again. The silk was soft against his skin and the scent of rose-water and camphor helped calm his nerves: God knows, he thought, they needed it. Tearing the letter in two, he hurried into his parlour. It was quieter here, the thick stone walls kept the city at bay: and cooler. Pulling his cloak tighter round his chest, he crossed over to the unseasonal fire blazing in the hearth and delicately wiped a bead of sweat from his hooked nose. Why hadn't Audley paid up? What did that damn fool of a prior think he was playing at by requesting his presence in Cranborne? He, a physician, on what promised to be the hottest day of the year? Surely the man knew that with Jupiter in the ascent and the vapours humid it was vital he stay where he was if the humours were to remain in harmony, not go gallivanting round the countryside. Anyway, he had no intention of releasing Audley from their agreement. Old habits die hard, even after eighteen years. There was still pleasure in guessing which of the two sacks hid the purse. He chuckled, then cursed. Audley was cunning for a monk. His sending a letter instead of payment had a reason. It had to be a trick. But what was he planning, and why?

Like a predatory weasel stalking its prey, Buckle circled his parlour. Eighteen years ago he had dressed in rags, lived in a fly-blown hovel in the city slums and survived by adding colouring and hemlock to water. The discovery that an unknown Benedictine novice, like all monks sworn to chastity, had fathered a bastard had been accidental. It had also changed his life. After delivering the child he had returned home to find a gang of lepers occupying his room. One had attacked him with a cudgel. Instead of resisting, he had fled and vowed never to return. That night he had decided on blackmail. By dawn he had composed his first demand for payment, giving it and his last shilling to a pardoner travelling to Tewkesbury Abbey, where the monk then dwelt. And now? He glanced round at the black oak chest beneath the window, the surgical knives and saws on a table, the cloth of gold tapestry decorated with the four quarters of the moon hanging from the hammer-beamed ceiling, the burnished copper, the shelves of potions, powders and salves. Times had changed. Brother Roger was now Prior Audley of Cranborne, and he, Nathaniel Buckle, boasted the wealthiest apothecary's practice in Sarum.

He permitted himself a sly smile. Then reached a decision. He would send the boy in his place. That would remind Audley of the risk he had run in sending the monk empty-handed. Picking up a whip, he closed the parlour door behind him and walked along the passage that led into the garden at the rear of the house.

*   *   *

11

'Come here, Sampson!' The whip cracked.

The young man picking rue into a trug at the far end of the garden turned as his master came striding towards him. Eleven miniature knots, each a blend of four herbs trimmed into a sign of the zodiac, separated them. Jumping the claws of the twelfth, he ran back along a raked gravel path to where Buckle stood waiting.

The physician ignored him. His whip was raised above the white hair lapping his collar, and the silver stars and comets embroidered on his cloak sparkled in the sunlight. An instant later an arm snaked from beneath the cloak and snatched at Sampson's basket. 'What's this for, whelp? Weaning swine? I ordered you to weed, not act the oaf.' He flicked the thong of his whip round the back of his apprentice's legs. Sampson flinched, but remained silent.

'Speak up, boy! Devil got your tongue?'

'No, sir.'

'No, sir; yes, sir; three blind mice. Forgotten what happened to them eh? Take that scowl from your face or it'll be another night in the cellars!'

Sampson backed away. Even after five years of gathering the fungi that sprouted from their walls, the thought of the cellars still made him shudder. They were damp and dark, the air was chill and stale, and the grotesque, distended toadstools that spilled across the floor in search of light wrapped round his ankles whenever he entered. Buckle had traded on his horror by making a night in the cellars the remedy for all his transgressions, however minor. He would lead him by the ear to the top of the steps, cackling as he pushed him into the darkness. The bolts would slam behind him, and there he would remain till dawn, terrified and shivering, his only company the water dripping from the ceiling and the rats scurrying through the puddles.

'Yes, thought that'd cure your insolence,' growled the physician, running his whip through fleshless fingers. 'But for once you're spared. I've work for you. An' Lord help you if you ain't back before the cathedral bell tolls four 'afore midnight tomorrow. Want you to go to Cranborne and collect the herbs that self-righteous monk should 'a delivered this morning.'

Sampson disguised his excitement. In five years he had never once been allowed to leave the city. But where was Cranborne?

Although two sacks of herbs were sent from its prior twice a year, he knew only that it was a village on Cranborne Chase. He'd get there. What mattered now was showing indifference to the journey before Buckle realized his excitement and changed his mind.

'I don't know where it is,' he said sullenly.

'Find it!' snapped Buckle. 'Now stop dithering and get out of sight 'afore I take the whip to you.' The physician reversed it and thrust the stock under Sampson's chin. 'One thing, boy, tell Audley your name. Should amuse him. Too serious by half, monks. A surfeit of prayer may get a man to Heaven, but it makes 'em as dull as a pauper's grave when living.'

A sudden sense of misgiving filled Sampson. The physician's mood unnerved him. He had long ago learnt that every order given by his master had a purpose, usually nefarious, always self-serving. An hour ago, when Brother Peter arrived with a sealed letter from his prior instead of the usual consignment of herbs, Buckle had become hysterical, needing to be cupped of an ounce of blood lest rage inspire an excess of bile. What had caused the change? He was now smiling, his hooded eyes were closed and he seemed unaware of his apprentice's presence. Sampson's questions faded as he thought of the journey ahead. He edged back a step, then turned and ran quickly toward the house.

Buckle listened to his footsteps recede over the gravel, first opening one eye, then the other. Suddenly he began laughing, filling the garden with a shrill wheeze that continued to echo between its walls even after he had returned to the parlour.

Once inside again, he sprinkled some balm on the fire and sat down on his canopied bed. It was here that he took his pleasure with the wives and daughters of the city burghers. The stout, the skinny, the comely; all had known the touch of his bony fingers and dry unwrinkled skin. Still lost in thought, he glanced across at the reason for their eagerness to enter his sheets. A large brass retort was balanced on the unlit stove. One end of the copper spiral rising from its neck described a series of loops before falling towards the funnel shaped lip of a crucible. Beside it stood a press for pulping herbs, beside that a pestle and mortar. On a nearby table were a set of scales and a row of lidded pots containing the quicksilver, brimstone, dried Jew's ear and crushed gold that had made him rich.

13

He smiled at his reflection in the retort. Immortality, all wanted it: abbots, knights, merchants – and their wives. Even the queen had recently sent a page from Clarendon to purchase a flask of the elixir. He had given it to her, royal favours might one day be useful. But she was no different to the others; all would pay any price for the impossible. Oh yes, and he sold it to them as fast as he could distill and bottle it. Eternal youth! The panacea for all ills! Teeth lengthened, hair turned grey, the grave yawned – and he grew richer. Giving a short laugh which sounded as if it had been squeezed through the bellows beside the stove, the physician took two keys from beneath the bed mattress and shuffled over to a door let into the parlour wall, his pointed slippers soundless on the flagstones.

As he unlocked and entered his study, the cobwebs which hung from the ceiling, shrouding the entire room in their curtain, lifted slightly, revealing two vellum charts tacked to the wall. One depicted the human skeleton, the other the planetary influences on the circulation of the blood. Both had faded, curled at the corners. An astrolabe stood on a table, and beside it, deep in dust and dead flies, a bundle of uncut goose quills leant against a sealed jar containing a pickled hare's heart.

Buckle knelt and pulled a small iron-bound trunk from beneath the table. Glancing quickly behind him, he unlocked and opened the trunk, lifting out an abacus and a battered ledger. The heavy pages crackled as he turned them. Every now and then a finger would reach out and flick at the beads on the abacus. 'Eighteen years. Two payments in each. Could double it again,' he muttered, suddenly pushing the ledger aside and returning to the parlour. 'He's no choice. 'Tis pay or the gutter.'

The thought pleased him. He smiled, picked up a small bag, loosened the string, and emptied its contents into a tall glass jar standing on a plinth near the fire. The water inside it turned scarlet. 'Patience, my beauties,' he murmured as the fat leeches lying on the bottom, still torpid after bleeding a lawyer earlier in the day, began wriggling towards the surface. 'He'll be yours one day,' he added, watching their translucent bodies turn opaque as they sucked in the dried ox's blood. 'Two dozen of you fastened to an artery apiece and Roger, Prior Audley won't know what's happening till you've drained the first quart. By then it'll be too late. Much too late.'

Sampson ran happily through the city. After weaving his way through a group of women hurling rotten vegetables at a baker being hauled through the streets on a sledge for selling underweight loaves, he turned into the market place. Ahead of him a raised patchwork of canvas stretched away towards the line of pot-shops and ale-houses that bounded one side of the square. All was bustle and confusion. Barefoot peasants in coarse homespuns mingled with liveried servants, pedlars, beggars and city matrons wearing wimpels and robes of damask and velvet. Oxen lowed, geese hissed. Here a flock of sheep were being herded into pens: there a travelling juggler tossed his skittles into the flawless blue of the sky. Sampson peered through the dust. He could smell horse leather and roasting beef; hear a grey-robed friar preaching eternal damnation from the steps of the Poultry Cross; the costers calling their wares:

'Fresh 'errin' an' oysters! All native an' new from the brine!'
'Birch besoms!'
'White Lombard wine, to wash the red meat down!'

After vaulting a bewildered pig rooting through the filth from the fishmongers' shambles, Sampson dived into the shade beneath the awnings and began running between two lines of cloth stalls. He slowed to a walk as he entered the narrow alleyway leading into Smiths' Row. Here the waves of hot air coming from the forges washed round him and the rhythmic tap of hammers deadened all other noise. Once round the corner, he broke into a run again. Facing him, at the far end of a broad street, stood the tavern. Pausing for a moment, out of habit, to tilt the wooden arm of the ducking-stool and send it splashing down into the foul waters of the channel flowing the length of the street, he looked up at its steep gables, half-timbered façade, and the three tiers of mullioned windows with diamond shaped panes that his mother despaired of ever keeping clean. He was nearly home. Kicking aside the hens scratching through the sun-baked mud in the courtyard, he ducked through a low door and entered the kitchens.

In front of him was a long scrubbed table covered with half-rolled pastry, a piece of silverside, marrow bones, spices, salted

15

flounder, cheeses and a basket of cabbages. In a recess, a whole lamb dripped fat into a pan as it turned on the spit before an open fire. Beside it, behind a heat shield, a small nondescript terrier was treading the slats inside a revolving wooden wheel connected by cogs to the spit. The dog halted and began wagging its tail. The two maids standing at the far end of the table smiled a welcome. Briefly.

'Beatrix! Stop grinning! If I want a mule for a maid I'll ask Mervyn to bid for one at the market.' A moment later a stout middle-aged woman burst into the kitchens from the pantry with one fist wrapped round a rolling-pin. Suddenly she saw her son. 'God bless my soul! Buckle taken leave of his senses?'

Sampson smiled at the sound of that familiar high-pitched squeak. He walked round the table and kissed her brow. There was an angry glint in her grey eyes. Her plump cheeks, normally wrinkled like a windblown russet, were streaked with flour.

Ignoring her son, Widow Hooke turned towards the maids and pointed to the heap at her feet. 'Agnes! Get them blankets off the floor. Come on lass. Jump to it! Times I told you girls to be done with wash-day 'afore the river turns into a midden.'

'It weren't us, honest it weren't,' protested Beatrix.

Widow Hooke slammed the rolling-pin down on the table in disgust. 'Weren't us! Who in Hell was it?'

'The butchers' boys were scrubbing carcasses upstream,' muttered Beatrix.

''Tis true, ma'am,' added Agnes. 'An' the dyers were cleaning out their vats.'

''Tis a wonder you didn't bed 'em there an' then,' retorted Widow Hooke. 'Look at 'em, every blanket we own reeking of offal and stained watered-down Burgundy. Beatrix! Stop gawpin' at our Sampson and earn your keep 'fore I take the pin to you. Put the blankets in the tub, new straw on the beds and change the parlour rushes.'

Sampson smiled sheepishly as Beatrix scurried from the kitchens. Five years ago she had crept into his room at night, her long hair braided, dressed only in a chemise, and squeezed up beside him in his truckle bed. Her coal black eyes had glittered in the moonlight coming through the shutters and her warm, plump body had smelt sweet and musty. Without saying anything, she had placed his hands on the soft rise of her breasts. He

16

had blushed, uncertain what to do. She had grinned and lowered her chemise from her shoulders and rolled her weight over his. That summer they would meet in the attics and stables. And now, with only one year of his apprenticeship to serve, he was leaving the city for the first time since the two of them lay together in the long grass on Harnham Hill, heady on Gascon wine, so that afterwards, still trembling, they had tripped and stumbled as they ran past the flocks grazing its slopes.

Widow Hooke sensed her son's thoughts. 'I ain't deaf,' she said suddenly. 'Nights I heard 'er creepin' round the house like a cat on heat.'

Sampson reddened. 'I might have wedded her had I stayed.'

'And sired fools,' said Widow Hooke promptly.

Sampson sighed. There were times when he thought otherwise. The familiar daily round of tavern life seemed part of another world. For five years he had been subject to Buckle's whim: the thrashings, sudden trantrums, a working day that begun before dawn and only ended when his master locked him in his box garret at the top of the house.

He was fourteen when they first met. An impressionable open-faced boy with tousled fair hair, he had sat spellbound in the parlour as the physician told a group of pilgrims lodging in the tavern how to cure the ague with a drench of mandrake root and rubified water and explained the art of blood-letting when the moon was in Taurus. His appearance had reminded Sampson of his childhood hero, the legendary magician Merlin. And when he suggested to Widow Hooke that her son become his apprentice, Sampson had been overjoyed, experiencing a delight so unbridled his imagination transformed Buckle into a scholar and sage, the healer of the incurable, the most renowned physician in all England.

It had taken him a year to learn the truth. Buckle's reputation rested on a talent for charming his patients, long-winded but meaningless diagnoses that exaggerated their ills and his fee, and an elixir as fraudulent as its creator. As to his supplying leeches to the Tuscan court? That too was a lie, a means of gaining the patronage of the many Italian clerics in the service of the bishop. In short, Nathaniel Buckle was a quack.

Sampson glanced at his mother. There was no point in discussing Buckle with her. Although Widow Hooke had long ago decided that all physicians were charlatans it was she who had insisted that Sampson become his apprentice. Yet there was a coldness in her attitude towards his master that continued to puzzle him. It was as if, he occasionally thought, the physician had some hold over her. When the matter had first been discussed, she had refused to listen, saying that she intended Sampson to help manage the tavern. That night Sampson heard them arguing. In the morning her eyes were red-rimmed and her decision reversed. Sampson woke to find his bundle packed and the terms of his apprenticeship agreed, signed and sealed.

Hearing Beatrix and Agnes giggling into their aprons as a drunk pilgrim tottered in from the street, he put the mystery from his mind. He smiled, once it had been his task to guide home the lodgers who had drunk too much of the porter brewed by the sexton in the cathedral belfry. He rose to his feet.

'I must go. I came to borrow a horse. Buckle's ordered me to go to Cranborne Priory to fetch some herbs. If I'm not back by sunset tomorrow it'll be a thrashing for sure.'

'You'll live,' snorted Widow Hooke. 'I've taken a strap to you myself 'afore now. Hit that rump o' yours till it was black an' I blue. Oh be gone with you,' she added as Sampson began pacing the flagstones. 'You're worse than a pilgrim. All this toin' an' froin' ain't normal, an' that's a fact. No one can stay put these days. All got fleas in their boots as well as their beds.'

Sampson grinned at her. Once close, the years of separation had forced them apart. She would quickly change the subject whenever he mentioned Buckle's treatment of him, choosing to make light of his misfortunes by appearing more hard-hearted than she really was.

'And can I ask Mervyn for a mount?' he asked.

'Aye, that you can.' Widow Hooke turned towards the parlour. 'Beatrix! Our Sampson's bound for the Chase. He'll need custard pies, ale an' a capon.'

As the two women busied themselves preparing his provisions, Sampson slipped unnoticed into the courtyard. Snatching an apple from the tree overhanging the well, he walked across to the stables and bellowed: 'Mervyn!'

A moment later an old man with a grizzled leathery face emerged from the gloom. His one eye lit up in delight. Tossing aside a pitchfork, he playfully punched Sampson in the belly.

'Paid your respects to mother?' he asked, in the lilting accent of the Welsh Marches.

'Yes.'

'That's my boy. Come on then, I've something to show 'ee.'

Sampson followed him into the stables. Mervyn pointed to one wall. Hanging from a hook was a salmon. Its eyes were glazed, loose scales flecked its silver body and a few sea-lice still clung to its jaws. 'A fresh run thirty pounder if she's an ounce,' said Mervyn. 'I took her at dusk from Bishop's Pool.'

Sampson gave a sad sigh as he jealously touched the salmon. Four years ago Buckle had burnt his rods and promised him a whipping if he ever went fishing again. 'One more year,' he said wistfully, 'an' I'll be free of Buckle an' able to apply for an apothecary's license of my own.'

Mervyn chuckled as he threw a sack over the fish. 'In time to keep line runnin' through an old friend's fingers a little longer I hope.'

Sampson looked at the ostler, the replacement for the father he had never known. His blue eyes still twinkled, and his laugh still threatened to become the full-throated roar he had heard so often as a child. And his second eye? The clay still needed a scrub, and the crudely painted pupil still seemed to stare straight through him.

The two men moved further into the stables. They were dark and cool and the single beam of sunlight coming through the hole in the thatch was speckled with dust. Sampson glanced round. Up there, amidst the hay, was where he had sat and listened to Mervyn tell and retell the story of Bannockburn. And there, hanging from a beam, were the ostler's sword and the now rusty spearhead he had torn from his eye during the battle.

'An' there it'll stay till they measure my winding sheet,' he said, noticing Sampson's glance. 'How's friend Buckle?' he added.

Sampson grunted. 'Last night, whilst you were playing with that salmon, I was scrubbing out the leech cupboard. I dropped one of the jars.'

'Pity you didn't smash 'em all.'

'That would 'a made it worse. It was an accident, Buckle thought otherwise. He nearly locked me in the cupboard till natural breeding replaced those killed.'

'Pah! The man's a rogue,' growled Mervyn angrily. 'You still doin' book work an' studying the texts?'

Sampson nodded. A year ago he had found the key to Buckle's study. Since then he had spent hours poring over manuscripts and charts whenever his master was out.

'You keep a hold of that tongue o' yours,' went on Mervyn. ''Tis all very well you tellin' me that the sun don't rule a man's heart and the moon his right side an' belly. I don't understand such things. But I know enough to be sure that there ain't a quack livin' who'd agree with 'ee.'

'I believe in healing the sick, not helping them die by draining half their blood and blistering skin to exorcise demons.' Sampson paused. 'I've made up my mind to stop studying the stars and drawing up a man's charts before deciding what ails him.'

Mervyn smiled at Sampson's earnestness. 'Calm down, lad. You're too reckless for your own good,' he said gently. 'If you tell that to the guild when asking for a license you'll end up being examined for heresy.'

'Oh, I'll keep silent – for the moment. But I intend becoming a great physician an' that's all there is to it.' Seeing Mervyn's concern, he added: I'll be careful, I promise,' before changing the subject by asking the ostler to tell him how to get to Cranborne.

Mervyn frowned. Tugging thoughtfully at the stubble on his chin, he knelt and drew a rough map in the dust. ''Tis a four hour ride westward. Take the Exeter highway an' then bear south. The track's poor, for the Chase is a God forsaken place; all moor an' forest an' chalk cliffs as white as the Brecknock Shire snows. An' keep awake. 'Tis a haunt of the outlawed an' other riff-raff. Only last week a brace were taken an' hung in the market place.'

Sampson bowed his head. 'I know, Buckle bought their corpses from the hangman. They're in lead coffins in the cellars, rotting. He's mad!'

'And dangerous,' added the ostler, staring at Sampson. 'Why's he sent you?'

'To fetch some herbs.'

'You staying?'

'Overnight.'

'Leave at dawn an' keep to yourself. I don't trust him.'

20

'But why?'

Mervyn ignored the question. 'Enough of Buckle. The very thought of the man gives me the apoplexy.' He paused. 'Take a sword.'

'Something is troubling you, isn't it?' said Sampson quietly.

'Aye.'

'What? Tell me.'

'You'll be safe.'

'Mervyn! What is it?'

'Enough. Something happened, many years ago. I thought it forgotten an' it maybe I'm wrong.'

As if to evade further questioning, the ostler turned and started walking past the horses in the stalls, calling to each one by name and then scratching their muzzles as they came up to him. Halting, he nestled his head against the flank of a grey. There was silence; the only sounds the swish of tails and the munch of hay. He straightened, smiled and said: 'Woah, girl. You'd best take *Beauty* here. She's in need of country air an' a gallop.'

The mare nudged at Sampson's outstretched fist, then pricked up her ears and whinnied.

Mervyn laughed. 'I'd hand it over if you want to stay friends.'

Sampson did so. Her stained teeth crunched into the apple and she stamped her hooves in pleasure.

'An' what do you two think you're up to? Life ain't of a span to waste words on beasts that don't talk back!' Both men turned as Widow Hooke came hurrying into the stables. She stood there for a moment, panting and out of breath, then dropped a wicker basket at her son's feet. 'You be wary,' she continued, poking a finger at Sampson. 'There's wolves an' dragons an' Lord knows what up on the Chase.'

Sampson laughed at her fears and began saddling *Beauty*. But twice before climbing into the stirrups and turning towards the courtyard arch he noticed the worried look on Mervyn's face and thought of questioning him. Both times, afraid of adding to his mother's misgivings, he decided against it.

*   *   *

It was nearly noon before Sampson breasted the summit of Harnham Hill. Looking back over his shoulder he could see the

21

slate and thatch rooftops of the city shimmering in the heat; the Avon, like a silver ribbon, winding its way through the streets and out into the meadows below; the vast stone flank of the cathedral rising up towards the unplumbed indigo of the sky. Masons were moving amidst the wooden scaffolding that enclosed the central tower. Baskets of mortar and huge blocks of cut stone were being swayed up to the frail platform that marked the summit of the still uncompleted spire. Sometimes he dared not look at it for fear it might collapse, at others its magnificence overwhelmed him. The work had been going on since he was a child and he could not imagine it coming to a halt, being complete, not eternally soaring upward like a fine Spanish needle toward the God it was built to praise. He turned and urged *Beauty* into a trot. Ahead lay open moorland, its emptiness broken only by ragged clumps of thorn and windswept juniper. Above him, wings outstretched, a lone kite turned effortlessly in the still air.

At first he felt apprehensive. His initial excitement at the prospect of the journey had been dulled by Mervyn's mistrust of Buckle. Born and brought up in a city's din, he was unused to the immense silence that cloaked the countryside. Relieved when the moor turned to rough pasture and the road dipped down into a small hamlet, he passed a group of peasants leading home their oxen from the fields, forded a stream, and started climbing a long coombe that led on to the rolling chalk downland now opening up ahead. His nervousness gradually faded. Here was the peace he had been searching for. He kicked *Beauty* into a steady gallop. Her hooves pounded beneath him, the warm breeze ruffled his hair. Buckle, Mervyn, the mystery that surrounded his journey; all were forgotten as they raced along the summit of the downs with the world spread out beneath them.

He finally reined in when reaching the stone cross marking the divide in the road. A rutted grassy track led southward. Its verges, unlike those of the main highway, had not been cut back to deter ambush and footpads. Sampson turned on to the track. He was alone now, completely alone. Earlier he had passed a chapman, naked but for a leather apron tied round his waist, stumbling slowly towards Salisbury with a block of salt strapped to his back. For a while he had travelled alongside a scrivener – his tally, parchment rolls and pens a neat bundle on his mule's withers. He smiled as he remembered the scrivener's eagerness to reach habitation. Outlaws? Dragons? Both seemed fanciful, mere imaginings. The woods on the horizon drew closer. Lichen encrusted oaks rose round him, turning the sky into a canopy of green. Suddenly his doubts returned. He touched the sword at his waist and goaded *Beauty* into a canter.

CHAPTER THREE

Thomas Woodward lay motionless along the branch overlooking the track, the sole sign of tension a reflex – a torn finger nail rasping against his bowstring. The leaves overhead had provided scant shelter from the heat, and he could feel the sun's scorch on the nape of his neck. A woodpecker drummed for grubs. Beneath him a herd of roe moved listless and sluggish through the undergrowth, their heads hung low in the late afternoon heat. In the last hour he had begun to question what Matilda had told him. But it made no difference. He had no choice but to wait – if not for Buckle, for one of the few merchants and pilgrims who travelled the track. At noon a chapman had passed beneath the tree; his back bent, his bare feet stirring the dust in the ruts. Thomas had let him pass. What good was slab salt to a man without food?

He carelessly flicked at the flies swarming round his face. There was a flash of scarlet and black. He tensed, suddenly aware that the woodpecker's hammering had ceased. A moment later he heard hooves and the clatter of harness. He lifted himself to his knees and raised his bow. Notching an arrow into place, he angled it through a break in the leaves and drew back the string until it was level with his shoulder and the six foot longbow was bent into a crescent. Ignoring the dull throbbing in his arm, he waited. The noise grew louder. He peered along the track, then quickly ducked his head as he caught sight of a horse and rider cantering towards him. Certain it was the physician, he carefully took aim. Within minutes he would have killed. He brutally banished the thought. Composed now, all emotion stilled, he levelled the steel-tipped arrow-head at the physician's chest and waited for the range to shorten.

Some inner sense of danger must have caused the rider to look up when he did. Suddenly he kicked his feet from the stirrups. Thomas cursed and let go his bowstring. The arrow skimmed the hide bracer on his wrist and sped forward as the rider dived from the saddle. He cursed again, angrily reaching for a second arrow as the first thudded into the base of a tree on the far side of the track. An instant later the roe herd burst from the undergrowth and jumped the lane, the stags' freshly frayed antler points scattering the sunlight. The now riderless horse shied, then ambled into the shade and began tugging at a stand of hazel. There was silence: the distant bark of a fox. Thomas waited, breath held tight in his chest, his left eye unblinking as he stared along the arrowshaft to where the physician had fallen and vanished. Despair threatened his concentration. He crept along the branch, cursing yet again when he brushed his remaining arrows with the foot of his bow and sent them sliding over its rim. The brambles stirred. Glimpsing a moving russet surcoat, he loosed his last arrow towards it, then watched helpless as a figure broke cover and darted across the track. Tossing aside his bow, he threw himself from the tree. It was a full fifteen feet fall and his injured arm buckled at the elbow as he landed. He gritted his teeth at the pain, then rolled sideways as he caught sight of a young man armed with a sword advancing towards him.

A second later there was a flash of steel in Thomas's hand. He rose to the crouch. The stranger halted in mid-stride. Thomas lunged forward, his dagger scything air; then began circling, a cock in its pit, hoping to panic his opponent. The stranger gripped his sword hilt with both hands and lifted the blade parallel to his chest. Thomas pounced again. Steel met steel as the stranger parried his thrust. He could feel himself shaking. No physician would know how to counter his attack. The stranger was too young to be Buckle. Perhaps it was a trap, his opponent a decoy? Confused and anxious, he struggled to clear his brain.

'Where's Buckle?' he hissed.

The stranger lowered his sword arm. Thomas leapt forward again, his dagger leaving a long rip in his opponent's surcoat. The stranger backed away. The suddenness of the ambush had left him dazed, mention of his master's name now added to his bewilderment. 'Sarum,' he said finally.

As Sampson spoke he noticed the hesitation in the outlaw's eyes give way to panic. He took in his rags, scarred legs, pinched cheeks, the arm hanging loose at his side. His confidence grew. Surely Mervyn had taught him enough to outwit someone armed only with a knife? But it was five years since he and the ostler had last crossed swords in the tavern courtyard. And Buckle, what part did he play in this attack? He glanced at the arm again, measuring the distance between it and his sword. And began planning.

'You're alone, aren't you?' demanded Thomas.

Sampson paused before replying. 'No.' He smiled to himself as the outlaw's eyes swept the surrounding undergrowth. It had rooted, that first seed of doubt.

'Where are you bound?'

'Cranborne Priory.'

Thomas tightened his grip on his dagger. 'You know Audley?'

'No. I've been sent to collect . . .'

'He's evil, a devil in monk's habit,' shouted Thomas, suddenly hysterical.

Now! thought Sampson. He jerked his head, gazed over the outlaw's shoulders into the woods behind him and bellowed: 'He's here!'

As Thomas turned to face this new threat from his rear, Sampson jumped forward, slashing at the outlaw's injured arm with the flat of his sword. Thomas screamed, lost his balance and fell sideways to the ground. Within seconds Sampson was standing above him, sword poised to plunge downward into his chest.

Both breathing deeply, Thomas moaning at the pain in his arm, the two men stared at one another. The silence lengthened. Still baffled by all that had happened, Sampson placed a boot on the outlaw's chest. It was a reassuring gesture, one that proved his supremacy – if only to himself.

'Who are you?' he growled finally.

'Thomas Woodward.'

The name meant nothing. 'And how had you heard of Buckle?'

Thomas's body slackened. 'With Audley dead, mother an' I

would have been safe.' He was barely conscious of what he was saying. It no longer mattered. He had been tricked. And soon would be dead . . .

'Why ambush me?'

'Audley's ailing. The physician was to treat him. I thought you were he. 'T'was today he was expected.'

'An' you would have killed him?'

The outlaw nodded.

Sampson felt suddenly uneasy. Nothing Woodward had said made sense: and yet. . . ? And now what was he to do? The two dead men in Buckle's cellars had sacked a farmstead on the Plain, robbing then murdering its occupants. Woodward was also an outlaw. He too had tried to kill. By rights he should share their fate.

Thomas sensed his thoughts. 'Why not be done with it?' he whispered.

Sampson lowered his sword and let its weight rest on the outlaw's throat. His hands began trembling. He could hear Woodward's breathing begin to quicken, smell its stench. He pressed downward on the hilt, pinking the skin.

'If I bind an' take you to Cranborne, what'll happen?' he said softly.

'I'll be hung.'

'Why?'

Thomas looked up at him, bitterness in his gaze. 'For seven years Audley's pigeons had been growing plump on our corn. I shot some, strung 'em across a crop of millet to protect it. For that I was to lose an eye an' father a hand. Last harvest I drew the bow at Audley. I missed. For that 'tis the gibbet.'

'And you've been living in the woods since then?'

Thomas smiled palely. 'You call being hunted like a wolf, livin'?'

Sampson stared down into empty expressionless eyes, the eyes of someone who had tried to kill him. An eye for an eye . . . Yet still he hesitated: not certain whether he owed the first stirrings of sympathy to a shared suffering that somehow linked them together, Buckle's whip, Audley's lack of mercy, or a conviction that the broken figure lying prone beneath him was already doomed. Or was it weakness, a shirking from duty? Suddenly he knew he could not kill him. He lifted and sheathed his sword and walked out on to the track, returning leading *Beauty* by the reins. Opening the basket slung over her saddle, he tipped the capon and pies on to the grass and said: 'Take them.'

Thomas gazed upwards; at timber and foliage that hung over him like a shroud. 'You've spared me. Why?' he whispered.

'I haven't. Or did you not mean what you said? Their eyes locked for an instant. Sampson smiled, and as he mounted *Beauty* and turned toward the track he glanced up at the oak in which Thomas had hidden, seeing again the sunlight on steel that had made him dive from the saddle. 'I'm returning to Salisbury at daybreak. We may meet then. Splint and bandage that arm, otherwise your aim 'll be no truer when next you draw a bow.' He grinned. 'One last word. I'm Buckle's apprentice, but I'd not have shed a tear if you'd killed him; 'tis no more than he deserves.' He kicked *Beauty* into a trot. When Thomas next looked up, he was gone.

*   *   *

Thomas gazed up at the sky. Stars patterned the darkness with small splinters of light. It was colder now, time to crawl into the set and wrap himself in skins. The half-moon had risen, and the ground mist hugging the bracken seemed almost aglow with its light. He could hear an owl beating its wings against the ivy behind him in hope of disturbing a mouse, a sounder of boar grunting as they trampled through the undergrowth. He closed his eyes. What would happen to him now? Must he begin all over again, scavenging pence as boar do roots? He flinched as he tried to straighten his arm. Even if he cut a new splint it would be a month before it was mended. He would remain hunted, Audley would live: life would go on as before. And what would become of mother? He sighed, too weary to invent a future. That was her task. And yet how long it now seemed since the night of the storm and the first proof of her powers. He was ten then, the third of seven children but the first to survive infancy, a lonely solitary child condemned by the constant blink in his right eye and the twitch in his feet to be despised by his own family and regarded as a simpleton by the rest of the village. That too belonged to the past. Yet he still had not forgotten the morning his mother began feeding him raw caterpillars and snails in the hope that their placid, unruffled behaviour might drive out the demons she thought were tormenting him. The results had exceeded her expectations. Thomas grew sluggish and leaden, his eyes glazed. Even now he could recall the bitter taste of his diet and night merging with day as he lay apathetic and languid on the rushes by the fire. His last memory, before delirium began and stomach convulsions started lifting his entire body from the ground, was of gazing up at his father's thick red beard and hearing him mutter: 'T'aint't right, Alice. You mark my words. Them worms'll be eatin' him, not he them, 'afore long,' and his mother replying. 'Demons ain't mortal, same as you or I. They got to be cast out, taught that our Thomas ain't their natural home.'

Only afterwards did he learn that his mother, thinking his spasms to be a form of levitation and proof that God was now her ally in the struggle for his soul, had one evening invited her neighbours to witness the departure of the demons. It was Matilda who later told him that during the night Lydia Shears, the village wise-woman, had touched his forehead and announced that she could sense the presence of death and was not staying to keep it company.

After her departure an electrical storm broke over Cranborne. Lightning forked the sky: thunder caused the very ground to tremble. The villagers barred their doors, awaiting dawn or doom. A panic-stricken ox uprooted its tether and ran amuck. The priory dovecote was struck by lightning. Shortly after midnight the new prior, Roger Audley, interrupted Lauds and ordered the monks to sprinkle holy water round the priory and ring its bell in an attempt to drive away the storm. Next day two novices scaled its walls; the moss that clung to the outer stonework had been scorched and the cross on the summit fused into a single ingot of molten bronze. As for Lydia Shears, she was found dead in bed with her once green eyes colourless and wide open.

Afterwards Thomas discovered that at the height of the storm his father had pushed his mother to one side, removed the wedge she had placed in his mouth to aid the demons escape, wrapped him in a blanket, and fed him bread dipped in warm milk. By dawn his fever had subsided. Within a week he could walk. After two the cramp had left his belly. As for Alice, the combination of so much that was both miraculous and inexplicable laid the foundations for her career as village wise-woman and the years of conflict with Prior Audley.

But it was Hereward who finally cured Thomas of his blink and twitch. Even now, nine years later, every detail of that morning his father first took him to the butts was still vivid. They stood at the far end of a meadow on the outskirts of the village. They were made of earth, straw roundels lay embedded in their centres, and from fifty paces the six red bull's-eyes seemed small and indistinct. All that day the two of them stood side by side: one a teacher, the other so enthralled by the arrow's flight that his nervousness fled. By noon the itch in Thomas's feet and the tic in his eye had both departed. Hereward had smiled at the success of his plan: his time had not been wasted. Mastery of the longbow was dependent on concentration, poise and a steady eye. By late afternoon Thomas's shoulders ached with fatigue and his arms felt wooden and heavy. But the pain did not matter; his last two bolts had reached the target.

In the days that followed he had become obsessed by the faded red circle that marked its centre. Every morning at dawn, and again in the evenings when the day's work was done and he could exchange bill-hook for bow, he ran across the fields and loosed arrow after arrow at the target. A month after first lifting a bow two successive arrows struck its straw heart. He left them where they were and hurried homeward.

His mother scoffed when he told her what he had done. 'Aye,' she said, 'an' t'will bring nothing but trouble. No archer in this family has ever died an old man.'

Hereward smiled. 'Pay no attention to her prattle, ain't nothin' goin' to happen to 'ee.'

'That's what you all say,' cried his wife. 'But it doan' stop half of 'ee fallin' in battle an' t'other half finishing your days at the end of a rope.'

'Ain't no Woodwards amongst 'em,' replied Hereward, grinning at his son. 'Us buggers is too sly for 'em.'

Alice snorted. 'Your day'll come.'

She was right. It came eight years later on the day Thomas lifted his bow at Prior Audley. And now? The owl began screeching, waking Thomas from his memories. He turned, smoothing his prints with a handful of bracken as he eased his way, feet first, down into the set. He pulled the skins up over his shoulders and lay his head against the sand. For a moment the faces of the apprentice, prior and his family revolved like a kaleidoscope in front of his eyes: then came emptiness and sleep's abyss.

CHAPTER FOUR

'That's Cranborne for you. Right now you're lookin' at as God forsaken a vill as any in Albion.' The potter steadied his oxen and walked back to his cart, returning with the earthenware pitcher he had been drinking from when he and Sampson first met. 'No one not in his dotage could live here an' stay sober.' He lifted the pitcher to his lips. 'I can't even look at the place without coming on thirsty.'

'Who owns the village?' asked Sampson.

The potter grunted. 'The manor's held by Lady de Burgh, but she ain't ever here. Don't blame 'er. Land's leased to the priory. None can wed or leave without his worship's consent. When any of 'em drop he buries 'em so fast you'd think they'd the pox, then he helps himself to their best ox and doubles the tithe.'

'And the're all serfs?'

'Serfs, sir! The're lice-ridden, unwashed, half-starved, penniless chattels. Throw 'em a clipped farthin' an' they'd fight like toms over it. Aye, they're serfs alright; every man Jack o' 'em but the miller and reeve.'

Sampson smiled as the potter spat a stream of ale into the hedge and guided his oxen round another of the potholes in the lane leading down to the village. A barrel-like, florid faced man who only stopped talking to drink, Sampson had met up with him when the track through the woods merged with a drove road. He had kept silent about his encounter with the outlaw, and although the past hour had given him time to reflect on the ambush and its outcome he was still as bewildered as ever by what had happened. He ruffled *Beauty*'s mane and looked down into the valley.

'That's it,' muttered the potter. 'One mill, some thatched hovels I wouldn't kennel a hound in, a manor house and the Chase court, a market place, two dozen sanctimonious monks and their priory.'

Sampson followed the sweep of his hand. Far below a line of cottages straggled along both banks of the narrow river that wound through the valley. On the far bank stood an open square, beyond it he could see the priory church and a cluster of buildings. At either end of the village lay open fields, their ridge and furrow strips patterning the valley floor with lines of shadow. To the south of the priory orchards and the manor house the ground sloped upward, pasture and coppice gradually receding into open downland that stretched away to the far horizon.

'The prior, have you met him?' asked Sampson finally, his mind on the meeting ahead.

'Only once, when his damned cellarer made me recite ten score *Glorias* as penance for selling him a cracked gallipot.' The potter took another swig from the pitcher, spilling ale down his beard and bare chest. He belched. 'Every time I set foot in the place I swear I'll never return. Half a dozen stalls, Mistress Woodward and her sorcery and four score peasants with purses as empty as their bellies don't make a market. 'Tis more like a miser's wake. Be lucky if I part with an egg-crock.'

Still abusing his potential customers, the potter goaded his oxen forward and began the descent into the valley. The hill suddenly steepened. Their yokes rose up over their heads as the weight of the cart and its load bore down on the shaft. One of the team stumbled, its splayed outer horn gouging a furrow in the track. 'Woah now! Steady!' bellowed the potter, slowing their pace by deftly looping hobbles round their front legs. As the cart jolted downhill, its wheels bounced in and out of the ruts and its wattle sides creaked and bellied as the straw-packed pottery shifted position.

Sampson followed on *Beauty*. When the track levelled out the hobbles were removed and more ale uncorked. They went on; passing a flock of geese grazing a field of stubble before skirting the mill-leat and crossing the stone bridge that led into the village.

The potter turned to Sampson. 'Well, lad. We're here.

Priory's up yonder. Still sure that mother o' yours don't need a gross of best chamber-pots for them pilgrims?'

Sampson grinned. 'Quite sure.'

The potter nodded gravely. 'Aye, they're all too busy pacing the pilgrim-ways an' swopping holy relics to have time to piss a pint 'a porter,' he muttered, before climbing aboard his cart and whipping his oxen into a lumbering walk. 'Will the potter is 'ere again!' he bellowed. 'Old pots mended, new pots sold! Crocks, pitchers, pipkins, noggins, gallipots, basins an' bowls! Best Do'sset clay, glazed and baked for three days an' nights in a pit of oak!'

Sampson watched him head towards the market place before dismounting. After taking *Beauty* down to the river to drink, he led her past the cottages that bordered the lane. Outside the first an old woman, her beard tied into a bun on her chin and dressed only in a torn shift, was puddling earth and water into mud and smearing it on the wattle and daub walls of her home. A pig lay sprawled in the entrance to the next whilst a hen pecked the fleas from its belly. Smoke seeped through the roof of the third, and outside it a group of children were packing raw wool into sacks. Sampson glanced back along the line of hovels; not one had either windows or a chimney. The children looked up at him, wide-eyed, their thin faces streaked with dirt. Sampson smiled at them. 'Got business 'ere 'ave 'ee?' said a voice. A moment later a woman with a baby at her breast and a face scarred by disease appeared through the smoke billowing out of the doorway and pushed the children back into the gloom. Sampson turned away: no medicine yet invented could cure suspicion and hunger. Suddenly, for the first time, he began to realize the hardship and poverty of the world in which he now found himself; the world from which Woodward had fled. Feeling glad that he had not brought him back to be hung, he entered the market place and looked round.

The villagers were still returning from the fields; the men carrying hoes and mattocks and the women clutching small baskets filled with gleanings from the stubble. There were dogs everywhere, most of them mastiffs whose front paws had been lamed with mallet and chisel to prevent them chasing game. A group of urchins were throwing sticks at a cockerel tied by one leg to a post whilst their elders wandered amongst the stalls. Few were buying anything, and seeing on their faces the mixture of resentment and apathy that belongs to those too poor to buy anything not vital to their survival, he began to grow angry. Twice now he had encountered the results of Prior Audley's dominion, and yet the prior was still a stranger to him. The thought tempered his anger with apprehension, and to appease it he turned towards the centre of the square. It was then he saw the stocks. They stood surrounded by hurdle pens empty but for a handful of cattle, sheep and swine. A tall bearded man was sitting inside them. His chest was bare, sinew and muscle knotted his shoulders, and he all but dwarfed the wooden slats locking his arms and legs.

Glimpsing Will unloading his wares, Sampson went over to him and asked him who the man was.

'Hereward Woodward,' grunted the potter. 'Poor fool. His missus is a witch, he's an outlaw for a son, and the only wench in Cranborne worth courtin' for a daughter.'

Sampson frowned and looked at him more closely; then he turned away in disgust. Poking through one of the armholes in the stocks was the swollen stump of a wrist. 'What's he done?' he asked finally.

'Nothing. 'Tis one of Audley's little jokes. He gets slapped in there every market day at dawn and freed at dusk. It'll keep happening till that son of his is at the end of a noose.' The potter paused and indicated the small crowd gathered under an elm tree in the far corner of the market place. 'That's his missus over there. You say you're apprenticed to a physician, well five minutes listening to her an' you'll know why half Cranborne's fit for the grave. Dress her up how you like, the woman's a witch.'

Sampson wandered towards the tree. As he approached he heard a shrill voice shout: 'Live slugs for warts, wormwood for the shingles, a paste of Black bryony for chilblains an' the gout, a sprig of St John's wort to keep the littl'uns safe from tempests an' storms, me very own spittle to . . .'

'What about my *Jericho* then, Alice?' cried one of the women in the crowd, interrupting the speaker in mid-sentence.

'Fetch her to me now,' shouted the voice impatiently, 'an' 'tis a fact she'll be milkin' by mornin'.'

Surprised by the sincerity in the voice, Sampson remounted *Beauty* and looked down over the crowd at the woman sitting

35

behind a trestle table under the elm. He smiled to himself: she was short and shrewish, and her bright eyes and leathery bewhiskered face reminded him of the mice he had once hunted in the tavern stables.

'Where was I?' The two eyes sparkled and flashed.

'Your own spittle,' snapped an old gaffer standing near the front of the crowd.

'Don't you scorn!' she screeched, angrily waggling a calloused finger. 'I've cured more mules of colic with a drop o' spit than you've had swine in farrow.' She paused before continuing. 'I've frogs for the throat, dowsing hazels, ewe bones for cramp, runes and spells, plaintain for the flying venom, and a new found charm to give widows an' babes protection against gremlins.'

As Alice finished the crowd parted and a woman led a brindled heifer with a swollen udder that almost trailed in the dust up to the table. 'My *Jericho*,' she glowered.

Alice knelt beside it: the crowd fell silent. Closing her eyes, she slowly passed her hands over its udder and murmured: 'This beast has udder-ill, take it Lord if it be your will.' After placing her lips to each of its teats, she turned to the woman. 'If it ain't milkin' by morning you'll be wanting a tallow to keep the spirits from the byre.' The woman glared at Alice, mumbled something under her breath, and pushed a coin across the table. Alice bit it suspiciously, then dropped it down the front of her dress.

Sampson watched spellbound. He had never seen a village wise-woman practising her trade before, nor had he heard a voice speak with such passion and certainty. Her eyes were too open for cunning, and when she spoke it was without the flattery employed by every other physician he had met when dealing with their patients. Still thinking of her, he turned away as the crowd gathered round to watch her smoke out the worms thought to be causing a girl toothache, and headed *Beauty* up the lane leading to the priory.

Glancing casually over his shoulder, he suddenly noticed a young woman squeeze between the pens in the centre of the square and walk towards the stocks with a basin of water. He pulled *Beauty* up as she brushed the hair from her face and lifted the basin to the prisoner's lips. Suddenly he realized that the woman must be Woodward's daughter. Dipping the hem of her dress in the water, she began wiping her father's brow. Her

36

movements were gentle and graceful. Her face and arms had been tanned by the summer sun; chaff tossed out whilst winnowing corn spangled her hair. Her dress was sodden with sweat and its cloth clung to her waist and thighs, cupping her breasts and moulding the long shape of her legs. She suddenly looked up. Her eyes found Sampson's, cutting through them like a knife. For an instant he thought of returning to the market place and telling her that he had met her brother and spared him his life. But there was no warmth in her gaze, only indifference and contempt, and instead he turned in the saddle and kicked *Beauty* into a trot.

Ahead the lane divided, one fork leading towards the north door of the church, the other into a cobbled courtyard. He guided *Beauty* into the yard, forcing himself to forget the woman. In front of him was a long stone building that stretched the length of the yard; its only windows were narrow slits high up in the wall. Beside it the church tower and nave rose into the evening sky, casting their shadows over the stables, cowstalls and neat hayricks that lined a second side of the yard.

The difference between the village and priory struck him at once. Instead of being tumbledown and squalid, the buildings clustered round the yard were sturdily built and their walls had been white-washed with lime. In the centre of the yard two scullion lads were netting carp from the fish-still. Laughing, their leather buckets brimming with fish, they ran across the cobbles to a round stone outhouse, obviously the kitchens, abutting the cloisters. Next to the kitchens and scullery was a bakehouse, beside which and all but hidden behind a stack of barrels, was the priory brewery and a timber clad granary perched on staddle stones which ran back towards a poultry yard crammed with geese and capons. The granary doors were open, and outside it a group of novices chanted canticles as they unloaded sacks of corn from a waggon.

Seeing a stranger, the monk keeping count by cutting notches in a wooden hand tally gave it to one of the novices and headed towards Sampson. He smiled and said: 'Laudate Christum,' making the sign of the cross as he spoke.

Sampson dismounted and knelt. The monk took a small wooden crucifix from inside his habit and placed it to Sampson's lips. After repeating the Blessing, he lifted him to his feet.

'Welcome to the House of the Lord,' he said. 'This is Cranborne Priory, of the Order of the Blessed Saint Benedict. How can we help you?'

'My name is Sampson Hooke. I've been sent here by Master Buckle, physician and apothecary of the free city of Salisbury, to wait on his worship the prior.'

'And he's expecting you?'

Sampson nodded. 'Good,' said the monk. 'Come. I will see that your horse is fed and stabled.' He turned, walked under an archway dividing the two halves of the cloister wall, and knocked at a heavy iron-studded door. When it opened he spoke a few words to the doorkeeper, another monk wearing the black robes of the Benedictines, and returned to his work. The second monk beckoned Sampson inside. The door slammed behind him, its echo a reverberant counterpoint to his own quickening heart beat. Nervous and tense, fearful that Prior Audley might have learnt of his encounter with the outlaw, he looked up. In front of him, half in sunlight, half in shadow, lay an open expanse of clipped grass enclosed on all sides by the cloisters. To left and right ran a covered flagstone walk, its emptiness broken by a raised stone water-trough and the shadows traced by the buttresses and delicate stone arches that fronted the cloisters. Apart from the distant murmur of a monk repeating the Rosary and the drip of water into the trough there was complete silence.

'Wait here,' said the doorkeeper in a guttural Norman accent. 'His worship is engaged in business with a pedlar.'

As Sampson watched him walk towards the well in the centre of the cloister garth, he noticed two men standing amidst a pile of cages. One was wearing a serge jerkin and cross-gartered leggings, the other a scarlet edged cassock and a fur lined cowl that fell across one shoulder. He was a tall, dark-skinned man with a lean face and eyes placed close together above a straight, almost Roman nose. Aware that he was in Audley's presence, Sampson lowered his gaze as the pedlar lifted a pair of pure white pigeons from one of the cages. Audley took them, smiled, and tossed them into the air. They circled for a moment, then rose above the cloisters, quickly becoming white specks against the blue of the sky. First one, then the other, collapsed its wings. They fanned their tail feathers and began falling, tumbling and turning as they plunged through the air. Suddenly, when it seemed that both must strike the ground, they opened their wings. An instant later, amidst a flurry of feathers, they landed on the rim of the well and began cooing.

'Bravo!' cried Audley. 'I'll give you a groat for the pair and not a farthing more.'

The pedlar opened his mouth to protest, but seeing the waiting monk Audley waved him into silence. The monk bowed slightly and indicated Sampson. Audley glanced towards him and nodded his head.

'His worship will see you,' said the monk after returning to the cloisters.

As Sampson walked out on to the grass he felt his heart start thumping against his chest.

The narrow eyes fixed on his, then shifted to the pair of tumbling pigeon. 'He shall defend thee under his wings, and thou shalt be safe under his feathers,' said Audley slowly, in a soft languid voice that never rose above a whisper. 'The ninety-first Psalm of David, the work of an unknown scribe with a gift for verse; but wasted on this idiot, and on you too I've no doubt.' He paused, mockery curling one lip, then added suddenly: 'Where's Buckle?'

'In Salisbury, your worship. I'm his apprentice.'

The pedlar coughed. 'The ring doves an' homing pigeons, your worship,' he said hesitantly.

'I've seen enough,' said Audley curtly, not taking his eyes off Sampson. 'Brother Robert will give you your groat. Return in a month.'

'But they cost more 'an that to rear an' train . . .'

'Your error, not mine.'

'But . . .'

The prior turned to the pedlar, suddenly angry. 'Are you deaf, man? Or merely venal? Do as I say and be gone.'

The pedlar gave a last despairing look at his birds and began loading the cages on to a hand-cart. Audley waited for him to go in silence. And as that silence lengthened Sampson felt that he was employing it to solve a riddle brought into being by his own arrival. The sound of the cart grew fainter.

'So,' said Audley finally. 'Buckle refused to hazard the journey. Tell me, master apprentice, was the way clear?'

'Someone loosed his bow at me. Luckily he missed. I rode on.'

'The Lord is not always so merciful.' The prior's eyes were as green as the pieces of Turkestan jade sold in Sarum by a Venetian merchant. They wavered, then held Sampson's in a steady inscrutable stare that seemed to bore right through him. The hammering in his chest quickened. For a second he felt certain he was about to be accused of deceit, then Audley turned away and began pacing the grass, his robes swaying from side to side as he moved through the shadows now lapping the garth. One of the pigeons fluttered onto his shoulder. He reached up and began smoothing the down on its breast. Suddenly he spoke.

'What's your name, boy?'

'Sampson Hooke, your worship.'

He halted in mid-stride, knocked the bird from its perch and raised his head. Sampson backed away, suddenly frightened. The blood had left Audley's face, dulling it to a pale ashen colour, and his eyes, though open, seemed shuttered and blind. When he finally spoke his voice was almost inaudible.

'You are Sampson?'

'Yes, your worship.'

'And Nathaniel Buckle is your master?'

Sampson nodded. Audley began trembling. 'Go,' he whispered. 'We'll meet in the morning.'

Sampson did so in bewilderment, not daring to look back until he had reached the cloisters. He turned. The prior was kneeling. His whole body was shaking and he had buried his face in his hands.

*　　*　　*

'Pater de colis deus, miserere nobis.'

'Fili redemptor mundi deus, miserere nobis.'

'Spiritus sanctus deus, miserere nobis,' chanted the monks on both sides of the choir, their now combined voices echoing back out of the darkness as they begged God's mercy. An instant later one of the novices, his unbroken voice rising out of the muttered Amen that followed the responses, sung the first verse of the psalm. The monks repeated it, then continued on, filling the priory church with a sustained wave of plain-song that lifted and fell as verse succeeded verse.

Sampson peered into the gloom. Through the ribbed tracery

in the carved wooden screen that divided the chancel and nave he could just make out the faces of the few villagers attending Compline. To his left, beyond the two lines of monks facing each other across the choir aisle, stood the High Altar; bare but for an alabaster figure of the Virgin Mary and a silver cross, its cloth-of-gold hangings mirrored the light from the single candles placed at the sanctuary entrance. There was no other light in the church. It was damp and cold, and Sampson rubbed the backs of his hands as a bat flitted through the darkness.

As the psalm ended a voice said 'Cremus'. The monks knelt, their tonsured heads almost touching the flagstones that fronted their stalls. Led by the officiating priest they began reciting the Paternoster. Sampson joined in and, as always, the familiar Latin taught to him by his mother when still a child, calmed and steadied him. For the first time since reaching the priory he felt his spirits beginning to rise: that strange meeting with Audley had been followed by a bowl of fish broth in the refectory – hastily swallowed when the Compline bell begun ringing – and there had been no time to ponder the day's events. He glanced across the choir aisle at the high, canopied stall of the prior; and froze. Audley was staring at him. He closed his eyes and mouthed the final words of the Lord's Prayer. But the spell had been broken. He shivered slightly. Question piled on question. Why had Buckle sent him here? Why had the prior so nearly fainted when he told him his name? And how had an outlaw, alone in the woods, known that Audley was expecting a visit from his master? Gradually he sensed that he too was part of the mystery, and that the answers to his questions would not be an end, merely a beginning. The thought unnerved him, and to take his mind off it he began examining the carving on the nearest panel of the chancel screen. He turned away in a daze. It depicted a naked man being swept headlong towards the lip of a whirlpool.

'Dominus vobiscum.'

'Amen.'

'In pace, in manus tuas domine.' Sampson struggled to allay his fears as the monks, the Litany and Creed now over, turned to face the altar whilst their prior commended their souls to the Lord's care. They knelt and repeated the Blessing. One rose and began circling the sanctuary, swinging a censer as he went. The smell of incense mingled with that of candle smoke as the remaining monks left their stalls and crossed in front of the High Altar, genuflecting to the cross before slowly filing out through the small door that led into the cloisters.

Sampson followed. It was now dark outside, the only light came from the risen half-moon and a rush taper placed above the water-trough. Each of the monks washed his face and hands and climbed the narrow staircase leading to the dormitory. Audley had vanished. After washing, Sampson followed the monks up the stairs into a long vaulted room that stretched the length of the cloisters. A line of straw pallets ran down both sides; in the centre, lit by a single tallow, was a small wooden carving of Saint Benedict. Some of the monks were kneeling in prayer, others removing their gowns or climbing under rough, horse-hair blankets. One led Sampson into a small alcove adjoining the dormitory and indicated a mattress and quilt.

'Thank you, father.'

The monk smiled slightly, his vows preventing him from replying.

Sampson looked at him. His cheeks were pale and sunken, his eyes exhausted by the eternal round of prayer that marked the passing of the days: then he was gone. As Sampson pulled the quilt up round his chin he could hear one of the monks intoning the Rules that governed their lives. There was silence, the click of beads as someone completed the Rosary: the candle flickered, then gutted and went out.

Sampson lay awake in the darkness listening to the distant bark of a dog and the slap of sandals on flagstones as the duty monk went his rounds. Unanswered questions and Audley's stare circled endlessly through his brain. He slept fitfully. At midnight he was woken by the ringing of the dorter bell. A taper flared in the dark. He could hear the monks pull on their cassocks and shuffle downstairs for the first offices of the new day, Nocturn and Lauds. He woke again when they returned, tossed drowsily for a moment, then slid back into sleep. Dimly, as if in a dream, he woke once more before dawn broke. Moonlight was streaming through the narrow window above his head, silhouetting the ghostlike outline of a cowled figure moving silently away from his bed.

'A monk's business is not to teach but to mourn. Saint Jerome's words and still true,' said the prior, lifting the latch on the massive wooden door in front of him. 'Even here we are able to offer comfort to the dead by singing the Lord's praises.'

Sampson glanced behind him. Although the orchards hid the priory from view he could still hear the distant chanting of a solemn dirge. It seemed, he thought, out of place. The sun was hot on his back, the sky cloudless, and a gentle breeze lifted the apple laden branches that surrounded him.

'But even the living need comfort and song,' added Audley with a smile. 'And here is where I find it.' He pushed open the door and entered his dovecote.

Sampson followed him inside. Its circular stone walls were pierced by tier upon tier of arched holes that filled the chamber with light. The brick floor was thick with guano and fragments of egg-shell. In the centre was a wooden post that rose from the floor to a socket in the roof, at each end of the post a single arm joined it at right-angles. Audley pushed the ladder linking the arms. 'A potence,' he explained. 'Both ladder and post revolve. 'It makes it easier to collect the eggs without disturbing the birds.' He paused. 'Listen.'

As the echo of his voice faded Sampson became aware of a dull lingering hum that seemed to emanate from the walls. Audley clapped his hands: the noise grew louder. Suddenly Sampson realized that he was listening to the cooing of not one, but literally hundreds of pigeons. He looked up at the tiers of nesting squabs. Pink eyes gleamed back at him as the half-fledged chicks, deserted by parents out feeding, paced their boxes and stared down at the two men, their heads cocked to one side.

He turned to Audley; his head was tilted to the noise and a smile edged his lips. It was almost as if each was imitating the other. He sighed. Overnight the prior's attitude towards him had completely changed. After ignoring him throughout Mass and the sparse meal of haddock, bread and beer that followed, he had suggested they inspect his dovecote whilst the herbs were packed and taken to the stables. The invitation could not be refused, but apprehension had returned as the prior, holding him lightly by one arm, had led him through the orchard.

Audley remained silent as they walked, and Sampson had sensed that he too was on edge. As they approached the dovecote his mood had changed; one moment taciturn, he suddenly became a courteous good-humoured cleric showing a guest his domain.

'When I first came here I had two pairs, now I've nearly five hundred,' said Audley, lifting his voice against the din. 'Each requires four bushels of corn a year to breed.' He frowned. 'A harmless bird, but there are those who don't share my affection for them.' For a second Sampson was certain he was thinking about the Woodwards, then he smiled and added. 'Tell me about your master?'

Sampson's bewilderment at the sudden change of subject must have shown, for Audley added: 'I was made an oblate in our abbey at Tewkesbury when still a boy. If nothing else a lifetime of prayer has taught me that it is easier to speak the truth than to invent it.' He paused, stemming Sampson's diffidence with a disarming smile. 'Is he a good physician?'

Sampson shook his head.

'And you could do better?'

'I think so.'

'And your father, does he approve of your choice of profession?'

'My father is dead. He died before I was born.'

Audley lifted his hands, as if acknowledging his regret. 'And your mother?'

'Is mistress of a tavern.'

'She must be proud of you. To heal is to make whole again.'

'I'm not sure she'd agree, your worship. My master's example has taught her otherwise.'

'Ah. So serving a successful physician with courtiers for patients has taught you their tact.' Audley laughed, then added: 'Why do you dislike Buckle?'

Gradually the prior began to draw the truth from Sampson, learning first about the realities of his apprenticeship and then about his childhood and life in a city tavern. He himself said little, and Sampson – although unable to prevent it – more than once sensed that he was playing the puppeteer, standing outside their conversation, aloof and detached. Suddenly he switched back to Buckle, carefully guiding Sampson – against his wishes – into a long explanation of his theories about diagnosis and

44

disease. Eventually he pushed himself away from the ladder and gestured towards the door.

'I'm afraid that the affairs of this priory mean little to those who administer our Order. Cranborne is a backwater, its income small. I have no chamberlain or precentor and there is much to be done before Chapter.'

Dismayed by Audley's abruptness, Sampson followed him out into the sunshine. As they retraced their steps through the orchard, he suddenly realized that Audley had deliberately invited him into his dovecote, not to show it to him, but to listen to him talk. He had succeeded, and, as a result, he now knew as much about him as any man but Mervyn.

'You are wondering why I questioned you,' said Audley, noticing Sampson's frown. 'I will tell you. Curiosity. Monks live in seclusion, yet we presume to understand the world and its follies. There are times when I'm not convinced that we do.' He patted Sampson's shoulder. 'An answer, and honest, but not the one you'd hoped for.'

They turned into the courtyard. Sampson could see *Beauty* standing tethered outside the stables. A groom was strapping the two sacks of herbs to her saddle. The knowledge that he would soon be leaving gave Sampson courage.

'When we first met,' he said, 'you asked my name. It seemed . . .'

Even as he spoke Sampson knew he could not finish. The prior's eyes had tensed; his face became bland, a mask without feature.

Audley turned towards him. 'Do you have secrets, things you hide.'

'Of course.'

'From God . . . ? I don't. No monk does. That's the price we pay for serving Him. He is our shepherd, therefore we lack nothing and can conceal nothing. Audley paused and glanced at *Beauty*. 'Wait here a moment. I have something I want to give you before you go.'

As Audley hurried towards the cloisters, Sampson perched on the edge of the fish-still. Once again he knew he had been rebuffed, but this time he felt certain that Audley was keeping something from him, hiding it behind a riddle. He looked down at the carp, too pre-occupied to be aware that the prior was now standing in the shadows under the archway staring at him.

That stare was shifted by a distraction. One of the women winnowing and flailing corn in the granary had emerged from the dust carrying a sieve laden with grain. She tossed the grain into the air. It glittered and hung for a moment, then fell back to the sieve as the chaff was borne away on the breeze. She looked up, saw the prior and spat onto the cobbles before turning away.

Audley's lips whitened with rage. Even now, with Sampson so near to going, the sudden appearance of the Woodward girl had reminded him of how much he was still haunted by yesterday's events. He shook his head, reproaching himself for not guessing that Sampson would be Buckle's apprentice and that the physician would suspect a trap. Thank God Woodward had missed. He smiled slightly. In fooling the girl into thinking he was dying he was now certain she knew where her brother was hiding. He'd have her followed, trap them both, prove the mother a witch and watch all three of them hang. The thought calmed him. He left the shadows and walked towards Sampson, making one final effort to appear composed.

'Give this to Buckle when he next threatens you with a whipping,' he said, handing him a small glass phial.

'What is it?'

'A corrective for melancholy. We prepare it in the infirmary. Although monks spend their lives contemplating the world to come, there are times when they too find this one hard to endure. The corrective calms them. Each flask has been blessed. Inevitably I believe that makes some difference.'

Sampson held it up to the light.

Audley smiled. 'Ah, you doubt me. You think healing is a science, not a province of faith. Try it and see what happens.'

Sampson placed the phial in his scrip and mounted his horse.

'You are always welcome here.'

'Thank you, your worship.'

Audley repeated the Blessing. But the words sounded forced, like a plea. The two men looked at each other for a moment, then Sampson turned *Beauty* into the lane and away from the priory.

Audley watched him round the corner before hurrying back through the orchard. He bolted the dovecote door behind him, revolved the ladder until it was beneath a small dormered window let into the dome of the roof, and climbed past his pigeons. Already he could feel tears on his face. He broke the window glass with his fist and looked out over the village. Suddenly, through his tears, he caught sight of a lone rider cantering up the track leading on to the Chase. Knowing it was Sampson, he bowed his head; unable to watch his son merge with the woods that lined the horizon.

CHAPTER FIVE

'Out strumpet, out! Before I take a whip to that pretty little bottom of yours.'

Sampson stood in the doorway of his master's parlour not daring to move. Suddenly the curtains surrounding the bed were thrown open and a naked girl fell onto the floor. She rushed past him crying. Her hair was tangled and scratches welted her back.

A moment later the physician's head appeared round the curtains.

'Back at the eleventh hour, eh? Dainty creature. New parlour-maid. In need of instruction, bites like a mule. Well! What you standing there for, whelp? Fetch my robes an' slippers an' bring in the sacks!' Buckle smiled and rubbed his hands together as Sampson retrieved his clothes from the flagstones and carried in the herbs. 'Knife!' he snapped, climbing out of bed and into his gown. 'So he changed his mind, did he? Thought he might. Sight of you must have jogged his memory.'

'I . . .'

'I, I, I . . . that's all you ever say! Ninth letter, third vowel, Greek *Iota*, but said alone it's wasted breath!'

Sampson handed his master the knife. Buckle grinned slyly and turned to his apprentice. 'You too, out! Work to be done; leeches to be fed, elixir to be bottled, cellars to scrub.'

As soon as his apprentice had left the parlour, Buckle locked the door and shuffled towards the sacks. 'Paid up, knew he would,' he muttered happily, prodding each of them with a spindly finger. 'Wants to be an abbot. No choice but to pay. The boy must have told him his name.' He cackled, then plunged the knife into one of the sacks and quickly sliced a large hole in its side. 'Small purse, leather, should hear 'em clink,' he murmured as armfuls of dried lavender piled round his legs. He started growling. The sack was nearly empty. He turned it inside out, shook it, cursed, tossed it to one side and reached for the other. This time, wheezing heavily, he stabbed and slashed at the sack like a man possessed, not pausing until the parlour floor was awash in yarrow and torn strips of sacking. Saliva gathered on his lips as he hurled the knife into the fireplace. 'So he thinks he can outwit Nathaniel Buckle, does he?' he whispered hoarsely, his crabbed face now quivering with rage. 'One letter, that's all it needs, and Audely 'll be out of that priory and into the gutter so fast he'll not have time for an Amen.' An instant later, a frenzied glint in his eyes, he unbarred the door, screamed 'Boy!' and began flailing his fists against the wall.

As Sampson entered the parlour, Buckle pounced. Lunging out, he grasped his apprentice by the hair and pulled him forward until their faces were only inches apart. 'What you tell him?'

'Nothing!' cried Sampson, flinching at the pain.

Buckle growled and pitched him to the floor. 'Where's the purse?' he hissed.

'What purse? What are you talking about?'

The physician looked down at his apprentice. His hooded eyes narrowed slightly. A finger uncurled, describing a small circle in the air. 'Ah, of course, should have guessed. You an' Audley been conspiring. Blood's thicker than loyalty to me.' He paused, a malevolent smile creasing his smooth unwrinkled skin. 'And damn me if it ain't time we drained a bit of yours.'

Sampson hurried to his feet as Buckle locked the door and reached behind the bed curtains. An instant later a whip cracked and a steel-tipped thong snaked towards him. He staggered backwards, a thin trickle of scarlet oozing from his neck.

'Well, whelp. Tongue any looser?'

The whip cracked again, drowning Sampson's protest. 'One, did you tell friend Audley your name?'

'Yes.'

'Good, that's better. Then what happened?'

'Nothing.'

'Try again, boy. Two, then what happened?'

Sampson repeated himself before raising his hands to his face and retreating into the corner. The physician was advancing towards him, whip aloft, a thin smile playing round the corners of his lips. Suddenly the whip dropped, its steel tip lashing Sampson's face and gouging a deep gash above his eyes. He cried out as he fell to the floor. A red film filled one eye and for a moment he could see nothing but shadows. There was a kick in his ribs.

Buckle growled, gave his apprentice a second kick, and entered his study. He stood there for a moment in the half-light, breathing deeply and nibbling a knuckle. 'So the boy still doesn't know,' he murmured. 'High time he did. Not everyone's a prior's bastard. Father an' son. Soon both be begging for crusts in the street. No more gold though. Pity, could have redoubled it if he'd become an abbot.' He grunted, pulled the iron trunk from beneath the table and hauled it into the parlour. He glanced at Sampson, now kneeling and swabbing the blood from his face, and snapped: 'Wine!'

Sampson rose and lurched towards the flagon beside the bed. Although the pain above his eyes had dulled to a steady throb he knew he was not yet out of danger. He lifted the flagon. Why had Buckle attacked him over a missing purse within minutes of his return from Cranborne? Cranborne. The prior's parting gift... He glanced over his shoulder; his master was rummaging through a trunk, his back was turned. Sampson eased the phial from his scrip, uncorked it and carefully poured the contents into a goblet, adding wine and mixing the two with a finger. He turned towards his master.

'More! Fetch more!' Buckle snatched the goblet and lifted it to his lips. Sampson reached for the flagon. A moment later there was a hideous scream. He spun round. His master had risen to his feet and was clutching his throat. Only the whites of his eyes were visible. The goblet slid from his fingers, shattering as it hit the flags. He opened his mouth to speak, but instead of words bile and phlegm bubbled from between his lips. His legs buckled and he toppled slowly towards the floor. Suddenly his whole body stiffened and arched upward. A reflex bucked in one leg, a hand shuddered, there was a faint hiss as air escaped from his lungs. Then silence.

*   *   *

50

As Sampson closed the parlour door behind him and ran headlong into the street, a small long-legged spider scurried out of a crack between the flagstones and climbed up Buckle's hair. It paused, then slowly picked its way across his forehead, over the white of one eye and down the bridge of his nose. Suddenly it stopped, clamping its feeler pads to the side of a nostril. Warm air fanned its abdomen. As it ran quickly down the physician's neck and back to the safety of its lair, the recumbent body heaved, twitched once, and then was still again.

*   *   *

'He's dead, mother! I swear it. Audley poisoned him!'

Widow Hooke had risen from the window seat in her room as her son burst through the door. Now she collapsed back into it again.

''Tis true,' went on Sampson. 'After stabling *Beauty* I paid a carter to take the sacks to his chambers. There was supposed to be a purse in one of them. He couldn't find it. Thinking I'd taken it, he attacked me with a whip. Audley had given me a specific to calm him when he next lost his temper. I mixed it with his wine. He . . . , he . . .,' Sampson's voice trailed into silence as the shock of what had happened spread through his body.

'You're sure he's dead?' whispered Widow Hooke, only now realizing what her son was saying.

Sampson nodded. His face had turned pale, the wound on his brow had opened as he ran through the city and blood caked his hair. 'I felt his heart, there was nothing.'

'But that's murder . . .'

'Exactly.' Sampson bowed his head in an effort to shake off the image of his master's eyes staring sightless and blind at the ceiling. 'The phial smelt of bitters. I began opening the bottles on the shelves to try and find out what it had contained.' He paused, his voice becoming a whisper. 'T'was henbane, a venom. Buckle used to mix one drop into an infusion to ease the pain of women in childbirth. More than four are fatal.' He looked at his mother. An embroidery hoop sat forgotten in her lap, her mouth hung open and her whole body seemed to have gone lifeless and slack. 'For God's sake say something!' he

51

screamed.

She lifted her head. Dusk was falling. On the far side of the street a group of apprentice tanners in blackened aprons laughed and joked as they diced in a pot-shop doorway, a water-carrier was rinsing out his barrels in the street channel, a knight, followed by his page, clattered by on his way to Clarendon; his lance pennon hung slack in the still evening air and his helm and plate-guards glowed gold against the sunset now spreading over the city. Worlds within worlds. But none of them the one that harboured all the lies and half-truths she must have told him since he first asked after his father. She turned towards him.

'Tell me about him.'

'Who?'

'The prior, Audley.'

'He's a monk like any other. He keeps pigeons, he . . . oh mother, none of this matters!'

Widow Hooke pressed her face against the window. She opened her mouth to speak, then, as if the words were trapped in her throat, let her unspent breath mist the panes, reducing the worlds to one. Her hands began shaking. 'Was he missing a finger?' she whispered calmly.

Sampson froze. An image of Audley so fleeting he had hardly noticed or been aware of it until now rose up before his eyes: yesterday evening, after tossing the tumbling pigeons into the air, the prior's hands had continued upward and for a split-second his splayed fingers had been etched against the sky. He nodded, then murmured 'Yes' as he once again saw the gap where a forefinger should have been.

As he spoke his mother slumped into her seat. Her embroidery frame cracked, then snapped beneath her weight. Sampson rushed to her side. Tears wetted her face. 'T'was the left hand,' she said slowly.

'You know him, don't you?' cried Sampson shaking her by the shoulders. 'So does Mervyn.'

'No! Mervyn knows nothing!' She lifted her head, and as Sampson breathed in the familiar musty scents he had known as a child he suddenly saw her as she was now – an ageing frightened woman with sunken eyes and cheeks so lined they might have been cut from the cracked, baked earth in the courtyard below.

'Tell me,' he said tenderly.

She tried to look him in the eye, but failed and so took refuge in evasion. 'You must flee, tonight. When the sheriff learns of Buckle's death he'll order a hue an' cry. It don't matter who did the killin'. 'Tis you who'll hang. No court will take your word against Audley's. Why should a prior plot murder? Hide, anywhere. Mervyn 'll get word to you soon enough. Now go. Scrub that face o' yours and bandage your brow. I'll fetch food, there's some shillings in the bed chest.' She started to stand, but Sampson held her firm in his grip.

'I've done nothing to be ashamed of, mother. Runnin' is proof of guilt an' if I'm to be hunted like a hart 'afore hounds I must know why.'

'God forbid that you should ever know. I swore once I'd not tell you, an' I meant it.'

Widow Hooke rose and pushed past her son, turning when she reached the door. 'Buckle is dead, for now the rest don't matter. To find out you must live, and to live you must flee 'afore they clap irons on you.' The door slammed behind her.

Sampson stood stunned and unable to move for a long time after she was gone. He knew she was right: no court would believe him. He must leave. Fear knotted his belly as he thought of the uncertainty ahead. Where would he go? How would he prove his innocence? What secret was his mother keeping from him? The questions multiplied as minute succeeded minute and twilight, like a tide that cannot be stemmed, flowed in through the leaded windows overlooking the street.

When Widow Hooke returned neither she nor Sampson spoke. He sat on the edge of her bed as if in a trance whilst she bathed and bandaged his brow. She handed him a bundle and purse, then pressed his face to hers. His skin was cold, the bone behind it unyeilding to her touch. She kissed his lips. From downstairs in the parlour came laughter and the smell of roasting pork. Trenchers clattered, a lone minstrel struck up a tune on his lyre. Suddenly Beatrix's voice merged with the music.

> A woman is a worthy thing,
> She do the wash and she do the wring.
> She baste's the spit, she do push the hoe,
> Yet without a man she hath but woe.

she sang as Sampson straightened and wrapped a cloak round his shoulders. It was time to be gone. Already the tavern seemed distant and remote. He rose, opened the door and walked downstairs without once looking back. Widow Hooke turned to the window. A cloaked figure moved across the street, quickening pace as it vanished into the dusk.

*　　*　　*

The room was in darkness when the door next opened. A candle flickered, washing the low-beamed ceiling in splashes of light. 'Betty, you here?' Mervyn's head rounded the door. His one eye narrowed as he heard a rustling from near the window. The boards creaked as he crossed the room and lit the two rush lights bracketed to the bed-posts.

'Mervyn,' whispered a voice, 'that you?'

The ostler knelt beside the crumpled figure lying in the window bay. 'What in Hell an' thunder do you be doing up here?' He paused, suddenly aware she was crying. Placing a hand under each shoulder, he lifted her on to the seat and asked the cause of her tears.

'Buckle's dead,' she blurted. 'Sampson's fled. He'd a hung for it.'

'Lord alive, lass. What you prattlin' about?'

''Tis true.' As Widow Hooke raised her head, Mervyn saw bloodshot eyes and cheeks that were blotched and swollen. 'A monk at Cranborne made Sampson give him a venom.'

A sudden sense of foreboding made Mervyn sink to his knees. 'Audley!' he whispered sharply.

'T'was he who gave Sampson the poison. He said t'would calm Buckle when he next took the whip to him.'

'This is madness!' cried Mervyn. 'You're sure the man's dead?'

'Aye. Sampson left him where he fell.'

'An' where's the boy now?'

'He's fled.'

'What else do you know?'

'Nothing.'

'You're lying, Betty,' said Mervyn gently. Widow Hooke turned away and lifted her skirts to her face. ''Tis nigh on twenty years since you last saw him. He was Brother Roger then. It was spring. Will had been buried no more 'an a month when he lodged here.'

'Stop it!'

'Betty, if Buckle's really dead I'd be the first to hope him in Hell. But Sampson's to be hunted. No, the time has come for the truth to out. You can't keep it hid for ever.'

Widow Hooke began sobbing. 'So you knew,' she murmured.

'Aye, and many's the day I've rued that I did.' Mervyn lowered himself to the seat. 'The Lord in his wisdom may 'a taken the sight from an eye, but I can see that night as clear as if it were yesterday. I'm guilty too, if only for never saying that I'd hoped to court an' wed you when Will's mourning had ended. He was a good husband to you. I was happy to wait . . . No, don't say anything, let a man finish his piece.' He paused, closing his eye before continuing. 'It was raining, the tavern was crowded with Easter pilgrims. I came upstairs to find you. I opened the door. You were lying on that same bed. The monk was with you. Huh! you should 'a seen me later. I went from inn to inn till there was porter to my gills. Mervyn the pot-valiant, fisticuffin' with all who'd take him on. But it made no difference. For weeks afterwards I intended leaving an' going back to the Marches. Then you were with child. Sampson was born. He needed a father. There was no one else. So I stayed. T'was that simple.'

There was a moment's silence, then Widow Hooke whispered: 'You should have told me. For all these years we've both known the truth an' not dared speak of it.'

'What was I to say? That I'd seen you in sin? No, such things are best forgotten.'

'I didn't know what I was doing,' said Widow Hooke quietly. 'I was lost without Will. I was in mourning, he comforted me. That evening he'd heard my confession. We were praying together when he suddenly touched me. I couldn't stop him. After it was over I felt only shame. He left. I didn't even know his name. For years I've thought him dead.'

'He was alive, Betty, and prospering. A year later, on the eve of St John's Feast, I saw him at mass in the cathedral. T'was then I found out who he was and where he came from. Seven years ago some pilgrims mentioned his name in the parlour. I asked who he was, new Prior of Cranborne they said. I thought little of it till yesterday when Buckle ordered Sampson to go there. Buckle was too cunning for that to have been chance. I realized then that he knew, 'afore that I wasn't certain.'

'I told him,' admitted Widow Hooke. 'When I realized I was with child I became frightened. I'd heard friars in the market place tell of bastards born with tails as punishment for the sin that beget them. For weeks I tried to hide myself. When it became impossible I asked Buckle into this room and offered him money to stop the birth. I'd seen him touting his purges. He sold me a physic. I was sick, but my belly kept growing. I begged him to try again. He said it was too late. I tried reasoning with him, but he wouldn't listen. So I told him what had happened. He demanded six gold sovereigns. I gave them to him. He told me he could do nothing until I'd borne the child. The day after Sampson's birth he came to my bedside, bringing with him the master an' council of the physician's guild. I was still weak. I hadn't dare take the swaddling robes from Sampson for fear of what I might find. They gathered round the bed . . .'

'I know,' interrupted Mervyn. 'I was watching from the door when they examined you. I heard one say: "As the boy has no blemishes, tail or webbed feet, it seems certain he was conceived in wedlock. But it's a rare case, Master Buckle, a rare case." The others agreed. Fools, I thought, since when has a babe been born a newt. But for a moment I nearly believed them. Perhaps the boy was Will's, perhaps he had been eleven months in your belly as Buckle said.'

Widow Hooke smiled slightly. The knowledge that Mervyn had always known what she had most feared telling him had drained her of all emotion, leaving her light-headed and strangely dizzy.

'Aye,' she murmured. 'T'was Buckle who convinced 'em that the child was Will's. I'd 'a done anything for him then, but he wanted none of it. He hardly came near the tavern till the day he asked me to let Sampson become his apprentice. I couldn't say no, not after all he'd done.'

'And now he's dead,' added Mervyn, 'and I doubt if even the most ravenous of worms will find him to their taste. The man was a rogue, and none but a few pampered matrons with more money than brain will mourn his passing. Fate plays strange tricks. He treated Sampson worse than a galley-slave, yet t'was Sampson's own father that killed him.' He paused, sighing to himself. 'And now there's no more to tell. Was it that hard a task?'

Widow Hooke shook her head as he reached out to her and clasped her hands in his own. 'Betty, look at me. You an' I are growing old. But I love you now as I loved you then . . . No, lass. Don't turn away from me. Tonight is one for plain speaking an' I'll not keep silent.'

'How can you say such things when you know what I did?'

'Should we not leave the Almighty to do the judging?' Mervyn paused, and then whispered: 'Betty, shall you an' I be wed?'

Without thinking Widow Hooke leant her head against his chest and began crying again.

'Tears are no answer.'

'They're mine.'

'And mean yes?'

She nodded. For a moment neither spoke. Candlelight lapped round them as she lifted her face and placed her lips against Mervyn's cheek.

'Sampson must never learn that the prior's his father,' she said suddenly.

'He may have to. Does Audley know that you bore his child?'

'No, not unless Buckle told him.'

'So why should Audley murder the man? To silence him? But why? If we can find proof of a reason, Sampson can return to Sarum a free man.' Mervyn rose and hurried towards the door. 'I must go to the house, tonight.'

Widow Hooke pleaded with him to stay, but he ignored her. 'If the watch had found his corpse they'd 'a called on you 'afore now. You'd best go down into the parlour. I won't be long.'

'Mervyn.' He turned in the doorway. 'Be careful.'

He smiled. 'Aye, lass. I'll be that. I've waited nigh on eighteen years to make you my mistress an' I'll not fall foul of man or beast till that be done.'

The city was almost deserted. At the far end of the street, where it narrowed to the Milford Street Gate, a porter's brazier flickered in the darkness. Mervyn slid silently through the shadows, keeping close to the tall overhung houses that fronted the cobbles. Once he had to crouch behind a cart as two night-watchmen armed with pikes passed by. Shortly afterwards, glimpsing the movement of a draw-latch or foot-pad in a doorway, he doubled back and crept through a warren of passages and courtyards. Suddenly he was on the edge of the market place. The slam of a pot-shop's shutters echoed across the empty square. A cat hurried by with a rat between its teeth. Mervyn moved on, ducking as he stole through the crimson net of light cast by a baker's ovens on the cobbles outside his shop. The smell of freshly baked loaves receded. He started running, finally reaching Buckle's house as the cathedral bell began tolling the hour.

He pushed open the door, closing it carefully behind him. From somewhere ahead he could hear the sound of a kitchen-maid tossing in her sleep. Aware that the entire household would have been roused if their master had been found, he lifted the latch on the parlour door and stepped inside. He stared round in bewilderment. The fire had dwindled to a dull glow. Buckle's corpse had vanished.

For a moment he felt certain that either Sampson or Widow Hooke had dreamt of the murder. Then, in the light from the embers, he saw a square of black cloth lying on the flags. On it someone had lain a small wooden crucifix; the sign of a death in the room. He gazed despairingly at the cross. 'So he's dead,' he muttered. He frowned thoughtfully, troubled by the doubts now nagging at his brain – the absence of soldiers or a priest, the maid asleep in her wall cupboard – then walked over to the fire and tossed a bundle of faggots onto the ashes. They crackled and flared, lighting up an iron trunk standing open on the flagstones. Kneeling beside it, he quickly lifted out a succession of purses each heavy with coins. Beneath them lay a leather-bound ledger. Not yet certain what he was looking for, he carried it closer to the fire and began skimming its pages. A sheet of faded parchment fell to the floor. Curious, he picked it up and glanced at it. It was the draft of a letter dated 1327, the year of Sampson's birth, and as he began reading both rage and dismay spread over his face. It was signed: 'Nathaniel Buckle, physician, to be reached at the Blew Bore tavern, 3 Cup Chequer, New Sarum.' Laying the letter to one side, he lifted the ledger to the light and looked through it again, this time carefully. Yes, each of the two annual payments demanded by Buckle from Audley in return for his silence had been entered. 'Blackmail!' whispered Mervyn. Aware that Audley must have discovered that Sampson was his son during the course of his stay in Cranborne, he cursed, then hurriedly continued his search through the trunk. Suddenly he heard voices, the clatter of hooves in the street outside. A horse whinnied, a fist began beating the door.

'In the king's name! Open up!'

Mervyn sprang to his feet. The years of working in the stables had slowed his reactions. He stood there, as if welded to the floor, as the parlour door was thrown open and soldiers burst into the room. The last to enter wore a surcoat emblazoned with the golden leopards of the royal coat-of-arms.

He stepped forward and began reading from a parchment roll. 'By order of Philippa of Hainault, wife of Edward, King of England, Lord of Ireland and Duke of Aquitaine, I, John de Godwin, knight-banneret and Captain of Her Majesty's Guard, am required to command . . .'

Mervyn stepped backwards. 'Look cap'n!' cried one of the soldiers, instinctively drawing his sword.

Knowing that he himself had betrayed the existence of the pile of purses and rifled trunk, Mervyn raised his hands in horror as the knight cried: 'Take him!'

Mervyn stared at the advancing soldiers, too terrified to move or protest his innocence. Suddenly fear made him panic. He moved back, plucking a glass jar from a table and hurling it at the soldiers in an attempt to delay their advance. One raised his sword, his boots trampling the broken glass and wriggling leeches that now covered the floor as Mervyn turned and dived towards the study door. But he was too old, his legs had lost their spring. The sword, its blade glinting in the firelight, swept sideways in a vicious scything arc that cut deep into his side. He fell to the floor. For a moment there was no pain, only a strange feeling of warmth that spread outward from his belly and into his limbs. Then it came; he screamed and tried to staunch the wound with his fist. He lifted his head. He could see the soldier standing above him, sword poised to fall. A moment later his head lolled against the flagstones, his arm straightened and finally went limp.

The soldier shifted uneasily as he gazed down at the body. There was a long silence before he sheathed his sword and said: 'That's one that'll never see the hangman's halter.'

'A robber,' said another. 'An' caught in the act. Perhaps the leech 'll reward us with one o' them purses?'

'Fetch a cart for his corpse,' snapped the knight. 'We've business to attend to. If Her Majesty wants Buckle and his machines for brewing that damned elixir she's taken to, she must have them. The man must be somewhere. Lawe, wake the maids! Jeffery, search the house!'

As the men obeyed their captain's orders, two of the soldiers began gathering up the papers scattered over the floor. One picked up a sheet of parchment, it was the draft of Buckle's letter to Audley. He gazed at it blankly.

'What do it say?' asked the other.

The soldier scratched an ear. He was a fighting man, not a scholar. It was all he could do to mark a cross beside his name on the guard roll. He pretended to read it. 'It be just words, they doan' mean nought,' he said finally, crumpling the letter in his fist and tossing it to the flames.

CHAPTER SIX

Sampson lifted his hands in protection against the brambles tearing at his face as he stumbled through the woods. He was moving blind, for the moon was hidden behind cloud and the branches overhead exaggerated the darkness by smothering any hint of light. Hunger had weakened him, and his legs had stiffened after the long walk from Salisbury. The fear of arrest had made him cautious and he had only travelled at night, hiding on the first day in a deserted shepherd's hut and on the second in a copse on the edge of the Chase. Yet despite having reached his goal he now felt more frightened than ever, for although darkness had fallen each step he took seemed to find an echo in the unfamiliar sounds of a wood at night. Deer, badger, even a woodcock's cry had sent him diving to the ground in expectation of attack. Again and again he had cursed his decision – made even before he had swum the Avon and left Salisbury behind him – to return to Cranborne Chase and take sanctuary with the outlaw who had ambushed him on his way to the priory. But it was now too late to turn back, and, after pausing to draw breath, he moved on again, tripping over fallen trees and changing direction whenever he blundered into another of the thickets of bramble that rolled through the forest. He was lost, he knew that, and when he finally glimpsed a faint break in the blackness ahead he hurried towards it, intending to try and find shelter for what remained of the night. Suddenly, out of nowhere, a hand passed in front of his face and clamped his mouth, stifling a cry. An instant later he felt breath on his neck and cold steel at his throat.

'Don't move,' hissed a voice.

Sampson felt the blade press tight against his skin. For a moment he surrendered to the certainty of death. Then, as the pressure on the blade slackened, his brain cleared, despair became defiance. Stealthily lowering a hand, he reached for the knife at his waist.

'Leave it be!'

The invisible arm locking his mouth gripped tighter. It felt rigid, as if it had been bandaged. A splint! Woodward's broken arm! He tried to speak. The hand lifted long enough for him to blurt: 'I'm Sampson Hooke, the apprentice who . . .'

The blade jerked upward. 'Stay in front of me an' start walkin'.' Then it left his throat for the small of his back, forcing him to move. The next few minutes spanned an eternity. Apart from a bandaged arm, Sampson had no grounds for thinking his attacker to be Woodward and he half-expected the knife to plunge into his back with every step he took. His captor led him across a ride that cut through the wood and into a labyrinth of coppice and undergrowth. He seemed certain of where he was going, for never once did they collide with a tree or wade into bramble. The ground levelled, turning to thick bracken.

'Stop,' ordered the voice. Sampson glanced down, at his feet were the embers of a small fire. Twigs were tossed onto it, the ashes began to glow. 'Sit.' He did so. The knife moved away from his spine. He looked up: kneeling facing him on the far side of the fire was Thomas Woodward. Sampson threw himself headlong into the bracken. Suddenly his fear and tension both faded, leaving him weak and almost numb.

Thomas grinned nervously. 'I couldn't take chances, even when you said your name. I thought you'd left Cranborne days ago.'

'I did.'

Thomas's confusion showed itself as a quizzical frown. 'Then why are you here?' he demanded. 'I was hunting an' heard you crashing through briar. I thought you were a boar left wounded by the keepers. You were walking in circles.'

'I know,' admitted Sampson, hauling himself to his haunches. 'I was searching for you. I need help, and only you can give it. There's much to tell, but first I must eat.'

'We must be wary, the keepers rode by at dusk and I daren't add to the fire,' replied Thomas, walking over to the entrance to the set and returning with a leaf-wrapped carcass. 'Here, the remains of a roasted pigeon. 'Tis all I have.'

As Sampson drew close to the fire and began eating he told Thomas all that had happened since their meeting, beginning with his arrival at the priory and ending with his flight from Salisbury. Thomas sat silent and thoughtful whilst he spoke, but it was he who broke the silence that followed.

'And now you wish to stay here with me?'

'Yes. Where else can I go?'

Thomas shook his head in disbelief. 'But I'm villein born, a peasant an' outlaw. You're a free man, a physician's apprentice an' son of an innkeeper.'

'My father and Buckle are both dead. I'm no longer free, but a fugitive like you,' said Sampson fiercely. 'It doesn't matter what we were born. We're both here because of Audley, and if I'm to discover why he poisoned Buckle and prove my innocence I must stay close to him.'

'But you can't hunt or use a bow . . .'

'I can be taught.' Sampson gave a wan smile. 'Please, let words wait on the morrow. I need sleep.'

'I'll keep watch outside,' said Thomas quickly.

Hearing his mistrust, Sampson shrugged his shoulders and crawled into the set. Thomas waited until he was silent before trampling the fire, then he drew his cloak round his chest and lay down in the bracken, first making certain that his knife was within reach. Overhead the moon threaded its course through a mantle of scudding cloud. Delight and suspicion muddled his thoughts. For a year he had been longing for companionship, but Sampson's tale was so unlikely and his arrival so unexpected that he could not be sure it was fact. Perhaps he and Audley were in league? Anyway, what if he had told the truth? Alone he knew how to survive; a city apprentice could only add to his problems. He smiled at his doubts. Sampson's optimism had already eased the despair and sense of failure that had haunted him since the day of the ambush.

When Sampson woke the sun had already risen. He climbed from the set and looked round at the horizons of his new world. Behind him a wall of sand, drilled near the surface by a skein of roots, rose vertically to a wilderness of furze and underwood that all but enclosed the clearing. In front of him the bracken, now steaming in the sunlight, tumbled headlong into a dense jungle of bramble, beyond which oak and beech towered skyward. The perfect hiding-place, he thought admiringly, glancing towards Thomas.

The outlaw was paunching a rabbit. Muscle rippled his shoulders, and his bare nut-brown back offered an unlikely contrast to his ashen hair and gaunt unwashed face. All externals. What mattered was how he thought, and in this Sampson already had his misgivings. 'You've been busy. I could have helped,' he said.

Thomas grunted. 'An' told every coney on the Chase we were after 'em? No, we must eat and be sure of it. That's the first lesson to be learnt.'

'And the second?'

'Silence. We've four ears, but two tongues, an' 'tis they we must guard against.' Seeing the crestfallen look on Sampson's face, Thomas grinned. 'After twelve months alone a man ain't used to speech.' He paused, again thinking of Audley, then waved a blood-stained knife at the encircling forest. 'There's keepers, foresters an' those who'd slit a throat for the chance of a shillun' out there,' he added, deftly skewering the rabbit with a length of green hazel and balancing it over the fire. 'Or perhaps you ain't 'afeared of them?'

'You don't trust me, do you?'

'No, an' it'd be a fool who did.' Thomas glanced up. 'But I've yet to thank 'ee for advisin' this,' he said gruffly, tapping the splint on his wrist, 'and for sparing my life as you did.'

Sensing that the outlaw was attempting to make amends for his suspicions, Sampson smiled. ''Tis I who should be grateful. Last night you could 'a made use of that knife on me.' He chose his words with care, aware that Thomas might still resent the outcome of their first meeting and the insight it had provided into his state of mind. 'Anyway,' he added, 'until you've taught me to hunt I'll be beholden for every meal.'

'Aye,' muttered Thomas. 'I've a line of snares on the far side of the wood. Once we've fed I'll take you to 'em.'

The two men knelt in the bracken to eat. Together with the previous night's sleep, the meal revived and strengthened Sampson: his thoughts turned to the future. 'Does Audley ever leave the priory?' he asked suddenly. 'Perhaps we could ambush him.'

Thomas gave a mocking laugh. 'Oh, he leaves alright. But never without an escort of pikesmen and archers.'

'I must question him,' said Sampson angrily. 'How else can I find out what happened?'

Thomas sighed wearily. 'I been here since last Michaelmas an' I'm as near the gibbet as when I fled. You've been outlawed, there'll be a price on your head. You can forget about returning to Sarum. There's only one way you'll leave the Chase; feet first and in chains.'

'There must be some who get pardoned.'

'Not murderers of physicians or serfs who lift their bow at a prior.'

Sampson said nothing. Suddenly Thomas realized that he had told the truth. Instead of relief, he felt saddened. 'That's fact,' he said quietly, 'an' let's not talk of it again. I thought as you once, now I know better.'

'But I haven't done anything! I'm innocent!'

'The snares, Sampson. Follow close and do as I say.'

Thomas vanished into the wood. He moved fast at first, only slowing the pace when he heard the snap of twigs to his rear. Sampson did his best to imitate him, but whilst the outlaw moved nimble and sure-footed through the undergrowth, he found his own movements hindered by the roots and low branches that blocked their route. Every now and then his mentor would pause and point to the ground; in turn showing him the slotted tracks of a roebuck, the imprint of a badger's toes, the splayed spoor of a fox. Gradually his spirits lifted. Breathing in the scent of dampness and rotting leaves that clung to the shadows even in the heat of summer, he began to look round. The inquisitive physician in him reasserted itself. In the glades and along the rides he glimpsed banks of herbs – here the violet cups of the periwinkle, there the tall bent stems of fennel and foxglove – and he began to list the medicines that made use of them.

Entering a gorse filled dip in the wood, Thomas knelt and indicated a small leather noose hanging from a hazel peg. 'The warren's at the far end of the coombe. This here's the lead run,' he whispered, lifting the snare. 'I'll take 'em in till dusk, but first you must learn how to set one.' He glanced at Sampson. 'See the grass in the run; some's flat, some's standing. The flat's where a coney lands. You set just past the jump. The snare should be four fingers above ground, but don't touch the run, for it hold's a man's scent long after he's gone,' he added, shaping the noose with a twig before leaving its circle spread open across the run.

As they gathered in the remaining snares, Sampson began to realize the extent of his helplessness. Yet he was determined not to be dependant on Thomas for longer than necessary, and he listened carefully as the outlaw told him how to place the peg and showed him a rabbit's spoor, indicating where the hind legs landed ahead of the front ones. As Thomas talked his mood changed. But as his surliness left him, his nervousness became more obvious. He kept jerking his head up or touching the shaft of his bow. His movements were hurried, his manner agitated, and he seemed incapable of relaxing. For now these things did not matter, but Sampson knew that it was they that would shape their relationship, perhaps even hinder his intention to do all he could to outwit Prior Audley.

Returning to the set they crossed a narrow spit of pasture that jutted into the wood. Here they sat on the grass and gazed out over a landscape of turf that stretched downhill in a sweep of green, then rose to where an outcrop of chalk and a spinney of pines shimmered in the haze. Sheep were cropping the valley slopes, and every now and then the tinkling of bells would come drifting up on the breeze. A hare loped across the hillside. Overhead a solitary lark rose to sing, tracing a spiral in the air before rising upward in a succession of aerial leaps to become a buff speck against a backcloth of blue.

'I'm glad you came,' said Thomas quietly.

Sensing a nakedness, an admission only half revealed by words, Sampson smiled. He knew now that Thomas trusted him, even needed him. For the first time since being ordered to go to the priory by Buckle he felt at peace. It was almost as if the emptiness of the Chase had absorbed all the unanswered questions that still nagged at his thoughts, leaving him drained but content. 'And so am I,' he murmured, closing his eyes against the hot August sun.

★　　　★　　　★

Summer gave way to autumn, and with it came rain and a chill wind that gusted through the trees and sent a continual flurry of leaves drifting across the clearing, covering the now dying bracken in a mosaic of yellow and bronze. At first the change of seasons passed unnoticed by the two outlaws. By day they hunted, and soon Sampson could be trusted to place a line of snares, skin a deer or snatch a trout from the stream that tumbled through the heart of the forest. Thomas began teaching him archery as soon as his own arm had healed, but it was not until a morning in early November that he finally embedded an arrow in an oak tree at the far end of the clearing. It was a cold, blustery day and massed banks of cloud, their bellies heavy with rain, marched slowly southward as he turned to his companion.

'An' about time,' laughed Thomas. 'Keep that arm straight and remember to use the weight of the body to bend the bow. Now, again.'

Sampson notched a second arrow to the draw string. Placing his left foot slightly ahead of the right, he drew back the string until it was level with his shoulder. The longbow slowly bent, the yew heartwood on the inside edge compressing as the elastic sapwood on the back stretched outward to take the strain in the curve.

'Steady,' whispered Thomas. 'Aim high.'

Sampson stared along the arrow's shaft. Raising his left arm slightly, he took his fingers from the string. The bolt sped forward, nudging the scrap of red cloth fixed to the tree. He grinned happily. 'Damn it, I'm an archer!'

'You think you are,' said Thomas curtly. 'But you still don't breathe as you should or hold the arrow steady enough. Now watch, and watch carefully.' He raised his own bow, taking aim at a shred of bark above the target before slowly sucking in air and holding it in his lungs until his body felt balanced against the spring in the bow. He fired. A split-second later his arrow hung quivering in the tree, its steel head impaling the cloth. 'Now 'tis your turn,' he said, pulling the hood of his cloak up over his head.

Thomas smiled to himself as he watched Sampson take aim. Since August they had grown close. At night they would lie alongside one another and talk of their lives. Sampson had insisted they gather herbs, and though they had once come to blows –

when Sampson made him drink a daily infusion of elder and nettle to sweeten his breath – their friendship had prospered. Yet he knew that much had been left unsaid. Fearful of doing anything that might hasten their capture, unable to see any reason why their present way of life could not continue indefinitely, Sampson's growing impatience to strike back at the prior had made him apprehensive. Sampson was restless, but was he reckless as well? Thomas could not be sure, but he knew that now his companion had mastered the bow it would only be a matter of time before he suggested some plan for forcing Audley to make a move. Of recent he had made him select sites for an ambush . . .

There was a sudden movement in the undergrowth. Thomas dived for his bow. A moment later the brambles parted and Matilda stepped into the clearing. On seeing Sampson alone in its centre she stopped in her tracks. 'You?' she cried. Thomas rose and called her name. Glancing angrily at Sampson, she ran towards her brother. 'For God's sake, Thomas. He . . .'

'Sssh.'

'But he an' Audley . . . !'

Thomas did his best to calm her. ''Tis alright. Sampson's been outlawed. He's been here since soon after you last came. I owe him my life.'

Matilda turned to Sampson. He blushed, stammering an apology for frightening her. She studied him warily – the square face, unkempt beard, hint of freckles beneath umber eyes – smiling to herself as she realized that he still had not forgotten the look she had given him when comforting father in the stocks.

Thomas, not knowing of their one encounter, introduced them as he took tinder and flint to a pile of brushwood and spitted a slab of venison. Matilda's arrival had made him talkative, and even as they ate he seemed unaware of the silence between Sampson and his sister. Matilda listened, but watched Sampson.

Suddenly Thomas stopped his account of all that had happened since their last meeting and asked after his parents. Matilda frowned before replying. 'Father's losing his sight,' she said finally. 'He's told no one. We owe Audley forty days' woodwork and since Lammas we've been cuttin' hurdle coppice. He keeps missin', and with a billhook. He never did that 'afore.' She paused, worried lest the truth fuel Thomas's despair. 'We had a poor harvest as well. Come Christmas we'll have to buy in priory grain in exchange for more days work. 'Tis the same for all, but father can't keep pace. Since you fled he's been away to the fields at dawn and not home till after dusk. His arm's troublin' him. Mother's tarred it with pitch, but it's started swelling near the stump.'

'Tell her to bathe it in betony,' interrupted Sampson. 'I have some here. It'll ease the swelling and help the wound to heal.'

Matilda rounded on him, blue eyes flashing. 'An' what do you know of us peasants?' she cried. 'Or of what it means to have a father without a hand?'

'Matilda, stop it!' shouted Thomas.

'Why should I?' She rose and stared down at the two men, hands on hips, long raven hair stirring in the breeze. 'Hark at him speaking of betony as if he was mother herself. I don't trust him. Who told you that Audley poisoned his master? He did. Three months back I saw he an' Audley entering the dovecote. They weren't feuding then. Perhaps 'tis all a plan to see you hang?'

'That's nonsense,' protested Thomas.

'Of course it is. It wouldn't fool you if it made sense.'

'But he could 'a killed me 'afore now.'

'So what? It ain't just you Audley's after. 'Tis common talk in the priory that he wants all us Woodwards' in the grave. To do that he needs proof that we know where you're hiding. He could give it,' she added, pointing at Sampson.

There was silence. Then, seeing the doubt on Thomas's face, Sampson said: 'She's wrong, Thomas. Every word I told you is true.'

'Prove it!' demanded Matilda.

'Stop it, both of you.' Thomas turned to his sister. 'When you last came my belly was empty, my arm broken. You called me a cornered rat and asked how long I'd live. Now what do you find? A brother who offers you venison and can lift his bow again. I no longer lie awake thinking of the noose. I've changed, Matilda, changed. And why? Because of Sampson. Two men can't spend their days together and their nights in the same hole in the ground and live a lie.'

Matilda kept her eyes on Sampson whilst her brother spoke,

and again, as in the market place, he felt that she was looking through him, not at him. Suddenly she lowered herself to the ground. 'I must believe you,' she said softly, 'for what he says is the truth.'

Sampson accepted her change of heart by giving her some betony. She took it, but even as she did so he sensed that she was still holding some part of herself back, resisting his offer of friendship. He thought of Beatrix, the few city girls he had pleasured with for a night. Suddenly he found himself longing for her to be gone and wishing that she would stay. He shivered uneasily and turned away.

Later that day they went into the wood to take honey from a hive Thomas had found in the trunk of a rotting tree. After returning they sat round the fire. Matilda was staying overnight – Audley was away, and as the reeve had ordered her to shepherd home some sheep from the far side of the Chase she had ample excuse for her absence from the village. Dusk fell early, slowly reducing their world to a small heap of ashes and the blurred outline of the surrounding trees. The night was cold, and Thomas raised his hands to the warmth as he asked for news of his mother.

Matilda grinned. 'A month back Audley had her arrested for sending a plague of fleas to infest the priory. 'T'was the week of the abbot's visitation and he arrived to find every monk in the place busy itchin' an' scratchin'. She denied it, said Prince Lucifer himself could strike her dead if she ever took such a liberty in a House of God.'

'And Audley?' asked Sampson.

'Something's agitatin' the man. Mother, the abbot – no one can be sure. He spends more time with his doves than he do at prayer.'

'But nothing else? The sheriff's men haven't called on him?'

'No, I'd 'a heard. But 'tis to Sarum he's gone.'

Sampson fell silent as brother and sister began discussing their mother's feud with Audley. Mention of Alice reminded him of his own mother, and he sat there in the shadows feeling exiled and slightly homesick. Suddenly Thomas stood, whispered 'Good night' and disappeared into the set, leaving his sister and Sampson alone by the fire. His absence made both of them tense. The only sounds were a log's spit and the rustle of wind in the trees. Sampson glanced at Matilda. Hair hid her cheeks, her knees were drawn up under her chin, and the play of firelight in her eyes made her seem hard and forbidding.

'When I first saw you, that day in the market place, I nearly rode across to tell you that Thomas an' I had met,' he said finally.

'I wouldn't have believed you.'

'Because you don't trust me?'

'Because I've heard it before. I'm not yet wed. I've no brother to protect me. There's a saying: 'When the Chase is hareless and Cranborne whoreless, the world will end. It brings men to the village who chase after women such as I as if we were hind or doe.'

'And you ignore them?'

'If I can. Some pinch and paw, others court my maidenhood with Malmsey or gold. But it don't help 'em.'

'What would?'

'God knows, I don't.' Matilda lifted her head. But instead of her sorrow, Sampson saw only the shadows edging her cheekbones and the fire glowing red in the black of her hair.

'Do you trust me now?' he asked.

'I do as my brother commands.'

'But not as you feel?'

Matilda laughed. 'I've two sisters an' a brother to cook an' care for, a mother due to bear a child in the spring but who still thinks only of her spells, a one-handed father going blind, and a brother who's been sentenced to the gallows. And you talk of how I should feel!'

'I'm sorry.' Sampson leant towards her. She shivered, then turned her face to his. Before she pushed him away his lips touched hers: they were cold and lifeless. Her eyes held his for a moment, seeming both to mock and draw him forward to kiss her again.

She brushed her mouth with the back of her hand. 'Now we're equal,' she murmured. 'You've claimed payment for sparing Thomas, I've made amends for doubting your story.'

'And next time?'

'Will be because I wish it,' she answered, rising and melting into the darkness.

*   *   *

71

'We must strike!' cried Sampson angrily. 'How much longer are we to go on skulking in a hole like curs 'afore a fire?'

'Some fire,' said Thomas, hoping to calm him.

'Some dogs. Even a lady's lap-dog remembers how to bite.' Sampson sighed. 'Aye, and some fire,' he added, punching a fist into the February snow.

Nearly three months had passed since Matilda's visit. For weeks the memory of that one kiss had stayed with Sampson; then she receded from his thoughts, leaving him restless and impatient. The short winter days grew monotonous. He became irritable: first out of boredom, then from frustration, but most recently because of Thomas. His companion's acceptance of his fate had grown more irksome as the days shortened and they spent more time together in the set. Again and again he had proposed they mount an ambush, but on each occasion Thomas had been quick to find fault with his plan. The months of outlawry had helped him reconcile himself to his status, and to the latitude it permitted his actions. For although he had given up believing that Audley would hang for Buckle's murder, he had spent hours trying to persuade Thomas to help him harry the lanes linking the priory with the outside world. Such a move, he argued, would undermine Audley's authority and prove him an incompetent incapable of maintaining the King's Peace on the Chase: it might also lead to his dismissal.

And it was this that he was thinking of as he gazed up out of the set at the snow that had swept across the clearing during last night's blizzard. He turned to Thomas, determined to win the inevitable argument that now lay ahead.

'It's three weeks since the first snows, and apart from foraging for food we've done little but watch it fall. I'm as good an archer as I'll ever be. We're outlaws, let's act like them. We've nothing to lose. 'Tis the grave if we fail, but if we succeed it will unnerve Audley and show him what we're capable of. He doesn't know you've a companion, and no one'll expect an ambush in weather like this.'

Thomas plucked at his bow-string. 'You're mad. It'd never work.'

'Aye, and it's sitting here that makes me so,' said Sampson angrily. 'Listen,' he went on. 'We'll block the track with a fallen tree and hide nearby. Someone's bound to pass.'

'No, I won't do it!'

'Can't you mean! There's a craven's blood in your veins Thomas Woodward an' 'tis time you knew it!'

Despite the accusation of cowardice – an accusation that would have made Sampson reach for his bow – Thomas just stared at him, mouth agape, nerves making one eye blink. Sampson sneered, then climbed out of the set. 'Matilda once called you a cornered rat,' he snarled, looking down at him. 'She was wrong. A trapped rat fights back. I intend an ambush, and with or without you it'll take place.'

Sampson made ready in silence: first binding loose fox skins to his legs, then tightening the thongs threaded down the front of the thick pelt jerkin he had stitched together with gut and wooden needles earlier in the year. After strapping on one of the two pairs of snow-shoes he and Thomas had made when the first snow fell, he slung his bow and a quiver of arrows over his shoulder and set off, his breath freezing to ice on his lips as he clambered over the drifts and entered the wood.

Although Thomas's refusal to join him had added to his own misgivings, he moved quickly towards the track. His wattle snow-shoes squeaked as they slid through the snow. Above him leafless trees merged with the slate of the sky. Apart from the occasional muffled thump of snow falling from a branch the forest was silent. No birds sang, no rabbit darted across his path, and the only signs of life he met were the tracks of a wolf and a muddy, leaf-strewn break in the snow where deer had been scraping at the frozen earth in quest of food.

Sampson halted when he reached the lane. A waggon had recently passed by and the tread of its wheels still showed as indentations in the overnight snow. For a moment he nearly turned back: what chance had he of success alone? Knowing he could not admit failure to Thomas, he put down his bow and began hacking at the trunk of a beech tree overlooking the track with his knife. At dusk the tree was still standing. He returned to the set to find Thomas grim-faced and morose.

'Where have you been?'

Sampson told him.

'You're a physician, not an archer. You're wasting time an' risking death.'

'But I'm also an outlaw. So are you. Or must we now dress you in skirts and call you ma'am?' replied Sampson contemptuously.

Thomas turned away, retreating into silence. That night, whilst Sampson slept, he struggled to allay his nervousness. He was no coward, only cautious, and he knew that Sampson was courting disaster by mounting an ambush in mid-winter: any soldiers sent to track them down would soon find their trail and surround the set. In the morning he tried to make Sampson see sense, but it was no use. Sampson scoffed, then vanished into the woods.

Light snow was falling when Sampson finally tied a rope round the beech, took the strain and watched it fall towards him across the track. Walking along its trunk, he suddenly noticed that someone had ridden by before his arrival. He stared down at their hoof prints for a moment, then smiled as the germ of a plan took shape in his brain. That afternoon, whilst Thomas watched curious and silent, he sat outside the set and patiently turned a pair of shaped arrow heads and two lengths of hazel into a set of blacksmith's claws and fashioned a rough hammer out of a stone and piece of wood.

Next morning he retraced his steps and built himself a hide in the shelter of the tree stump. He was now ready. The reality blunted his excitement, made him uneasy and on edge. By day's end his fear had turned to petulance. No one had passed, and he growled angrily when he returned cold and hungry to the set to be met by a mocking smile.

'You're a fool, Sampson.'

'Aye, and so's the jester who eats off gold and sleeps on silk at Clarendon palace. Someone'll come. They've got to.'

Sampson was right; they came at noon on the third day when his fingers were numb, frost rimmed his beard and he was stamping his feet to keep warm. Suddenly he heard voices and the jangle of harness. After cupping and blowing air into his hands, he quickly lifted his bow and placed an arrow to the string. The noise grew louder as fear made his bow hand tremble. He peered up the track. A moment later a line of monks escorted by two soldiers rounded the corner. Their palfreys moved slowly through the drifts. The eight monks led the way, chattering and laughing as they approached the fallen tree.

74

Sampson ignored them, concentrating on the soldiers. Both were armed, but neither seemed perturbed by the presence of the tree; one was gazing glumly ahead, the other tilting a wine-skin to his lips. Sampson ducked and closed his eyes, suddenly terrified and uncertain what to do. He could hear the rattle of his arrow against the shaft of his bow, feel his heart pounding. Struggling to remember all that Thomas had taught him, he raised his bow again and took aim at the nearest soldier. The trembling in his hands worsened. Suddenly his fingers slipped. Helpless and horrified, he watched his arrow sail over the soldier's head and vanish into the trees. Disbelief delayed the soldier's reaction. There was a pause, then he pointed at Sampson, discarded his wine-skin and reached for his bow. Sampson fumbled for a second arrow as both soldiers took aim. There was a hum, a flash of steel. A split-second later one of the soldiers fell from his horse, snapping the arrow now lodged in his shoulder as he hit the ground. His companion cried out in bewilderment, then screamed as an arrow-head pinned his wrist to his saddle pommel. The monks began shouting as they turned their palfreys and kicked them into a trot. Suddenly Thomas stepped from the undergrowth, blocking their escape.

'Dismount, all of you,' he snapped, levelling his bow at the leading monk.

Sampson collapsed against the beech tree, too dazed by his escape and the suddenness of Thomas's intervention to be able to think. Finally he pulled himself together and ran toward his rescuer, grinning foolishly. 'Never do that again!' he cried. 'I could 'a sworn I was dead an' buried!'

'You'd 'a deserved it,' answered Thomas sharply. 'Truss the soldiers an' stop shudderin'.'

One of the monks began to protest at being held-up. 'We are the Lord's servants. Sworn to poverty,' he insisted.

'It's the outlaw Thomas Woodward!' added another.

Thomas smiled at being recognized. 'Aye, 'tis me, Brother Peter. And if you wish to reach the refectory alive you'll do as I order and dismount.'

The monk's lips curled in contempt as he climbed from his horse. 'The prior won't rest till you're in chains, Woodward.' Seeing Sampson dragging one of the wounded soldiers towards the fallen tree, he added: 'So you've found a companion, another gutter scouring to join you on the gallows.'

''Tis the apprentice lad who stayed with us last summer!' cried another of the monks.

Thomas growled. 'Save your speeches for Audley.' When he next spoke there was even less humour in his voice. 'Take the panniers from your palfreys, remove your robes and lie face downward in the snow. That should cool your ardour to see me swing. Move!'

The monks began shivering as they took off their sandals and cassocks and squatted in the snow dressed only in coarse knee-length horse-hair shifts. As Thomas watched, Sampson tied the two soldiers to the fallen tree. Removing their swords, he tossed one to Thomas, who caught it and asked: 'Well, master outlaw. What now?'

'We'll take the two best horses and hobble the rest. I've a plan.'

Thomas gave a scornful laugh. 'Some plan! If I'd not followed you you'd be food for carrion.'

'And if you'd not played the valiant none of this need have happened.'

Thomas glanced at the monks lying prostrate in the snow. 'The argument will keep. 'Tis time we were gone.'

Sampson began emptying their saddle-bags. 'So you're sworn to poverty,' he said finally, lifting two purses.

'That money belongs to God,' exclaimed one of the monks.

'In which case you won't object to it being spent on food and clothing for two of His most lowly subjects.' Sampson smiled as he tossed both wine-skin and purses into a pannier and slung it over his shoulder.

'You'll hang for this!'

'I think not. Let's go, Thomas!' Sampson turned and vaulted into the saddle of one of the soldiers' horses as behind him Thomas did the same. A moment later both men had vanished into the woods, leaving the half-naked monks to shout and curse and shake their fists in their wake. Thomas dropped their cassocks and sandals into the snow and spurred his horse to the canter. Its hooves pounded the snow and cold air rasped at his throat as he ducked and dodged the overhanging branches that swept in front of him as he sped through the forest.

'Audley'll order a search! They'll find our tracks!' he shouted, drawing alongside Sampson.

Sampson glanced over his shoulder. Suddenly he reined in his horse and jumped from the saddle. Taking the blacksmith's claws and hammer from inside his jerkin, he lifted one of its hooves. 'I wish 'em well, for they'll freeze to the marrow 'afore finding us,' he said, scraping the balled snow from its hoof and drawing out the first of the nails holding on the shoe.

Ten minutes later the outlaws remounted. Retracing their steps, they cut off at an angle across a glade. Sampson turned in the saddle and grinned. Behind him a line of hoof prints receded through the wood, each of them certain proof that they were riding in the opposite direction: the halt had been spent reversing their horse shoes.

Thomas smiled happily. 'You may be a fool, Sampson, but at least you've wit for both of us.'

Sampson laughed. 'I need another lesson with the bow. From now on no one's to be safe who crosses the Chase; merchants, knights or monks. We've horses an' gold. Audley's rule has ended.' He paused and took the wine-skin from the pannier. 'I'll give you a toast. Woodward and Hooke, the scourge of the Chase!'

CHAPTER SEVEN

Ten days later the outlaws struck again, ambushing a papal courier as he hurried over the Chase on route for Canterbury. Their next victim was a travelling clothier robbed of forty nobles and a bale of broadcloth by two men disguised as charcoal-burners. Shortly after that, as warmer weather melted the last of the snow, they attacked a knight and his page fording a river on the southern edge of the Chase. On the following day, four hours hard ride to the north, a party of monks was held up outside a lonely wayside inn on the ox-drove and relieved of a hogshead of sack. This sudden spate of robberies, so different in pattern and character from those expected of the cut-throats in hiding on the Chase, baffled the local villagers. Their hall-marks were speed, surprise and superb archery. Within minutes of mounting each attack the two outlaws seemed to vanish into thin air, a talent which made credible many of the more improbable rumours now beginning to circulate about Thomas Woodward and his mysterious companion. Although Prior Audley had ordered his bailiffs to read out an edict forbidding mention of their names, conversation at weekly markets, in tavern parlours, and at the compulsory archery practice which took place on village greens after Sunday mass was dominated by talk of their deeds. Women discussed their daring whilst their menfolk debated Audley's reasons for not requesting military support to help hunt them down. Was he wary of drawing attention to his failure to maintain law and order on the Chase, or did he have some other motive for not informing the sheriff of their depredations? His hatred of the Woodwards was well known. Armed robbery was a capital offence. His temper had worsened and his moods grown more changeable whilst the outlaws were at large. Why then had he made no attempt to have them brought to justice?

Cranborne's reeve was as puzzled as anyone by the prior's behaviour. But as he entered the priory one March morning he knew that Audley now had no choice but to demand assistance. The reeve was a straightforward man who despised procrastination, yet he hesitated before striding across the cloister garth towards the west walk: why was it always he who had to break the news? He turned into the cloisters. The monks were sitting at a line of trestle tables illuminating the pages of a psalter. The only sounds were the scratch of quills on vellum and the steady thump of gold-leaf being pounded in a mortar. As he walked past them towards the hunched figure sitting in the pale wintry sunshine at the far end of the walk he caught odd glimpses of their work; half-finished centaurs, gold unicorns, fuchsin mermaids and blowzy angels with the features of geese, coneys and foxes. He coughed nervously as he approached the prior.

Audley lifted his head. Circles ringed his eyes and his cheeks were wan and lined, like creased paper. 'Well, what do you want?' he snapped.

The reeve touched his forelock. 'One of the verderers is just back from Bockerly Covert, your worship . . .' He paused, preparing himself for the tantrum to come. 'A troop of mounted archers has been ambushed. Their bows have been taken. They were found trussed to a tree. 'T'was *they*, your worship.'

'They! And who are *they*?'

'You gave orders not to say their names, your worship.'

Audley's fists curled, the knuckles showing white as he rapped them against the table top, rose to his feet and shouted: 'Get out! I've listened to enough of your fables. How could a pair of common thieves disarm mounted soldiers?'

The reeve stood his ground. ''Tis true, your worship. They were bound for Portsmouth under orders from the king. His majesty'll hear of it. He won't like it, your worship. Not one bit he won't.' That was the nearest he dare get to warning Audley that unless the two outlaws were hung, and soon, the king would fine him for failing to keep the peace and perhaps request his dismissal. If Audley fell, so would he, and he had no intention of allowing a prior's pride to be the cause of his return to serfdom. 'The tolls are falling fast,' he added pointedly. 'Many merchants and wayfarers are now avoiding the Chase for fear of being robbed.'

Audley's eyes narrowed angrily. 'Are you trying to tell me my duty?'

'I'd not presume to do that, your worship. 'Tis jus' that . . .'

'Go! Before I have you sold to a drover to spade mule dung!'

The reeve backed away. Audley had taken leave of his senses. It was no use arguing with him. But he'd see reason soon enough. It was common knowledge that he hoped to be made Abbot of Sarum, but unless Woodward and Hooke were dead and in the charnel-house within a month there'd be no chance of that.

As the reeve's footsteps faded Audley heard his brother monks begin whispering amongst themselves. He knew they were watching him, waiting for him to let slip some unguarded phrase that they could repeat, distort and use to hasten his ruin. He closed his eyes, almost too weary to think logically any more. Did the monks hate him, or was he imagining that they did? Ever since learning that Sampson had become an outlaw he had been prey to morbid imaginings that had unbalanced his humours and plagued his sleep. The wish to protect his son whilst capturing Woodward had become an obsession that seemed incapable of exorcism. Twice he had written to the sheriff requesting soldiers, twice he had burnt the letter. Indecision had confused him still further. Tiredness had added to his despair, leaving him melancholic and vindictive. He looked down at the pile of illuminated pages on the table, seeing in the strange beasts with human heads and animals' bodies that had been drawn in their margins the same fantastical creatures that tormented his sleep. He pushed his fists into his eyes. Each day he found it that much harder to keep a grip on reason. Fearing that he was sliding towards madness, he rose and began pacing the deserted north walk of the cloisters. But as he walked images of his son began to haunt him again. Ever since that first mid-winter ambush he had postponed ordering a hue-and-cry in the hope that Sampson would leave the Chase. Now he could delay no longer. Village gossip could be ignored, but not the king. England was at war with France. Edward intended to invade it. Even now he was gathering an army on Southsea Common, near Portsmouth, and he would brook no excuse for the inability to guarantee safe passage for his soldiers and baggage waggons over the Chase.

But why had Sampson joined Woodward, the one man he had sworn to see hang? When had they met? He bowed his head as he moved through the shadows. None of that mattered any more. He had been trapped, manoeuvred into a position that compelled him to strike back. To the monks, reeve, local merchants and his neighbouring landlords, Sampson was a thorn to be grubbed out and destroyed; a human wolf whose head belonged on a spike in the market place.

Realizing where his thoughts were leading him, he began trembling. He forced it from his mind. But it was too late. And he gave in to it. He was a monk. He had served his Order since childhood. Whilst Sampson lived there was always the chance that someone might find out that the boy was his bastard. It was folly to risk the future for one moment of weakness, an act of sin that had taken place more than twenty years ago. He glanced up, then dipped his face to his hands. In front of him, carved into a niche in the cloister wall, was a stone effigy of Christ on the cross. Tears blurred his sight. He too had no choice. Like God the Father it was now his turn to sacrifice a son.

It was some time before the monk standing patiently in the shadows risked disturbing the prior by announcing his return from Salisbury. Audley raised his head, took in the monk's mud spattered travelling habit, then stared at him blankly.

'You asked me to inquire after the physician, your worship.' Audley remained silent. 'His maids are certain he's dead,' continued the monk. 'But the beadle has no record of his burial and no masses have been sung for his soul in either St Thomas's or the cathedral.'

'Saddle a fresh mount and return to Sarum after None. Dead or alive, the man must be found.' Ignoring the monk's protests, Audley turned across the garth and entered the church. The sanctus bell would soon begin tolling and he needed a moment's peace before celebrating the office. The choir was empty. He knelt on the sanctuary steps and tried to pray. But even as he did so his concentration wavered and the words of the Ave died on his lips. Opening his eyes, he stared up at the cinque-sided panes of grisaille glass that filled the lancets of the east window. So Buckle still couldn't be found. He must be dead! Why else would Sampson have fled? Something had gone wrong. The venom must have been too strong. His death should have been slow, gradual, one which would have aroused no suspicion. And now? Now he must watch his own son hang limp from the gallows. Rising to his feet, he walked under the chancel arch and into the nave aware that in accepting the inevitability of that death he had also killed some part of himself. Suddenly he was filled with a longing to put the hanging behind him, to be able to forget.

'Good day, your worship.'

He looked round, but saw no one. He shook his head, certain that he was being haunted by some imaginary voice.

'She's comin' on, your worship. 'Tis a fair likeness.'

He turned again, taking his hands from his ears as he noticed paint splashes on the flags and two ladders leaning against the wall of the nave. His eyes climbed their rungs. Seeing the two men perched at their summits with buckets and brushes in their hands he suddenly recalled that it was he who was responsible for their presence. Shortly after the Feast of the Purification he had ordered a Doom depicting the Day of Judgement to be painted on the wall facing the north porch, the entrance into the church used by the villagers. He stepped back and studied its progress: the tree sprouting from a woman's head, the flames scorching its seven branches and the naked man on each being burnt alive for his sins. One of the men was painting a claw-footed Devil with a tail, the other filling in the blue of the woman's vast, circular eyes.

'Do you want her name scribed on it, your worship?' he asked. 'No.'

'Aye, you're right,' agreed the painter. 'It's take a blind palmer not to recognize our Alice. But I don't know that she'll take too kindly to it.'

'That doesn't concern me. This mural is intended to remind each and every one of you that the woman's a witch, the Devil's sibling.'

'Very good, your worship.' The painter winked at his companion. 'You're sure about them cherubims? They're fourpence the pair an' cheap at the price.'

'Quite sure. Get back to work, both of you.' Audley turned, simultaneously deciding that once None was over he'd have the entire Woodward family arrested and thrown in the manor cellars. A whipping would soon persuade the girl to reveal where her brother was hiding. It would then be simple to trump up charges proving the witch to be in league with her son. He shivered, suddenly horrified by the ease with which his new and unfamiliar self had emerged into being: the man of God who could attempt murder, connive at the death of his own son, conspire to watch an entire family hang.

The journeymen painting the Doom waited until None was over and the church was empty before speaking.

'The man's as mad as a March hare,' said one finally.

'Aye, Thomas an' Hooke have proper mazed him.'

'That's as may be. But 'tis Alice he's after. And she'll need more than spells and bats' wings to save her now.'

His companion agreed. ''Tis her own fault mind. Last Sabbath a dozen or more of them monks were found downin' a pickled boar's head an' a tun o' best London ale when they should 'a been fastin'. John the malster says he's heard 'em blasphemin' against the Lord instead of reading from the Hour Book. 'Tis Alice that done it to 'em. This Judgement won't help her keep her head on her shoulders.'

'That's as Audley intends.' The painter growled, then spat towards the floor. 'There's days I wish he'd sprout feathers like them birds o' his an' take wing for Heaven.'

'You certain's that where he's bound? Anyway, he'll not do that till every Woodward alive has had its neck wrung.'

'There'll be another of 'em soon. Alice has been calving since dawn. You'd a thought there was a brace of yoked oxen inside her the way she was bellowin' come daybreak.'

'Lord have mercy on the babe,' murmured the other painter. 'Audley means trouble, an' bairn or no it won't be long in comin'.'

*   *   *

The baby had still to be born when Audley gave orders for the Woodwards to be arrested. It was mid-afternoon, but the smoke rising from the small turf fire inside their cottage made nonsense of the sunlight outside it. Shapes emerged, then vanished again: a hen scratching through the layer of dung, bone and rushes that covered the bare clunch floor; the ram and two ewes standing penned in one corner; a sow in farrow waddling through the doorway.

Alice was lying on her back on a pile of straw beside the fire, her knees lifted and spread open. Occasionally she would twist at the pain or bite at the piece of wood in her mouth as another contraction reached its height. Sweat drenched her pelisse. The blood vessels in her eyes were livid and swollen from the strain of trying to push the baby from her womb. Her three youngest children, all of them under twelve, stood in a line beside her. Wide-eyed, thumbs in mouths, they watched spellbound as they waited for her to produce the new brother or sister that had been growing inside her for so long.

Matilda dipped a kerchief in the cauldron balanced on the fire and began wiping her mother's face. 'You alright?' she said anxiously.

Alice smiled. 'I'll live, lass, so will the babe. Don't forget I've spawned seven of you 'afore now.'

'Mistress Warren has offered help. You're nearly due. I'll send Ranulf to fetch her.'

'Keep her away. I'll have no one say Alice Woodward needed succour when lying-in. 'Tis as simple as shellin' peas . . .' Her words turned to a moan as the muscle in the uterine wall began to stiffen and contract, forcing the foetus towards the floor of her pelvis. 'Fetch your father,' she gasped.

Matilda peered through the smoke to where she could hear the rasp of a blade on a whetstone. To occupy and calm him she had suggested he sharpen a knife in readiness for cutting the cord. She called out to him.

As he approached he stumbled against a storage jar containing the last of the bacon joints he had salted down in the autumn. He cursed. Since New Year he had been training himself to remember the exact position of every object in the house before he finally went blind. It was a thankless task, for Alice kept moving things and he dare not ask her to leave them be lest she guess the reason. He was determined to keep it a secret. If the news reached Audley his lands would be granted to another tenant and the family would be forced into beggary. But his sight was failing fast. Distances were already hard to gauge, and he knew that the film slowly spreading over his eyes would eventually turn all he looked at into an indistinct blur. He knelt beside his wife and lifted her wet hands to his cheek.

'Soon be over,' he said softly.

''T'will that.' Alice paused to fight back the ache in her belly before adding: 'Be best if t'were a boy. With Thomas gone we need a man's hands to help 'ee.'

'Sssh, that rests with Our Lord.'

They gazed at each other. Alice seeing in his weathered face the furrows etched by a lifetime spent in the fields and woods; Hereward remembering her as she once was – the sloe-eyed eleven year old he had married in the church porch on his fourteenth birthday.

Seeing them together, Matilda smiled as she prepared for the birth. After taking their only heirloom – a copper pap-boat – from the chest behind the door, she layed out the swaddling robes she had woven for the child and scrubbed her hands with ashes and warm water. Though unable to conceive the day when she would be in childbed, she felt strangely calm, as if guided by an instinct that could be ignored but never suppressed. Gradually birth's mystery washed round her, leaving her silent but somehow aware of what lay ahead.

Suddenly a sharp scream exploded the silence. Hereward retreated as his wife began panting. Matilda knelt beside her and lifted her pelisse. 'Careful now, lass. If it comes out feet first promise to turn it widdershins 'afore slicing the cord.'

Matilda smiled at her mother's superstitiousness: revolving a child in the opposite way to the sun was thought to counter the misfortune prophesied to those not born head first. She reached up towards her mother's thighs: there was still no sign of the babe. But realizing that the birth was imminent, she turned to her brother. 'Ranulf,' she said, 'milk one of the ewes an' fill the pap-boat. Quickly! Girls, one of you fetch a blanket, the other take care of the knife till I ask for it.' Suddenly it dawned on her that her sisters were not looking at her, but at the door. A moment later she saw a soldier advancing through the smoke. She cried out as five more followed him into the cottage.

One drew his sword. 'Are you Matilda Woodward?'

She nodded blankly.

The soldier glanced at Alice, the line of children. He hesitated, then said: 'You're all charged with aidin' an' abettin' the outlaw Thomas Woodward. I've orders for your arrest.'

Matilda's eyes widened in horror. 'Are you mad?' she screamed. 'My mother's in childbed. Look! Leave us in peace.'

85

The soldier shook his head. 'Can't be done. Prior's orders. An' 'tis a week in the stocks an' no pay till quarter day if you ain't all under lock an' key within the hour.'

'But my mother!'

'We've a cart. She'll have to chance it. Now come on, all of you.'

As Matilda stared at him in disbelief, a second soldier intervened. 'You heard 'im. Now get those brats outside 'afore I take a sword to 'em.'

Matilda sneered, then reached for the cauldron of boiling water beside her. 'Stay your hand, lass,' murmured a voice. 'They'd as soon see us dead as show mercy. Do as they say. Help me to my feet.'

'But, mother! What'll happen if it's born?'

'Babes been dropped in stranger places than the back of a cart,' grunted Alice, pulling herself to her haunches and trying to stand. She was almost upright when another contraction started. Stifling a scream, she clutched her belly and collapsed to her knees. Two of the soldiers began hauling her to her feet again. There was a snarl, a bellow; then Hereward loomed out of the smoke, grasped one of the soldiers and hurled him across the hovel. There was a dull crack as a cheek-bone hit the king-post supporting the roof, then the remaining soldiers jumped on Hereward. Two pinnioned his arms whilst a third slammed a fist into his groin. He grunted and fell. The watching children began crying. The soldiers turned to Alice and half-dragged, half-carried her towards the door. Matilda screamed, picked up the knife, blanket and her youngest sister and ran after them, followed by Ranulf and her other sister. Her mother lay curled into a ball on the floor of the cart. She climbed aboard and knelt beside her as Hereward was hauled feet-first through the mud and tossed over the tail-board. The soldiers surrounded the cart. A whip cracked and it moved off towards the market place, accompanied by a small but angry crowd that quickly grew larger. Matilda straightened her mother and pillowed her head with loose straw as the crowd began taunting their escort.

'I can feel the babe. 'Tis near out,' gasped Alice.

'Don't speak.' Matilda placed the blanket between her mother's legs.

Suddenly Alice cried out, her back arched upward. The cart

had bounced into a rut and for a moment her whole body was lapped by an intense searing pain. Then the pain ebbed slightly and she continued bearing down on the unborn child.

'Push!' cried Matilda.

'I can't!'

'You must. I can feel it. Push!' Matilda's finger-tips had touched the baby's head. It was damp and warm and she had felt the hair lying matted and flat against the curve of its skull.

From then on she was oblivious to the presence of the soldiers and the noise of the crowd, the sway of the cart as it trundled across the square and up the lane past the priory. All she could think of, and feel, was the wet slippery creature now being squeezed from its mother with each successive contraction. Supporting its head with one hand, she used the other to chart its progress; first feeling its neck, then a shoulder, finally its chest. Suddenly the baby fell forward into her hands. She felt herself trembling as she cut the slender lifeline connecting it to the womb that had cradled its growth, then she wrapped it in the blanket and carefully pulled it clear of the hem of her mother's pelisse. She lifted it towards her. Its face was blue and puckered and spotted with blood, but its eyes were wide open and it coughed and sputtered as it drew in its first breath. Its cheeks turned pink as its bloodstream absorbed oxygen. After wiping the mucus from its nose and mouth she gave it a gentle shake. It whimpered slightly, unclenching a fist. Its throat gaped open as the whimper gave way to a scream.

Matilda grinned. ''Tis a boy, and was born head first.' She lifted it towards its mother.

Alice smiled weakly. 'I knew it.' She looked at her son for a moment, then sighed and closed her eyes. 'Show him to the village folk,' she whispered. ''Tis time they learned what us Woodwards is made of.'

Matilda raised the baby to the peasants clustered round the cart. Some roared their delight, one threw a stone at the soldiers. Their mood worsened. They began jeering and shaking their fists and an old cowherd tried to halt the oxen hauling the cart, insisting as he did so that Audley leave the priory and baptize the baby. The soldiers lined up behind the cart. Stones began falling all round them: then the din receded as the cart entered a walled courtyard and drew up in front of the deserted manor house that stood like a brooding stone ghost on the edge of the village.

'Out! All of 'ee!'

Hereward spat at the soldier. No one else moved. The soldier lifted his sword. He was a squat, brutal looking man with a vinous and battered face, and as Matilda watched him advance towards her father she sensed the danger of violence. She stood, handed the baby to Ranulf and asked her father to help lift Alice from the cart. Her mother's face was pale and bloodless and her whole body was shaking. The rest of the family gathered round her as the soldiers closed ranks and led them through a small overgrown garden to the rear of the house. A door opened at the bottom of some steps. The Woodwards were pushed through it and into a long vaulted cellar. The door slammed and the bolts slid home. After lowering her mother to the floor Matilda walked towards the narrow slitted window that looked out at the encircling downland. Her baby brother began crying behind her. In front of her, secure in his greenwood refuge, was another brother. She smiled as she thought of him. And slid exhausted to the floor.

*   *   *

Two days later Matilda was taken from the cellar and led upstairs into the great hall. Prior Audley was waiting for her. He demanded to know where Thomas was hiding. She said nothing. In response Audley ordered his men to strip her naked. They began whipping her. After the first ten lashes she revealed the existence of the badger-set. On the following day the process was repeated. That morning the set had been surrounded. There was no one there, nor was there any evidence to suggest that there once had been. Audley accused her of lying. Her dress was cut from her body. She fought back, viciously scratching both prior and the soldiers with her fingers. After thirty lashes she swooned and fell to the flags. Blood dripping from her back, she was removed from Audley's sight. The prior felt weak. He walked over to the fire-basket in the centre of the hall and stared up at the smoke-blackened louvres high overhead. He could feel a sharp pain where she had torn the skin from his cheek. He pinched the wound, increasing the pain in the hope that it might help him forget Sampson, the nightmare that plagued his days. Still haunted by his son, he slumped against the basket as the sergeant commanding the manor guard entered the hall.

'God forgive me,' he muttered absent-mindedly, 'but it had to be done.'

The sergeant stirred uneasily. 'Two score lashes 'd make a mute find its tongue, your worship,' he said finally.

'Yes, yes. You did your duty.'

'We could try again tomorrow.'

'No. I'll have no more thrashings.'

'Shall we send 'em home? The woman ain't touched food since we brought 'em in and the babe's still poorly.'

'Not yet. I want them kept here till I say otherwise.'

The sergeant smirked. 'Very good, your worship. T'ain't often we get the company of a lass in here.'

Audley's eyes flashed angrily. 'If any of you lays a hand on that girl I'll see him hung for it. Is that understood?'

'Yes, your worship.' The soldier shrugged: one minute he wanted the skin peeled from her back, the next he was treating her like a daughter.

Audley began pacing the hall. Suddenly he halted and said: 'Order one of your men to saddle his horse. I've a letter for the sheriff. You might also let it be known that two chests of silver are shortly to be taken from the priory and sent to Salisbury.'

The sergeant grinned. 'Bait, your worship?'

'How else do you catch a fish?'

'You mean two, don't you, your worship? Kippers an' outlaws come in pairs.'

Audley smiled, and the first tear did not mingle with the blood on his cheek until he had turned and left the room.

CHAPTER EIGHT

Sampson laughed as the old hermit began huffing into the snow-white beard that reached down to his chest. 'Don't fret so, Joshuah,' he said jokingly, ''t'was easier than plucking a fowl. We waited for them where the track narrows in Bockerly Covert. They hadn't a chance. Thomas's aim had never been truer and he'd unsaddled two before a bow had been drawn.'

'Huh! You lads reckon you could outwit the Devil himself,' grumbled Joshuah as he lifted another oat-cake from the stones circling his fire and handed it to Sampson. 'But it doan' impress I. I seen too many o' you hot-heads being led past in chains for a meeting with the hangman to be fooled by luck and a longbow. They were the king's men, bearing his orders.'

'They aren't any more.' Sampson swallowed the oat-cake and took a sheet of parchment from inside his jerkin. 'Look, sealed by the king himself. From now on we're excused all tolls and given the right to demand food and shelter for the night.'

Joshuah snorted, then poked a wrinkled grubby finger at the mounted knight stamped in red wax at the bottom of the parchment. 'If you two keep up this nonsense much longer there'll be a couple o' hundred of them on the Chase soon, and all of 'em questing for you.'

Sampson laughed at his fears. ''Tis a week now since the attack. You've heard nothing, nor have we. ''Tis all forgotten.'

'Believe that an' you'll soon be dead.' Joshuah looked up as Thomas returned from tethering the horses, dropped a pannier at his feet, grinned and said:

'Here, another fifty shillings in pence to bury in the hut.'

Joshuah growled. 'I won't have it. How can a man contemplate the divine mysteries when sleeping on stolen coin? Anyway, there ain't no more space. ''Tis already fit to bursting.'

'We'll build you another,' said Sampson.

'Oh no you won't.' Joshuah pointed at the round turf hovel that stood beside the highway. 'That there's been my dwelling for nigh on . . .' He paused, a twinkle in his eyes. 'Never you mind. T'aint right for man to speak of his age.'

Sampson smiled as he glanced at the hermit's home. Gorse and blackthorn had rooted in the thick sods of turf that covered its roof. A pilgrim's staff protruded from one wall, and from its crook hung a bell and a bleached human skull in which a pair of wrens had begun building their nest.

He and Thomas had first met Joshuah after ambushing the monks on the ox-drove. Riding homeward over a deserted wind-swept stretch of downland in thick fog they had suddenly heard the tinkling of a bell. A moment later an old man with wizened cheeks and the sharp face of a hawk had appeared out of the mist reciting the Beatitudes and clutching a begging bowl. It was Joshuah. Since then they had discovered that he was almost a legend to those who travelled the Chase. No one knew his age or when he had first settled beside the lonely crossroads in front of his hovel. He spent his days in prayer and meditation, and few travellers passed by without tossing him some food or drawing water from the holy well that stood near the road. To many he was part of the landscape, an image strengthened by the moss that sprouted from his broad-brimmed hat and the tufts of white hair that cascaded from each of his ears. His past was a mystery. It was rumoured that he had accompanied King Edward I on the last of the Wars of the Cross, more than sixty years earlier. No amount of questioning would persuade him to discuss the inter-vening years, and local gossip had filled them with a history that he himself would neither confirm nor deny. Some, convinced that the skull hanging outside his cell was that of a Saracen, believed that he had been captured by infidels and sold into slavery; others, that he had seen a vision of the risen Christ during the siege of Acre and forsaken the sword for the cross. A shrivelled palm leaf decorated his hat brim – proof that he had been to the Holy Land – and the rows of pewter badges and ampullae sold as souvenirs outside shrines and now sewn onto his cloak added further weight to the belief that he had once been a pilgrim.

Despite his love of solitude an unlikely friendship had developed between Joshuah and the two outlaws. He was old enough to be their great-grandfather, but Sampson's high-spirits and resourcefulness and Thomas's timidity had awoken some long forgotten echo from his own youth. He had soon realized who they were, but said nothing, leaving them to decide when to tell him. When they finally did so he had immediately started cackling. 'I knew that when I first clapped eyes on 'ee,' he had said at last.

'How?' asked Thomas in amazement.

Joshuah tapped the side of his head. ''Tis all in here. A dog don't pup, a wench play the cuckold without ol' Joshuah getting the knowing of it.'

The two outlaws had smiled at his boast. Like most who met him they regarded him as harmless but feeble-minded, and it was several weeks before they realized that his eccentricities masked a knowledge of the Chase perhaps greater than that of any other who lived within its borders. Shepherds and swineherds stopped to chat with him. Merchants and tinkers passed on their gossip, telling him who was bound where, with what and why. Foresters sheltered in his hut from the rain and the Chase verderers joined him to grumble about poachers over a flask of mulled ale. In time the two outlaws had recognized his worth. He became their confidant and only ally, an extra set of ears and eyes, and a source of information that had already proved invaluable in their struggle to discredit Prior Audley.

It was Joshuah who had told them that a squad of archers was travelling over the Chase, and as this was their first meeting since the ambush Sampson was eager for news. Whilst Thomas hid the money they had stolen from the soldiers, he and Joshuah sat by the fire and debated the chances of Audley ordering a hue-and-cry.

'He'll never find us,' he insisted. 'Since leaving the set we've always kept moving. I'm certain he thinks we've a hiding-place.'

Joshuah grunted. 'Aye, an' I reckon he'd be forgiven for suspecting that this was it.' He paused, glancing at Sampson: the bright impetuous eyes oblivious to all danger, the open intelligent face unmarked by the disappointments and compromises that come with age. 'There's days I wonder why I befriended you,' he went on. 'Right now I wish the pair of you in Hell for disturbing an old man's peace of mind. Me innards ain't been the same since you left for the covert.'

Sampson smiled. Joshuah was troubled by an unending catalogue of maladies that owed more to imagination than fact. One day he would complain of a fever, on the next of the stone or a quavering in the kidneys: a hypochondria he humoured by supplying the medicines and potions that formed the basis of the hermit's diet.

''Tis the black bile again, ain't it?' added Joshuah suspiciously. 'T'ain't no purpose in pretending. I've cheated Death often enough to know when she's come to claim me.'

Sampson suppressed a laugh. 'Nonsense. You've an excess of phlegm. It'll be gone come nightfall. Now tell me what gossip you've heard.'

'Pah! You quacks are all the same – prattle first, a man's welfare second. Joshuah paused, suddenly grave. 'Aye, I've something to tell 'ee, but it don't make dainty listening.'

Catching his mood, Sampson was instantly serious. 'What is it?' he demanded.

'Thomas must hear it as well. 'Tis he it concerns.'

But even when Thomas finally joined them beside the fire, the hermit remained silent. Suddenly he glanced at Thomas. 'You'll not like it,' he murmured. 'I heard it two days back from a huckster.'

Thomas felt his heart beat quicken as he waited for Joshuah to continue. The ease with which he and Sampson had robbed during the last few months had made him think that he had at last conquered his nervousness. He now realized that he had been guilty of self-deception, but not of deceiving Joshuah. 'Tell me,' he said.

Joshuah hesitated, then said: 'Audley's arrested your family and placed them in the manor cellars. Your mother was in childbed when they came for her. She dropped the babe in a cart. T'was a son. It died three days later. As it hadn't been baptized the soldiers cast it on a dung-heap. Some folk found it and buried it in a copse near the river. The day before it died the soldiers searched the set. ''Tis thought Audley took a whip to your sister to find out where it was.'

There was silence. Thomas crossed himself and buried his

face in his hands, Joshuah reached out for his arm. 'I'm sorry. I had to tell you. I've said prayers for its soul. ''Tis those who suffer as that babe that God most loves.'

'Audley must die,' cried Sampson. 'We'll snatch him from his dovecote, break into the cellars and hang him in the woods.'

'Be silent, lad!' snapped Joshuah. 'Let a man mourn 'afore plotting revenge.'

Thomas lifted his head, tears flecked his cheeks. He smiled wryly and said: ''Tis alright, Joshuah,' before turning to Sampson and adding: 'Now, perhaps, you can understand what us Woodwards mean to Audley, how much he hates us. We've no hope of outwitting him.'

'We've done it 'afore. We can do it again,' retorted Sampson. 'You're a better archer than any of his soldiers.'

'And what will you do? Plan an' scheme an' tally the dead we leave in our wake.' Thomas scowled his contempt, then turned and looked out over the Chase. The day was overcast, and the humped downs that rolled away to the horizon faded one into the next, as if in ignorance of the valleys and coombes that lay between them. The March pasture was still withered and rank. The few stands of trees that broke the emptiness stood gaunt and bare, the sap still dormant in their shallow roots. It was a grim, forbidding landscape; even the tracks that intersected at the crossroads seemed to deny man's attempts to tame it, and Thomas felt a sudden longing to leave it, to be free of the endless suffering it seemed to spawn.

'Why don't we seek right of sanctuary?' he said finally.

Sampson leapt angrily to his feet. 'And be forced to walk the highway, bare-footed and carrying a cross, and then to be exiled from England for crimes we did not commit?'

'Perhaps we should part,' replied Thomas. 'You always said we'd make Audley act, and we have. I've a corpse for a brother and a family locked in a dungeon.'

'You're wrong, Thomas! In three months we've halved the amount of goods being carried across the Chase. We've horses, food, money and small caches of arms hidden near every track. We've kept moving, never biding anywhere long enough for Audley to trap us. Don't you understand? We're winning!'

'You call robbing monks and merchants a victory?'

'Yes! Audley's made no move to snare us. Why? Because he's

afraid of us. We're like fleas feeding on an open wound. It festers and poisons. Sooner or later his patience must fail: 'tis then he'll make a mistake.'

'Meanwhile my father an' mother, aye, an' Matilda too, must rot forgotten in a cellar.'

'He'll release 'em soon enough. He's trying to panic you. He's nothing to charge them with, and knows it.'

'That's right,' agreed Joshuah.

The three men lapsed into silence. Sampson had detected the sharp look Thomas had given him when mentioning Matilda. He closed his eyes: recalling her kiss, imagining the scars that now patterned her back. And yet, despite his horror at what she had suffered, he was not surprised by news of her arrest. He had known it might happen, just as he had feared that Audley might employ force to make her reveal where Thomas was hiding. He had known, but done nothing. Feeling corrupted in some way for his failure to try and protect her, he cursed his own cold-bloodedness, the ruthless pragmatism that had made him insist they abandon the badger's set within days of that first mid-winter ambush.

'I've something else to tell 'ee,' said Joshuah eventually 'A tranter came by yesterday. Before leaving he told me that two chest loads of silver are to be taken from the priory to Sarum.'

Sampson's mood changed. He grinned. 'They'll never arrive. We'll mount an attack in the woods, show Audley that we can't be silenced.'

'Don't be so hasty.' Joshuah frowned, a sudden premonition of danger making him pause for a moment. 'Why should Audley choose now to move bullion?'

'Because he's certain we'd plan an ambush,' ventured Thomas.

'No!' cried Sampson. 'He thinks he's safe, that having surprised the king's archers we'll be wary of showing ourselves.'

'Aye, an' so you should be,' added Joshuah. 'For 'tis odd timing, an' that's a fact.'

Thomas agreed. 'Let's leave 'em be. The chests 'll be guarded. No man sends silver across the Chase without an escort.'

'Of what? A dozen ruffians grown idle on guarding the manor house and dragging your own mother from her childbed? We're not unarmed peasants to be cowed with one blow of a cudgel, but fugitives, outlaws who've learnt to live by their wits and the bow. We must attack. We'll set a trap. There's only one road they can travel. Listen, and listen carefully . . .' And a moment later, as the seed finally germinated, Sampson began explaining how they could snatch the chests.

Thomas remained silent whilst he spoke. He still did not doubt that they would eventually be caught. The past few months had seemed an illusion, a dream, a brief pause between the year he had spent alone and that final walk to the gallows. And now that pause had been stretched to breaking-point. Knowing that each attack hastened the inevitable, he begged Sampson to reconsider.

Sampson ignored him and strode hurriedly towards his horse. Mounting it, he turned to Joshuah. 'When we next meet we'll be as wealthy as any man in the kingdom.'

The hermit spread his hands. 'A deep purse can still be cut.' He paused, gripping Thomas's hands in his own. 'Go with him, my friend. He needs you just as you need him. You're in God's hands. Let Him be your guide, not the fear in your belly.'

''Tis folly to tempt fate,' replied Thomas. 'No cunning can match Audley's, not even Sampson's.'

'Was it fate that took your brother or laid the lash on Matilda?' The hermit smiled. 'Now go, and God speed your arrows to their mark.'

Thomas rose and walked over to his horse. Glowering angrily at Sampson, he climbed into the saddle and forced it into a canter. Joshuah watched the two outlaws ride out of sight before kneeling beside the fire and beginning to pray.

*   *   *

The waggon lurched and swayed on its unsprung beams. Its massive nailed wheels bit into the mud as the drover goaded his oxen up the long hill that led into the woodland ahead. 'Git up!' he bellowed, raising his voice against the wind blustering over the rim of the gully. He lifted his whip and cursed the prior – and not for the first time that morning – for making them leave for Sarum on so foul a day. Rain had dogged every inch of their journey. Mud had seeped through his hosen, water was trickling down the inside of his jerkin. A sudden squall made him turn, and he cursed again as he thought of the soldiers sheltering beneath the hooped canvas covering his waggon whilst he waded through the quag. Soon it might reach the axles, he thought happily, forcing them to jump out and push. 'Aye, that'd do none of 'em any harm,' he growled, catching a brief glimpse of the mounted archers riding to the rear of the waggon.

The five soldiers huddled inside it were in no mood for risking their necks. They had been roused at dawn, only to be thrown this way then that by the constant jolting beneath them. The track's potholes made dicing impossible, they had long ago drained the flagon now rolling across the boards, and the two chests kept chaffing and then snapping the ropes holding them in place.

'Ben 'll be dead of the ague 'afore long,' growled one of them as he watched the drover flounder through the mud.

'Aye, an' it'll be that damned fool Audley who's to blame,' added another, glancing at the two monks squatting in the back of the waggon. The monks shuffled uneasily and raised their cowls. One took out a rosary and began repeating the *Gloria* in expiation of the soldier's blasphemy: the other hooked a finger beneath the canvas and placed an eye to the opening. Behind the escort the track sloped downhill, but he could just see the massed body of soldiers standing beside their horses at its bottom. He was young, a novice, and he felt a moment's sympathy for the two outlaws as he thought of the hundred men levied by the sheriff and the score of Cheshire archers sent by the king to make certain that neither of them escaped. Trees rose up round him as the waggon entered the wood. He lowered the canvas as he saw the soldiers mount and begin moving into position. The trap was about to be sprung.

The waggon rumbled on. The men guarding the chests strung their bows and sat grim-faced and tense in a silence punctuated by the sound of rain-water dripping on to the awning from the branches overhead.

'They'll not do it,' muttered one.

'They're as good as dead if they do.'

'Poor buggers. Sir Godfrey's men should have circled the wood by now.'

'And all for these,' added another, kicking the side of one of the chests.

Even as he spoke the waggon lurched to a halt. Within seconds an arrow had sliced through the canvas and embedded itself in the boards. One of the monks screamed, then all was confusion as the oxen began lowing and a succession of arrows flighted in on the waggon. One of the soldiers looked out. The drover and the two leading teams of oxen had vanished into a pit that must have suddenly opened up beneath them in the track. His confidence fast ebbing, he reached for his bow, then cried out and spun round as an arrow slammed into his spine. A moment later a giant oak tree toppled slowly across the track, cutting off the waggon from its escort.

*   *   *

Sampson lowered his axe as the oak ripped through the surrounding coppice and fell behind the waggon. He could hear the sergeant commanding the escort shouting orders to his men, and he knew it was vital that they cripple the waggon before the soldiers unhitched it. He ran back through the undergrowth, only halting to gather breath when reaching the cart they had stolen from an isolated farmstead on the previous evening. The two cobs standing patiently in the shafts watched curiously as he picked up a coil of rope. It led upwards to a thick, high branch that overlooked the track; beneath which he could just see the rounded outline of the boulder he and Thomas had hauled into place during the night. He peered through the undergrowth, and smiled: they had dug the pit in the perfect position, boulder and waggon were directly in line with one another. Pulling on gauntlets so as not to scorch his hands when the rope ran free, he quickly slashed at the short stake holding it down. It leapt through his fingers. The boulder dropped, plummeting towards the waggon and vanishing through its awning before reappearing as it tore a jagged hole in the boards. There were screams. A soldier with an arm smashed to pulp fell into the mud; another, a huge splinter dangling from his chest, rolled through the torn canvas and lay lifeless on the ground.

Sampson turned and started running past the dozen longbows mounted on posts along the edge of the wood, pausing to loose an arrow from each as he went. He could see Thomas now, steel cap low over his head, calmly picking another arrow from the heap at his feet and firing it at the soldiers squatting behind the oak.

'How many down?' he bellowed.

Thomas glanced at him before taking aim. 'Six, four of 'em dead.'

So finally they had killed. But there was no time to dwell on it. He had long known it would happen. And these men were soldiers, trained to kill. After a moment's remorse, he shook the thought from his brain and unshouldered his bow as a crossbow quarrel tore past his head. From now on it was take life, or have it taken.

Unlike Sampson, Thomas had chosen to ignore all such equations as he stood, sheltered by a tree, notching arrow after arrow to his bow. For now that the attack had started he felt lucid and clear-headed, as if mind and body had been welded into one by the proximity of death. There was a gruesome simplicity to his labours, and his concentration never faltered as he carefully took aim, fired, marked the shot and reached for another arrow. The soldiers defending the waggon were still wasting shots on the longbows lining the perimeter of the wood. Winding back their crossbows had slowed their firing rate, and he knew that their chances of beating back the attack were rapidly lessening. With his bow in his hand and Sampson beside him, he felt a companionship between them that had been absent throughout the three days spent preparing for the ambush. He grinned contentedly. Once again Sampson's optimisim and planning had proved him wrong. Then his grin faded as he remembered the plight of his family and deliberately took aim at the unguarded face of one of the soldiers. The man reeled back, clutching at the shaft now deep in his cheek. A moment later he heard Sampson shout: 'Keep me covered! They've fled.'

Thomas looked up as the handful of surviving soldiers dropped their bows and ran for safety. Then Sampson was gone, swerving and keeping low as he broke through the undergrowth on to the track and boarded the wrecked waggon.

Thomas quartered the woods for signs of a counter-attack before keeping a close watch on the wounded soldiers lying sprawled in the mud. Time seemed to slow, then come to a standstill. Lucidity became fear as he waited for Sampson to cut the rope from the sling wrapped round the boulder and tie it to the first of the chests. Suddenly a hand poked through the canvas: the signal for the lift. He dropped his bow and began hauling in on the rope. It tautened, he heaved, inch by inch the chest rose through the awning and into the air. Sampson reappeared Pulling the chest behind him, he walked back across the track and forced his way through the brambles. The chest clattered against the side of the cart. Thomas took up the strain again. The chest rose, swinging over the wattle sides of the cart and dropping into place as he slackened the rope. 'Now the other one,' said Sampson, untying the rope and beginning the return journey to the waggon. A split-second later he heard a horn sounding and the clatter of armour. He looked round in bewilderment, diving for cover as an arrow sped past him.

'Take 'em!' bellowed a voice. 'There's a silver noble for the first to bring me a head!'

Then Sampson was beside him again, his face torn by the brambles. 'Quickly,' he cried breathlessly. 'It's a trap! There's a line of archers on the far side of the track.'

'There's more here!'

Sampson followed his companion's gaze, suddenly seeing a solid wedge of mounted men-at-arms advancing towards them through the wood. 'We're surrounded! Come on, 'tis time to be gone!'

The soldiers began to close in as Sampson jumped aboard the cart and snatched at the reins. It was already moving when Thomas tossed his longbow and a bundle of arrows over the tailboard and threw himself alongside the chest. Sampson whipped the cobs into a canter. The cart bumped and swayed as Thomas steadied himself in a corner and picked up his bow. 'Force a gap!' screamed a voice in his ear. He turned and peered over Sampson's shoulder. Ahead of them stood a line of pikesmen, the long wooden shafts of their pikes lifted to the ready. He glanced round. The archers had crossed the track, the men-at-arms were circling the cart. A whip snaked overhead. A horn shrilled. He turned again as Sampson steered the cobs towards the line ahead. He lifted his bow and fired. One of the pikesmen toppled from his pony. 'Now his neighbour!' yelled Sampson. Thomas notched another arrow into place and tried to take aim. The cart's motion made accuracy impossible. He waited. The line drew closer. He fired at point blank range. He could see a mottled stain spread over his victim's throat, his arrow's flight feathers etched cream against scarlet. Then the cart was driving through the narrow gap in the line. A pony swept past him, knocked to its knees by the force of the charge. The curved head of a pike slid past his face, its steel tip only inches from an eye. Then they were through and bouncing down a steep slope. He glanced back, suddenly horror-struck. A knight in full armour astride a grey charger had plunged over the top of the bank, followed by a throng of archers and swordsmen.

'Which way?' cried Sampson.

'Keep to the woods! We've no hope in the open!'

'The cart 'll fall apart!'

'Keep going!' Thomas ducked as branches skimmed his cheeks. The wheels skidded beneath him. Mud was being thrown up all round him. He could hear hooves pounding the soft earth and the shouts of the soldiers giving chase. Lifting his bow again he began firing at those nearest the cart. Gradually the gap closed. Soon he could see white foam spilling from the horses' mouths, the drawn faces of the soldiers, the coat-of-arms on the knight's surcoat. 'Faster!' he shouted.

'We can't!'

Suddenly the knight lowered his visor and lifted his lance. He began flailing the flanks of his charger with his spurs. It quickened pace, drawing nearer with every stride. Thomas took aim at its rider. Steel plate guards covered his body and limbs, a square helm hid his face. He lowered his aim slightly, knowing that their only chance of escape lay in laming the horse. His first two arrows went wide. The third struck a fetlock. The massive charger stumbled, one leg collapsed beneath it and a moment later the knight flew over its mane and crashed helpless to the ground. A few of the men-at-arms reined in their mounts, but most kept moving and Thomas watched in dismay as the archers in the van lifted their longbows and began firing at full gallop from the saddle. Only one squad of soldiers could do that, the legendary Cheshire bowmen chosen by the king to serve in his bodyguard and who dressed in green and white. Replying to their fire, he saw a hint of green beneath a jerkin. He dropped behind the chest. He had to stem their advance. Sampson would soon be hit. He felt the chest pressing against his ribs. He banged a fist on its lid, then acted. Without it the cart would go faster. The chase might be halted if the silver was recovered. After manhandling it to the rear of the cart he waited for a sudden bounce to help him jettison it. When it came he gritted his teeth and kicked the chest with his feet. It crashed through the wattle, dissolving into splinters as it hit the ground. A sack of stones exploded into the air. A moment later the first wave of horses smacked into the flying mass of timber and stone now checking the charge. Men fell, horses whinnied and stumbled. The second line of archers collided with the first, adding still further to the confusion. As the distance between the soldiers and cart increased, Thomas looked back on a muddled heap of horse and man.

'Stop!' he yelled 'The cobs 'll soon tire. They're still saddled. We've a chance to cut the traces.'

Sampson nodded and shouted 'Woah!' as he pulled back on the reins and forced the cobs to a halt. 'Cover me whilst I cut them free!' he cried, jumping from the cart and taking a knife to the harness. The first arrows had already began falling round them, and though Thomas did his best to return the fire he had seen the pikesmen and men-at-arms fan out in readiness to charge the cart. Sampson started shouting at him. He stood, vaulted on to one of the cobs and kicked it into a gallop as his feet groped for the stirrups. Then they were off again, swerving in and out of the trees as they plunged deeper into the wood.

'This way,' he bellowed, suddenly changing direction and vanishing into a stand of gorse. Eventually he saw a break ahead. Ordering Sampson to follow him he headed towards it, oblivious to the thorns tearing at his face and hands. The wood ended without warning, giving way to open moorland that climbed upward towards an anvil shaped ridge of down. Neither of the outlaws looked back till its summit lay behind them; then, falling exhausted from the saddle, they crawled back to the top of the down and gazed out over the moor. It was deserted, not a soldier could be seen. They rolled on to their backs, sucking in air as the blurred outline of all that had happened gradually found focus. For a while neither of them spoke, each still too stunned to order his thoughts.

Finally Sampson grunted and gave a wry smile. 'So much for the silver. To think we risked our necks for two hundredweight of pebbles.'

'We must flee the Chase. Audley won't rest till he finds us.'

'But where can we go?' Sampson closed his eyes, the closeness of their escape making him plot their future with untypical care.

It was some minutes before he answered his own question.

'Those archers we ambushed,' he said. 'Where were they bound?'

'Portsmouth, to join the king's army.' Thomas paused, shrugging his shoulders as he realized what was being suggested. 'Why not?' he added. 'I've not left the Chase since the day I was born.'

Sampson grinned. ''Tis time you did, my friend, 'tis time you did.'

Part Two

THE FIGHT

CHAPTER NINE

Thomas was convinced that they were nearing the sea. It was mid-morning, and the two outlaws were leading their horses up a steep serpentine track that climbed a hill being grazed by goats. He could not see or hear it, but the breeze blowing across the slopes carried a bracing and unfamiliar tang; sea gulls wheeled overhead, wing tips curled slightly, legs and feet flat against their plumage. He broke into a run, excitement overcoming his fatigue. Throughout the two previous days, as they skirted the New Forest and rode through the Forest of Bere, his thoughts had kept returning to the moment now approaching – his first glimpse of the sea. Sampson had told him that it stretched to the edge of the world, beyond Samarkaland and the lands of the Northerlings, and that those who sailed over its rim fell into a fathomless abyss from which none returned. That he understood. He had once seen some illuminated seascapes worked by the monks in the margins of the Holy Book. He knew about its bounds, as also he knew about the creatures that swum in its depths and the whirlpools and waterspouts that disturbed its surface. It was its appearance that mystified him. Only this morning had he finally decided that it was an immense silken void swathed in mist and tufted with white growths.

But nothing born by the imagination had prepared him for the sight that finally met his gaze when he reached the summit of the hill. Below him lay three spits of land, each shaped like a pincer, divided by broad inlets that turned to marsh at the foot of the down. Beyond them lay the sea. It was not blue, but slate; not smooth, but storm-tossed and choppy; and the growths he had assumed to be static were a rolling surf of waves that broke before sliding into the troughs formed by the swell. For a while he just stared out, as if intoxicated, to where sunlight glittered on the horizon. Then his heart thrilled as he caught sight of a small boat heeling before the wind as it rounded a headland and entered calmer waters. Waves spilled beneath its bows, its single sail was bent into a taut arc, and he twice glimpsed the underside of its hull as a sudden squall laid it on its beam. Never having seen a boat before, he watched spellbound as it tacked towards the town huddled along the lee shore on the central spit of land.

'That's Portsmouth. The goat girl was right, we're nearly there,' said Sampson drawing alongside his companion. 'Look!' he added suddenly.

Thomas waited until the boat was out of sight before turning to where Sampson was pointing. A moment later the ocean was forgotten.

An open expanse of flat ground lay to the left of the town. It was fronted by the sea and nearly five miles distant, but from their downland peak the two outlaws could see the brightly coloured chequerwork of tents and pavilions that now decked it. 'The army,' exclaimed Thomas.

'Aye, an' God willing we'll soon be archers in the royal pay.' But Sampson made no move. Apprehension and excitement muddled his thoughts as he gazed down at the vast encampment. Ahead lay a new beginning, a world outside his experience, one which could blow him this way then that like a reed shaken by wind. Pennants flew, armour glinted, and an endless caravan of men and waggons moved along the causeway linking it with the town.

Finally they remounted and quickly picked their way downhill. The track merged with a highway and soon they were no longer alone. Foot soldiers and mounted knights clogged the lanes. Victualling officers in close-fitting skull caps sat perched on waggons heaped with fodder and grain; royal purveyors with tallies and empty purses dangling from their waists cantered to and fro; carts piled high with bundles of arrows, horse shoes, timber, bales of fustian and broadcloth trundled past them. The sound of wheels, laughter, song and impatience filled the air. Neither outlaw had ever seen so many men. Some were craftsmen carrying the tools of their trades in bag-rolls on their backs. Others were leading strings of war-horses and mules. Yet more were driving the cattle, swine, sheep and fowl being brought in from the surrounding countryside to help feed the army.

No one paid any attention to the two fugitives. They mingled with the mud splashed throng, letting themselves be shoved and cursed as they moved closer to the walled ramparts ahead and squeezed through a fortified gateway into a warren of narrow streets. Either side of them tall, shingle-hung houses leant precariously over the cobles. They could hear costers calling their wares, women screaming 'Away!' as they emptied their slop-pails onto the heads of the human tide moving beneath their windows. Suddenly the streets gave way to an open square bounded on one side by warehouses and fish stalls and on the other by the harbour. Thomas tried to halt, but it was impossible, and he turned in the saddle to look at the vast armada lying alongside the quay or wallowing at anchor in the fairway. Masts and spars rose in profusion. A gang of shipwrights were shaping the keel of a half-built cog still sitting in the stocks. He could see sailors, small as mice, clambering amongst rigging, carpenters adding small battlemented castles to the bowls and stern of a merchantman. Then the road turned away from the port. They passed through another gateway and into a swarm of tents and hovels hastily thrown up by the camp-followers who lived off the army. Sampson looked round, his inquisitive medical eye seeing ample need for the skills he had been forced to abandon. Cripples on crawling blocks or crutches lined the causeway, thin-faced mendicants held up begging bowls and a group of peasants with scrofula, or the King's Evil, sat waiting for the king to pass by in hope of being healed by his touch. The presence of these wretches offered a grim contrast to the good-humoured banter of the tumblers, jesters, stiltwalkers and jugglers busy performing in hope of a coin. Sampson smiled at their antics, instinctively crossing himself as he noticed a circle of hovels set well back from the causeway. It was a lazar, recognizable by the cross mounted on top of a post, and although most of its inmates had hidden their affliction behind a shawl, he could see on some the shining white scales that branded them as lepers. One, his gloved hands beating a pair of wooden clappers as a warning to others, stood beside the road selling honey from a barrel. Sampson threw him a silver penny, then turned away, ashamed of the charity that had always been his only response to the contagion, as the leper dipped his ladle into the barrel and lifted it towards him.

'An' can 'ee spare a groat for me, soldier. I'll make it worth your while.' Sampson looked down as a hand began pawing his leg. 'Come on, dearie, they'll be no time for wooing when you reach France.'

'No thank 'ee.' Sampson blushed. For a split-second he had substituted Matilda and a different reply for the flashing eyes of the girl walking alongside his horse. Her lips were rouged, flour blanched her cheeks and she wore the striped hood that symbolized her profession.

'Another day p'rhaps?' She smiled coyly, then dropped back to accost someone else.

When the squalid township finally receded and the entrance into the encampment drew closer, Sampson rose in the saddle. 'Look!' he shouted suddenly. 'The king is already here.' The army was camped beyond a palisade, above which he could see the massed canvas awnings of the soldiers' billets and the pavilions of the barons and knights who were to command them in the field. A brilliant patchwork of colour, some bore coats-of-arms on their sides or had been draped in arras or silks. Heraldic pennants fluttered from the finials supporting their guys, making them seem like ships under full sail. One towered above all. Its octagonal walls were of cloth of gold and white swans had been painted on to the powder blue panels that formed its canopy. A gilded crown circled its summit, and a vast scarlet flag quartered with golden leopards and fleur-de-lys trailed from its flagstaff.

The two outlaws stared awe-struck at the royal pavilion before turning to each other and grinning nervously. 'What if we're questioned?' asked Thomas as they slowly approached the gateway.

Sampson shrugged the question aside. 'We're journeymen glaziers given leave by our master to enlist. No one 'll demand proof. Who needs glass to wage war?'

Thomas nodded uneasily and reined in his horse as a brawny black-bearded sergeant returned the transit papers to the carter ahead of them and waved them on. He raised a hand. 'Halt! Your names and shires of birth?'

Sampson replied for both of them.

'And your business?'

'To serve in France for the king.'

The sergeant glanced at their horses, at the well-worn bow over Thomas's shoulder. He hesitated, frowned, then – as if too harassed to care – suddenly ordered them on. A moment later they found themselves facing a wide mile-long avenue lined with pavilions and tents. They dismounted and looked round: lost, confused, uncertain where to go or what to do next. The noise was deafening. Soldiers poured past in all directions, each of whom seemed to be speaking in a different accent. Thomas listened, the manor serf to whom the soft growl of the East Anglian shires or the unhurried Saxon of the northern dales at first seemed like new languages. 'There's little enough chance of being recognized here,' he shouted as a waggon laden with scaling ladders rumbled by.

Sampson laughed. 'Aye, an' so much for Woodward and Hooke, the scourge of the Chase. We might be blades of grass for all anyone cares about us now. Yet three days back some of these lads were out hunting us.'

'We should have stayed.'

'No, Audley would 'a found us 'afore long. Let him search in peace. After a few weeks traipsing the woods there won't be a cottager on the Chase not mocking him for a fool. We'll return, for we've not yet finished with the man, but for now let's wish him in Hell and earn an honest shilling killing a few Frenchies.' Seeing a red-faced archer wading through the mud, Sampson paused. The man carried a yoke, clay slopped from his buckets. Shouting 'Will!', Sampson grinned and ran towards him.

The archer turned, looked blankly at Sampson for a second, then his face crumpled into a smile and he shook himself free of the yoke. 'Well I'll be damned,' he cried. ''Tis the widow's son. Come to patch an' mend us in France have 'ee?'

Sampson's grin faded. 'Would that I had. No, my days as a healer are over.'

'Damn'ee. What then?' demanded the potter, thumping Sampson's shoulders.

'I've a companion with me, we're hoping to enlist as bowmen.'

Will grunted. 'You must both have heads stuffed with mill grist. The pay's twopence a day, the ale tastes like mule's piss an' you'll soon have a lance through your belly.'

'And you, have you stopped potting?'

111

Sorrow drifted across Will's face. 'Trade worsened. A man can't feed a wife an' three babes on hawkin' gallipots. No, lad, I'm an archer, what pots I make go to the kitchens for a few extra pence.'

'But you just said . . .?'

'I know, an' I'd as soon forget.' Will turned angrily and reached for his yoke.

'Wait!' Sampson jumped in front of him. 'Can you help us? Like you we've no choice but to take up arms.'

Will looked at him for a moment, then smiled broadly and smacked his hands together. 'That I can, lad. Who's your companion?'

Sampson introduced him to Thomas.

'God damn it!' bellowed the potter. 'From Cranborne eh, and the witch's son to boot. Well, better a corpse in France than one of Audley's serfs.' He paused, a shrewd look in his eyes. A question formed on his lips, then he glanced keenly at Sampson and told them to follow him.

As they trudged through the mire the two outlaws studied the surrounding bustle. A mood of tense and restless expectancy pervaded the encampment, and there was no doubting its purpose. Ever since mobilization preparations for the invasion had continued without pause, and even now the craftsmen accompanying the army were busily plying their trades. Armourers were hammering steel into shields, swords and breastplates. Skinners were cutting leather into the padded hauberks that would be worn by the archers. Coopers sat knee deep in barrel staves. Fletchers, surrounded by sacks of goose feathers, trimmed arrows and fitted their heads and flights. As they walked Will told them all he knew about the army's formation.

''Tis said there's fifteen thousand of us going to France, an' most of 'em archers; as well as smiths, waggoners, cooks, surgeons, carpenters an' Lord knows who. The king's even raised a minstrel band to play him into battle. As for me, I'm serving under Sir Ned Horton in the retinue of Thomas Beauchamp, Earl of Warwick.'

'Will he take us?' asked Thomas.

'Horton? Why not? To be blunt, you're an outlaw, though I've no ears for knowing how you an' Sampson met or why you've fled the Chase. That don't concern me. But to have kept your head on its neck these past months you must know how to draw a bow. Horton's short of good bowmen. He's contracted to arm six knights, a dozen men-at-arms and four score archers. He'll hire you,' said Will, leading them between a row of tents towards a bell-shaped pavilion. 'Sir Ned!' he bellowed.

A falcon perched on a mailed fist was emblazoned on the pavilion awning. It lifted, to be replaced by a tall lean-faced knight with a clipped beard and a scar on one cheek. 'Will the potter, isn't it?' he said gruffly.

'That's right, sir. These lads are friends of mine. They want to fight the French.'

Horton grunted as he looked them up and down. 'And so does every able-bodied wastrel from here to the Scottish border. What's your trade?

'We're glaziers, sir,' replied Sampson.

'Huh! Since when could a blower of glass lift a longbow?'

'Try us, sir. You won't find us wanting,' said Thomas quietly.

'Come with me.' Horton led them through the maze of tents and past a mobile windmill milling oats for the thousands of baggage oxen and chargers tethered in the horse leaguer.

'You first,' he said, indicating Sampson, when they finally reached the area of common set aside for archery practice.

Sampson unshouldered his bow and glanced down the line of archers all taking aim at the butts. The air hummed with arrows and the shouts of the marshals calling the range. His heart drummed nervously as he drew his bow. His first shot went wide of the target, his second struck its outer ring. 'Enough!' cried Horton. 'If you can hit straw at three hundred paces youll hit a charging French knight at fifty. Now you, sir.'

Thomas picked up his bow, greased the string with the wax from inside his ears and notched an arrow into place. He breathed in, closed his left eye and took aim. A second later his arrow was deep in the centre of the bull's-eye. Horton looked at him, a faintly quizzical expression edging his scar. 'Luck or skill?' he said finally. 'Again.' Thomas said nothing, but his second arrow skimmed the first. Horton smiled, pulled a nearby stake from the ground and walked towards the butts, only returning when he had balanced a silver coin on its top. 'Hit that and it's yours.' A moment later the coin was spinning through the air.

113

'Bravo!' cried a voice. 'Who'se the archer, Ned?' Thomas turned as a sanguine faced man wearing chain-mail leggings and a plum velvet doublet strode towards them followed by his entourage of clerks, knights and pages.

'A glazier from Sarum, my lord,' replied Horton.

'If he can stain glass as well as he can shoot he's doubly blessed. Let me meet him.'

Suddenly Thomas found himself face to face with the Earl of Warwick.

'What are you being paid?'

'I'm not yet enlisted, my lord.'

'God damn it, Ned! If you don't hurry I'll have him for myself. Whatever Horton pays you, I'll double it. We need men like you if we're to teach the French a lesson in the arts of war.' Warwick snapped his fingers. A clerk rushed forward with a purse. 'Here, and don't squander it on whoring – or if you do, keep free of the pox.' The earl smiled as he tipped a handful of coins into Thomas's cupped palms. Then he was gone, his retinue scurrying after him like hounds round their huntsman. One knight remained for a moment, a thoughtful expression on his face as he stared at both Thomas and Sampson. Then he too turned and followed his master. The two outlaws glanced at one another, too relieved to hear Horton telling them that by the grace of God and Edward, King of England, they would henceforth serve at the king's pleasure as archers in his retinue. Five weeks earlier they had ambushed that same knight as he and his page forded the Stour, leaving them naked and penniless and tied to a milestone.

*　　*　　*

'I'll lay five to one on the king!' shouted Will, raising his voice against the roars of the crowd gathered round the tournament field.

'I'm for Warwick,' cried Thomas. 'I've still the mark he gave me that day at the butts.'

''Tis as good as mine, lad. No one's unseated the king for twelve month or more. Look. Here he comes.' As Will spoke a fanfare of trumpets sounded and a grey war-horse pranced through a gap in the fence surrounding the field and cantered to the far end of the lists. The crowd hurrahed and cheered as their king, only recognizable by the crown surmounting his helm, snatched a lance from the turf and waited for Warwick.

Leaving Thomas and Will to scorn each other's wager, Sampson gazed round at the now familiar encampment. The pavilions ranged along the avenue that ran through its heart were awash with banners, all of them billowing in the gale force south-westerly that had delayed the army's departure for France for over two weeks. He and Thomas had been in camp for nearly three months. During that time the Chase, Audley, Joshuah, his mother and Mervyn, even Matilda, had faded to a blur; a miscellany of faces, memories and events that grew dimmer as each day passed. Even Thomas spoke less of his family. It was as if, he thought, they had both conspired to shutter the past, to exchange it for the easy companionship of those in their troop and the unending task of preparing for the campaign ahead. He smiled ruefully and looked round at the grinning faces on whom his life might soon depend: the stocky miners from the Forest of Dean whose days were spent dismantling and re-erecting their enormous siege engines; the hobilars, Gascon and Irish mercenaries who would act as scouts and couriers when the army reached France; the savage Welsh tribesmen, so unlike Mervyn, trained to thrust their long knives into the eye slits of a fallen knight's visor; the pink-cheeked pages, many of them nine or ten years old, who dressed their masters and groomed their chargers; the knights themselves, bannaret or bachelor, who now stood in the tiered lists overlooking the tilting yard; and the great sprawling seethe of men just like himself, English freemen or villeins who cursed, drank, brawled and whored together, and who gathered in the butts each morning to perfect the trade on which victory or defeat would finally depend. And now it was they who were waving their bows and tossing their steel caps into the air as Warwick and his monarch lifted their lances and turned to face each other.

Drums rolled as the two knights saluted the Queen of the Lists, the queen herself, sitting surrounded by courtiers and her ladies-in-waiting in the stands. A herald waved a flag. They lowered their visors, dug their spurs into the sides of their horses and charged. Warwick was the first to gather speed. His crest plumed out behind him and the clusters of bells hanging from his horse trappings and the armour covering its head sparkled in the sunlight as it reached full gallop. He levelled his lance, shaking its stock clear of his left armpit. As the two men thundered towards one another they raised the small triangular shields strapped to one arm. A moment later they met. Each turned his buckler to deflect the other's lance, then they were passed and reining in for the turn. Sampson watched in silence as the king's charger gathered momentum again. Its trappings hung almost to the ground. On each side was an embroidered leopard rampant with jewels for claws and eyes. The king's armour had been silver-plated and both his surcoat and shield bore the red cross of St George. In combination horse and rider made an awesome sight, and Sampson held his breath as they suddenly clashed with Warwick again. They met head on, slamming into one another with a noise so loud it could be heard above the roar of the crowd. Dust rose round them. The king tottered in his saddle. For a moment it seemed he must fall, then they separated and he pulled himself upright as his charger, as if by instinct, turned for the next mêlée. They quickened pace, each digging in his spurs until their horses were at full gallop and their hooves flailing the turf. As they met the king's lance struck Warwick high on the chest. Its wooden shaft snapped in half, but the impact was so great that the earl could not retain his balance. He toppled backward as the king broke and rode on, then slid from the saddle and fell heavily to the ground.

'I warned 'ee, lad,' shouted Will, holding out a hand towards Thomas as the king raised his broken lance to acknowledge the cheers of the crowd.

Thomas grinned, too excited to regret the loss of his money, then watched in delight as his sovereign was winched from his charger and lowered to the ground. Pages swarmed round him and began unbuckling his armour. His helm was removed, then the leather and silk caps that prevented chafing. He shook his shoulder length hair as he waited for the greaves and sabatynes to be taken from his legs. Picking up the remains of his lance he walked over to where the vanquished earl lay helpless on the grass, unable to move beneath the weight of his armour. After placing a mailed foot on Warwick's chest in token of victory, he lifted him to his feet and unclasped his helm. The crowd roared its approval of the gesture as the two knights embraced.

116

Warwick spoke, the king laughed and stroked his beard before giving orders to an attendant herald and joining Queen Philippa in the stands. Suddenly Thomas realized that Horton was with Warwick. The knight turned and began searching for someone in the crowd. His gaze fastened on Thomas and a moment later he began striding towards him.

'God's tooth, we ain't done yet!' bellowed Will in his ear.

'Look!' added Sampson. 'They're placing targets at the far end of the field.'

Then Horton was shouting at him. 'The jousting's over, but Warwick and his majesty have agreed to a wager. Each has sworn he has an archer who can outshoot the other. You, Woodward, are to champion the earl.'

Thomas swallowed, started trembling. 'No, I can't do it!' he cried as Horton tossed him a surcoat bearing the Beauchamp arms.

'You can, lad, and you will. There's four hundred pounds and a thousand acres of best Norfolk loam at stake.'

Thomas's eyes grew wide with fear, his face paled. He stared round in dismay, reminding Sampson of a hunted beast uncertain which way to run. His legs began shaking: an eye blinked, once, then twice. An instant later Horton was leading him out into the centre of the field to the cheers of the archers massed round it, many of whom had witnessed his skill in the butts and recognized him. Then Sampson chased after him and thrust his longbow and a quiver of arrows into his hands. 'Forget everyone. Pretend you're hunting roe. Remember what you told me when teaching me in the woods. You can do it, Thomas. I know it!' Then he was alone, surrounded by a meaningless confusion of sights and sounds that dazed his senses. He tried to focus, catching a brief glimpse of Warwick and the king laughing together in the stands. Then the mist descended again as a sturdy bowman in the green and white of the royal colours joined him in the middle of the field.

Horton drew him aside as the crowd fell silent, content to wait for each archer to try and prove himself the champion in the only art of which all Englishmen never tired. 'Longe's a good bowman, consistent and accurate. He triumphs by outstaying his opponent.'

Thomas nodded blankly, too bewildered to listen to the

knight's advice. Suddenly the trumpets sounded. The royal champion bowed to his patron and stepped to the mark. 'Let this tourney between my Lord Edward, sovereign king of England, and Thomas, Earl of Warwick, now begin!' cried a herald. The two archers glanced at each other, their faces impassive and unsmiling. Longe lifted his bow, a six foot length of unpolished elm that bent into a crescent as he sighted his first arrow at the target. Thomas turned away as it struck red, then shook his head as the next eleven arrows stitched a neat cluster round the rim of the bull. The points were called. Thomas moved into position. His mind wandered as he wiped the sweat from his hands and waited for his heart to cease thumping. He could delay no longer. Notching an arrow to the string, he took aim. It was away, skimming the leather bracer on his wrist before glancing off the side of the target. The crowd booed its disgust as he fought for concentration. His second arrow hit the outer ring. The next ten moved slowly inward toward the bull, the last of them striking the edge of the red.

One target was removed, the other set back a further forty paces. Longe took aim again. Once more his arrows circled the bull. Thomas stepped forward. He relaxed his muscles and breathed in, gradually aware that he was at last finding the composure he needed. He lifted his bow, deaf to the heckling from the crowd. His first arrow drove deep into the heart of the bull. The second lodged alongside it. He smiled inwardly, heedless of all distraction, aware only of the bowstring's twang, the distant target and the sudden hum of the goose feathers guiding his arrows as each hurtled towards its goal. Then he realized that his four final arrows had piled one on top of the other and that the crowd's abuse had turned to applause. He withdrew from the mark, determined not to let their cheers break his concentration.

He watched in silence as a thin wand was placed in the ground in front of the target. Longe took aim, emptying his quiver of its last dozen arrows. All hit the bull, but only one nudged the wand. As Thomas exchanged places with him, he remembered something said by his father when they first went to the butts: 'If you can become the bow, the arrow will fire itself.' He took up position, waiting until his entire body was in harmony with the spring in the bow before taking his fingers from the string. His arrow sped through the air, its head glinting in the sunlight. A second later it split the wand, slicing it from crown to foot before impaling the centre of the bull. For a moment there was silence, then the crowd began yelling. He notched another arrow to his bow, firing it through the narrow break in the wand and placing it beside its predecessor. Nothing mattered now, he knew he had won, and he quickly emptied his quiver, describing a large W, for Warwick, across the face of the target with his remaining arrows. Then all was a dream as the crowd stamped and roared and Horton led him into the stands. He knelt, looked up into the blue eyes of his king.

Edward smiled and glanced out over the field. 'A popular champion. But soon it'll be men not wands you'll be cleaving,' he said quietly before turning to Warwick. 'You've made Lord Thomas master of yet more land.'

The earl spread his hands in apology. 'But you, my lord, will soon be adding an entire kingdom to your estates.'

The king sighed, eyes half-closed against the glare as he looked down at the crowd. 'I hope so, Thomas, I hope so. If not, those who acclaim us now will have widows for wives.'

Suddenly Thomas realized how exhausted he was, how much effort it required to smile and jest. His face was grey with fatigue, his cheeks were sunken and lined. Then Warwick was speaking.

'I once gave you a mark. Do you still have it?'

Thomas grinned. 'No, my lord. I wagered you'd unseat his majesty.'

'And lost.' The earl laughed. 'Half of the money you won me is yours.' He paused, eyes twinkling as he shrugged aside Thomas's thanks and added: 'Time may suggest some other reward,' before glancing at the line of ladies' maids seated behind the queen.

'I suspect you of plotting again, Thomas,' smiled the king, slapping Warwick on the shoulders. 'And you, sir,' he said turning to Thomas, 'will be serving under the earl when we land in France. My son will be your commander in the field.' He rose, leading Thomas towards a young man, of no more than sixteen or seventeen, sitting beside an oval-faced woman dressed in crimson, pearl-trimmed silk. Thomas bowed to her as her husband continued speaking. 'My son, Edward. Look well, one day he will be king.' He stopped, his smile turning to a scowl as a

119

hook nosed man with straggly silver hair leant over the queen's shoulder and handed her a small glass flask. Thomas watched as she uncorked it and lifted it to her lips. The man nodded his delight, rubbing unwrinkled hands along the hem of his planet embroidered cloak as she swallowed.

The king stormed towards him. 'Get that damned quack out of my sight!' he snapped. 'You, sir, will sail with us to France as a surgeon – though God have mercy on those you treat. I look forward to learning how that elixir you brew performs on someone with six inches of French steel in his guts.'

The physician gave an obsequious bow. 'I am honoured, my lord,' he whispered. 'The moon is in Cancer, the humours changeable. Perhaps you require cupping, my lord?'

'Pah! I'll spill my blood in battle, not feed it to the leeches.' The king pivoted on his heels, ordering Thomas to follow. He smiled tersely and said: 'You may only be an archer, but at least you are spared the prattle of quacks and diviners of the stars. Now be gone. The crowd is waiting to salute you and I've much to attend to.'

'Thank you, my lord.' Thomas turned and left the stands. The crowd cheered as he raised his bow and walked across the field to where Sampson and Will were waiting.

*   *   *

It was dark when the three men finally returned to their bivouac. All were slightly drunk and they lay on the grass and stared up at the sky as the smoke from the cooking fires drifted across the encampment. An evening of revels had followed the jousting. Its last echoes washed round them; here a group of soldiers urging on a performing bear, there the laughter of those still watching the few buffoons and mountebanks who had not left the camp. Sampson listened for a moment, smiling as he thought of all the ale and ox he must have downed since Thomas's victory. 'You're wealthy now,' he said finally, rolling on to his side. 'You've money enough to buy your freedom and become a yeoman farmer or baron's steward.'

Thomas sighed. 'From serfdom, yes, but not the gallows. Two hundred pounds for slicing a wand! ''Tis more than father 'll earn in a lifetime.' He chuckled. 'Who in Cranborne will believe I've spoken to the king? Me! An outlaw!'

'Hark at Will. He must have emptied a hogshead.'

Thomas listened to the potter's snores for a moment. 'I nearly failed out there this afternoon, Sampson,' he said quietly.

'I know, yet I said you'd do it.'

The two men fell silent, lost to their thoughts. Neither noticed the approach of a lantern through the darkness. 'Woodward!' cried a voice.

'Aye.' Thomas turned lazily onto his stomach.

'My lord Warwick wants you.'

Thomas climbed unsteadily to his feet and looked down at Sampson. 'Who'd be a champion? There's no time for rest when you win land for an earl.'

The soldier laughed and led him through the encampment. Suddenly he doused his lantern and ushered Thomas through the awning of a small pavilion. He grinned. 'You'll not get much sleep tonight, my friend.' Then melted into the shadows.

'Come here, master archer,' whispered a voice.

Thomas peered through the candle-lit gloom as a black-haired girl, naked but for a chemise, rose from the pile of quilts in the centre of the pavilion and padded across the furs strewn over the grass.

'Warwick promised you a reward,' she said. 'I am it.' Her eyes flashed green and then she was against him and her chemise was sliding to the floor. 'Come.'

He was too dazed to resist. She led him to the quilts, pushing him backwards with a giggle. A moment later her breasts, pendulous and soft and ivory, were blinding his eyes and her long legs were arching and twisting round his. She rose above him, legs splayed, her hair a curtain of fire-flies glowing ebony in the light from the candles. He closed his eyes as she loosened the ties on his jerkin and laid her lips against his. She tasted sweet, the scent of musk clung to her skin. She giggled again and moved back onto her haunches, dimming the candles with the shape of her body; rounded hips, slim waist, the pattern of her ribs. Then he groaned as she slid forward, trailing her breasts across his belly and chest.

If Thomas slept that night he was hardly aware of it. He dozed, was woken, fell asleep again and was woken once more as the first signs of dawn coloured the pavilion above them. They spoke little. He was an archer, she a maid in the countess of Warwick's household. There was no need to justify or explain. Thomas had coupled before, with village girls who stood stiff and shy against the daub of a cowshed. Yet when he was finally woken by a drum roll and the sound of waggons, he turned towards her and kissed her gently on the brow. She smiled and stirred in her sleep. Suddenly he was fully awake. He could hear tents being dismantled, men shouting, the clatter of hooves. He looked up at the ceiling. The canvas was still. The wind had dropped. He dressed hurriedly and lifted the awning. 'Time to rouse yourself, friend!' cried a passing soldier pushing a hand-cart laden with bows. 'We're sailing for France on the next tide!'

CHAPTER TEN

For the next six days the fleet lay at anchor in Spithead. Even as the army went aboard the wind rose again, turning the open waters of the Channel into a humped mass of spume tossed rollers. Only one vessel ventured from safety, putting to sea on the second day under the eyes of the watching fleet. Its voyage was short. A rogue wave washed over its stern as it set a course for France. It yawed broadside to the swell. Water sluiced over its decks and its mast and hull dipped from view, never to reappear. There were two survivors. The rest of its crew and complement of archers were drowned, victims of the gale force south-westerly blowing up Channel.

And it was the wind that Thomas and Sampson were cursing as they hung over the gunwhale of the cog *Fortune* and gazed longingly at the solid motionless shape of Wight Isle, half-a-league to starboard. For six nights the *Fortune* had been their home, their prison, the cause of the sickness that had emptied their bellies within hours of stepping aboard. Overnight the wind had abated and veered northwards, but as yet its change of direction had done little to relieve Thomas's misery.

He groaned and muttered: 'I'm never leaving land again.'

'You must, or grow old in France,' replied Sampson as his companion's face turned a bilious green and he retched up the daily ration of bread and salt pork he had only just swallowed.

Sampson shook his head in silent commiseration and looked down at the other archers crammed aboard *Fortune*. Most were sprawled on the open deck, shivering beneath their capes, but a few were tossing knuckle-bones or warming their hands over the brazier near the mast. A carter was checking the chocks on two baggage waggons, whilst a farrier threw fodder to the horses and hogs penned dejectedly in the waist. He turned away, casually glancing at the other ships in the fleet. Suddenly he saw a hint of white standing out against the grey of the sky. 'Look!' he shouted. 'The *Thomas* is raising sail!'

Those round the brazier quickly joined him, laughing and chattering as they picked out the ponderous outline of the king's flagship. Her single sail was being hoisted. The wind filled it. A moment later she was under way and a string of signal flags was being run up her halliards.

'Loose sail!' bellowed a voice from high on the poop.

'Aye, aye, sir!'

A whistle shrilled as *Fortune*'s crew leapt into the shrouds and began climbing towards the yard-arm.

'Haul anchor!'

Sampson watched as the cog's master bellowed instructions to the two sailors standing beside the massive steering-board lashed to one side of her stern. 'Weather the Foreland, lads, an' keep to windward of that rabble. Get among them an' we'll finish the day as fish food,' he added, pointing to the remainder of the fleet.

Even Thomas forgot his sea-sickness as *Fortune* prepared for the passage to France. Hearing the rattle of the anchor chain, he stared up at the sailors crawling along the yard-arm. The sail's ties were slipped, and suddenly the sky disappeared behind an enormous square of patched and grubby canvas. The crew began hauling in on the sheets. The sail billowed out in front of the mast, and an instant later he felt the sea's motion beneath his feet as the cog gathered way and the first waves crashed under her bows. A ragged half-hearted cheer rose from the waist.

'We'll never see such a sight again,' shouted Sampson in his ear.

'Thank God for that.'

'But look, Thomas, look!' The entire English fleet was now under way. Sailcloth all but hid the horizon, and all round them the sea was awash with tall sided cogs like their own; galleys captured from Moorish pirates, low and fast, straining before the wind like greyhounds at the leash; ungainly fishing boats and merchantmen pressed into service by the clerk of the king's ships from every port and anchorage on the English coast.

Sampson had been told that there were more than seven hundred vessels in the armada, and each of them was now tossing and pitching as spray burst over its decks and the long Channel swell lifted it high in the hull, then dropped it with a sickening thud back into the troughs.

Throughout that day the fleet buffeted its way toward France. Once clear of land it spread out, patterning the sea with small canvas squares that dipped and danced under a leaden sky. Aboard *Fortune* the excitement that had marked the beginning of the voyage soon dulled. Someone produced a pair of fighting-cocks from a sack, a barrel of porter was broached and drained, but most of the soldiers sat listless on the decks. Sampson joined Will in the lee of a waggon. Silent and glum, they tried to sleep or listened to the wind in the rigging and the creaking of the timbers beneath them. Thomas remained at the gunwhale, too ill to notice the constant corkscrewing of the cog or the steep white-capped waves driving beneath its hull. Occasionally he would raise his head and, after deriving a moment's comfort from watching the bows of the nearest herring cobble plunge head-long into the swell, try and recapture the pleasures of his last night ashore. But for much of the time he just stood there, salt stinging his cheeks, the foul taste of bile on his lips, clutching at the gunwhale as his stomach heaved and fell.

When night came the wind dropped slightly. The sea turned silver, became the coruscated backcloth to a galaxy of bobbing red lanterns. The livestock aboard *Fortune* lay down in the straw and the soldiers slept as high overhead a thin slither of moon travelled the sky. Thomas huddled in the scuppers, only rising to his feet when dawn's first flush stained the eastern horizon.

Daybreak found the fleet scattered. Throughout that morning it slowly reassembled again, gathering round the royal flagship like chicks to a hen. The faster galleys hove-to until the main bulk of the fleet had formed station. The sound of trumpets and tabors echoed across the water as the armada sailed on. The tension aboard *Fortune* grew as hour succeeded hour. All kept glancing at the figure of the look-out perched high on the mast-head. Hot broth thick with mutton slabs was ladled out from a cauldron. Then it came:

'Land ahoy!'

The archers crowded the shrouds and stared out over the

bows. 'There 'tis!' cried one of them.

Sampson pushed his way through the now cheering throng towards Thomas. 'France!' he shouted. 'If the wind holds we'll be there by noon.'

'Aye, an' dead by dusk,' predicted Will as he joined them.

Thomas lifted his head. In the distance he could just see a long ashen smudge rising over the horizon. He smiled wanly. 'I wouldn't care if we were driven ashore inside the hour.'

'Come on, you lads. Stir yourselves!' ordered a bearded knight from the narrow deck overlooking the waist. 'String your bows and prepare for landing. I want a dozen of you in the forecastle, some aloft on the yard and the rest lining the sides.'

'So the Frogs are waiting to welcome us, are they?' cried someone.

'No, not unless they've the second-sight. The master's orders were sealed. No one was told our landfall till after we'd sailed. The French think we're bound for Gascony. But that . . .' The knight paused, indicating the coastline. '. . . is Normandy.'

It was low and flat and capped by cloud. Sampson and Thomas kept glancing at it as they donned their steel caps, tightened the lacing down the front of their leather hauberks and wiped the salt from their bows.

The *Fortune* luffed to windward and began sailing parallel to the coast. They could see villages now, hear church bells pealing the alarm. Suddenly they rounded a headland and entered a small sheltered bay. A town stood on the foreshore. The vanguard of the English fleet had already dropped anchor, and a confused skirmish was being fought between the town garrison and the first troops ashore. Fishing boats manned by oarsmen were ferrying reinforcements between the fleet and a shingle beach. There was a quay, protected by a breakwater, and as Sampson watched a small force of men-at-arms, flanked by archers, began running towards it from either side of the town. As *Fortune* hove-to and its crew climbed aloft to begin furling the sail, a group of French crossbowmen entered the square fronting the harbour. The English halted, the archers lifting their bows. The first arrows fell amongst the French, who turned and ran as the men-at-arms continued their advance. Soon the waterfront was in the hands of the English and a flag was being waved from the quay.

It was nearly dark when the signal was given for *Fortune* to berth alongside the other ships unloading onto the quay. She kedged in, grinding against the piles lining the harbour wall as mooring-lines were tossed ashore and she finally made fast.

'Waggons first, ten men to each shaft!' shouted the marshal in command of docking. A pair of gangplanks were lowered. Thomas and Sampson jostled for a place at the head of a shaft. 'Take the strain! Carefully now, get those wheels on the planks.' The waggon began rolling toward the cobbles. Suddenly Thomas felt land beneath his feet for the first time in a week. He grinned. And was promptly sick again.

*　　*　　*

'Come on, lads! There's bedstraw a'plenty in here!' The soldier laughed, battering the door down with an axe before vanishing inside the hovel.

'Aye, an' I wager they'll be as louse-ridden as the rest of 'em,' shouted one of the archers in the column.

'At least the lice make 'em jump a bit!' added another, breaking ranks and disappearing into the darkness. Those round him laughed. There was a scream. A young woman rushed through the doorway, saw the endless column of men marching through her village and fell crying to the ground. Three other women appeared in her wake, followed by the soldiers.

'Who's for the dame?' cried the archer.

One of the three was bearded. Age had shrivelled her cheeks and chapped skin gaped through the rips in her gown. She spat at her attacker, screamed 'Cochons!' and began beating his chest with her fists. The archer laughed, sent her spinning to the dust. Her companions soon had their clothes plucked from their backs. They stood naked, wide-eyed with fear, clutching at themselves. They were driven back into the hovel. Screams gave way to whimpers. A group of archers gathered in the doorway to joke and watch and take their turn.

Hearing Thomas shift uneasily beside him, Will laid a hand on his wrist. 'Leave 'em be. Wenches an' wine are the regards of war, its booty. They'll tire of it soon enough. T'was raiders from these villages that sacked Winchelsea and Wight last summer.'

'So it must be rape for rape till the account's squared?'

growled Thomas angrily as he watched lighted torches being tossed on to the thatched roofs of the cottages clustered round the market square. 'In a week's marching all we've done is plunder deserted villages.'

Will slapped his shoulder. 'Don't fret so, lad. You'll be drawing that bow of yours 'afore long. 'Tis thought we'll reach Caen tomorrow. The Frenchies won't give that up without a fight.'

'A week?' Sampson sighed. 'It seems an eternity since we landed.'

Will grinned and inspected the soles of his boots. 'And in another it'll be I who's doing the pillagin' – for a pair of Norman clogs.'

The three men sat on the cobbles and watched the endless convoy of baggage waggons rumble through the smouldering village. Behind them they could hear the crackle of flames, looters rolling barrels into the street. They closed their eyes, glad of the pause, too tired and foot-sore to care what went on round them. In the two weeks since reaching France they had marched more than seventy miles through the low-lying Normandy countryside. The first five days had been spent in St Vaast helping unload the sixteen hundred waggons needed for provisions and equipment. The abandoned port had soon resembled a fortress. Carts, horses and siege engines choked the narrow streets. The waterfront vanished beneath a mountain of sacks and casks. The king had given orders that the work was to continue without pause. At night mutton-fat torches were scattered along the quay, bathing the soldiers in their dim yellow light. Merchantmen docked, were unloaded, and as soon as one cast off another appeared out of the darkness to take its place.

There too, on that same waterfront, the king had knighted his heir, making him Prince of Wales and a divisional commander. Then he moved inland, leaving orders that the fleet was to sail eastward and burn coastal shipping as soon as the last cog had been unloaded. The advance began. Marsh gave way to a landscape laid waste by the fleeing French. The fields were empty, the crops blackened and charred, and women and children and men too old to fight were the only occupants of the villages through which they passed.

The cowed, bewildered faces of the Norman peasantry had

awoken Thomas's sympathy, however irrational. War, he thought, meant a battle – longbow against knight, sword matching sword – not looting and raping and the firing of abandoned homes. Sampson was less equivocal. To him the campaign was a means to an end – Audley's eventual death – and he saw its realities as the inevitable consequence of conquest. Had he not robbed, killed, even once, with Matilda – and this he found harder to accept – known the desire to bed a woman against her will? But nonetheless he sighed wearily when Will lifted him to his feet and the three of them took their places in the advancing column.

Once clear of the village he was able to see its entire length. The sight rekindled the excitement he had felt when the march first began. The road curved slightly and for once, beneath the permanent pall of dust that charted the army's progress, he could see the banners and standards that heralded its vanguard. To the rear of the king and his bodyguard rode the knights, their armour and lances sparkling in the July sun. Behind them were the hobilars and mounted archers, followed by a vast cavalcade of baggage waggons, carts and French tumbrils. Then came the archers, nearly nine thousand in number, each carrying his bow, two sheaves of arrows and a pair of steel-tipped stakes. Behind him were the last of the archers, the Welsh spearmen, more waggons, the herds of livestock not yet slaughtered, and, mounted on mules, the clerks, surgeons and chaplains that the king took with him on campaign. It was an awe-inspiring spectacle, made almost intoxicating when he heard the distant sound of pipes and fiddles begin drifting towards him from the van.

Suddenly the column lurched to a standstill: the day's march was done. Couriers galloped by bellowing orders. A troop of scouts rode off across the fields towards a windmill. Its sails stopped turning, three figures fled, a moment later a semaphore mirror began flashing from its summit. The column slowly disintegrated as along its length small groups of men built cooking fires, fetched water and helped pitch tents or lift ovens from waggons. Oxen were freed from the yoke, horses unsaddled, and soon the surrounding fields were dotted with their grazing silhouettes. Smoke and the scent of roasting pork wafted on the evening air as the sun slid beneath the horizon. Dust gave way to darkness and a fat moon began climbing the sky.

Horton and his entourage appeared out of the night. Jumping on to a waggon, he waited until a torch had been planted in the ground beside him before shouting: 'Tomorrow, my friends, we attack Caen!'

A cheer went up from those squatting round fires on the roadside. It faded, then re-echoed throughout the army. Everywhere commanders were rejoining their men and giving them their orders for the morrow.

'His majesty,' continued Horton, long adept at such speeches, 'promised to spare life and property if they submit peaceably. The Bishop of Bayeux imprisoned his envoy. When next you prepare for sleep, God willing, it'll be His servant the bishop who rots in a dungeon.' He paused until the cheers had ended. 'We'll be striking camp at dawn, there's a three hour march still ahead of us.' His audience groaned. 'My lord Warwick has been chosen to lead the assault. That, lads, means you!'

'Action at last!' whispered Sampson eagerly. Will and Thomas both nodded, but said nothing.

'You'll not be so thirsty for blood when you've seen it spill,' growled a grizzled archer sitting on the far side of the fire. 'I served with the king and Sir Ned in the '40 campaign through Flanders. It won't be they who'll get chopped into pieces, neat as a butcher's joints, by French steel.'

The archer's words haunted Thomas's thoughts as he tried to sleep. Wrapped in his cloak by the roadside, he kept imagining a cleaver hacking into a side of beef, the marbled fat peeling back as the blade cut deep into the lean. Others shared his fears. All round him those who had never seen service before stared thoughtful and subdued into the embers of the fires. Every now and then someone would cry out as he slept.

At dawn the sleeping army was roused by a trumpeter. The column reformed and the advance continued. Mist hugged the ground. From stirrup, waist and wheel down it seemed as if the army was moving through a veil of cloud which deadened sound, muffling the clank of armour and the rumble of the waggons. It gradually lifted, revealing the sun, crimson and distended, as if it had only recently been born, shimmering in the haze which still hung over the horizon – and Caen.

Sampson was amongst the first to catch sight of the city: the

130

stone walls of the castle rising above the northern boundary of the old town, the spires of its churches, the masts of the shipping at anchor in the tidal river that separated it from the new. When less than a mile from the nearest tenements, the army divided into three columns, one wheeling north, one south, and one marching on towards the earth ramparts surrounding the old town. Just out of crossbow range the order was given for the column to halt. A hobilar went on ahead, climbing to the top of the ramparts before turning and waving a flag.

'Fall out!' cried Horton. 'The old town's been abandoned.'

'Called it a day, have they, sir? I had a mind that the sight of us lot might curdle the milk that once gave 'em suck,' shouted Will approvingly.

Horton smiled. 'You flatter yourself, Will potter. They've fled the old town and fortified the new. We'll be storming its two entry bridges as soon as we've eaten.'

'You're men ready, Ned?'

Horton turned as Warwick rode up accompanied by a young knight in black armour with a gilded coronet for a crest. He looked round at the queue shuffling towards a waggon and said: 'Not yet, my lord. The cooks are still lighting their ovens.'

'Send a courier when they've eaten.' Warwick paused, lifting a gauntleted hand toward the knight at his side. 'His royal highness will command the reserve. I'll be leading the assault.'

The prince's unshaven face broke into a smile. 'The choice is not mine, Sir Ned. I'd gladly give up this coronet for the chance to join you and Warwick at the bridge-head.'

'Your chance will come, my lord.' Warwick turned to Horton, the time for courtesies now over. 'I'll be back when you've deployed. Make certain the archers are issued with swords. It'll be cut and thrust once we've fired the gate.' Then he was gone, cantering away toward the small pavilion serving as the king's headquarters.

As soon as the men had eaten they formed into a long line, six deep, composed of both archers and men-at-arms. Warwick returned, fully armoured and flanked by his household knights armed with battle axes and maces.

The order was given for the advance, the archers reaching for their bows as the line began moving. Sampson looked round, strangely calm, even curious. On all sides men were cheering and shouting as they waded through the knee-high flax and millet being grown in the common fields that surrounded the town. His muscles felt stiff, sweat trickled from his chin as he forced his way through a patch of nettles and up the slopes of the ramparts passed a rubbish dump. He smiled as he caught sight of a child's toy, the model of a horse, lying forgotten in the grass. The sun had blistered its paint, one leg had snapped off. Then he emptied such trifles from his mind as he loped down the far side of the ramparts and began running along cobbled streets. But again it was detail that distracted him: the flies swarming round a basket of eels in the market place, doors and windows flung wide, a half-plucked goose dropped during the evacuation. Finally the streets merged into one, and as he ran past a horse and cheese laden cart standing in a pool of shadow under a tree he saw the walls of the new town rising sheer from the river. A bridge straddled the water and on the far bank stood a fortified gateway. The gates were barred. Sunlight glinted on the steel helmets of the garrison high on the battlements.

'Halt!' bellowed a knight. 'Archers forward!'

The archers took up positions as two men carrying a bucket moved amongst them. Each dipped his arrow in the boiling tar, a torch was passed from hand to hand and the arrows fired. Flames soon pin-pricked the gate. The blaze spread, turning it into a wall of flame. Black smoke billowed upward as the advance continued. As Warwick and his knights clattered on to the bridge the first volley of crossbow quarrels began to fall towards them.

'Clear the battlements, lads!'

Now that the attack had been mounted Thomas's fears had vanished. Lifting his bow, he took careful aim at a French archer rewinding his crossbow, watching the passage of his arrow through the air when he finally fired. The Frenchman fell forward, his screams deadened by the roar of the flames as he splashed into the river.

The gate suddenly collapsed, toppling into a white-hot heap now fanned by the draught funnelling through the gateway.

'Look!' cried Sampson, pointing through the smoke at the line of knights waiting to stem their advance.

'Fire at will!'

The French wavered and reeled back as a volley of goose-quilled arrows poured through the gateway and into their midst.

A banner was raised. The knights charged, slamming into Warwick's men now busy picking their way through the charred timbers that blocked the entrance into the town. The English fell back across the bridge as the French turned and prepared to launch a second counter-attack.

Warwick lifted his visor and shouted. 'Back into the breach! We've not survived the sea to be sent packing like curs with docked tails!'

His words rallied the attackers. Thomas and Sampson were swept forward by a surging mass of archers and men-at-arms. The dash continued. Men began cheering, Sampson amongst them. 'Your sword, Thomas!' he cried.

Thomas grinned, wiping away the sweat and soot that streaked his face. 'I'll place my trust in English yew. Look, here they come again!' he added hoarsely.

The French knights had begun their second charge. Leaving shadow for sunlight, their immense armoured *destriers* thundered under the gateway and onto the bridge. Then all was chaos and tumult as each man fought to stay on his feet. Horses whinnied, the wounded screamed and steel parried steel as the wall of lances moved slowly forward. Thomas and Sampson were soon parted. Sampson cursed and winced as a hoof trampled his feet, then began slashing out with his sword. Horse trappings and limbs kept hemming him in and he was twice knocked to the ground, once rolling sideways under a French charger as its rider's lance plunged toward his cheek. Suddenly he came face to face with a French soldier. Large, startled eyes stared at him for an instant, then the soldier raised his double-edged battle sword in both hands and lunged towards him. He sidestepped. The Frenchman grinned as he blocked Sampson's riposte. His blade flashed through the air again. Sampson fell backward. The soldier smiled and lifted his sword. 'Vous êtes un Anglais mort,' he snarled, wrapping his fists round its hilt in readiness for the *coup de grâce*. Suddenly his mouth gaped open, his face contorted with pain and he began falling. Sampson gazed up at him, too terrified to see the steel head jutting from his chest or the blood on his lips. His sword slid from his hands, clattering harmlessly on to the bridge. His legs sagged as he began toppling toward Sampson. Then he was sprawled across him, now only a corpse whose arms twitched and jerked. Sampson pushed him

133

away and climbed unsteadily to his feet.

A moment later Thomas was at his side. 'You wounded?' he shouted.

Sampson shook his head. 'Was it you who . . . ?'

'Aye, I could hardly miss at . . .'

'Watch out!'

Thomas turned. A French knight, lance poised, was charging towards him. He threw himself upwards and sideways, just clearing the parapet of the bridge as the lance raked his thigh. Suddenly he hit water. Weed and filth clogged his throat, his lungs fought for air. Pain and panic mingled as his feet touched mud. It began oozing round his ankles. Lifting his legs, he swam upwards, finally breaking surface alongside the bobbing hull of a dead horse. Gasping for air, he headed towards the bank, reaching it in time to see the French fall back to regroup and the English surgeons begin clearing the bridge of the dead and wounded. He tore a hole in his breeches. Blood stained the wound. Badly shaken, he bandaged it as best he could and limped off in search of Sampson. Suddenly he heard a trumpet sound and the soldiers begin cheering.

'Talbot's men have forced the other bridge. The French are surrounded!' explained a passing archer.

Others surged round him as Warwick's knights mounted a fresh attack. Thomas followed in their wake, determined to witness the town's surrender. The gateway was already deserted and only a mound of corpses marked the struggle that had taken place beneath its arch. He could hear yet more cheering echoing out of the distance. Then Sampson was grinning and running towards him. 'Thank God you're safe,' he blurted. 'We've won. The French are in flight and the town's ours.' He paused, suddenly noticing Thomas's bandaged leg. 'So the lance caught you. I couldn't be sure. Is it badly punctured?'

'No, I don't think so.'

'Let me look at it.' Sampson knelt and removed the bandage. After examining the wound he stood and said 'Wait here' before vanishing into the maze of alleys that branched off the main boulevard. When he returned he was carrying a bandage roll and part of a fleece. He smiled. 'I broke into a physician's lodgings. This is best lamb's lint. Buckle made do with ewe's fleece bought from a slaughterer.'

134

Sampson's delight at being able to practise his trade was contagious. Thomas forgot his pain, and after his leg had been dressed and bound the two outlaws climbed on to the battlements. To the north a white flag fluttered from the castle. To the south they could see an English squadron sailing up-river on the tide. Plumes of smoke from burning wherries and galliots mapped its route, and every now and then another would slip beneath the surface, its back broken by the blaze in its holds. Behind them the looting had already begun. The dead littered the cobbles, many of them unarmed townsfolk who had been cut down as the English streamed triumphantly through the streets.

'So this is war,' said Thomas softly.

Sampson sighed. 'No, Thomas, you're wrong. This is the price paid for defeat.'

'Found at last! Huntin' for you two's like questin' for phantoms.' Both turned as Will came striding along the battlements with a barrel over one shoulder.

'Burgundy,' he announced, dropping it beside them and sinking to his knees. 'And with or without you I intend drainin' it dry 'afore standing again.'

'When you won't be able to.' Sampson grinned.

The potter chuckled and slapped Thomas's thigh. 'Something ailing you?' he asked as the outlaw winced at the pain.

Thomas told him.

'It'll mend, lad, it'll mend. The soft parts don't matter. 'Tis only bones an' offal a man can't do without.' Will loosened his hauberk and leaned back against the wall. 'God, I could sleep till Judgement.' A moment later, still cradling the untapped barrel, he began snoring.

*   *   *

'Silence that man!' whispered Horton angrily.

Sampson quickened pace and placed a hand over Will's mouth, stifling his snores. The potter opened his eyes, realized he was both upright and marching, and growled: 'Where in Hell am I?'

'An hour's march from the Somme.'

'And the date?'

'August the twenty-fourth. 'Tis more than a month since we

took Caen and eight days since we crossed the Seine. You were sleeping. How could you?'

'Too damned easily.' The potter rubbed his eyes. 'Aye, I was napping, an' dreaming of philandering with my Nellie,' he muttered, automatically placing one foot in front of the next. 'Pah! I should 'a known that were a fancy.'

'We'll be there soon.'

Will grunted gloomily, finally aware of the purpose to his marching. 'I can't swim, an' that's a fact.'

'Ssh.' Sampson peered into the darkness. Although dawn had still to break he could just detect the blurred outline of the surrounding marsh and the backs of those ahead of him. The silence was uncanny. He could hear footsteps, the squeak of wheels, a heron flapping through the reeds: but for once men and horses were silent, the former because the king had ordered it, the latter because their hooves had been bandaged to reduce the noise made by the army as it stole through the darkness towards the estuary of the Somme.

He smiled to himself at Will's bewilderment on being woken. So much had happened since storming Caen that there were times when he too woke uncertain as to where he was or why. Yet all he had now were memories, some fleeting and already fading, others that would endure for ever. Two remained most vivid, and each was dependant on the other: dust and marching – always the marching. Since leaving Caen the army had marched more than two hundred and fifty miles through the August heat. There had been mornings when his legs had refused to obey him, others when his ankles had swollen like dough, once so badly that he had had to cut the boots from his feet. The villages and towns through which they had passed rolled one into the next as he tried to relive the long march along the south bank of the Seine: the avenues of poplars, contaminated wells, the broken ribs of each bridge they came to, the French army looking down from the high lime cliffs that lined its north bank. And then, one morning, their tents had vanished: the king's bluff had succeeded. The French had hurried on towards Paris, now certain that Edward intended to besiege it. It was a mistake that had cost them dearly. For whilst he and Thomas and the remainder of Warwick's division had added to the deception by burning the villages surrounding the capital, the king's carpenters had worked day and night to rebuild the bridge at Poissy. The Seine had been crossed. Closing his eyes, he searched for some memory from the forced march, seventy miles in eight days, that had brought the army to its present position. Only one remained distinct: that of some children sifting through the ashes that had once been their home whilst their mother skinned a dead dog for their supper. It was a march he preferred to forget. For five days he had lived on unripe fruit and unleavened bread made from stale chaff and ale-tub dregs. Many of the horses had died from lack of forage, and the flesh of their replacements, French cart-horses, already hung loose from their bones. And now they were to cross another river. He stared ahead again, confused by an excitement, an expectancy inside him that seemed to thrive whenever he sensed a battle ahead. A faint glimmer of light coloured the sky and he could just see the hunched shapes of the knights accompanying Warwick in the vanguard. Beside him a voice whispered:

'We're there. I can see the river.'

He turned as Thomas pointed through a break in the reeds towards a grey expanse of open water. For a moment he thought it was the sea, and then he glimpsed the pale contours of the woods on the far bank.

Thomas shivered as he stared at the river. 'It's madness. We'll never make it!'

'The king's certain it can be forded.'

'Because a Frenchman told him so. What if it's a trap?'

Sampson did not reply. Like every other soldier in the army he was only too aware of the risk the king was taking. He too had seen the prisoners captured yesterday being led into the royal pavilion at dusk, heard the rumours of the king's intention to offer a reward in exchange for information on how best to cross the Somme.

'What if the tide turns when we're half-way over?' continued Thomas. 'To hazard the entire army on a mile-and-a-half long causeway in knee deep water is folly!'

Sampson grinned. 'Or genius. The king's no numskull, he proved that on the Seine. Anyway, 'tis he'll who drown if the tide turns.'

'Aye, an' while he's perishing in the rear we'll be butts for the bowmen on the far bank,' muttered Will, still unable to forgive

Warwick for suggesting that his division be the first to cross.

The three men fell silent as they slowly drew nearer to the river. When they finally halted a knight spurred his horse down its bank, quickly retreating as the tide swept him downstream.

'Now what?' demanded Will as a tense looking Horton rode by.

'We wait.'

The archers leading the column broke ranks and gathered on the river bank as the rest of the army closed up behind them. Soon the narrow track leading on to the invisible causeway thronged with men, horses and waggons. Couriers galloped back and forth between the king and the two earls in command of the assault. Every now and then a knight entered the river to test its depth, reporting his findings to Warwick and Northampton who were impatiently pacing outside a hastily erected tent. The tide slowly ebbed. A pale sun sparkled on the water. Suddenly Warwick strode into the river. It lapped his knees. He stood for a moment, gazing out over the two thousand yards that divided its banks, then turned and cried: 'Forward!'

A hesitant cheer broke the tension. Knights and men-at-arms remounted their horses as the first line of archers plunged into the water, eleven abreast, and began the long trudge towards the far bank. Thomas, at Warwick's insistence, was in that first line. The causeway was slippery underfoot, his wounded thigh was still weak and the tide tugged at his legs as he waded further into the stream. Lifting his arrows and bow high on to his shoulder to prevent them getting wet, he stumbled. A thickset arm reached out and steadied him. He glanced at its owner, a bearded mason – the guild badge depicting a cold-chisel, hammer and block of cut stone betrayed him – whose lop-sided and toothless grin revealed rather than hid his fears. He looked at the other archers in the line. All were silent and grim-faced, alone with their thoughts, the tightness in the belly.

'If we live, all England will know of this day,' growled one of them.

'And if we don't?' ventured another.

'We'll reach Rye as clean as boiled bones.' It was a poor joke, but all laughed at it as they splashed onward through the chill water. Thomas looked round. To his left waves were breaking in the river-mouth, to his right the estuary narrowed, behind him

138

he could hear the distant shouts of the waggoners goading their oxen into the water. He noticed Sampson, tight-lipped and three ranks to his rear.

Soon the French were clearly visible on the approaching bank. A force of several hundred knights had gathered at the end of the causeway in readiness to repulse the column as it advanced up the bank. Flanked by some two thousand crossbowmen, their pennons fluttering in the offshore breeze, they seemed a solid and immoveable wedge unlikely to be easily shifted. Minute by minute the distance between the two armies lessened.

'The bastards 'll open fire soon, we're nearly in range,' said the archer beside Thomas, silently crossing himself.

'Unshoulder your bows!' shouted the mounted knight leading the attack. 'No one's to return fire till I give the order.'

Thomas ran his fingers down his bowstring, checking it for signs of weakness.

'I want the first twenty ranks within two hundred paces of the bank before we counter-attack. Each will fire when I call its number.'

Soon Thomas heard a French knight barking orders at the crossbowmen lining the shore. Suddenly the sky went grey. He ducked, then stood, ashamed of his fears as the hum overhead grew louder. All round him men began screaming and crying out as the first volley of quarrels raked the silent column. As the dead and wounded floated seawards on the tide, others hurried forward to fill their places. The advance continued. There was a lull whilst the French rewound their bows, and then a second volley cut its grim swathe through the English ranks.

'Take aim!' commanded the knight.

Thomas lifted his bow.

'One!'

And took his fingers from the string.

'Two . . . three . . .' And so it went on until all twenty ranks had loosed their arrows and the count restarted. There was no pause in the English fire and soon an unbroken fusillade of arrows was pouring down on the French. The column halted when less than a hundred paces from the shore, bringing several thousand bowmen within range of the enemy. Thomas closed his mind to all distraction. Arrows splashed into the water, men died alongside him, but all he heard was the repetitive roll-call of numbers and the rasp of arrows being drawn from quivers as volley after volley streamed toward the shore. Gradually the French fire slackened. Longbows could be fired at six times the speed of a crossbow when in well-trained hands, and the archers leading the English advance were amongst the best in the land.

'Cease fire an' move to the sides! Make way for the horses!'

Thomas squeezed to the edge of the causeway as the first of a long column of mounted knights splashed passed him. The French galloped forward to counter the attack and the mud-flats bordering the river bank soon echoed to the clash of swords and lances.

The archers reformed ranks, covering the assault by lowering their aim and turning their bows towards the crossbowmen, a move which slowed their firing-rate still further. The pitched battle along the foreshore raged merciless and loud. But suddenly the French turned and fled, spurring their chargers back up the bank and heading inland, a detachment of English knights hard on their heels. Seeing the rout of the cavalry, the hard-pressed crossbowmen began a retreat which swiftly turned to headlong flight as the remaining English knights charged their ranks.

Thomas grinned, then did so again as the burly mason who had steadied him when he stumbled began embracing him. All round him men were shouting and laughing as they sloshed on through the blood-stained water and clambered up the bank. Thomas followed them, pausing as he reached its crest to look back over the river. The slender column stretched like a thread from shore to shore, and he could hear cheers recede along its length as the news that the bank had been gained passed from man to man. He smiled happily, then turned away as he noticed the colour of the water and the half-submerged corpses of horse and man being washed up-stream by the incoming tide. He recoiled in horror as he turned. The surrounding grass was thick with the dead and wounded. Some lay silent and at rest, as if only sleeping, others cried out as they clutched at the arrows in their bodies. He walked amongst them, as if mesmerized, heedless of their cries, only halting when he stood waist deep in a field of oats, gold and clean, whose ripple and rustle muffled the noise behind him.

The memory of that walk still haunted him when, on the following day, the army marched on through the forest in which it had camped after crossing the Somme. The contrast between today's peace and yesterday's carnage still lingered in the thoughts of those who had fought in the van. Everyone seemed dazed and light-headed. Smiles turned too quickly to laughter, the most foolish of jokes amused.

In late afternoon the army halted on the edge of the forest. Tents were pitched and fires lit. Scouts hurried by, leaving behind them the rumour that the king had selected a battlefield and intended to stand and fight. The banter ended. Some of the men grew maudlin, others irritable, but most were content to lie in the grass and stare up at the sunlight filtering through the trees.

Thomas, Sampson and Will were listening to an account of the crossing by one of the archers who had accompanied the king in the rear.

'The French reached the causeway as the last of the baggage entered the river. There was a skirmish. The Frogs grabbed a dozen of the waggons and a few prisoners.' He paused, chuckling. 'There was a waggon load of surgeons ahead of us. One of 'em wouldn't stop howling so his mates tossed him overboard and 'ee 'ad to walk like the rest of us. Water was chest high by then, an' this 'ere quack offered fifty pounds in silver to be carried.'

'Did anyone take it?' asked Sampson with a grin.

'Lord no. No one believed him. In the end we had to gag 'im. Had a bray worse than a mule. Buckle was his name. Nathaniel Buckle . . .' The archer turned to a passing courier. 'Hey! Where are we?'

The courier pointed eastward through the trees. 'Nowhere you'll want to tell the missis about. There's a small village up yonder. Crécy they call it.'

*   *   *

'He was dead, I'm sure of it!' repeated Sampson angrily.

'You heard the archer's description of him. 'Tis no use pretending, Sampson, 't'was Buckle – and you know it.' Thomas rolled over in the darkness. 'For God's sake! How many more times must we go over it? The man's alive, an' that's all there is to it.'

'But why did he disappear? Why's he in France?'

'Because the king ordered it. I've told you, on the day of the tournament.'

But Sampson refused to believe. 'When I last saw him lying on the parlour floor, he was dead!'

'Why doan' the pair of you cease prattlin' an' sleep,' interrupted a gruff voice from amongst the bodies sprawled round the ashes of the fire. ''Tis near dawn already.'

'Exactly,' added Thomas. 'By day's end none of it may matter.'

Thomas pulled his cloak up under his chin and was soon asleep, but, as the realization that Buckle was still alive slowly rooted in Sampson's mind, any chance of his doing the same quickly faded. The physician's sudden resurrection meant that he need never have left Sarum or become an outlaw. Yet now it was too late. He was wanted for murder, and if and when he returned to England he could not go back to the tavern or resume his apprenticeship. Confused, angry, clinging on to the last of his doubts, he tossed restlessly until morning finally came and the army was roused.

When no marching orders were issued the men gathered in small groups to discuss the likelihood of a battle. Marshals hurried by with orders from the king. A worried looking Warwick rode up to confer with Horton, who then turned and began shouting at his knights.

'The scouts report a French advance. All horses are to be taken to the baggage leaguer being formed in the rear. If we fight, it'll be on foot. Now hurry, and have the men fall in!'

'We're giving battle, are we, Sir Ned?' yelled someone.

'If God wills it, yes. The army's to be drawn up in three divisions: his majesty commanding the reserve, Northampton the rear-guard, and the Prince of Wales, together with Warwick and Oxford, the vanguard on the right.'

The column formed. Once out of the forest they passed the baggage park – an open square bounded by waggons and carts and already teeming with horses – and marched up a slight rise to a road. To his left Sampson could see Northampton's division trudging westward. To his right lay the thatched roofs of Crécy. Above him a stork, unperturbed by the presence of soldiers, flapped through the dust and landed awkwardly on the church tower, its spindly legs folding beneath it as it settled on to its nest. Watching it, Buckle left Sampson's thoughts for the first time since the previous evening. His mood change, anger giving way to anticipation as he climbed the summit of the ridge and gazed out over the site chosen by the king from which to face the French.

Below him lay a wide, undulating valley of meadow and pasture that fell away towards thick woodland, perhaps a mile distant. To his left a wooded plateau merged with the pasture. To his right sedge and yellow flag irises rose from the stream that skirted the forest. It was a superb defensive position, made stronger by three terraces in the centre of the valley. Studying them, each a natural obstacle to charging cavalry, he noticed Northampton's men begin moving down the slope. Some four thousand in number, a quarter knights and men-at-arms, the remainder archers, they were pelting each other with hay and vaulting the neat stooks left behind by the French. From a distance they seemed like puppies at play. Finding their indifference to the fact that those same stooks might soon mark their graves curiously reassuring, he turned towards the stone windmill that nestled beneath the ridge. The royal pavilion had been placed beside it, and he could see the king poring over battle plans with his commanders. Clerks were busy copying out orders at a table, marshals and scouts hovered in attendance. The king glanced up as his vanguard passed. His bearded face was wan and drawn, yet it broke into a smile as an impromptu cheer went up from the men. Sampson joined in, the privations suffered in his name all forgotten as he realized the extent of his achievement in leading a fifteen thousand strong army through a hostile land and now, finally, bringing it to a place of battle of his own choosing.

The king rose, silencing their cheers with his hands. His eyes scanned the column. Recognizing Thomas, he called out: 'God guide your aim, soldier. 'Tis English elm that will win or lose us this day.'

Thomas blushed at being singled out. 'Say something,' urged Sampson.

And blurted: 'I'll not let you down, my lord.'

'Nor will any of you I trust.' The king paused. 'Philip has

143

raised the oriflamme, the sacred banner of St Denys. You know what that means? No quarter will be given, no prisoners taken. If we are routed, not one of us will leave this valley alive.'

'A pretty speech,' whispered Will, 'but carrion ain't fussy. Eyes is eyes to them, French or English, an' it don't make no difference which they dine on.'

The men began chattering amongst themselves as they continued on down the slope. Warwick and the Prince of Wales had joined them, and it was Warwick who ordered the halt. Soon the division was being formed into position; archers on the flanks and in the centre, men-at-arms drawn up between them.

'Woodward.' Thomas turned as Horton approached. 'My lord Warwick has suggested you serve in the prince's bodyguard. The rest of you will be told exactly where to stand. Knock in your stakes to mark the spot and then begin digging pot-holes in front of the line.'

Sampson and Thomas looked at one another as Horton finished speaking. 'So finally we are parted,' said Sampson.

Thomas smiled, sadly. 'Forget Buckle. Remember all I taught you on the Chase. We'll live, somehow I know it.' He reached forward and embraced him. 'God keep you.' Then he turned, quickly, and disappeared.

''Tis alright, lad. I'm still here to keep 'ee company.' Sampson grinned as Will wrapped a massive arm round his shoulders.

'Hooke! Potter! These are your marks.'

The two archers moved into position and began hammering in their stakes, angling them so as the points would impale any French chargers that managed to cross the pot-holes in front of the line. As they worked, waggons trundled to and fro through the division, leaving in their wake bundles of spare arrows and bowstrings. Carts carrying grindstones lined up to the rear of the men-at-arms, and each took it in turn to sharpen his sword. A black robed priest carrying a pyx and flask of sacramental wine wandered through the ranks, occasionally pausing to hear a confession or administer communion. Four field surgeons wearing skull-caps and leather aprons arrived and began laying out their instruments on a square of canvas: a stove for melting pitch, saws, forceps for removing quarrels and an assortment of scalpels and bistouries. Sampson watched, curious as to how they intended treating the wounded. Suddenly he saw the familiar cadaverous figure of Nathaniel Buckle climb from a cart and join them. Even though he had come to accept that his old master was still alive, the reality of seeing that pallid face with its permanently soured expression momentarily stunned him. Dazed, visibly pale, he stood rooted for a second, then pushed his way through the lines towards him.

'Master Buckle!' he cried. ''Tis I, Sampson.'

The physician glanced up. For a moment the shock of recognition showed on his face, then it turned to a featureless mask.

'You must be mistaken, soldier. I've never seen you before,' he said finally, in that soft whispery voice Sampson knew so well.

Sampson halted in amazement. ''Tis I, Hooke, your apprentice from Sarum!'

Buckle smiled at his brother surgeons. 'A condition, I suspect, that you each know well, but nonetheless worthy of study. Fear of combat, disturbed humours, withdrawal into delusion.' He paused, hooded eyes fixed on Sampson. 'My name is indeed Master Buckle. But unless you are a courtier disguised as an archer there is little chance of our having met. I do not number common soldiers amongst my patients, not as personal physician to her majesty,' he added pointedly, as if reminding his companions of his status. 'And now I would suggest you return to your post before I have you hung for cowardice.'

'But!'

'I mean what I say, boy.'

Master and apprentice stared at one another for a moment, then Sampson turned and moved away. As he did so he heard Buckle say: 'A pity, but every pack has its craven.'

His fists tightened, but he continued on.

'You seen 'em too, have you, lad?' said Will as he returned to his position. 'I damn near keeled when I first clapped eyes on 'em.' Sampson looked at him, uncomprehending and still too stunned to notice that those round him were climbing on to each other's backs. 'I've seen six of 'em,' added the potter. ''Tis said they shoot boulders and balls of iron.'

'What are you talking about?' snapped Sampson impatiently.

'The cannons, lad, the cannons! Ain't you seen 'em? Look, over there!'

Sampson followed Will's outstretched finger. Suddenly he

glimpsed a line of six iron tubes mounted on timber sledges being hauled into position near the centre of the division. 'Cannons?'

'Cannons, crakeys, bombards – call 'em what you will. Some say they spit flames and make a noise like thunder. The balls come out of the ends. Though God knows what a ball can do that a bow can't do better?'

'But what are they for?'

'For killing, lad! The very employment us archers get tu'pence a day for.'

'Everyone back to their posts!' bellowed Horton. Still mystified by the strange instruments of war now amongst them, the soldiers shuffled back into their ranks.

'Here comes the king!' cried someone.

Sampson rose to a tip-toe and peered over the helmet of the man ahead of him. Suddenly he saw a banner emblazoned with the Wessex dragon moving towards him. The king was beneath it, riding a grey palfrey. He was unarmed and wore no crown, but carried a short white staff and was dressed in white hose and a crimson surcoat decorated with golden leopards. Every now and then he paused to speak with his troops. Behind him, in a suit of black armour, rode his son and field commanders, Warwick, Northampton, Oxford, Sir Godfrey Harcourt, the Bishop of Durham – a mitre cresting his helm. As he passed each contingent the men cheered and lifted their helmets. When opposite Sampson he again halted, speaking for a moment with a veteran of an earlier campaign before continuing the review. The archer turned, grinning proudly. 'Thirteen years an' he still knew my name. He an' I ain't met since he was a nipper in '33 an' we skittled the Scots at Halidon Hill.'

'Three cheers for his majesty!'

Once again the hurrahs rose from the four thousand throats in the division. Horton returned and waved his own retinue into silence. 'There's still no sign of 'em!' he cried.

'I reckon they've gone home!'

'To spawn yet more of the buggers!'

'Who can blame 'em? A Frog's a frog an' will be till it croaks!'

Horton smiled at their banter. 'Food's been prepared in the leaguer. You're all to fall out and eat. Leave your helm or bow to mark your position. If the trumpet sounds, return at once.'

'Come on, lad.' Will pointed to the cook-waggons lined up on the slope. After placing their bows on the ground, they joined the scramble for the roast baggage oxen that the king had ordered slaughtered. After eating they found Thomas, and the three of them sat on the grass and gazed out over the valley. It was a period of limbo, made unreal by the sweet scent of hay, the chirp of crickets in the grass, the song of a pipit and a vixen playing with her cubs on the edge of the wood. Towards the hour of Vespers there was a sudden shower. Everyone ran back to his post, unstrung his bow and placed the string beneath his helmet to prevent it getting wet. The sky lightened, the sun broke through and the little groups regathered to joke and jest or wager how many Frenchmen each would unsaddle.

It was Thomas who saw the look-out posted on top of the windmill begin waving a flag. A troop of minstrels appeared on the edge of the ridge where the king was now stationed with the reserve. He started to speak, but his words were drowned by the sudden blast of trumpets sounding the *call to arms*. Someone cried 'They're coming!', then all was pandemonium as orders were bellowed and twelve thousand men returned to their posts and stood to. There was a pause, a silence, then the sharp-eyed began pointing towards the far right hand corner of the valley, nearly two miles away.

Sampson and Will and those round them watched speechless as the French vanguard entered the valley. A column of cross-bowmen led the advance, behind whom rode a seemingly unending cavalcade of knights and men-at-arms. Soon the entire base of the valley glittered with armour, horse trappings and banners. Each knight held his lance upright, and the woods lapping the horizon appeared as if bounded by a forest of steel.

Someone in the English ranks began reciting the Paternoster. Others followed suit, and gradually its words spread like a contagion throughout the entire army. As the final Amen faded, each soldier put on his helmet and lifted his bow or sword.

'Would that it were Amen,' muttered Will as another French division entered the valley. 'Ain't they ever going to stop?'

Yet Sampson felt grimly confident as he followed their progress. They seemed disorganized, as if they had been marching all day and only stumbled on an enemy by chance. 'How many do you think there are?' he asked.

147

'Six thousand crossbowmen, maybe. Ten, twelve thousand knights. Start tallying that lot an' you'd end up half daft, or asleep.'

And so they watched in silence as the first of the foot-soldiers marched into the valley. Column succeeded column. Each was thought to be a thousand men strong, and Sampson gave up his addition when reaching thirty. The sun began setting over the sails of the windmill behind them, leaving only a sky brindled coral and gold when it finally dipped beneath the summit of the ridge. He was certain that the French would halt, make camp and give battle on the morrow. But he was wrong, and slowly, like a tide washing over sands, the great army spread out across the valley and began advancing up the slope. Once or twice the Genoese mercenaries in the van paused to redeploy, but on each occasion they were finally forced onward by the sheer weight of those behind them.

Sampson glanced across at the Welsh spearsmen lining the terraces between the two divisions, and then at Northampton's division itself: the flank archers standing in their wedge-like herces, projecting forward from the front of the line like the bastion flanking the curtain-wall of a castle; the knights and men-at-arms swollen to an unnatural size in their ungainly armour; the support teams in the rear – surgeons, armourers, priest and courier, the waggons piled with spare swords and arrows.

He turned again, his heart tolling its own alarm as he realized that battle would soon be joined. The Genoese crossbowmen were already within range, the first bolts began to fall. Occasionally they would run forward a few paces, as if to panic the English into breaking ranks. 'Hold firm!' shouted Horton, and dimly, through the din, Sampson heard other unit commanders repeating the same words to their men. The three hundred yard gap between the two armies shrunk by a third. The swarthy, sallow faced crossbowmen in their mail leggings and black breast armour drew closer. They fired again. Sampson began trembling as their quarrels fell. A clarion sounded: the waiting was over. Sampson lifted his bow and pulled back on the string, aiming low to allow for the slope.

'Fire!'

Three thousand Englishmen took one pace forward and fired.

The sky darkened. To Sampson it seemed as if a flock of starlings had flown overhead. Their wings turned to goose feathers, their heads to steel. He watched them rise, curve, dip lazily and begin falling. Suddenly the Genoese line broke into fragments. Men spun, reeled, staggered backwards, began screaming. A moment later there were a series of thunderclaps; flames and smoke belched from the mouths of the cannons and balls of iron hurtled forward into their densely packed ranks. Sampson stood dazed, then reached down and plucked another shaft from the ground. He fired again, pausing to watch the flight of his arrow before notching another to his bowstring. All round him his brother archers were doing the same. The crossbowmen struggled to rewind their bows. They closed ranks, only to be decimated by a second fusillade of balls. Suddenly they turned and began retreating. As they did so the knights and men-at-arms to their rear spurred their *destriers* to the gallop and levelled their lances. The English line fell silent as it watched the knights charge through their own vanguard, trampling the wounded and dying. The Genoese, panic-stricken and trapped on both sides, turned in self-defence and opened fire on the knights; and then the first wave of pennons broke through their ranks. Again came the order to hold firm. Sampson felt the ground begin trembling beneath him as the advancing hooves pounded the turf. All he could see now was horse and plume and the massed line of lances. He shivered and took aim at a square helm bent low over the neck of a charger.

Seventy paces to his left, Thomas stood facing that same swirl of mane and armour and lance. But here the advancing knights seemed more numerous, more purposeful. He knew the reason. Not twenty feet away from him stood the slender boyish figure of the heir to the English throne, surrounded by his household knights and branded by the red cross of St George on his surcoat. And it was the prince who gave the order.

'Fire!'

Thomas stepped forward and loosed his bow. A second later the line of galloping knights broke and stumbled in front of him, dissolving into screaming and whinnying heaps of dead or wounded horses and fallen knights weighed down by their armour. Some were literally crushed alive under their horses, armour buckling and splitting at the seams as the great beasts rolled on to their sides. Others hauled themselves to their feet, only to be knocked down again by those behind them. Some came on, miraculously surviving that first withering stream of arrows and driving their spurs deep into the trappings covering the flanks of their chargers; chargers who could only shy and stumble as they galloped blindly into the pot-holes protecting the English line. Those that crossed them were next confronted by a yelling horde of men-at-arms wielding swords, pikes and maces. By now a second wave of knights had joined the battle, and across the breadth of the valley the air echoed to the clash of steel as the struggle to break the English line began.

Dusk gave way to darkness. The moon rose, bathing the battlefield in its silvery glow. The king's tactics continued to take their toll; for as the French knights forked either side of the archers in their herces they were herded together in front of the men-at-arms, their flanks unprotected and exposed to the English crossfire. Yet they still kept coming. Hundreds fell – many to whom death was the sudden lunge of a Welshman's knife through the slits in their visors – but more took their places. Thomas began to sense the pressure on the line. Firing at point blank range into the wall of armour ahead of him, always aiming at a horse or visor, he realized that numbers alone might decide the day. Many of the French were now on foot, and the most hard pressed archers were using their stakes to beat off the attack. Suddenly, through the darkness, he saw Sir Godfrey Harcourt leave the Prince of Wales's side and start hurrying towards the rear.

'Where's he bound?' he asked a companion.

'To the king, for reinforcements.'

At once an angry cry went up from those who overheard his words. 'Fetch 'im back, we doan' need 'em!' shouted someone.

Thomas glanced at the prince. He had removed his helm, light glinted in eyes made crazed and wild by the moon's brilliance, his sword scythed the air as he fought off a pair of knights. In front of him the dead lay in a mound.

The French attack gradually faltered and for a few minutes the valley slope loomed empty and deserted out of the darkness. Thomas and his fellow archers immediately ran forward to retrieve their arrows from the dead. The ground was slippery and scored, blood stained the dew damp grass and he could hear the wounded groaning and crying out. Retracing his steps he saw Harcourt returning to the prince's side. The two men spoke. The prince smiled and looked round at his men, all of whom stood silent, leaning on their bows and swords as they quietly awaited the next attack. 'Lads!' he shouted. 'No help is coming. His majesty believes us capable of holding firm.'

'What did he say, my lord?'

The prince grinned. 'Let the boy win his spurs!'

Those who heard him began laughing and cheering, then their laughter faded as the next wave of knights appeared out of the darkness and charged towards them.

And so the battle raged on beneath an indifferent moon. There were lulls, silences made eerie by the hooting of an owl, sudden and bloody mêlées during which the French were pulled from their horses or had them slaughtered beneath them as they probed for a weakness in the English line. The heap of dead turned into a wall, over which the living had to clamber. As they did so, the archers fired into their ranks, heightening it still further with every volley. To Thomas the battle took on the aspect of a dream. The moonlight glinting on armour, the knights and foot-soldiers advancing up the hill, the hum of arrows and screams of the fallen all seemed unreal, as if no imagination could have conceived of so grim a reality. He lost all sense of time. Assault followed assault, each in turn being checked and repulsed.

Suddenly he realized that the French had scattered. He heard Warwick order the cease fire and his words being repeated throughout the division. Laying down his bow, he listened to the distant sounds of a skirmish being fought on its far flank. Then came silence, and all could be heard were the cries of the wounded. Horses stood riderless, reins dangling, in the middle of the battlefield. French knights and soldiers were crawling back down the valley on their hands and knees, only falling when the night had swallowed them up. He looked round. A few torches had been lit, roll-calls were being taken. No one seemed certain if the battle was over or who had won it. What had happened to Northampton's division? Had the reserve seen action? As these questions found answers the mood changed. Doubt gave way to the beginnings of celebration. Thomas stood dumbfounded for a moment, then, as the extent of the victory began to dawn, he felt suddenly too exhausted to think or care. On all sides men lay sprawled on the grass, their bows beside them, content to sleep where they had fought. He glimpsed the prince kneel in prayer, then make a pillow of his surcoat and lie down amongst his men. Suppperless, their throats dry, the entire division began settling down for the night. Thomas dropped and fell forward to the grass. After joining in the whispered prayer being said by those round him he closed his eyes, certain that he would never sleep with the sound of the battle still ringing in his brain. But he was wrong, an instant later he slid into sleep.

CHAPTER ELEVEN

Morning. In his impatience Sampson stamped his feet as he gazed out over the invisible battlefield. 'It must clear soon,' he said again.

'By whose command?' growled the soldier standing ahead of him in the long line shuffling towards the field kitchens parked near the windmill. 'The dead must wear their shroud. 'Tis God's work. You'll see it soon enough, and when you do 'tis more than likely you'll wish you hadn't.'

Sampson turned his back on the valley. Thick fog had fallen during the night, and even now, more than two hours since being roused by the royal minstrels, he had yet to see beyond the abandoned stakes that marked the front of the English lines. He breathed warmth into his hands. The air was dank and chill, the men round him subdued and melancholic. It was as if, he decided, the invisible presence of the dead was made tangible in their mood. Smiling feebly at Thomas, standing remote and distant beside him, he tightened his cloak and listened to the shouts of the water-carriers and breathed in the smell of mutton scrag drifting towards him from the cook-waggons.

'They still haven't finished,' said Thomas, indicating another of the clerks ordered by the king to count the dead vanish into the mist with his tally.

'Nor will they 'afore dusk,' added a water-carrier, stopping his cart beside Thomas and handing him a ladle. ''Tis said the field's as black as a plague of crows. Cobham's men have already counted more than a thousand knights and men-at-arms, and they reckon there's ten times that number of foot-soldiers that won't see the morrow.'

'And our losses?' asked Sampson.

'A dozen knights an' no more than nine score archers dead.'

As Thomas tipped the ladle to his lips he thought of the fourteen notches in his longbow, one for every knight he had unseated.

The water-carrier nodded wisely. 'I'll tell you lads something. No cattle will graze this valley for ten year or more, no ploughshare turn the clod. 'Tis a battlefield, a place for dead men's bones an' the red dog-rose.'

Thomas handed Sampson the ladle and looked down at the valley, shivering slightly as he wondered how long it would take him to forget all that had happened there. Discarded arms and equipment littered the ground. A group of surgeons were tending the wounded. A waggon piled high with corpses was moving slowly across the slope, occasionally halting to add to its cargo . . .

Suddenly he realized that he was not looking at the English lines but at the battlefield itself. ''Tis lifting,' he blurted.

Those round him turned. For a moment there was a stunned silence, as if none could believe what they were seeing. Then the water-carrier whispered 'God have mercy on their souls,' and Thomas sank to his knees as the fog gradually dispersed, revealing the full measure of all it had been hiding.

It was the desolation that struck him first: the turf broken and torn from the ground by hooves and the charging soldiers, so that the valley seemed like the surface of a sea whose surf was the wall of corpses straddling the front of the English lines. Everywhere he looked limbs poked stiff and rigid and dead, gaping eyes stared back at him. Further down the slope, in a landscape scarred by prostrate horses and twisted armour, French peasants in hodden grey were dragging their dead countrymen towards the burial pits being dug where the dead lay thickest. Monks moved amongst them, either administering the last sacrament to the dying or comforting the wounded. Once a group of horses, panic-stricken with thirst and hunger and the stench of blood, galloped the length of the valley and vanished into the last of the mist. A squadron of English knights was circuiting the field; every now and then one would dismount and place a fallen lance upright beside its owner, a sign that the dead man was a knight. The royal clerks were still counting them, a task which meant dismantling the mounds of corpses and laying out the bodies in lines. As the work went on a breeze broke up the mist and the sharp reek of putrefaction began to float over the English lines. The men seemed indifferent to it. Joking and chatting, their initial gloom turned to elation, they downed their food and went back to sleep again. But by the time Thomas had reached the ovens and a trencher of bread heaped with scrag had been thrust into his hands he had lost his appetite.

He sat on the grass beside Will and Sampson and said: 'What will they call this battle?'

Will grunted. 'A massacre.'

'The Crécy Fight? Who knows? Let the chroniclers decide.' Sampson paused, gazing round at the little groups of soldiers sprawled across the hillside. 'One day we will meet some of those who served beside us and stay up till dawn over a pitcher of ale. I wonder how we will see it then? When now all we want is to sleep and forget.'

'Aye, but not for long, for I reckon we'll be at it again soon,' said Will watching a line of armourers move across the battlefield and gather the thousands of spent arrows into heaps to be collected later.

'Here comes Warwick,' said Thomas suddenly.

The three men turned as the earl and his entourage left the king's pavilion and began walking towards them. They could hear him call out to the men under his command, jesting and laughing as he thanked them for their services.

'Sir Ned must be proud of you,' he said, approaching Horton's retinue. 'And so will all England when the couriers have posted news of what you have done in every church and shire in the land. So far fifteen hundred French knights have been counted dead, amongst them the king's own brother, his nephew, two archbishops and the King of Bohemia.' He paused, sadness softening his voice. 'The king was blind. He was found strapped to his horse and its reins were still tied to the knights who had led him into battle. He was a true paladin, and his majesty has asked my lord Durham to preach a requiem for the repose of his soul. As for the rest of the French army, it no longer exists.'

Thomas had stopped listening. Amongst those in Warwick's entourage was the knight he and Sampson had ambushed on the

155

Chase. And the knight, a thoughtful frown on his face, was now staring at him. He turned away, pretending to be restringing his bow.

'My lord!' Thomas felt himself go cold inside as the knight's voice rose above Warwick's. 'Those two archers are outlaws! 'T'was they who robbed me as I crossed Lady de Burgh's Chase! You, come here!'

Thomas and Sampson rose and shuffled towards him.

Warwick stared at them both for a moment, then said: 'Are you certain of this, Sir John?'

'Yes, my lord. Even when we were in camp at Southsea I had my suspicions, their faces were familiar. Now I'm sure of it.'

'And would mar our victory by demanding that the past be revenged?'

'One is your champion, of that I'm aware. But robbery on the king's highway is punishable by death, my lord.'

'I know the law.' Warwick scowled and turned towards Thomas. 'You, Woodward. What have you to say to this?'

Pale and terrified, Thomas shifted from foot to foot without replying.

'Come, come,' insisted Warwick. 'Sir John Baynton has accused you of outlawry. You are my champion and as good an archer as any in the army. I've no taste for seeing you hang. But if it's true you must both be led before the king to plead his mercy. Now, answer me. Are you guilty or nay?'

As if in a dream Thomas heard himself murmur: 'Yes.'

'And you?' Warwick turned to Sampson, who hesitated and glanced at Thomas before silently nodding his head.

The earl glared angrily at Baynton and slapped his gauntlets together. 'With one word you have sealed your own warrants. Take them away! Though God knows the king has sufficient to attend to without dealing with a pair of felons.'

Sampson opened his mouth to protest.

'The matter is out of my hands. Spare your pleas for the king.' Warwick looked sadly at Thomas for an instant, then moved on.

Neither outlaw spoke as they were led away towards the baggage park. Both were still too stunned by the abruptness of their exposure and arrest to be aware of its implications. They walked slowly, heads hung low. Those who had not witnessed the incident spat and cursed as they passed, thinking they were

156

to be tried for cowardice on the field.

Reality only struck Sampson as they entered the narrow entrance to the leaguer. Horses, oxen, grooms and waggoners milled round them. Everyone was laughing, a mood of jubilation hung with the dust in the air. The Chase seemed so distant; yet there they had robbed a knight, merchant and papal legate, ambushed monks and left for dead at least two dozen of the soldiers sent to hunt them down. Aware that all this would be made known to the king before they were sentenced, he shook his head in despair as their escort led them towards a pair of covered waggons with iron bars for sides. Some soldiers were sitting nearby. On seeing the prisoners approach, one rose and spoke with their guards, who then handed them into his charge and vanished.

'Outlaws, eh? Well you picked a fine time to be snared.' Their new jailer was short and stocky. Black hair pelted his arms, and only a kindly grin saved him from the callousness characteristic of so many of those who shared his trade. Stabbing a finger at the two waggons behind him, he added: 'They ain't Newgate, but they does. In one we've a pair of cravens who'd rather swing than fight Frogs and a third who spent the battle skulking under a cart.' He paused, indicating the prisoner in the neighbouring waggon. 'As for him, he used the Fight to settle an old debt. Scuppered his own lord of the manor, gut to gizzard with six inches of steel.' The jailer grinned. 'Take your pick.'

Sampson nodded at the first of the waggons.

'I don't blame 'ee.' Their jailer laughed. 'There's just one morsel I ain't let drop. Our third craven's as mad as a Cheapside hatter.'

Sampson followed his glance. The two deserters were lying at one end of the waggon. At the other sat a slumped figure dressed in a torn silk doublet and breeches. His thin fingers were twisted round the bars, every now and then he cackled into his silvery beard.

The two outlaws entered their prison. As the bolts slammed behind them their companion began banging his head against the bars. 'Pull him off, lads,' shouted the jailer. 'King's orders, we're to keep him alive.'

Sampson walked over to him, knelt, grasped his hair and turned the bent head. It was Buckle.

157

The physician stared up at him, emptiness in his gaze. 'The pox, the gout, the itch, the stone. Buckle can cure 'em all, cure 'em all . . .' He began giggling, grinding stained teeth from side to side.

Sampson's astonishment quickly vanished. Rage took over. He brutally slapped the physician's face to silence his giggles and said: ''Tis I, Sampson.'

'Oh, very good.' Buckle tittered, pulled Sampson towards him and, after first making certain no one was listening, whispered: 'Comets. Showers of them. All last night. Rats' tails in the sky. Had to hide. No choice . . .'

Sampson hit him again. 'Listen to me!' he snapped. 'You may be mad but you can still talk. 'Tis due to you that I'm here. Why did you pretend to be dead when you weren't? Without knowing that I've no chance of escaping the noose. Why?'

'Dead, stiff as mutton. Basted, boiled and . . .' Suddenly a glimmer of recognition appeared in Buckle's eyes. 'You!' he croaked.

'Yes, me!'

He nibbled at his lower lip. 'You've a father, so had I,' he said finally. 'One lies dead and one's alive. 'Tis a riddle, boy, a riddle.'

Sampson slapped him again. 'You've not answered my question.'

The physician ran his fingers across his cheek, smiling slightly. 'Oh but I have. You and he were after me. Had to die. Can't kill a corpse. Can't be done. But I'll get you yet. Father and son and the Holy Ghost, all together on the same gibbet. . .' Then he began giggling again and his words turned to a meaningless babble.

Buckle's insanity and brief moments of lucidity angered Sampson still further. Unaware of what he was doing, he began hitting him again, methodically and calmly, as if blows would give birth to the answers he sought. Finally Thomas intervened, dragging him to the other end of the waggon.

'Leave him be. One madman's company enough. This time tomorrow all three of us may be dead.'

The thought sobered him, and he spent the remainder of the day sitting hunched against the bars, head in hands. Occasionally he tried questioning Buckle, but each time he did so the physician's reply ended in delirium. During the night he began howling, only pausing to list the ingredients of his elixir. Eventually the guards could bear it no longer. Entering the cage, they bound and gagged him. His madness, which had taken hold at the start of the battle, added to Sampson's despair, and whilst Thomas sat brooding in the straw he paced back and forth in the darkness trying to read sense into the physician's chatter. The riddle meant nothing – both his and Buckle's fathers were dead – and he kept switching and reversing the order of the words in the hope of finding their meaning. But even if there was one, which he doubted, it continued to elude him, and finally, his thoughts confused by questions that lacked answers, he too lay down in the straw. Outside he could hear the crackle of flames from a bonfire lit by the waggoners and pages in celebration of the victory. But the battle seemed a world away. The past and present meant nothing now. All that remained was the future: that one short walk to the gallows.

*　　　*　　　*

The king slid the jesses from his fingers and placed his falcon back on its perch. Its pale eyes gleamed malevolently. It pecked savagely at the hands of its austringer as he lowered a hood over its head. The king ruffled its feathers and glanced up.

'My lord Warwick tells me you are felons,' he said quietly. 'Common outlaws who have robbed and pillaged over the rights of chase my ancestors granted to the Clares in Dorsetshire; that you ambushed a respected knight, Sir John Baynton, and that you killed a score of the soldiers once sent under my orders to apprehend you. What have you to say in answer?'

Thomas looked across at the king. Between them lay a table strewn with parchment rolls, wine, exchequer tallies, quills and a dish of sweetmeats. The Prince of Wales sat beside him, his marshals, household knights and secretaries were gathered in a small circle behind him. He could see Warwick, grim-faced, and a worried looking Will trying to push his way nearer the table.

'Come on, speak!' snapped the king. 'I'm waging a war, not presiding over a shire court. I've just condemned three cravens to death and sentenced the queen's physician to two years in the Tower.' He paused, banging a fist on the table. 'Answer me!'

159

'We had no choice, my lord,' said Thomas.

The king's face paled with rage. 'You are outlaws who broke the law. The choice was yours. I will not tolerate treason and murder, not even by the best archer in the land. What purpose is there in making France our vassal if ruffians like you roam free to rob the innocent? You will hang, both of you, at dawn tomorrow. And let that be a lesson to anyone else who contemplates abusing the laws of our realm.'

Thomas collapsed forward, then straightened and stared out over the battlefield as he waited for their death warrants to be signed and sealed. Suddenly another voice broke the silence.

'Father, both these men fought well. One may have saved my life. The Count d'Alencon was within feet of me when he fell. It was Woodward's arrow that unsaddled him. You say I have won my spurs, surely these men have won the right to live and serve you? For years you have been telling me that a king must temper justice with mercy, be as humble in victory as he would be in defeat.' He stood: black doublet, black hosen, Black Prince in all but name, and added: 'My lord, I now request that both men be pardoned.'

The king listened to his son in silence, then glanced at Warwick, who gave a slight nod. He smiled. 'If every criminal had my son to defend them we'd have no need of the hangman.' Whilst waiting for the laughter to fade, he pulled a roll of parchment and his seal towards him, then looked up at the two outlaws.

'Your lives are spared. You will serve as archers under the Earl of Warwick until we return to England. The royal charter of pardon for all your abominations will be drawn up and signed in my presence. Should either of you take to outlawry again and be caught you will be cut down from the gallows when still alive and be drawn and quartered. Now enough of this. In a week's time we march on Calais.'

Part Three
THE DEATH

CHAPTER TWELVE

'Hold tight! We'll be shootin' her soon! Get them nippers stowed safe, the Sabbath's no day for a dunkin'!' The boatman plunged his steering oar deep into the Thames. Sluggish and unwilling, as if aware of what lay ahead, the wherry rounded Temple Bend, finally gathering speed again as its bows straightened and the current quickened.

'The tide's ebbing fast. It'll be wetter than a mill-race 'neath the bridge,' shouted the man perched in the stern-sheets.

The boatman chuckled. 'A penny you paid, Jeb, an' scrubbed you'll get. The queen's laundry lasses couldn't wash 'ee as clean as the Thames in flood.'

'Aye, but I'd give tu'pence to let 'em try.'

'Shame on 'ee!' snapped the stout, fierce looking woman sitting beside Jeb. 'You'll be skulkin' off to to the stews 'afore long.'

'He already do,' laughed the boatman. 'Your Jeb may be a ratter, but 'tis Winchester geese not vermin he chases at Mistress Hapley's.'

Thomas Woodward, sitting opposite them, grinned as the woman began belabouring her husband with her hold-all for frequenting the south bank brothels owned by the Bishop of Winchester. Then his smile faded and his thin face turned woebegone and glum. He leant over the gunwhale, letting a hand trawl through the debris that kept slapping at the hull of the wherry as it floated down-stream. The August sun sparkled on the water and the Thames was crowded with shipping. Lighters were unloading wine and sea-coals at White Friar's Wharf; skiffs, lugsails filled, plied busily from bank to bank with those who had taken advantage of the pause in the rain to spend the day at the Bear garden in Southwark village or on the heath beyond. An episcopal barge, its canopy draped in silks, was being rowed against the tide, returning some bishop to his Strand side mansion from Mass in St Paul's. The breeze was warm, London's spires stood framed against a cloudless sky, and the muted sounds of a city at play echoed across the water. And Thomas felt as miserable as at any time in his life.

He looked round at his fellow passengers. Beside him sat an old seamstress whose hooked nose and the loose dry skin which hung in folds from her jowls were an exact facsimile of the solitary and disgruntled looking popinjay in the bird-cage at her feet. Next to her sat a merchant and his wife, whilst opposite lounged two apprentice lads homeward bound from Holborn Woods with their lasses. Whilst the merchant glanced at the girls, his wife, fussily dressed in voluminous skirts and a starched linen whimple, stared sternly ahead. Beyond them, and occupying the remainder of the wherry, were a glover and his wife and eleven children. They were moving house. Skillets and spits poked between pallets, a wooden hobby-horse hung like a figurehead over the wherry's bows and an assortment of pans and pewter plates lay piled on the duck-boards.

Listening to the children, Thomas felt suddenly homesick. Apart from Matilda he had not seen his family for three years. Though Sampson would have told them where he was, each day spent apart lessened his chances of rejoining them. Laying down his bow, he opened his purse and tipped its contents into his hand: he had eightpence left, sevenpence after paying the boatman. He glanced back over his shoulder. Beyond the river's leftward curl he could see the roofs of the Palace of Westminster rising above the marshes on the south bank. He sighed, the penny spent on the fare to Westminster Stairs had been wasted. Warwick was not at Court. His steward had been courteous but firm. His master had returned to his estates and there was little likelihood of employment in his household, even for the archer who had once been his champion. He could only suggest that Thomas call again when the earl was next in residence.

Thomas tightened his purse. Sevenpence! The next archery tourney was in the fields beyond Lud Gate in a week's time. How was he to survive until then? And even if he won what good would it do him? It was nearly two years since the Crécy Fight. England and France were at peace, and the city had grown tired of the discharged soldiers who thronged its streets. To reduce their number the mayor had ordered a reduction in the prize money offered by the Fletchers' Guild. At best he would carry home a boiling fowl or a basin of chitterlings.

He looked round again, temporarily forgetting his worries as he watched Tower Royal, Hanse Wharf and Vintry Steps speed by in quick succession. Suddenly the seamstress began bellowing in his ear.

'There it be, soldier! The nation's wonder, London's boast. There ain't nothing to match it on God's earth.'

He followed her gaze. Ahead of them, its twenty arches straddling the river and halving its flow, lay the ribbed outline of London Bridge. Hearing the distant roar of water the seamstress's parrot started squawking. Her attempts to soothe it were soon deafened by the noise. As the current gripped the wherry in its pull, the massive timber starlings that supported the piers loomed closer, Thomas glimpsed a flat sheet of water, spume-tossed and flecked with spray, surging between a pair of arches. 'Here she comes!' cried the boatman, hurriedly lashing his steering oar into the stern rowlock before guiding the wherry towards a narrow, central arch. Suddenly the shops and tenements that lined the bridge rose overhead, blotting out the sky. A child screamed as the wherry's bows dipped into the race. Its hull bounced against a weed covered starling, then skimmed another. Water, its boom amplified by the curve of the arch, splashed up, spilling down Thomas's face. A moment later the wherry shot the top of the tide-race and landed with a smack in the foam beneath the bridge.

Still dazed and blinded by the glare, Thomas wiped the spray from his face as the boatman sculled into slack water. After passing under the counter of a Flemish carrack laden with cloth, they nosed in amongst the merchantmen docked alongside Bottolph's Wharf. Refuse, empty barrels, even a discarded truckle bed bobbed beneath them. The noise was immense. Boatmen bellowed insults at one another, water carriers were loading their butts from a waterhoy come down from Marlow on the tide. A flock of sheep was being herded aboard a barge drawn up against the steps. Whilst gulls squabbled for fish heads on the quay, whores, porters and waterfront hucksters touted for trade. Down-stream, the White Tower stood sentinel behind a forest of masts and spars. The seamstress smiled contentedly and turned toward Thomas.

'London city,' she said. 'I'd rather lodge in the Fleet than not wake to the sound of Bow Steeple.' Seeing his bow, she added: 'A soldier, eh?'

'Discharged.' Shame made Thomas hesitate. 'Now I earn what I can with my bow. 'Tis better than turning to beggary.'

'That's what they all say,' scoffed the seamstress. 'Another month an' it'll be a mendicant bowl you'll be holding, same as the rest of 'em.'

Thomas blushed angrily. 'T'aint I who's to blame. My lord Warwick gave me some money at the time of the peace. I invested it with a group of merchants engaged in the draining of Moor Fields.'

'God take you for a fool! That swamp's soaked up more gold than a Lincoln's Inn serjeant. A fen it was made and a fen it'll stay!'

Thomas sighed as he shouldered his bow. 'Aye, I know that now. In six months I . . .'

'Had been milked for every groat you had,' snapped the seamstress, glancing at the crowds on the quay. 'There's no lack of cheats an' dupes for them to prey on in London city, an' that's a fact.' She paused, poking a finger into his ribs. 'Go back to the shires, lad. Get out whilst you've still the penny for the toll. This city ain't the place for countryfolk. There, that's my advice, an' 'tis free,' she added, scooping up her bird-cage and stepping ashore. Thomas watched for a moment as the porters haggled for her custom, then he handed the boatman his fare and stepped on to the quay.

'She's right, he thought, yet in another three months he would not be a serf but a free man who had won his freedom by living inside London's walls for a year and a day. But at what price? Shrugging the question aside, he entered Bottolph's Lane, intending to return to his lodgings. The seamstress's words lingered in his thoughts. By reminding him of his failure to turn his dreams into a reality they had opened a wound that had only recently healed. How long it now seemed since the October morning he had entered the city behind his king and Warwick over the bridge he had just been swept under. It had been a triumphant entry: Calais had fallen, Brittany was in English hands and the French had sued for peace. Cheering citizens had thronged the streets and for weeks afterwards, as a member of the earl's bodyguard, he had attended the succession of feasts and jousts that followed. At night the countess of Warwick's maid had led him into the attics of her master's mansion. The pleasures he had found in her company and the city's welcome had made him light-headed and reckless. Warwick had offered him permanent employment, but he had rejected the offer. In London he would grow rich, in time becoming a burgher wealthy enough to buy the release of his family from serfdom. And now? Now he had sevenpence in his purse and paid a ha'penny a night to sleep packed between two cheapjacks on a straw pallet with his head at its foot.

He looked up, suddenly aware that he had been paying no attention to where he was going and had strayed into one of the many slum quarter courts that bordered the river. The stench of fats hung in the stale, rank air and no sunlight lit up the ramshackle tenements that circled its perimeter. But the court itself was crowded with booths and stalls and fishgirls who hurried by with baskets of whitebait balanced on their heads, followed by packs of curs who fought over any that fell. Carts trundled by, their drivers ducking as they passed under the bundles of twigs tied to the ale-stakes hanging from the tavern doorways. A pedlar was selling best London ale spiced with pepper, another was broiling sheeps' feet on an open brazier whilst a third bellowed: 'Buy! Buy! What d'ye lack?' In the centre of the court, its cobbles their stage, a troupe of mummers was acting the tale of St George, and the watching crowd laughed and heckled as Little Johnny Jack, seven black dolls hanging from his breeches, tried to goad a pig into charging a stilt-walker dressed as St George. Thomas grinned as the stilt-walker lost his balance and toppled onto the pig's back. This was the London the seamstress loved, the one that had captivated him on his arrival in the city. He walked on, splashing his way through the rain-water, heavy with filth, that clogged the kennels as a kite strutted from the shadows and began scavenging through a pile of oyster shells, its beak drumming in time to his own quickening footsteps.

He froze. Amongst the pedlars' cries was a voice he recog-

167

nized. But whose was it, and when had he heard it? He listened for a moment.

'The Judgement is nigh, my friends! The Lord's vengeance is great, and will be amongst us before the sun enters the house of Libra! Hark! A fire column has been seen over the papal palace at Avignon! Stars erratic fill the night skies, whilst by day Heaven's floodgates discharge rains and hailstones! The Death comes! Saturn and Jupiter, the constellations of torment, have joined in the House of Leo! Evil vapours have been drawn from the earth and kindled into fire! Take heed! A tempest of frogs, serpents, lizards and other venomous beasts has been seen falling over the lands of the Tartars! The hour of Apocalypse has dawned . . .!'

Thomas turned. Suddenly, through a break in the crowd, he saw the face of Nathaniel Buckle. For a moment he stood riveted, his head reeling as if from a blow, as the physician harangued those passing by listing the portents of God's wrath. Yes, it was Buckle alright; but a Buckle grown old in the Tower and now but a caricature of his former self. He was dressed in horsehair, his bare feet were black with dirt, his beard hung matted and knotted and there was a wild, almost demoniacal look in his eyes.

Thomas's first instinct was to walk away. Prophets of Doom had been a common sight in London that summer. The endless rain, the reports of blackened crops and a murrain of sheep coming in from the countryside had fuelled their speculations, already given substance by the strange pestilence – the Death some were calling it – known to be raging on the other side of the Channel. But Buckle was no ordinary seer, and Thomas, seeing someone he knew for the first time in months, was irrevocably drawn towards him.

His breath reeked of wormwood and eau de vie. His eyes were glazed and shot with scarlet. A grey patina of filth ingrained his cheeks and filled the lines across his brow. Seeing Thomas, he waved the spirit flagon he was holding and shouted: 'You can still be saved, friend! A penny buys a physic, a groat will purchase a measure of the only true elixir manufactured in this realm . . .!'

Thomas shook him by the shoulder. 'Master Buckle, listen to me. You an' I have met before. In the prison waggon after the Crécy Fight.' Seeing the vacant expression on the physician's

168

face, he paused. Buckle had been deranged after Crécy, and two years in the Tower – from which he must have just been released – could have only crazed him still further. He shook him again.

'I had a companion, Sampson Hooke, once your apprentice and now . . .'

Buckle silenced him by lifting a conspiratorial finger. Giggling slightly, he drew closer to Thomas and whispered: 'The boy's a bastard. Never told him, should have done. The Prior of Cranborne fathered him. Know him? No, don't expect you do. Audley, Roger Audley. The pair of 'em tried to poison me. Henbane, fickle herb, kills one day, spares the next. No gratitude. The boy's an outlaw now. You say your name's Hooke? Had an apprentice called that once. A prior's bastard. Ever been in the Tower? Rats the size of terriers . . .' His words turned to a meaningless whimper and he backed away as if still haunted by memories of his dungeon.

Thomas followed him. Then, as if trying to convince himself of what he knew must be a lie, he blurted: 'Sampson's father's dead!'

Buckle tilted his head to one side, pillowing it on a shoulder. 'Audley dead?' he murmured. 'No, but will be soon. Worms, fowl, hogs and man. All of us, dead as mutton.' He paused, perhaps finally aware that his mind had wandered into some confused echo from the past. Eventually he scurried off into the crowd. Thomas ran after him and tried to question him. But it was pointless, he was mad. Once he spoke of a whale he had seen beached on the shingle at Wapping before muddling Thomas with Sampson and demanding he gather the Jew's ear in the cellars.

Thomas halted, and after watching him disappear he sat down on the cobbles and tried to collect his thoughts. Despite Buckle's insanity, he knew that what he had said was the truth. Prior Audley, the cause of all that he and his family had suffered, had fathered his best friend, and Buckle had known it since the day of his birth. It was all so obvious. It explained Audley's attempt to poison Buckle, his delay in sending for troops when Sampson was at large on the Chase. Buckle's part no longer mattered. It was Sampson who now needed to be told the truth. Thomas sighed. He had last seen Sampson on the Calais wharf before sailing for England. During the siege he had been appointed a surgeon's assistant, and after the city fell Warwick's influence had gained him the post of garrison surgeon and the promise of a discharge after six months on condition that he return to Salisbury and continue to practise in the city. He would be there now.

Thomas rose to his feet, his thoughts in a turmoil, and headed east toward Ald Gate. The sun stood low over Hampstead Heights and the streets lay deep in shadow. The curfew bells were already ringing, and the hawkers from the outlying villages were hurriedly packing their wares to avoid being fined for not leaving the city before the gates closed. The smell of fish pie and roasted meats drifted through the doorways of the cook-shops in Belzettars Lane and Leaden Hall Street. Outside Allhallows Stonechurch a priest, barelegged and holding a lighted taper in his hand, stood doing penance for his sins whilst a group of street urchins played club-kayles on the cobbles.

Yet Thomas noticed none of this. Still dazed, he turned into the alley leading to his lodgings and climbed the stairs to his garret. When his bed companions finally returned, he lay between them on the pallet and stared up at the ground poultry bones embedded in the rough daub of the ceiling. Dusk gave way to darkness. The surrounding city grew silent; a place for the cut-purse, the knife and the watch. He fell asleep with the faces of Sampson and Audley circling endlessly through his brain. When he awoke it was still dark and the same images still plagued his thoughts. Suddenly the seamstress's advice came back to him. No, he thought, to leave London would be proof of failure. Yet he knew that that was an excuse, that what now held him was his fear of confronting Sampson with the truth about his paternity. Locked in indecision, he lay, hour after hour, erecting arguments that denied the facts, only to see them fall as Buckle's words echoed through his thoughts.

Dawn had broken when he finally reached a decision. Slipping from the pallet, he crept over to a loose board in a corner of the garret, lifted his charter of pardon from its hiding place and tucked it between his chest and jerkin. After shouldering his bow and quiver, he walked down the stairs and out into the alley.

The city was already stirring. A night watchman was tapping the shutters of the merchants' houses in Fenchurch Street with his pole, calling the hour as he roused their inmates from sleep. Thomas headed south toward the river, stopping briefly in a

Fish Street pot-shop to eat a bowl of gruel and a halfpenny's worth of pie. The bridge lay ahead of him, and as he walked on to it the four-storied houses that lined its sides rose overhead, turning it into a gloomy tunnel made noisy by the carts and waggons streaming in from the surrounding countryside with goods for the city's markets. To his left, through the breaks between tenements, he could see the hull of a cog sitting in the stocks of a boat-builder's yard and the mud-flats that stretched eastward along the river towards Rotherhithe. The drawbridge and postern gate were four arches from the end. Here two harassed gate-keepers were collecting tolls from the jostling crowd of pilgrims, carters and peasants waiting to enter the city, whilst an armed constable scrutinized each face to make certain none were lepers. Thomas and a merchant at the head of a line of pack-horses laden with broadcloth passed through the gate together. The merchant asked him where he was bound. Thomas told him. The merchant laughed. 'You're welcome to it. Sarum's a four week walk an' the road's a mire.'

'I'll get there.'

The merchant cursed at a group of pilgrims blocking the Pilgrims' Way and turned on to the Dover Road. Mounting his ambler, he glanced back at Thomas and shouted: 'You may get there, but you'll never return. Haven't you heard? The Death's landed in Dorset. A Gascon merchantman brought it ashore soon after the Feast of St John. Some feast. The whole shire's struck with it.'

Thomas trembled slightly as he looked back across the Thames. In the distance the wooden spire of St Paul's soared over the rooftops, nearer to hand the heads of the criminal dead grinned down at him from the spikes above the bridge gate. There was nothing to keep him. He turned, not once looking back till neither was visible.

CHAPTER THIRTEEN

The hens pecking through the mud on the river bank scattered as
Matilda dropped her water bucket and ran homeward. She was
already crying, and by the time she reached the doorway both
her cheeks and hair were wet with tears. After pausing to gather
breath and try and control her excitement, she ducked under the
lintel and plunged through the pall of scented smoke that filled
the cottage. Reaching the hooded figure squatting by the fire,
she halted, uncertain how best to break the news. Horror and
shock mingled with a joy inside her as she slowly sunk to her
knees.

'I've seen Thomas,' she whispered. 'He's on foot an' crossing
Goose High.'

The hood was lowered. Her mother's face turned towards her.
'Nonsense, lass. None but a rabid dog would come here now.'
Alice glanced absent-mindedly at her daughter before patting
her ladle against the cauldron balanced on the fire. 'We need
juniper, toads an' more borage if we're to keep it at bay. Fetch
the water, then go gather 'em.'

'Mother! It's Thomas! I swear it!' Matilda slumped into the
straw and thrust a handful of hair deep into her eyes. 'Oh God,
why couldn't he let us be? Why did he have to pick now to
return?'

There was a tapping. A moment later Hereward emerged
from the smoke pushing a stick ahead of him as he walked. 'If
'tis true, go bring him home, girl,' he said quietly. 'This is his
village. He belongs here. Even now.'

Alice lowered her ladle and looked at her daughter. 'You sure
it's him?'

Matilda nodded.

'Poor Thomas.' Alice smiled sadly, nerves making her bury her hands in the hem of her shift. 'Do as your father says. An' take Lillibet with 'ee. Thomas ain't seen her since she was bound and swaddled.'

A young girl with black hair and large watery eyes joined Matilda and pressed a hand into hers. The two sisters left the cottage and began wading through the quag towards the bridge. The overnight rain had only recently stopped and the September sky was overcast and ashen. Cranborne seemed deserted. The empty market place and the squeak of a door hanging wide on its hinges made it strangely forbidding, a place abandoned or hastily evacuated. A cart-load of rotting pease stood axle deep in the mud near the bridge, and though a few ribby pigs lay wallowing in the river the only sound was of wailing from inside one of the cottages.

'Who's that crying?' asked Lillibet.

'Mistress Hayward. Both Dorothy and Jane passed on in the night.'

'Will they go to Heaven too?'

Matilda bit at her lip. 'Yes.'

The noise faded as once over the bridge they began trampling through the still uncut corn in the manor fields. Ahead of them, a longbow and bundle over one shoulder, they could see a man moving towards them from the far side of the field. A hand lifted and waved. Matilda started running, dragging Lillibet behind her. Suddenly she checked in mid-stride and tried to staunch her tears. The man quickened speed and the corn parted like a curtain in front of him as he vaulted the ridges. Then he halted, and for a moment brother and sister stood staring at one another, knee deep in an ocean of gold.

Thomas grinned, opened his arms and began advancing towards Matilda.

'No! Stay back!' She raised her hands in horror.

Bewilderment spread over Thomas's face. 'What's wrong? 'Tis I. It'll be three years come All Saint's since we parted. Now come here an' give me a sister's welcome.' He moved forward again.

'For the love of God, stop! You must come no further. Has no one told you?' she pleaded, even now seeking an escape.

173

'Told me what?'

'Oh Thomas.' Matilda closed her eyes and collapsed into the corn. 'The village has been struck by the Death, more than three score have died. Now go, and leave us alone.'

For a moment sky and field revolved in front of Thomas's eyes, then his legs buckled and he dropped to his knees. He shook his head in disbelief, cursed himself for his blindness. The red crosses on doors, silent streets, staring faces; he had seen all of these during the last few days. Merchants, friars and fleeing peasants had all warned him that the whole of the West Country was gripped by the pestilence. Why then had he been so foolish as to believe that his own village might be spared? Still stunned, he rose to his feet. Through his tears he could see Matilda's raven hair and the confused face of the sister he barely recognized.

'Father, mother. Are they . . .?' He fell silent, unable to ask.

Matilda raised her head. 'Father's blind, but alive. So's mother.'

'But Ranulf's gone to Heaven, hasn't he, Matilda?' An' so's Kate,' said Lillibet gravely. 'They're angels now,' she added. 'I'll be an angel one day, won't I, Matilda?'

Matilda tried to smile, but failed, and when she finally spoke her voice sounded empty and hollow, as if she had been drained of all emotion during the three weeks that had passed since the plague first struck. 'Ranulf went first, Kate two days ago on the Sabbath. We buried her ourselves. Audley's forbidden the monks to hear confession or administer the sacraments to the dying.' She arched her neck and gazed up at the mantle of grey that lapped the sky.

'You may come home, Thomas,' she murmured, 'but 'tis only to die.'

Thomas hesitated, then moved towards her. 'Where else can I go?' he said firmly. 'I left London nearly a month back. Apart from a day's ride in a huckster's cart I've walked every mile of it. Plague or no plague, I'm here, and I intend staying.'

His stubbornness angered her. 'Are you mad, Thomas?' she cried. 'The Death's here, in this village. In three weeks it's turned the quick into beasts and the dead into a meal for carrion. Mothers have abandoned their babes, the sick are shunned and left to starve. It's taken Audley's bailiff, the miller, your own kin. Food's scarce an' some have whored for the price of a loaf.

At night wolves come down from the Chase and take the fowl. The swine, sheep and cattle have been left to fend for themselves. Look at this corn. The husks have burst. It's rotting but no one 'll harvest it. But the Death reaps. Oh yes, a harvest of corpses that no cleric will bury.' Suddenly she broke down, burying her head in her hands. 'What's happening to us, Thomas? Have you seen what it does to those it takes. Where does it come from? What is it?'

Thomas lifted her to her feet. 'Come, let's go home. I can't answer your questions. I only know that we've sinned an' must wait on the Lord's judgement. The Death's everywhere. I met travellers on the road who spoke of whole villages become graveyards. We can't flee from it or fight it. God giveth and taketh away, when and who He calls.'

Matilda tore herself from his grip. 'That's all everyone says.' Her eyes flashed angrily. 'It's meaningless, fools' talk, and as pious as a pardoner's chatter. Saul's son, the barcar, was the first to die. After his burial all of us, every man, woman an' child in the village, went in procession, bare-foot and heads bowed, through the market place repeating the litany and singing psalms. By the time we were done two more lay dead. So much for the power of prayer. The Holy Book tells us that the poor and hungry will be blessed. It took Kate three days to die. On Sabbath morn we found her lying in the pool of black filth that had spilled from her armpits and belly when the boils finally burst. She'd been screaming all night. She was eight years old.'

'Stop it!' cried Thomas.

'Why?' Matilda's face turned hard and savage. 'Why should a child die and Audley live? Every day I pray that the Death will claim him. Have you heard how he treated us 'afore you fled the Chase?'

Thomas sighed. 'Yes. Sampson an' I met a wayside hermit who lives near the highway. He told us what happened. 'Tis partly to revenge that day that I've now returned.' He paused, uncertain whether to tell her that Sampson was Audley's bastard. Instead, he soothed and calmed her, finally asking if she had seen Sampson since his return from France.

'Aye. T'was he who told us that you'd been pardoned and were in London. He's been granted a physician's license and taken rooms near the market place in Sarum.' She took his hands in hers. 'I can't forgive him and I still don't trust him. 'Tis best that you know that. You took him in, fed him, taught him the longbow an' the ways of the Chase and won him his pardon. Now that he's a free man again he's cast you aside as a serpent might its skin.'

'That's untrue,' said Thomas angrily. 'I love Sampson as I've loved no other man but father.'

'Well I don't. And if he's not to come between us it would be best for you to forget him. 'Tis Audley not Hooke who should concern you. The prior hates us Woodwards as much as ever. He's still determined to see you an' mother hang. Last Lammas, when he learned that father was blind, he took back most of our land. Since then he's never ceased preaching against her, accusing her of being able to turn into a hare, of sorcery and of bringing the rains. Last Sabbath he said t'was she who'd brought the Death.'

'But that's impossible!'

'Aye, you an' I know it. But no one else does. Mother's a wisewoman, a maker of charms and spells. The Death's no ordinary contagion. It's baffled us. We're helpless. When Audley said t'was our punishment for harbouring a witch everyone turned toward mother. His words gave them hope, someone to blame.'

Thomas felt suddenly apprehensive as he gazed out across the fields towards the priory. It was three years since he had lifted his bow at Audley, and he knew now that time had changed nothing. He lifted Lillibet on to his shoulders and walked on through the corn. At first Matilda tried to persuade him to take refuge in the woods, but seeing the set look on his face and sensing a rare obstinacy in his mood she finally fell silent. To Thomas no silence could have been more indicative of what lay ahead. The invisible presence of the Death haunted every step he took. The stench of rotting corpses and burning herbs filled the still air. As the river drew closer he heard the distant screams of a woman. Suddenly he came face to face with the reality. A crude red cross had been painted on the door of the mill. Then he shuddered as he walked over the bridge; all but two of the cottages in the lane bore the same stigmata. The taint of decay was now as powerful as the most pungent of perfumes. Dead swine and cattle lay piled on the river bank. The carcass of an ox lay half-submerged in the water and where it broke surface its skin was bloated and silvery. Then he gripped the parapet of the bridge as he realized that what he had seen was a living mass of maggot. He turned away, only now beginning to comprehend what must have taken place in the village since the first death.

Matilda sensed his horror. 'To begin with you don't think you can live with it,' she said quietly, 'that it would be better to die yourself. But now, after waking and feeling for the buboes under your arms, you try and forget it. You just want to live. Nothing else matters.'

A head peeped round a doorway, then vanished: curiosity, fear – each indivisible and the sum of the look Thomas had grown so used to walking through the silent plague struck villages on the last few days of his journey from London. Work and the fields forgotten, everyone would be indoors, terrified of exposing themselves to another's miasma or the poisonous vapours thought to carry the disease.

'Has it struck the priory?' he asked.

'No one knows. After Mass Audley ordered the doors to be barred and the gates shut. We're forbidden to enter it. The graveyard's full and we're using an old sheep pen as a burial ground.'

'If only Sampson were here. He'd be able to help us.'

'He'll not come,' said Matilda contemptuously. 'Anyway, mother an' Brother Gilbert have tried every drench and potion they know. Moher cut a rune-staff and beat the manor bounds with it. She's made spells, witch-broth and given every household a herb sack. But none of it's done any good.'

Thomas lowered Lillibet to the ground when they reached their cottage. The lane was still empty, only bird song and the cries of the bereaved broke the silence. Matilda gave a thin smile and pushed open the door. Tense and on edge at the prospect of the home-coming ahead, Thomas followed her inside, squinting as he peered through the smoke.

Hereward was the first to hear them enter. Calling out his son's name, he shuffled towards the door.

Thomas clenched his hands in disbelief as his father loomed out of the smoke. In three years his beard had all but fallen out, leaving in its wake only a few wisps of dappled hair which clung to his cheeks and chin. His back was stooped. His eyelids had grown heavy and leathery, like blinkers, and they sagged down over the small unlit chambers that had once been his eyes.

Suddenly Hereward's stick clattered to the floor. 'Come here.'

Thomas moved towards him, forcing a smile as his father stretched out his arms and began feeling the contours of his face with his one hand. It touched his longbow. 'So those days in the butts weren't wasted?' he murmured.

'No, father.'

''T'was the bow that made you an outlaw an' the bow that won you your freedom.'

''T'was you who taught me how to lift it.'

'Aye.' Hereward smiled slightly. 'You've changed. You're a man not a bairn now.' He turned towards Matilda. 'Lead us in a prayer, lass. The Lord has spared us and my son has returned. 'Tis right that we should give thanks.'

'Wait!' Suddenly Alice appeared out of the smoke. She was almost bald now, and the wrinkles on her face were as deep as furrows. But that same indomitable spark still burned in her eyes and Thomas marvelled as he pulled her into his embrace. She had buried five of her children, seen a sixth be hunted, watched her husband lose first a hand and then his sight, yet it all seemed to have washed round her, leaving her core still untarnished and untouched.

'So you're back from your gallivantin's, eh?'

This time Thomas's smile was unforced. In one sentence she had dispelled his nervousness and evoked a world without Audley or the plague, the world of his childhood. 'Tis good to be home,' he said.

'Aye,' she grunted, 'an' let's hope you stay put, take a wife, change your bow for a bill-hook and start taking care of your father an' I.'

'I may have changed, but you haven't, have you, mother?'

'Damme no. His worship may wish me a corpse, but I intend disappointing him. Enough of this. You'll be as empty as a bishop's brain. I don't promise no fatted calf but I reckon we can wring the neck on a fowl without temptin' the fates an' breakin' out in the buboes.' Even as she peered up into the rafters in search of a roosting hen, the door was thrown open and a stone clanged against the side of the cauldron.

'You're a witch, Alice Woodward!' screamed a woman's voice

from outside in the lane. 'That's Harold an' three of me babes you've struck dead with your sorcery! You're the Devil's daughter! The Death won't leave us be till you're in the grave!'

The woman's words turned to hysteria. Another rock flew through the door, then it slammed and the screams receded, leaving the family silent and uneasy.

'How long's this been going on?' asked Thomas.

'Forget 'em!' scorned Alice. ''Tis more bluster than meant. Three months back they was in an' out o' here from morn till midnight demanding simples an' spells. Now they curse an' hurl stones. Fools! They must reckon 'tis contagion not broth I keep in the cauldron.'

'That's the third time that's happened this week,' said Matilda, glancing anxiously at Thomas.

'An' no doubt there'll be a fourth. I've told 'em 'afore. The sun an' oceans are at war, and the waters have been drawn up as a vapour so foul with dead fish that the sun can't consume it or let it fall as wholesome rain. Divine punishment! Fiddlesticks! The Almighty'd be a mite fussier in who he took if t'was he who'd made it. And so would I! But 'tis Audley they listen to now, not me!'

'They've panicked,' said Matilda. 'They're confused and frightened. Try and understand them, mother. Soon it'll be too late.'

'Pah! The Devil take the lot of 'em. They're like medlars, not ripe till they're rotten.'

'Perhaps we should hide on the Chase,' suggested Thomas. 'They'd not trouble us there. I've the bow, we'd not starve.'

'You be silent, Thomas Woodward,' said Alice sharply. 'You may be an earl's champion but I can still take the strap to 'ee. I ain't movin'. I'll have no one say Mistress Woodward was afeared of a few stones. Let 'em come! They'll be as helpless as whelps 'afore long. You wait. 'Tis I, not Audley they'll be needing then.'

*   *   *

The news of Thomas's return reached Prior Audley on the following day. Despite it, and his terror of catching the pestilence, the prior was well-pleased with himself. On the previous evening the villagers had gathered outside the Woodward's cottage and, though Thomas's presence had prevented its destruction, he was now certain that the seed sown by his sermon had taken root. It could now only be a matter of time before the villagers resorted to violence.

Reflecting on the events of the past few days whilst waiting for his officers to leave the refectory after morning chapter, he smiled contentedly to himself, only glancing up when he heard the shuffle of sandals.

'Ah, Brother Gilbert,' he said. 'Chapter's over. You may return to the infirmary.'

'I must talk to you, father.'

Seeing the bewildered look on the monk's face Audley indicated a chair. A cadaverous scarecrow of a man who scuttled rather than walked, Brother Gilbert sat, coughed nervously into his habit and began dabbing at his cheeks with its sleeve.

'You heard them, I suppose?' Audley offered him wine.

'Yes.' He took it.

'Woodward won't stop them. If he even lifts that bow of his I'll have his pardon annulled and see him tried for treason. The woman's a witch and as good as dead.' Audley paused, lifting his wine cup. 'You disapprove. Perhaps you'd rather they blame us for the Death and march on the priory?'

'No mob is a court of law.'

Audley ignored the rebuke. If all went well he would soon be in Tewkesbury and a four day ride from his infirmarian. Neither his abbot nor the bishop would condemn him for fleeing if the villagers shed blood. But sensing Gilbert's disdain he tried to heal the rift between them by asking for other news from the village.

The monk sighed. 'Four more have died since yesterday. They need help. We sinned in locking the church. We are men of God and should be willing to go amongst them with the sacraments of penance and unction. Without God they are nothing.'

'They are nothing anyway,' snapped Audley. 'We are the Lord's servants, not peasants' grave-diggers. You forget that we agreed here, in chapter, that our duty is to praise God and pray for the salvation of souls. To do that we must live. I'll have no monk enter the village. They must be left to answer for their sins.'

'And what if we have sinned?' Brother Gilbert stood and loosened the girdle round his gown. Pulling it over his head, he lifted his arms, revealing, in the hollows beneath each of them, a solitary growth the size of a walnut.

For a second Audley sat staring at the sores, then he rose and backed away. Panic made him stumble. Half kneeling, he lifted his eyes to the *majestas*, the painting of Our Lord in Glory on the refectory wall, and began praying as Brother Gilbert gave way to his pain and coughed up the blood-stained phlegm that choked his throat.

'Prayer won't save you,' murmured the monk finally.

'Get out!'

'Nor will cowardice.'

Hearing the contempt in Gilbert's voice, Audley, his stomach tight with fear, climbed to his feet and hastily swallowed the last of his wine. 'You're a fool!' he hissed. 'If you hadn't insisted on being permitted to treat the villagers your life might have been spared.'

My task is to heal. Our Rule tells us to test the spirits, to endure the hardships through which we travel to God. I joined the Order to serve the people. If we don't do that they will one day rise against us.'

'The future, I suspect, will not concern you for much longer. Go. I'll order a Mass to be sung for your safety.'

'In three days I'll be dead.'

'You forget the words of St Paul: "the just shall live by faith."'

'My faith may comfort me, but it won't save me from the grave. Only a miracle can do that.'

Audley sneered. 'Then we must pray for one. Who else knows of your condition?'

'No one.' Now feverish and in immense pain, Brother Gilbert turned away in disgust as he saw the fear and cunning in his prior's eyes.

'Go to the infirmary. You are excused all further offices and duties. Tell no one you've the Death. I'll announce it at None.'

As soon as Brother Gilbert had left the refectory Audley poured himself more wine and returned to his chair. He could hear the solemn hum of the gradual psalms echoing in the cloisters, and as he sat staring at a marked candle burning away the hours under a glass dome on the table the familiar chant helped him order his thoughts. It would soon be time for None. If he did as he'd said the villagers would soon learn that there was a case of plague inside the priory. It might make them have second thoughts about blaming Mistress Woodward for their misery. But what if he kept Brother Gilbert in isolation? No one need know. The villagers would do as he hoped, Thomas would use his bow to defend his mother, and, by one means or another, both witch and her son would die. He smiled at his own shrewdness, then his smile vanished as he suddenly remembered Brother Gilbert embracing him before chapter. Rising from his chair he ripped open the front of his robes and felt both his armpits and groin. No lumps, no swellings, nothing but the sweat of fear. Pale and shaken and still trembling, he tipped the wine to his lips and swallowed.

*   *   *

Before crossing the bridge and entering the village Thomas lowered the roe carcass onto the parapet. It was dusk, his fourth evening at home, and he felt in need of a moment's solitude before facing his family's grief. Lillibet had died that morning, her frail five-year-old body wracked by a fever so intense that it had seemed as if she were on fire. Yet her death had come as a deliverance, and despite it Thomas felt calmer than at any time since his return. Walking back through the woods after leaving Joshuah had been to revisit the world he had known as an outlaw. Fallen leaves filled the glades, rose-hips, sloes and blackberries coloured the edges of the rides. As if through new eyes he had seen the oak from which he had ambushed Sampson and the badger's set that had once been their home. Breathing in the crisp autumnal air – untainted by death – he had felt a sense of place which gradually revived and strengthened him. But it was Joshuah who had initially rekindled his spirits. The hermit's roadside existence was the one constant in his life, and sitting talking to him Thomas had begun to see him as proof of the continuity denied by the plague. Joshuah's words had echoed his thoughts.

'Aye, lad, life 'll go on,' he had said. 'But there'll be pay an' repay 'afore the last corpse is put to rest. There's hard times ahead. Serfs are breaking bond and leaving the fields. Folk are fleeing the towns in hope of finding safety. Runnin' away won't save 'em. 'Tis as if the world has been taken by the tail, turned upside down and given a damned good shaking. Lord knows what it'll be like when the dust do settle.' He sighed. ''Tis Sampson I fear for now. A pedlar passed by earlier. It's broken out in Sarum.'

Thomas hesitated before speaking, and then, with barely a pause, he told Joshuah of his encounter with Buckle and the misgivings that had made him delay telling Sampson.

The hermit nodded approvingly. 'You did right. He'd a sworn revenge and left the city. He's a physician. They'll be needing him.'

'Have you seen him?'

'Aye, often, and he's still as fool hardy as ever.'

'My sister mistrusts him.'

'So she's told you already?' Joshuah smiled to himself. 'I met Matilda whilst you were in France. Once in a while she rides out to keep me company. She's a strange woman, Thomas. Most need a place to roost, babes at their skirts, a man to obey. But not Matilda. Since reaching womanhood every man she's met has tried to bed her. It's made her despise them, mistrust all men, not just Sampson. She knows you'd like her to wed him. Love isn't like that. To her it's something that wounds, something that can stunt or deform. She's frightened of giving herself. I've tried arguing with her, but she won't listen. ''Tis the way she is. Each of us must bear his cross. ''Tis hard to believe in charity when you've only known suffering.'

'She told you this?'

'I'm an old man, Thomas. There's no one without need of a confessor, someone to talk to.'

The conversation lapsed. Hands beneath his chin, Thomas gazed out over the downs whilst Joshuah ground oats in a hand-quern. The hermit's words had left him unsettled, made him feel that some part of the foundations to his world had been washed away. Until now he had thought Matilda impervious to fear. Blind to her beauty, scornful of the glances that greeted her every appearance in the village, it was she who had held the family together during the long years of its decline, she who had fetched and carried, mothered and mended, she who had comforted him when he first became an outlaw. And yet Joshuah's words had made her feel like a stranger to him. He now realized that her strength was also her weakness. She too had been scarred, made vulnerable and fragile. Uncomfortable in such terrain, his thoughts shifted to the plague.

'Is it true what they say?' he asked finally. 'That God has made this pestilence.'

Joshuah grunted. 'T'would be a wise man who could answer that. I've pondered it myself these last weeks. I don't think so. T'was He who fashioned us, why should He destroy what He once created?'

'Because we've angered Him?'

'And like those in Sodom must now suffer for our sins. No, 'tis too simple.'

'Then where does it come from?'

'No one knows. I've heard it said that two years back a Genoese trading-post on the seas of Crimea was besieged by Tartars who, having the Death amongst 'em, catapulted their dead over its walls. The Genoese took to their galleys, but t'was too late, for by the time they'd reached port more than half were dead. From Genoa it spread, either on the wind or by travellers.' Joshuah paused and a sad, almost despairing look spread over his face. 'There's one thing I do know, that whether God's work or the Devil's, the next few months 'll see men do unto others what none will admit to when 'tis over.'

And now Thomas remembered those words as he stood on the bridge whilst darkness slowly crept over the valley. Up-river he could see figures moving through the shadows. The pestilence had made the villagers nocturnal. By day they hid in their hovels, at night they buried their dead, fetched water and for a few hours let curiosity as to who had died or survived the day overcome their fear. Yet Thomas felt uneasy as he heaved the roe on to his shoulders and trudged homeward through the mud. There was, he thought, more purpose to their bustle than usual. Those he met were all carrying bundles of faggots towards the market place and each evaded his gaze as they passed. Finally he stopped someone and asked what was happening.

'You'll see soon enough,' said the man gruffly. 'T'aint you who's to blame, Thomas, but it has to be done,' he added in a strangely apologetic voice.

'What has to be done?' demanded Thomas.

The man shrugged his shoulders and hurried on.

Thomas stood for a moment. The mood in the village was in-

184

evitably strained, but there was a brooding, near palpable tension to it tonight that he had never detected before. His anxiety must have shown on his face, for as he entered the cottage Matilda looked up and asked what was troubling him.

He made light of it, choosing instead to talk of his meeting with Joshuah and stalking the deer as he hung it from a rafter. But though Alice was easily placated, Matilda's constant fidgeting and the pensive expression on his father's face told him that he was not alone in his fears. He listened, but could hear nothing, and so cut a joint from the roe and handed it to Alice to spit over the small fire burning in the hearth. He longed to talk alone to Matilda, but Lillibet's death still haunted the cottage and conversation was impossible. After they had eaten Alice and Matilda busied themselves jointing the remainder of the deer, leaving father and son side by side near the fire.

'Go out into the lane, lad,' whispered Hereward suddenly. 'I need eyes an' I ain't got 'em. I want to be sure what's going on out there. Go quiet, so as not to fret the lasses, an' tell only I what you see. I may be blind, but I've the ears of a hare. There's something a' stirrin' out there tonight an' I won't rest easy till I know what it is.'

Thomas rose, tip-toed across the rushes and stepped out into the night. Stars patterned the sky and a pale moon sat balanced on the church tower. The bats skimming the river in quest of food flashed dimly in its light as they weaved and curled through the darkness. The village seemed deserted. A door slammed, and for a moment he thought he heard voices coming from the market place. Then two children and a man carrying a spade loomed out of the night. All three were crying. The man spat at Thomas as he passed. Their footsteps faded and he listened again. But the village was silent, as dead as the wife and mother just buried by those who had passed him.

He went inside, rejoining his father by the fire. Hereward frowned as he told him what he had seen.

'It may be peaceful enough now, lad. But the night's a babe an' there's no storm without the hush 'afore it.'

'We're safe here,' insisted Thomas. 'I meant what I said when they came to the house. I've a bow, an' I won't think twice 'afore using it.'

But Hereward refused to be calmed. 'There's wickedness

abroad. I'll be glad to scent the dawn.'

*   *   *

They came just before midnight, when the Woodwards lay
asleep round the fire. Some carried hoes and bill-hooks, others
waved scythes, cudgels and mattocks as they moved up the lane.
Thomas heard them first, but by then they had surrounded the
cottage. Leaping to his feet, he crossed over to the door and
peered out into the night. In front of him, lit by the garish light of
torches, stood a line of grim faced villagers. For an instant he
stood stunned and too dazed to think, then he turned and roused
his family from the straw as an angry roar shattered the silence
and the first torches were tossed onto the thatch above his head.

'What's happening?' cried Matilda.

'They're firing the cottage! Quickly! Help father!' Thomas
lifted his mother to her feet. He could smell smoke and hear the
crackle of flames. A scythe pierced the wattle, an axe-head followed it. Above the shouts of the crowd he could hear his mother
whimpering as she clutched at his chest. She raised her head.
Confusion filled her eyes, her cheeks had blanched and drained
of all blood.

'Why?' she moaned. 'Why? Why?'

As if in answer a voice bellowed: 'Give us the witch! 'Tis only
she we want!'

'That's right!' cried another. ''Tis she who brought it. The
Lord 'll spare us when she's gone.'

Thomas glanced over her shoulder. His father and Matilda
were clinging to one another in the gloom, and for an instant,
before smoke billowed between them, he saw a look of such
hopelessness on his father's face that he felt like admitting defeat
and silently awaiting the end. It was Matilda who goaded him
into action. 'We must get out before the roof falls in!' she
screamed. A moment later the first sparks lit the ceiling. They
soon fanned out, turning into a sheet of flames as they kindled
the dry reed that lined the roof. Suddenly a molten wedge of
thatch fell to the floor. Flames licked amongst the rushes. The
air grew parched, the heat fiercer, and within minutes the entire
roof had become a blazing wall of fire likely to collapse on to their
heads at any moment.

186

By now the four of them stood huddled in the centre of the cottage. Matilda was crying, Hereward shielding his face with his one hand against the heat. Suddenly Alice broke from Thomas's grip. 'Let me go!' she screamed. ''Tis me the bastards want!'

'No!' Thomas pulled her back. 'We go together!' Covering his bow in his cloak and dragging his mother behind him, he dived through the flames to the door, quickly side-stepping as Matilda and his father burst from the smoke and fell in a heap in the mud. Matilda was screaming. Although she had covered her head with a blanket, tongues of scarlet danced amongst the black of her hair. Thomas jumped forward, smothering the flames with his hands before unwrapping his bow and rising to face the crowd as behind him their home turned into a furnace. Suddenly its walls and roof collapsed inward, leaving only the kingpost and a few burning rafters poking upwards into the blackness. As if awed by its passing, no one spoke for a moment.

An old crone waving a hoe broke the silence. 'Give us the witch!' she cried. Others repeated her words, turning them into a chant. Thomas drew his bow, aiming it at first one chest then another. A rock struck his legs. The noise grew louder. The sea of faces moved hesitantly forward. Mouths open, each chanting and waving their arm, their eyes lit up by the flames, they seemed to him unreal, as if reason had left them and despair transformed them into demons.

'Leave us be!' he shouted.

Beside him, his mother suddenly flung wide her arms and cried: 'Lord have mercy on you!'

''Tis 'ee who should be pleadin' for mercy, witch!' replied someone. 'There's no plague in the priory! There ain't a death token among 'em. 'Tis you who brought it!'

'Come on. Let's be done with it!' added another, and at once, as if driven by the instincts of the herd, the villagers surged forward, only halting when Thomas pulled back his bowstring and took deliberate aim at the nearest throat.

'I'll kill the next to move,' he cried. 'Spare us now an' we'll take to the woods. We'll not harm you there.'

'No! She must die!'

Alice turned to her son. Though crying, her face bore a look so tranquil that he began trembling as he pulled her towards him.

Her body was rigid, her hands cold. 'Let them have me,' she said softly.

'No.' He lifted his bow, choosing the same throat for a target.

Its owner opened his jerkin. A mottled rash discoloured his chest and the boils beneath his arms had burst and began suppurating. 'I'm doomed, Woodward,' he said. 'Nothing you do 'll save either of us.' Raising his scythe, he walked slowly towards Alice. Thomas allowed him four paces. Steel flashed. An instant later he gave a hoarse cry, toppled to his knees and fell face down in the mud, a steel arrow-head protruding from the nape of his neck.

There was silence. Someone yelled 'Kill her!' and then the villagers rushed forward as one. Thomas fired again, but they continued on, trampling Matilda underfoot and felling Hereward with cudgels as he tried to stem their advance. Alice was quickly encircled. Crying out in pain as a hoe gouged her brow, she crossed herself and closed her eyes. But she was still standing, and to his amazement Thomas saw a smile pass over her face as finally, her body battered and broken, she slowly slid to her knees and disappeared beneath the endless torrent of blows still raining down on her. Then Thomas himself fell, cut down by one chop from a spade. A sudden explosion of light filled his head, then his fingers slipped from his bow as the darkness descended.

Consciousness returned to him as if through a haze. It was still night, and the stars dimmed then blazed as he lifted his face from the mud. At first all that had happened was a blur. Gradually the night found focus. Clutching his neck, he climbed unsteadily to his feet and stumbled into the river, splashing his face with water before vainly looking for some signs of life. The two men he had killed still lay where they had fallen, but the survivors, as well as his own family, had all vanished. Hearing shouts and a tuneless, eerie chanting, he glanced toward the market place. The byres and hovels lining its sides shimmered in the light from a vast bonfire raging in its centre, round which, hands linked, the entire village seemed to be circling in procession. He headed towards it. Suddenly he saw his father trying to claw his way through the circle and Matilda slumped in the shadows. He looked again at the pyre, then turned away in horror.

'She's safe now. They can't hurt her any more.'

He lifted his head. Matilda was beside him, a vacant and dreamlike look on her face. Her dress had been torn from her body, but she seemed unaware of her nakedness. Bruises covered her back and thighs, blood caked her hair.

'She's dead, isn't she?' he whispered.

'I tried to save her.'

He looked up at the bonfire. Through the flames he could see the charred and shapeless remains of his mother hanging lifeless from the great post that had been driven through its heart.

'She was dead when they lit it,' said Matilda emptily.

'But she was one of them! For years she'd tended and helped them. Some are our kin!'

'None of that matters. They think God will take the Death from amongst them, that the flames 'll purify the vapours and their sins be forgiven when mother is ashes.' Matilda had been staring at the fire as she spoke. Without warning she started running towards it screaming: 'Father! Stop!'

Thomas glanced up, the terror in her voice making him afraid to look. His father had broken through the circle and was standing on the edge of the flames. Above the chanting he could hear him crying 'Alice! Alice!' over and over again. Even as he began running, his father plunged into the blaze, hauling himself over first one bundle of faggots and then another in an attempt to reach her. There was no hope of saving him. He was already a living torch when the fire collapsed beneath his weight and he fell deep into its heart.

Thomas buried his face in his hands and let the tears drench their palms. Matilda cried out and dropped to the ground. But there was no pause in the chanting and when Thomas next looked up he saw only a vast cone of light that licked at the darkness and filled the sky with its sparks.

He turned away, then froze. A black shape stood outlined against the lane leading to the priory. Its face moved, shifting towards him. For a moment the two men stared at one another, then Audley pulled his cowl low over his eyes and slid into the shadows, still smiling.

Thomas knew nothing after that. But later, his mind a void, Matilda lifted him to his feet, wrapped his cloak round his shoulders and led him back up the lane. They paused briefly beside the glowing shell of their home before crossing the bridge. A pair of mallard suddenly rose from the reeds. They called and circled, and then, as if offering themselves as guides, flew off in the direction of the Chase. By dawn Thomas and Matilda were deep in the woods.

CHAPTER FOURTEEN

John Swayne was the richest wool merchant in Salisbury. An artisan's son, he owed his wealth to his own industry, a carefully considered marriage and a willingness to be ruthless when necessary. He was also the city's mayor, an honour he had long coveted and one which had cost dear in the purchase of votes. But his sense of timing had proved unfortunate. Less than three months after taking office the plague had entered the city in the guise of a wandering friar who dropped dead in the Close. And now, five weeks later, his eyes were bloodshot from lack of sleep, his nerves frayed and his patience exhausted by the chatter of the physicians gathered in the upper chamber of the Guildhall. They were discussing the link between the spread of the Death and the movement of the stars, all of them, simultaneously. He banged his fist against the table.

'Silence! I called this meeting for a purpose. I want a cure, not a lesson in star-gazing. How are you to rid us of the Death if you can't even agree its cause? The city is in chaos. Corpses lie rotting in the streets. The pesthouse is overflowing. The burial pits are filled as fast as I order them dug. The homes of those who fled have been ransacked by felons. I need more constables, bearers, searchers and grave-diggers. I need men to distribute flour, to bake and keep the market open. But above all I need a cure. Find one! I'll give you a week, after that I'll have each of you tried for quackery and driven from the city.'

Ignoring the outburst that greeted this threat, Swayne paused and glanced at the young man sitting silent and alone to the rear of the other guildsmen. 'Master Hooke,' he went on, 'you've said nothing, not a word. You may be a surgeon, but is there no

191

physic you can suggest, no salve or drench?'

Sampson looked round at his fellow physicians. Some were scowling at him, the others making no attempt to hide their disdain. He hesitated for a moment, then rose to his feet.

'The rules of medicine are simple,' he said finally, his voice grave and resonant in the empty Guildhall. 'You examine symptoms, diagnose them and effect a cure. But in the case of the Death such rules are meaningless. It defies all logic. I've tried bleeding, surgery, poultices and various lozenges.'

'Using what?' asked Swayne

'Herbs, saffron, myrrh and aloes. All have failed.'

'Of course they have!' snapped a spindly, pinch-faced physician wearing an ermine skull-cap and eye-glasses. 'The contagion is carried by winged insects that invade the body through the mouth and nostrils. To halt them, you must build a wall round the city.'

'Nonsense!' interrupted another. 'Activity is fatal. The contagion penetrates the body when a man breathes. Sleep is the sole remedy, but not on the back, for that causes a stream of superfluities to descend on the liver. Heated, they flow back to the brain on waking and inflame the humours.'

'What proof have you of this?' demanded a third. 'My own experiments show that the Death is spread by aerial spirits escaping from the eyes of the sick and striking those nearest them. Seclusion and tranquillity are the only cure. 'Tis well known that sadness cools the blood, dulls the wits and deadens the spirit.'

And so it went on. Voices and tempers rose as each tried to convert the others to belief in his own theory. Sampson listened in silence. He had heard such arguments before and had long ago given up hoping that one might prove correct. He turned and looked out through a window casement into the market place below. Even now, in every ward in the city, men, women and children were dying. Nothing would save them. Time had taught him that the remedies concocted by his brother physicians were no more than a panacea, a vain attempt to demonstrate that those who had prescribed them still had some hold on the situation. But in recent weeks both cause and cure had changed character. No physician now bled, cut open the boils or bound them in a poultice. To touch the sick was to risk death, and all found safety in far-fetched speculation that made contact with their patients unnecessary. He did not blame them. Most of his fellow guildsmen had fled the city when the plague first broke, others had died and the handful that remained were eager to avoid their fate.

Hearing Swayne trying to restore order, he turned and glanced at the mayor. The pouches beneath his eyes were livid and swollen, his once bluff cheeks were hollow. His was a thankless task, for though the rich had abandoned their homes the city still contained some three thousand inhabitants: trades-men, craftsmen, day-labourers, beggars, those with nowhere to flee. Most lived in over-crowded tenements rife with infection. Some had formed gangs to terrorize the living, others murdered with impunity, drunkenness was widespread, the only doors that never shut were those of the taverns and brothels.

When the Guildhall was quiet again, Swayne pointed at Sampson. 'You were interrupted. Pray continue.'

'Sir!' cried one of the other physicians. 'Hooke knows nothing about the pestilence. Three years ago he was a common outlaw!'

''Tis the future, not the past, that now concerns me.' Swayne glowered angrily as he waited for Sampson to speak.

Ignoring the rage of those round him, Sampson rose again. 'There is no pattern to it, for its effects vary,' he said. 'One man may die and his neighbour be spared. A mother dies, her children outlive her for weeks. Some have succumbed within hours of the buboes appearing. Some spit blood and are fevered, some suffer only the swellings, others have both.'

'But none have recovered?'

He hesitated: so much was conjecture, so little certain. He answered cautiously. 'There have been cases where the buboes discharged and the victim survived: a handful, no more, but they may hold the key to a cure.'

'And if the boils are lanced?'

Sampson yearned to offer some comfort. 'It makes no difference,' he said finally. 'The Death despises all medicine.'

Swayne smiled glumly. 'So none of you can help me. Very well, you may go.' He shuffled through the parchment rolls in front of him. 'I've last week's mortality bills. Over ten score died, bringing the total to over seven hundred.'

'We must pray for deliverance,' muttered one of the physicians.

'You think that will suffice? I'm not so sure.'

The nine physicians, many holding bouquets of herbs of silk squares drenched in perfumes, left the Guildhall. Sampson was the last to leave. 'Master Hooke.' He turned. 'There are times when the burdens of this office weigh heavy. I'm a wool merchant, not a healer. I shall always welcome your advice.'

'And I will give it.'

'Thank you.'

Before closing the door, Sampson glanced back at the mayor. Head in hands, he lay slumped over his desk. The words of the Litany were just audible. He quietly lowered the latch.

Outside the Guildhall, the cobbled square was almost deserted. Although it was market day the booths and shops still open were only permitted to sell food, and the few women replenishing their larders found little to detain them before hurrying homeward as quickly as possible. Some wore veils, others beat the air with clappers as they walked in order to disperse the vapours. None spoke to one another. There were no dogs, cats or swine scavenging through the market refuse; pigs had been impounded, all other strays destroyed. A corpse lay bloated and black with crows in the gutter, and the watchmen were nailing boards over the doors and shutters of an Ox Row house in which the plague had broken out. No one seemed to notice the screams of those being walled up still alive inside it, and indeed, after a month, Sampson himself was hardly aware of the one sound that still pervaded the city. Wailing, lamentation, the hideous screams of the dying were as commonplace as the burial carts that rumbled by night through the streets, their drivers crying 'Bring out your dead!' For weeks now no bells had tolled in mourning, funeral processions had been banned inside the city for fear of spreading panic and there were moments when he feared that the Death might actually destroy it, only leaving it when grass sprouted between the cobbles and the derelict empty houses had become a throat for owls.

But for now it still lived. The air was chill, winter lay ahead, and leaves crackled underfoot as he crossed the market place, skirted Poultry Cross and entered his lodgings. After returning from France and obtaining his licence he had taken two rooms on the ground floor of a tannery. Both were small and dark, but though candlelight tired his eyes when working he kept the shutters barred for fear of infection. Entering the larger of the rooms, he removed his cloak and heaped the fire with sea-coals, breathing deeply of their sulphurous fumes before covering them with juniper berries, rue, mastic and camphor. He threw himself across his bed. Once again the weekly meeting with Swayne had led nowhere, but, as always in its aftermath, he was unable to resist sifting through all the evidence he had collated since the plague broke in the hope of finding some stone left unturned. But he was tired, more so than he cared to admit, and his concentration soon wavered. He fell into a restless sleep, to be woken, an hour later, by a woman's voice calling his name and a hesitant rap on the door. Thinking it might be his mother, he unlocked it. A middle-aged woman, reeking of garlic and hidden behind her capuchon, stood in the doorway.

'Master Hooke?'

'Yes.'

She lowered her capuchon. Sampson backed away as he saw the tell-tale stains that blooded its lining. 'Help me, I beg 'ee. I've money,' she blurted.

'Go home. There's nothing I can do. I'm sorry.'

'Who else can I turn to? You're a physician, your job is to mend.'

Sampson closed his ears to her despair. It was always the same. They pleaded and begged, some offered gold, others themselves or their daughters. And there was nothing he could do but turn them away.

'Have the searchers examined your house?'

The woman gave a slight nod. It was an offence to leave a building that harboured the plague. Once the doors and windows had been boarded its occupants were supposed to remain indoors for twelve days, until they either left in the cart or the contagion passed. Food was handed up by means of baskets and ropes. But many tore down the boards and moved freely about the city, spreading the contagion still further.

Sampson asked the woman to go. She refused, first imploring his help and then reproaching him for his inhumanity by standing head bowed and silent in the doorway. He paced his rooms. Suddenly he thought of Swayne's demand for a cure and his own reticence to mention the one remedy he still had some faith in. And now he had a chance to prove or disprove it. He decided to treat her. It was a risk, and whenever he touched a plague victim he spent the next few days constantly scrutinizing his body for any sign of swelling.

He made the woman remove her gown and shift and lie on her back on a table. Unashamed of her nakedness, she lay stiff and feverish as he pulled on some gloves and pressed the two boils beneath her arms. One was the size of a duck's egg, the other inflammed with poison. She screamed and began coughing up blood. He turned away, disgusted by the foetid stench of her body and breath. There was no hope for her, she would be dead by the end of the day. By rights he should send for the cart and have her taken to the pest-house before she infected others. Instead he took down a small glass jar from his medicine shelves and tipped its contents into a pestle.

'Will it hurt?'

'No.' He was lying. Lunar nitrate was a caustic that burnt and destroyed any living tissue it touched. Such pain was immeasurable. The only alternative was a red-hot iron; a treatment he had used but once and afterwards sworn never to repeat. Yet he knew that the only survivors of the Death were those whose buboes had broken, and he was convinced that they owed their recovery to a natural rejection of the poisons by the body.

He strapped the woman to the table with leather thongs and prepared a bran poultice. After smearing the bran with the caustic, he placed it over the larger of her boils and bound it in place with a dressing. He stood back, helpless, in dread of what lay ahead. For a moment she remained still, then, as the first wave of pain enveloped her, gave a wordless scream and tried to hurl herself from the table. Eyes closed, Sampson turned away and placed his hands to his ears. There was nothing he could do until the caustic had burnt away the outer kernel of the tumour and the poisons discharged. Her screams grew louder. They died as they were born, the progeny of torment. A hand slapped against the table. Silence. Sampson turned. Her eyes were wide open and she was staring blankly upwards from the stream of thick black blood still oozing from the poultice. Even before feeling her heart he knew she was dead. Exhausted and sickened at the manner of her death, he covered her body, opened the shutters and rang the hand-bell still permitted physicians. Once again he had failed, but pride made him look for excuses: the caustic needed dilution, the woman had left it too late. He cursed, suddenly angry with her for persuading him to attempt the impossible and be a witness to her death.

When the bearers finally arrived they tossed her corpse into the death cart. One recognized her and told him that her husband had thrown himself into a burial pit when still alive. 'There's plenty doin' that,' he added cheerfully. 'Death can't come too quick for 'em. Still, saves us toil, don't it?'

'Thoughtful, that's what they is, like the friars,' joked another. He shook his head and sighed. 'Aye, no one but a friar 'ed sew himself into his own shroud on finding the tokens so as to spare another the labour.'

'They're brave men,' said Sampson.

'So what? 'Tis easy to minister to the dying when you're bound for Heaven.'

Sampson noticed the scar left by a branding iron on the man's cheek. Like his companions, he was a convicted criminal who had been spared the noose to help cart and bury the dead. The work took a heavy toll, but those who survived had been promised their freedom. Grim humour kept them going and most practised some bizarre ritual in an attempt to stave off the pestilence. Some drank their own urine, others congregated in the latrines on Fisherton Bridge to inhale the stench; but neither habit stopped the plague from claiming them. The proximity of death made them profligate and reckless. At night they haunted the Culver Street stews or gathered in the slum quarter inns behind the butcher's slaughter-yard on New Canal.

After their departure Sampson scrubbed down the table on which the woman had died before shedding his clothes and washing himself from head to toe with vinegar. He dressed, sluiced the flags with rose-water and walked out into the street. For a moment he debated joining his mother in the tavern, but knowing that she would seize on his mood to try and pester him into fleeing the city, he turned north and began deliberating on his quest for a cure. Gradually, increasingly confused, his thoughts shifted from the search for a remedy to prevention. He was now almost certain that the contagion did not move through the air, but existed as an invisible venom which one infected person transmitted to another. Yet why had he, a physician, not succumbed to it? Did bodies differ? Were some made immune

197

by an unknown agent created by the humours? No, that was supposition and impossible to prove. Ignoring the body and its mysteries, he began looking for a more tangible answer. Suddenly he found himself making a mental inventory of the liquids, powders and herbs he used to purify his lodgings. Based on a wish to do something to protect himself rather than any knowledge of their merits, their initial selection had been random. But what if one, all, or some combination of them did keep the infection at bay?

When Sampson next glanced up he saw the Castle Street Gate ahead of him. The clatter of a wind-blown sign made him turn. Its gold leaf had peeled, but the words NATHANIEL BUCKLE were just visible. He halted. In the last few minutes he had come to realize the potential importance of his medicines. With the market closed and foreign trade at a standstill it had been impossible to buy more. Aware that the house was deserted and knowing that it might contain much of what he needed to perfect a preventive, he tried the door. It was bolted: he shinned the garden wall. Its once immaculate knots were overgrown and deep in weeds. He fought his way to the back door and kicked it open. The house was silent, his footsteps echoed in the ill-lit passageway. Uneasy, his thoughts haunted by memories of his apprenticeship, he entered the parlour.

A man was sitting with his back to him at a table. Long white hair hung down over the silk cloak draped round his shoulders. He seemed ignorant of Sampson's entry.

'Master Buckle.'

The man did not move. Sampson repeated the name and walked towards him. Confused and slightly frightened, he reached out and touched him. His shoulders felt bony and chill. He touched him again, this time pushing him forward. The man toppled sideways and fell loudly, his spine and the long limb bones that had once held flesh splintering as they hit the floor. For an instant Sampson was too horrified to move then, as a mouse jumped from the shattered rib-cage and the eyeless, polished skull stared up at him, he stumbled blindly from the room.

Later, much later, when he had finally recovered from the shock, he returned to the parlour, covered the broken skeleton with the cloak and gathered what herbs and powders he could find into a sack. The dead man was unrecognizable, but walking homeward he grew increasingly certain that it was Buckle's shoulder he had touched; a Buckle freed from the Tower who had come home to die, another nameless, unremembered victim of the plague.

Only when approaching the river did he begin to have doubts as to the man's identity. Yet what did it matter? Buckle, like Audley, could no longer harm him. Too weary for thought, he gazed out over the water-meadows on the far bank. The Avon was in flood and the wind licked at its surface, breaking it into boats of foam that sailed across the current. A cluster of flat-bottomed barges rubbed against the timber piles lining the waterfront. The quay was deserted, its warehouses looted. Suddenly he heard voices. It was the bearers who had collected the dead woman from his lodgings. They were dancing round an open burial pit on the far bank chanting: 'Hie! Hie for more shoulder work!' Each carried a corpse over his shoulder and held a flagon. Kites and crows hopped amongst the bodies still piled in the cart and two mastiffs were fighting over a leg left partially uncovered in a neighbouring pit. It was a grotesque, almost nightmarish cameo, and once again Sampson gave way to his horror and turned away in disgust. But even as he did so he sensed that what he had just seen was not rare, but a daily event in the city's life. He shuddered; soon it might be his corpse that the dogs fought over, his skeleton that sat forgotten at a table.

The two images stayed with him as he hurried on. Perhaps he should give in to his mother and leave the city whilst there was still time? Ahead of him the cathedral spire towered upwards above the rooftops. Against the whiteness of clouds he could see masons and carpenters moving amongst the scaffolding that encased it. For a moment he was so overwhelmed by its beauty, by seeing something that had been with him since childhood, something so different to the mockery of life he had just turned his back on, that he could not take his eyes off it. The men etched against its tapered stones were not friars supported by their faith, but craftsmen employed to complete a building even though the Death raged below them and the world itself seemed doomed to damnation. Each day they lifted its summit nearer to Heaven. Cold-chisels and plumb-lines were their tools, not prayer, and as he watched them his spirits rose and his doubts faded. If they could find a sense of purpose strong enough to support them in their work, so could he, and he suddenly knew that whatever the fate that awaited him he would not leave the city until the plague had passed.

*   *   *

''Tis St Nicholas Day,' said Widow Hooke, lifting two trout from the skillet over the fire and placing them on the kitchen table. 'We've been spared and should celebrate. There's still a hogshead of sack in the cellars.'

Sampson laid down his quill and listened to the rain beating against the tavern shutters. In two weeks it will be Christmas, he thought, and the Death will have been with us for four months. He sighed tiredly, gathered up his papers and glanced anxiously at his mother. Those months had aged her: her once plump cheeks were sunken and pale, the fire-light glowed dimly in her lack-lustre eyes and her once sprightly body had become stooped and thin.

'It still isn't over, mother,' he said finally. 'The bills show that nearly four score souls perished last week alone.'

She seemed not to hear him. 'Go fetch the lodgers. Tell 'em we've grayling in saffron an' plum pie an' custard.'

Sampson rose and walked toward the door. Suddenly he stopped, unable to go through with it. In the last few weeks the past and present had become muddled in her mind, leaving her prey to a blend of fantasy and fact whose boundaries had grown increasingly blurred. He rounded the end of the table so as to be near her if she needed comforting.

'Mother,' he said gently, 'there's no one here but you an' I. The cellars are empty. We've no lodgers, no custom and no maids; not even Beatrix since she vanished.'

For a moment he thought she was going to argue, but then the first low sob of reality broke from her lips and she began weeping into her apron. ''Tis the waiting that's crazed me,' she blurted between sobs. 'Why can't we go?'

'I'm a physician. I've told you before, I promised Swayne I'd help him. He needs me. The plague powder recipe I'm working on for him may succeed. I must stay and finish what I've started. Or would you rather I went back on my word?'

'Yes, if it means living I would.' Widow Hooke slumped

forward. 'Powders, cure-alls! What's the point to 'em? 'Tis the Lord's creation and no man alive can defy His will. If only Mervyn was here. You'd 'a listened to him.'

Sampson reached towards her and stroked her hair. 'I don't mean to hurt you. You know that. But please forget Mervyn. He's dead and nothing will bring him back to you. I'm not to blame for what happened.'

Widow Hooke nodded. 'You must do as seems fit.' She lifted her head and smiled palely, once again admitting defeat. 'There may be some ale in the parlour.'

Sampson took a jug from the dresser and walked through into the parlour. A month ago it had been looted by a gang of armed drunks. The torn shutters blew in the wind, puddles lay on the floor and the half-starved swine he had heard snuffling through it earlier in the week had shredded the rushes in their hunger. He drained the last of the ale into the jug and returned to the kitchen's warmth, carefully barring the door behind him. Since leaving his lodgings so as to protect his mother, the two of them had lived together in this one room, only leaving it when necessary and sleeping in front of the fire.

They ate in silence. To Sampson's amazement his mother suddenly opened the oven and drew four loaves from the heat. He frowned. 'Where did you find flour? According to Swayne the granary's empty.'

'I went looking for it. There's food a'plenty if you know where to find it.'

'I told you not to venture into the streets!' cried Sampson angrily. 'The Death's everywhere. 'Tis madness for both of us to risk infection.'

'I had to get out. This room's worse than a dungeon. At night I lie awake listening to the screams. By day I sit here, alone. Walls won't keep it at bay.'

Hearing her resignation, Sampson resisted another argument. He had his recipes, his work, his meetings with Swayne. She had nothing. Knowing that if he dwelt on it her suffering might make him leave the city, he rose and tipped more coals on to the fire. He was now virtually certain that its fumes gave immunity to those who breathed them. Or was it merely that the fierce dry heat of the coals purified the air? Of that, like so much else, he was still unsure.

The rain lashed against the shutters as the afternoon slipped by. He had spent the morning trying to persuade Swayne to enforce the law against emptying cesspits and ordure buckets into the street channels. The stench was almost unbearable, rats teemed through the filth. But Swayne had promised nothing: his scavengers were all dead, the watch too busy hunting the cut-throats who roamed the city. Sampson had suggested placing sulphur sacks on every street corner and was now planning the final combination of herbs to go in them. He picked up his quill. A moment later a faint banging on the courtyard door ended the silence.

Widow Hooke covered her face with her shawl. 'Don't go. 'Tis a trick. It'll be thieves. They're as brazen as best brass.'

Sampson took a knife from the table and crossed over to the door. He hesitated, then unlocked and opened it.

'Matilda!'

Bedraggled, sodden, swaying on her feet, she stood in silence with the rain drumming against her face and hair. Her cheeks were pale and splashed with mud. She opened her mouth as if to speak. Then her legs collapsed beneath her and she fell in a heap in the doorway.

*   *   *

'Drink this.'

The broth burnt her throat as she sipped it. Beyond his face, anxious, strained, close to hers, she could see fire-light mirrored in an empty copper. Sleep tempted her again, called her back to one world where she need not think or move or have to speak. Instead, she hauled herself upright and stretched her hands to the coals. He was still talking.

'Exhaustion made you swoon. You're safe now. Eat, you need strength.' She took the bread from his fingers, pouching some in one cheek like a squirrel and slowly swallowing the rest.

He smiled. Pouching was a form of security, a habit of the consistently hungry. 'When did you last eat?'

'Yesterday morn.' How distant that meal now seemed. Remembering the abandoned homesteads, the soldiers she had hidden from in a ditch, the taunts of those who had accosted her whilst tramping Sarum in search of the tavern, she shivered and pulled the blanket tighter to her throat.

'You walked from Cranborne?'

'From the Chase.' Seeing need for explanation, she added: 'I wouldn't 'a come but for Thomas.'

'But Thomas is in London!' Sampson placed the bowl on the flags and pulled her towards him. 'For God's sake tell me what's happened? Why have you come? When we last parted you said you hoped never to see me again.'

Ignoring the reminder of his attempt to woo her, she spoke slowly, harbouring her strength by pruning the details. But gradually it all came out: the coming of the plague, Thomas's return, the deaths of Alice and Hereward, their flight to the Chase and Audley's departure for Tewkesbury as the Death spread like a fire through the priory, engulfing two-thirds of its inmates in the flames; then the weeks spent foraging for nuts and berries whilst Thomas's grief ate into him like a canker, Joshuah's efforts to help them as Thomas grew frail and delirious.

'I had no choice but to come,' she said finally, the whites of her eyes red with fatigue and unshed tears. 'He's like a bird with a broken wing. It's as if father's death and seeing Audley made something snap inside him. You're a physician, his friend. You must help him.' Sensing an ally, she switched her gaze to his mother.

Numbed by mention of Audley, Widow Hooke had sat horrified as Matilda spoke. Until now she had believed him to be part of the past. The months he had spent trying to hang her son, his son, had been an unending nightmare. On his return from France Sampson had again asked her how she knew that he lacked a finger. She had made light of it, telling him that he had once lodged in the tavern and disputed the cost of his board, and since then she had always changed the subject whenever his name was mentioned. Yet now she spoke. And lied. 'I know nothing of the prior,' she said, turning to Sampson, 'but we've money enough to find Thomas an' take rooms in an inn till the contagion's passed.'

She could feel Matilda's eyes boring into hers, denouncing the lie, reproaching her for her cowardice. No silence could have been more eloquent. She blanched and turned away, certain of being unmasked. Then, as if through fog, the silence ended and she heard Matilda begin pleading with her son.

'He's with Joshuah. But 'tis you he needs!'

Sampson sighed, too tired to resist their attack. 'I must have time to think.'

'And what about Thomas? What'll happen to him whilst you brood?'

Sampson rounded on her, suddenly incensed by her petulance. 'You use your brother's name as if it were a sword. You forget that I'm a physician in a plague struck city. I can't just saddle a horse an' leave when the fancy takes'

Blind to Widow Hooke, Matilda tossed aside her blanket and rose stiffly to her feet. 'You think I hate you,' she cried angrily, 'that it was that which made me turn away when you came 'a courtin' in the summer. You're wrong, Sampson. I've seen too much hate to have any to spare for you. I've come to beg your help. Thomas needs mending 'afore he cracks an' breaks. You an' I may never be friends, but to Thomas you're like a brother.'

Bewildered by her rage and the suddenness of her onslaught, Sampson tried to calm her 'You're tired. You need sleep. No harm 'll come to him 'tween now an' morning. Tomorrow I'll ride to Joshuah's and fetch him. He'll be safe here.'

'And what of tonight?' She was almost hysterical, her voice was shrill with panic. 'He's my brother. All I have. Go to him, Sampson!'

'I will, but on the morrow.'

She reached for the clasp to her gown. 'I once let you kiss me to settle a debt. What payment would persuade you to do as I ask? Another kiss? Or would you take me now, on these flags and in front of your own mother?'

'Stop it!'

'You treat me like Audley! But I suppose that's to be expected from his . . . .' And then she stopped, choking back on the word as Widow Hooke buried her face in her hands. No, she could not say it. But fearing that she might be unable to check it for long, she snatched her cloak from the table and stormed towards the door. Her hand was on its bolt when it suddenly shook in its hinges and a voice cried.

'Master Hooke! Come quick! For the love of God, hurry!'

Matilda pulled it open, letting in a gust of wind and a young, frightened woman.

204

Widow Hooke was the first to speak. Aware that she had been reprieved and seeing the woman's striped hood, she rose to her feet and hissed: 'Get out! I'll not have whores in here! There's nothing he can do for you.'

The woman had blackened her eyes with charcoal and in the light from the fire they stood out like jewels in a setting of jet. Turning to Matilda for support, she said: 'T'ain't for me. 'Tis Beatrix. The tokens is on 'er. She said Master Sampson 'ed come.'

'You're wasting your time,' replied Matilda, glancing contemptuously at Sampson. 'He'll not budge: not for you, me, or anyone.'

The woman moved closer to him. 'She's at the sign of the Tabard. She works there, same as me an' the other girls. She swore you'd help 'er.'

'Beatrix? A Tabard slut? I don't believe it!' cried Widow Hooke.

'Believe what you want, ma'am. But she's there, an' poorly.'

Widow Hooke slumped to a stool. 'But why? What made her leave us?'

''Tis alright, mother. She'll have a reason. I must go to her. Bar the door and let no one in till I return.' Sampson swept up his medicine bag.

'I'm coming with you.' Matilda blocked his exit.

'No.'

'Yes. I want to see who it is that means more to you than Thomas.'

Beyond argument, Sampson relented. 'Stay close to me.' And then he was gone, following the woman through the mud beneath the courtyard arch.

He let her lead the way. Rain still blustered through the streets. Once they met a gang of bearers loading the dead into carts by the light of torches whose sparks streamed red in the wind. Occasionally they heard wailing or saw a figure flit through the shadows. Yet for much of the journey the city appeared deserted, or seemed it until they entered the slums. Here lights burned brightly, as if lantern and torch could keep the Death at bay. The taverns echoed to laughter and whores beckoned from doorways. Drunks and corpses shared the gutters and ragged street orphans with swollen bellies hovered like flies outside the pot-shops.

'We're there,' said the woman suddenly.

Pushing Matilda ahead of him, Sampson plunged behind her down a narrow alley towards a flicker of light. The woman stopped and ducked through a doorway: above it the torn tatters of a tabard blew to and fro in the wind. Inside, a line of barrels stretched the length of a parlour crowded with the city's flotsam: beggars, draw-latches, groups of ruffians armed with cudgels and knives. Women with floured cheeks and lips stained with cochineal moved amongst them. Caged fighting cocks hung from hooks on the rafters. A minstrel picked at a lute, the stench of ale and vomit filled the stale air and a grubby handwritten sign nailed to one wall promised that any woman who took money from a man would 'lie with him all night till a cock do crow.' Despite his revulsion, Sampson smiled: most stews kept cockerels specially trained to crow long before dawn.

'Please take me home!' Matilda was beside him, being pawed by a leering and drunken grave-digger who kept insisting that he had purchased her for the night.

'You asked to come. Now perhaps you'll understand why I'm here.' He shrugged the grave-digger aside as the woman led them towards the stairs.

He tried to reason with her as he followed her into the gloom. 'Go home,' he said. 'Leave whilst you still can.'

The woman halted, shoulders sagging as she glanced back at him. 'Home,' she said. 'What home? 'Tis boarded up. My husband an' babes lodge in a burial pit. Where else can I go?'

'You'll join them if you stay. A bawdy house is no place to mourn them.'

''Tis all the same. Holy place or stew, it makes no odds where you hide or who you are. The Death claims all. You're a physician. But what'll you say to Beatrix? How'll you comfort her? No, 'tis better to die full-bellied an' a whore than starvin' an' alone.'

Reaching the attics, she pushed open a door. 'She's in here.' For an instant Sampson saw grief cloud her face, then she was gone, vanishing into the darkness. He entered the room. A tallow fluttered then steadied as Matilda closed the door behind her. The garret was small, flies buzzed loudly in the angle of the ceiling and he could see Beatrix lying amidst the straw strewn over its boards. In her pain she had torn out whole handfuls of her hair, and they lay across the pillow beneath her head like seaweed left scattered on sand after a storm.

Hearing someone enter the room, she turned her chalk-white face towards his and croaked through cracked lips: 'Water, I must have water. 'Tis alright, Cicely. I'm still alive. You can bring it to me.'

Sampson glanced at Matilda; despair had touched her beauty, made it tender and gentle and filled with helplessness. 'There'll be a butt on the landing,' he said. She nodded and left the room, returning a moment later with a cup. Sampson lifted it to Beatrix's lips. She gulped greedily and fell exhausted to the straw.

''Tis you, isn't it, Cicely?' she whispered.

'No, 'tis me, Sampson.'

Looking up at him, she smiled slightly. 'So you came?'

'Yes.'

'The buboes, they hurt. Is it cold? I'm so very cold.' Sampson touched her face: it was hot with fever. She began whimpering and coughing up blood.

'Let me see them,' said Sampson when the pain subsided. She lowered her dress over her shoulders. The swellings were raw and inflamed and soft to his touch.

'You'll make them go away, won't you?' she said.

'You win, Sampson.' Matilda was behind him, tears drenched her face. 'You think you lose. You don't and never will. 'Tis just that you can't see it.' The door clicked shut as she left the room. Sampson shuddered and turned towards Beatrix again.

'Why are you here?' he asked gently.

'I needed money to feed my sisters. I couldn't take it from your mother. The tavern was empty.'

Sampson shook his head. 'You're a fool, Beatrix. She'd gladly have given it to you. So would I.'

'They're dead now. It doesn't matter any more. But you'll make me better.'

He closed his eyes. 'Yes, I'll make you better.'

She smiled again. 'I knew it. That's what I told Cicely.'

He opened his bag. It was hopeless, it was empty of anything capable of easing the pain or curing her. Suddenly she began screaming and tearing at the swollen lumps beneath her arms. He turned away. There was nothing he could do, nothing but wait for her to die and listen to her screams and watch her diseased body until it finally went still . . .

'Please, Sampson! Make me better! Please, please . . .!'

He rose and pressed his face to the wall as her screams grew louder. He locked his hands to his ears, it made no difference. He looked down at her. One boil had burst and blood trickled from its broken crust. There was no hope now. The pain would worsen, the poisons carry on bubbling up from inside her. The noise was deafening, a sustained scream of despair that taunted him for his impotence. Suddenly he could listen no longer. Snatching her pillow from beneath her head, he lowered it over her face. He pressed, pressed harder, then leant over her so that his entire weight bore down on the pillow. Her eyes went wide with horror. She stared up at him for a moment, suddenly understanding, and then began flailing the straw with her legs as her hands reached up to try and push the pillow from her face. He shut his eyes, keeping them shut and ignoring her muffled screams until her fingers left his wrists and he felt her body go limp beneath him.

Still hardly aware of what he had done, he sat staring at her until certain she was dead. Her face swam in front of him. The room was silent, but even in the silence her screams still echoed inside him. He lifted her hands, rested them across her breasts and placed a cheek against hers. What else could he have done? The pain would have worsened. She might have taken all night to die, maybe longer. He stood, knowing it was no answer, and still gazing at her walked backwards out of the room.

Downstairs, the stench and noise in the parlour hit him like a wave. As if a sleep-walker he pushed his way through blurred faces towards the door. The woman who had fetched him appeared out of the haze. She was drunk. Scarlet smeared her lips and one breast hung over the rim of her dress. Above it, the mark of her death, lay a sprinkling of livid black spots.

She giggled. 'Well, physician. Did you mend her?'

Sampson side-stepped and went out into the night. Afterwards, when he had returned home to find that Matilda and a horse had both vanished, he could not remember how long he had stood there; wind and rain lashing at his upturned face whilst behind him in the tavern the laughter of the doomed wove its music.

CHAPTER FIFTEEN

They left the city at first light, Sampson on a pack-horse with his plague powders in panniers, his mother on a mule. High on Harnham Hill, with Salisbury spread out beneath them in the dawn, Sampson dismounted and pushed a small cross into the turf. In happier days, somewhere on the sloping ground to his right, was where he had lain with Beatrix before being apprenticed. Widow Hooke wept as she watched him. He had taken life, and she knew that neither penance nor sorrow would save him from the retribution of the Lord. She asked him to hurry. After his return to the tavern, dazed and in shock, it had been easy to persuade him to flee. But now, fearful lest he change his mind, she longed to put the city behind her. Sampson stared down to where the cathedral spire stood etched in silhouette against the sky as he climbed into the saddle. Then he tugged at the reins and kicked his horse into a trot. At least masons and carpenters had a purpose, something to build. He could only stand back and watch or help to destroy.

The day did nothing to dispel the shame and self-hate that he felt that morning. For though the rain had stopped the wind was bitterly cold and the sky black with cloud. Flocks of lapwings flapped round them like leaves and the mournful cry of a curlew echoed across the furze. Widow Hooke tried consoling him, but hearing no answer she cacooned herself in her whimple and gazed stolidly ahead, leaving him to his misery and the image of Beatrix as he pressed the pillow to her face.

They rode on through the quag, following the highway as it dipped downhill and curled along the banks of a stream. After passing a mill, they entered a village. Peasants stared suspicious

210

and apathetic from the ruins of their hovels, and then, as if from nowhere, a horde of urchins rushed out into the road and began begging for food. Widow Hooke lifted the cloth from her basket and held out a loaf of bread. One leapt forward and snatched it from her grasp. Clutching it to his chest, he turned and ran, followed by his companions. One remained, a boy of about eight, eyes still fixed on the basket. Widow Hooke frowned at him.

'Where are your mothers?' she demanded sternly.

'We ain't got none. They're all up there.' The boy pointed towards the small stone church overlooking the village. ''Tis alright,' he added, as Widow Hooke raised the cloth to her face and backed away in fear. 'Ain't no one dropped dead for more 'an a week. Where you from?' She told him. He nodded knowingly. ''Tis in London too. Wilf the tinker told us. He said 'tis moving north as well.'

Sampson glanced at the boy. He was still a child, but his face had the lined, worn look of an old man. He turned in the saddle. The street had been cleared of corpses, but the harvest lay rotting in the surrounding fields and he could see the skeletons of what had once been oxen. Gradually he began to realize that though the Death had passed nothing would ever be quite the same again; that those who had been spared, whether young or old, had survived a nightmare that would reshape every aspect of their lives. Here, in this one village, was all England in miniature; its past, present and future.

As it lacked an inn they hurried on, Sampson rarely speaking or lifting his head as they rode through the other hamlets strung along the banks of the stream. Initially, most seemed deserted, and the survivors only finally emerged from their homes when the two strangers had passed by. No one spoke to them. In one they saw some women harvesting what was left of their corn, a thatcher cutting and stacking reed, but the next had been completely abandoned. The cottages stood roofless and tumbledown and a few blackened corpses still lay where they had fallen. Someone had tried to steal the church bell; upturned and brimming with rain-water, it lay deep in the mud at the foot of the belfry. The burial pit had been left uncovered and wolf tracks patterned the surrounding mud.

Few of the villages had inns, and the landlords of those that did refused them entry for fear of being infected. Widow

Hooke's tears and Sampson's anger left them unmoved. They were driven from one village with stones, in another Widow Hooke was dragged from her mule and pelted with refuse whilst Sampson was watering his horse. In late afternoon she began complaining of feeling feverish.

Sampson's guilt continued to obsess him, and Widow Hooke, who had never left Salisbury since being taken on pilgrimage to Canterbury as a child, grew apprehensive and frightened as they rode upward on to the downs and left habitation behind them. At dusk they halted on the edge of a small pine copse sheltered from the wind by the bluff behind it. Too weary to make a fire, they supped on bread and cheese and fell asleep on a carpet of pine needles. Once, during the night, Widow Hooke cried out as she slept. By morning she had begun coughing.

It was drizzling when she woke. Seeing no sign of her son, she rolled on to her back and let it cool her face. Her skin felt flushed, but her teeth started chattering as the coldness spread through her body. She coughed again, only screaming when she finally took her hand from her mouth and saw the blood on her sleeve.

Sampson was saddling his horse when he heard it. He turned and ran back through the copse. Suddenly he saw his mother stumbling towards him. Her eyes were wide, her face contorted, her clothes hung loose round her waist. Seeing him, she raised her arms and cried: 'I've the Death! Look! Two of God's tokens!' and then she slipped and fell and began sobbing into the damp earth.

Sampson stood stunned for a moment and then hurried towards her.

She screamed again, pulling herself on to her hands and knees and cowering away from him. 'No! Leave me be! I'll not be another Beatrix! If that's your only cure I'll place my trust in the Lord!'

Dazed at the venom in her voice, Sampson halted. 'I won't harm you. I promise,' he whispered, holding out a hand.

'Keep away!'

'You'll be alright. I can . . .' He paused, swallowing the lie, and inched slowly towards her. She retreated, crawling behind a tree. The movement irritated the swellings beneath her arms and to overcome the pain she began shredding the bark from its trunk with her finger-nails. Suddenly she threw herself headlong to the ground and burst into tears. Too weak to resist, she lay still, breathing heavily, as Sampson knelt beside her and quickly examined the buboes. He looked up, horrified by what he had seen. For a moment he deliberated yielding to her plea to be left alone, then, knowing that he could not sit by and watch her die, he carried her to the small clearing where they had spent the night. After lighting a fire and lying her beside it, he ran back through the copse to fetch the panniers containing his powders and herbs. Working quickly, and made tense by her sudden screams, he hurriedly felled some young pines, stripped their branches and built a rough shelter over her, using blankets to keep out the wind. That done, he heaped the fire with wet pine needles and a sprinkling of sulphur and camphor. Certain that both powders gave off a vapour that deterred the plague, he left his mother to breathe in the pungent yellow smoke that soon filled the shelter in the hope that they might break up the poisons and force the natural discharge of her buboes. After an hour he lifted the blankets. His mother lay drenched in sweat, but the fever had abated and her cough vanished. Only the boils remained.

For the next two days Sampson rarely left her side. Oblivious to time, driven to despair by his inability to stem her pain and in dread of catching the plague himself, he spent them comforting her, talking to her and bathing her diseased body with water. There was little else he could do. Her condition slowly worsened. The swellings grew larger, a rash spread upwards from her groin and both her fever and cough returned. For hours she lay silent as if in a trance. Once, in the darkness of the second night, her breathing faltered and her heart-beat slowed and for an instant he thought she was dead. At other times she would scream for hours on end, only falling silent when too exhausted to respond to the pain. But it was the convulsions he found hardest to bear. Before they began her eyes widened and her whole body went rigid. Eventually he learnt to anticipate them, but even sitting astride her he was unable to prevent her spine becoming an arc or a leg suddenly doubling back on itself.

Twice, during those two days, she begged him to put an end to her suffering. But he could not. Instead he sat beside her, a helpless witness to a pain he could neither comprehend nor assuage. On the morning of the third day she suddenly raised her head.

213

'It won't be long,' she murmured. 'I can feel it, see it on your face . . .'

'Ssh, lie still.'

She pushed his hand away. 'I'm so frightened.' She paused, panic now mingling with the fear in her eyes. 'I've sinned, Sampson. I've much to confess. The Holy Father knows it. He'll turn me aside, an' when I go it'll be to the kingdom of the Devil.'

'Don't say that, mother.'

'Why not? 'Tis the truth. I'll not see another dawn.'

'But the boils may . . .'

She shook her head. 'No. There's no need for lies. 'Tis too late for them.'

Sampson nodded and wrapped her hands in his. Suddenly aware that her torment was as much in her mind as her body, he said: 'I'm your son. Tell me. Confess it to me as you would to a priest.'

Yet still she hesitated. He was smiling. A child again; impulsive, quick to laugh, so keen to miss nothing that much passed him by. 'Kiss me,' she whispered. His lips were cool on her cheek. She closed her eyes, shame and the fear of losing his love on her death-bed still stopping her from speaking. But she could hold it back no longer.

'Once, 'afore you were born, I lay with a monk.' She turned away. 'That monk was your father.'

'But. . . ?' Half in a daze, half convinced she was delirious, Sampson let go of her hands and waited for her to continue.

'I nearly confessed it to you once before; on the night you fled after thinking you'd poisoned Buckle. Now 'tis done. There's no more to be said. You know who he is, don't you?'

'No, I don't!' cried Sampson in bewilderment. 'What are you trying to tell me?'

'Sampson, my child, sometimes you're blind.' She reached up and pressed a hand to his face. Only now, with death close and her guilt confessed, had she found the peace that had eluded her since Mervyn's death. But there was more to be said, and she was still terrified that Sampson might yet abandon her.

Impatient at waiting, Sampson pushed her hand from his face and began shaking her. 'What are you hiding? What is it?' He was shouting, her face had turned to a blur.

'Stop!' she screamed. He did so. She tried to speak but instead of words a scarlet bubble formed on her lips. She delicately wiped it away with her sleeve and said, in a firm clear voice that gave no hint of her suffering: 'It was Audley. He's your father,' before falling backwards and surrendering to the pain.

Sampson did not move. Eyes closed, his face expressionless, he sat there frozen as everything he believed in cracked then splintered inside his brain.

''Tis true, Sampson. I'm dying. Take my hand.'

The harder he clung to the lie, the more tenuous his hold on it became. Suddenly he knew that she was speaking the truth. He turned to her and took her hand, burying his face in its warmth as the first tears spilled from his eyes. 'Forgive me.' Her voice was a whisper. He nodded. 'No, say it. Let me hear it.'

'I forgive you.'

He lifted his head. Her hand opened and she began stroking away his tears with the tips of her fingers. 'Bury me here,' she murmured, 'amongst the trees.'

'If that's what you want.'

'The ground's not consecrated. I'll be spared the Resurrection of souls. I've sinned, 'tis best that way.' She paused and tried to smile. 'He may have fathered you, but you're not his son, not inside.'

'Why didn't you tell me?'

'There's craven's blood in all of us. Matilda knows, but even she, who has suffered so much because of him, couldn't tell you.' She paused again, banishing the past. 'You love her, Sampson, don't you? You tried to hide it, but I saw it on your face when she left with you to go to Beatrix. I'm glad. 'Tis right that you should love what your father would destroy.'

'Please . . .' He rose and pushed his way through the blankets into the chill winter air. It filled his throat, made him dizzy and weak. Behind him a long scream suddenly split the silence. High overhead a flock of rooks cawed noisily as they burst from the tops of the pines.

His mother must have tried to stand, for the roof of the shelter had collapsed, leaving her face and body outlined against the wet of the blankets. Her nose and brow and the hollows of her eyes stood out as clearly as if they were her death mask. He pulled them aside. Her mouth was an open circle and pine needles clung like splinters to her hands. Only the white of one eye was visible,

215

blood filled the other; so that side by side one looked like a moon and the other a sun at the moment of setting. He closed them both. High above him the rooks returned to their perches.

CHAPTER SIXTEEN

It was one of those rare December days when spring seems ready to bud. The breeze that carried its warmth tinkled in the bell hanging outside Joshuah's hut, and the pale wintry sun streaming through its entrance brushed Thomas's face in its light. But Thomas was as unaware of the season's reversal as he was of the figure framed in the doorway. Silent, motionless, his gangling limbs spread amidst strewn bracken, he lay on his back staring up at the domed roof of the hut. The bird with the broken wing.

'Go to him,' murmured Matilda.

''Tis up to you,' said Joshuah. 'We've failed. Neither prayer or comfort can mend him. He's not taken food in nigh on a week.'

Sampson glanced at Matilda and the hermit, then he turned and entered the hut.

Eight days had passed since his mother's death. He had spent one digging her grave and burying her beneath the pines, the others in a state of shock. Still horrified by his suffocation of Beatrix, his mother's death-bed confession had gradually evolved into an indictment so damning that he began to long for the Death to claim him. Unable to sleep, haunted by his mother's words and the wind's wail in the pines, he had waited for its first symptoms to appear. After seven days he knew he had been spared. And with reprieve came the slow return to sanity. A confused logic prevailed. Audley was his father, therefore it was his duty to destroy him, to cleanse his name in the blood of the man who had sired him, made Thomas an outlaw, whipped Matilda, caused the deaths of Mervyn, Alice and Hereward. The decision made, he had saddled his horse and left the copse, riding through the night and reaching the hut at daybreak. And now, a failed physician in the presence of the one patient he could not fail, he stood face to face with Thomas for the first time since watching him sail from Calais.

But it was a changed Thomas he now looked down on. The self-confidence he had gradually acquired after winning his pardon was absent, so too were the prudence and self-reliance that had helped both him and Will endure nearly a year encamped in the marshes outside Calais. The cycle had completed its circle. An eye blinked, a leg twitched. Lice crawled through unkempt hair that was damp and matted with fever. His skin had contracted, drawing itself tight as a drum across fleshless cheeks.

As Sampson knelt, Thomas's eyes shifted to his. They had sunk deep into their sockets and they stared outwards as if entombed in bone. There was a flicker of recognition, then they went empty again: a candle suddenly gutted.

Though appalled by his condition, Sampson forced a smile and said: 'I've left Sarum. Come to take care of you, make you well again.' His fingers began trembling as they smoothed Thomas's hair. 'Matilda's spoken to me of your meeting with Buckle. I know what he told you. You needn't hide it. I knew anyway. Mother's dead of the contagion, but she confessed it to me 'afore she died. Audley may be my father, Thomas, but I'm not to blame for what he made you suffer. I can help you avenge it. For even as he hunted us he knew I was his son. We'll destroy him, Thomas. You an' I. I can't do it alone . . .'

Finally Thomas spoke, forcing out the words through cracked lips. 'I prayed that you wouldn't see me like this, that I'd be dead 'afore you found me.' He paused, his eyes began blinking as the images that tormented him returned: the flames engulfing his father, Audley's face as he stood splashed in their light. 'He was smiling, Sampson. Father was fuel for his own pyre and the man who made you was smiling . . .'

Shame, rage, the sight of Thomas's wasted body filled Sampson's eyes with tears as he reached forward. ''Tis done,' he said softly, 'and can't be undone. 'Tis the morrow that matters. First I mean to mend you, make you as you were when we parted. Do you remember Will once saying that 'tis only bones an' offal a man can't do without? You've broken no bones, spilled no tripe.

218

'Tis demons that haunt you, phantoms of your own making. Understand that and you will begin to get well.'

Thomas's eyes glazed over, as if at will they could shut out anything that played no part in his madness. 'They won't go,' he whispered. 'I've tried to make 'em. 'Tis better that I perish than live in torment.'

'No, Thomas; you're wrong. That's to admit defeat, to give in like a trapped hart when the terriers have felled it. I can't heal a man who is already a corpse. You must help yourself, find the will to rebuild what's broken.'

'For what? To go on being hounded as 'afore?' Thomas slumped into the bracken. 'Leave me alone, Sampson. You bear his blood. 'Tis up to you to seek revenge, not me.'

Detecting his bitterness, Sampson stood. 'Believe what you wish. It'll make no difference. You won't die. I won't let you. I may have to force you to take food and resist the demons, but I promise you that I won't leave your side until you are mended.' He turned and left the hut.

Matilda was waiting for him. 'Can you heal him?' she demanded.

'I can try.'

She smiled. 'No, Sampson. You'll succeed. For by mending Thomas you'll be mending some part of yourself, atoning for what Audley has done to him. Pride won't let you fail, and you know it.'

Hearing that same bitterness in her voice, he brushed her aside and walked towards the well. Its shaft tapered into darkness and the pebble he tossed into it was reborn as a muffled plash. Thomas's face stared back at him out of the blackness as he tried to recall all he had read in the medical chapbooks and manuscripts he had found in Buckle's study when still an apprentice. He could bleed, but it did not need the turbid upper layer of blood in a leeching flask to tell him that the seat of Thomas's disorder lay in the mind. Yet he knew nothing about the diseases that can afflict it. Should he diagnose dementia, the possession by devils, and allow him to die? No. Yet something had snapped inside him. Ignoring all he had read, he began deliberating on the symptoms of madness he had seen in those who had suddenly turned craven when besieging Calais or gone berserk when struck by the Death. In such cases it was usually

219

the nerves or the inability to overcome shock that had made them lose hold of reason, inducing an inbalance in the liver and a superfluity of choler to flow to the brain. Unsure of his diagnosis, but glad of a base on which to build, his thoughts shifted to the plague powders and drenches he had brought from Sarum. But none was suitable, and he smiled slightly as he realized that Thomas's recovery would depend on plants and roots that grew wild on the Chase; the Chase that still threatened to destroy him.

'Come an' eat, lad. No man can heal on an empty belly.' Joshuah was behind him, his beard and gnarled ancient face making him seem like an Old Testament prophet.

''Tis Thomas we must make eat,' he replied. 'I owe my life to him, and my liberty.'

'Come.' Joshuah led him to where Matilda was sitting by the fire. It was still early morning and winter's scents, fresh and new and sharpened by the sun's warmth, mingled with the smell of a jugged hare bubbling inside a pot. Revived by food, Sampson began explaining how he hoped to cure Thomas.

''Tis nourishment he needs, for without it he'll waste into the grave within a week. But we must first dispel the demons, and that can best be done with soothe herbs – thorn apple, black bryony, cowslip – gathered now, whilst the moon still waxes, and brewed into an infusion we can add to his water cup. They may even tempt him to take food. But 'tis later, when he's on his feet again, that we must be most wary. 'Tis then we must guard against melancholy by suggesting he cut bow staves or practise his archery – anything that'll take his mind off all that's happened.'

Joshuah listened as Matilda joined in the discussion. Since fleeing Cranborne she and her brother had shared his cell. Unaccustomed to the company of women, it had taken him time to grow used to her presence. But as their friendship prospered he had begun to realize that her apparent strength masked a frail and complex character. Aloof, contemptuous of any show of emotion, her brief thaws into tenderness hinted at a fear of revealing too much of herself lest it result in further suffering. But despite his probing she remained an enigma, and he chuckled as he noticed that today she had plaited her hair into a single braid that fell like a question mark round the curve of her face. Then he frowned as he saw that her usually candid eyes kept shifting, evading Sampson's. Even Sampson, though intent on Thomas's cure, seemed ill-at-ease. It was as if, he thought, each was concealing something from the other, holding something back that had no connection with their conversation.

That afternoon the two of them walked to the woods and began gathering the herbs and roots they needed. Sunlight filled the rides. The trees were bare and their gaunt skeletal limbs laced the blue of the sky. Leaves swirled round them, occasionally lifting as a sudden gust swept them high into the air. Matilda partnered them in their dance. A sprig of bryony in one hand, ivy draped round her neck, her long waisted pelisse rising round her knees, she ran forward as if to give chase, spinning into a blur of skin and gown and falling laughing to the ground when the wind eddied and left them banked on the edge of a glade. It was then, as she lay deep in the leaves, her breath made a mist by the sun, that Sampson knew that he loved her. He called her name.

She turned, the ivy falling across the swell of her breasts as she rolled on to her side. His eyes betrayed him. She began trembling as she saw his love and knew that all she could offer in return was not her heart but a form of penance for all that love must now make him endure. In need of distraction, Sampson knelt beside her and began digging at the roots of a clump of St Peter's wort hurried into unseasonal appearance by the sun's warmth. She smiled as she watched him. Suddenly she said: 'Did the girl live?'

His body stiffened. Thomas's illness, Matilda's presence, the immense silence of the woods had all helped him forget. Now he paled and turned from her gaze as memory flooded back. 'No, I . . .' He stopped himself, taking refuge in a lie. 'The buboes burst. T'was too late to save her.' He paused, staring down at the petals of the cowslip. 'That night, in her room, you said I'd won. What did you mean?'

'She was a whore, yet you went to her. You must have loved her to have risked so much. She died in peace. Seeing her face, that smile she gave you, both were a victory over me for what I said in the tavern.'

Shamed into silence by her acceptance of his lie, Sampson pushed his fingers deeper into the earth. 'Look at me,' she whispered. She smiled as he did so. 'I once promised you that when next you kissed me t'would be because I willed it.'

221

'I love you, Matilda.'

'No. Don't speak of love. Love binds. I own no one, nor will I be bound.'

'But would you let me kiss you.'

'Yes.'

He leant towards her, then stopped. 'You could have told me that Audley was my father when you came to the tavern. Why didn't you?'

'You think it was love that made me stay silent, don't you? You're wrong. T'was to spare the mother in front of her son.'

'He once whipped you. For that alone I'd kill him.'

'And would now see his handiwork, whether the welts have healed.'

'No.'

'Yes.' Matilda's fingers began shaking as she unhooked her pelisse and lowered it over her shoulders. Her skin was milk-white where the sun had not reached it. His hands, still flecked with soil, left their imprint on her arms when he reached out and pulled her towards him. She smiled, murmured 'Wait' and slid on to her side. The marks of the lash patterned her back in a lattice of dull livid stripes that paled when he pressed them. She turned again, opening her eyes and gazing up at his face, brown eyes, the down of hair that ringed his neck. She felt his lips brush hers and his body go tense against her as he cupped her breasts. Inside her, fear and curiosity mingled with the first stirrings of pleasure as his fingers traced the outline of her ribs and slid towards her thighs. She lay back, hands fumbling with the knot that locked her plait before shaking it free and hiding her face behind a veil of hair. Suddenly, as if unable to be the possessed and not the possessor, she pushed him aside and rose above him, eyes bright with an animal need so long suppressed that she could not control it. Lifting her pelisse into a tangle round her waist, she savagely lowered herself on to him, crying out at the pain. Bewildered by an act in which he no longer played a part, Sampson lay supine as she rose and fell in hunt of love's rhythm. Her teeth glittered as she rocked, lifted, bore down on him. When she finally screamed the sound was carried away on the wind. Leaves swirled round them, smothering her flanks and thighs in bronze and gold. Above them the sun's light slowly

222

dimmed, fading and vanishing behind cloud as they fell apart and let the leaves lap their bodies.

*   *   *

What happened that afternoon was never repeated or mentioned during the days that followed. Matilda, more perturbed by what she had learnt about herself than the loss of her maidenhood, avoided Sampson's company, restricting her meetings with him to discussion about the bout of fever that preceded Thomas's gradual return to health. Despite her coldness, there was now an intimacy linking them that no evasion could completely disguise. Sensing this, and knowing that she had chosen to cut out all memory of their coupling as a surgeon might sever a decaying limb, Sampson honoured her silence by making no reference to their act of love. But though the act could be ignored, his love for her could not. Exaggerated by her presence, lowered gaze, sudden blush of remembrance, it nagged unceasingly at his thoughts. Gradually he began to believe that to win her he had to prove himself to her and give back what she held most precious – Thomas, his mind mended and his confidence restored. During the days spent nursing him the genesis of a plan began to take shape in his thoughts. But it was not until after Christmas, by which time Thomas had regained much of his strength and was able to lift his bow, that it finally matured. He eventually broached it one evening at dusk when all four of them were sitting round the fire.

''Tis time we moved on,' he said. 'The Death is on the wane. Merchants and travellers will soon risk venturing abroad. We've abused Joshuah's hospitality for long enough. We must make plans for the future and decide how best to trap Audley.'

'But where can we go?' asked Thomas.

'Nowhere. ''Tis the Chase itself we must make our realm.'

Seeing the dismay on Thomas's face, Sampson smiled and said: 'Listen to me. England is like a quilt that has been turned upside-down and inside-out and had the stuffing shaken out of it. Rape, looting, theft – even murder – are commonplace. Men are falling to the Death like corn 'afore the reaper in every shire in the land. Baron or pauper, no one is safe. It has struck London, from there it'll spread eastwards and into the northern shires.

Unless God stays it, one in three'll be dead before it's over. These are unnatural times, as near to earth become Hell as any man would wish to live through. Holy Church means naught, one lord bishop of Canterbury is already in his grave. The towns and villages have become charnel-houses for the dead. All round us are those who've fled their homes. Already Joshuah has heard tell of men, aye an' women too, who've been forced into outlawry to fill their bellies: franklins, friars, priests driven from their livings to become poachers. We must find these men; then train, feed and clothe them. We'll ride as one, an outlaw band no sheriff alive would dare to quarrel with. We'll let the poor alone, robbing only those whose purses need cutting.'

There was a silence, then Matilda rose angrily to her feet and sneered: 'As a dog returns to his vomit, so does a fool to his folly.

'And so does a fox skulk homeward to his earth when the keepers give chase,' retorted Sampson.

'Aye, where lads with spades wait to dig it out!' snapped Matilda, pointing to her brother. 'You say you wish to help him, then do so by leaving him in peace. Your work is done. He walks again, the phantoms have fled, what was broken is minded. We've said our thanks. Now return to Sarum and forget us peasants, Sampson Audley.'

Sampson smiled sadly. 'So you would mock me for the sin that beget me. I'll not wear that name, Matilda; nor have it thrust upon me – by you or anyone. I intend remaining with Thomas. Audley must pay for all he's done, and with his life.'

'He's your father, lad,' said Joshuah softly.

'Or I'm his bastard. He means nothing to me. He took my mother against her will and then abandoned her. Later, when he knew who I was, he tried to put my head – the head of his own son – on a market spike.'

'''Tis tempting the fates to stay here,' persisted Joshuah. 'Numbers alone won't keep you safe. The Death must pass. The sheriff an' his men'll take 'ee in the end an' they'll show no mercy when they do.'

'You're an old man in his dotage,' said Sampson harshly. 'For years you've done nothing but squat on this hill and pray that our souls'll be saved. From what? Laws that make men chattels from birth? The pestilence?'

'Fine words, but they won't save 'ee.'

'What will? Holy Church an' men like Audley? Thomas has been outlawed again. Bills have been posted offering gold for his corpse. How can I desert him when 'tis the man who made me that's made him suffer?'

'You must do as you wish,' said Thomas gravely. 'You're a free man, an' can point your boots where fancy turns.'

'I know, and that's why I intend staying. I belong with you, here on the Chase. With others beside us, armed and trained, Audley must fall. And when he does, the truth will out.'

Joshuah shook his head. 'Let the Lord be your shepherd, not the sword.'

'And then what will I lack?' Sampson paused in the hope that silence might make Matilda realize that it was she who had prompted his decision to remain on the Chase. But instead, with an honesty so brutal it made him cry out in horror, she answered his question.

'Me! You may fool Thomas an' Joshuah, but all this talk of robbing the rich is but a sham. 'Tis me you want, not Audley dead or Thomas pardoned. By saving him you hope to woo me, an' if that fails that he'll make me your wife whether I will it or no.'

'Stop it, Matilda!'

'No!' she cried. 'Tis time they knew the truth, time that they knew that you an' I coupled – aye, an took pleasure in it – but that it now means no more to me than dross I might pick from my gown. If Thomas puts his trust in you t'will be the end of him. A band of outlaws! A band of dullards with dust from the sawpit for brains! Have you yet asked my brother what he thinks of your scheming?'

Thomas's feet twitched with nerves as Matilda rounded on him. Feeling trapped by her gaze, still timid and uncertain and in need of solitude, he looked up at her. In the light from the fire anger made her face seem like a mask, and its owner a stranger to him. 'I'm an archer an' outlaw. I know no other trades,' he said finally. 'Sampson has offered to sacrifice his freedom to do as he believes best. 'Tis him I must listen to.'

Matilda dropped to her knees, stifling tears. Feeling betrayed and alone, she glanced across the fire at Sampson. 'So you've won once again,' she whispered. 'By returning Thomas into my keeping you've ended up taking him from me. Perhaps now you'll understand what I meant by saying that 'tis you who is always the victor.'

'But 'tis you not victory I want,' replied Sampson.

'If so, 'tis a defeat you've won for yourself,' said Matilda evenly. 'For I'm not staying. Cranborne is my home and I intend returning there, tonight. Those who killed mother an' father may themselves be dead by now. As long as the hungry want gander set roast on the table there'll always be need of a goose-girl.' She paused, encompassing both Thomas and Sampson in a single glance. 'And you, my only brother an' the lover I cannot love, I fear that when next I see you t'will be swinging 'neath the gallows.' She turned to Joshuah. 'I've sinned, I'm sorry.'

Joshuah smiled. 'There's no need to repent. There's not a man alive who hasn't erred an' strayed from the ways of the Lord.' He reached out and pulled her towards him.

She tensed, then relaxed against his warmth and said: 'I cannot help how I feel.' She looked up at his bearded face, now furrowed and creased with age. 'Bless me.' He did so, making the sign of the cross on her brow before wiping away her tears. She stood and embraced her brother. 'God guard an' keep you,' she said. 'I'll not speak against you or cease to love you. But I cannot stay here and wait for you to die.' She turned towards Sampson. For an instant she longed to run forward and throw her arms round him. Instead, she tightened her cloak and gazed out into the night and whispered: 'I won't forget you, Sampson. Nor what we did.'

Turning her back on the fire she stepped into the darkness as behind her a chill wind began moaning in the hollow skull hanging outside the hut.

*　　　*　　　*

Sampson glanced at the line he had drawn with his sword across one side of the clearing and pushed a stake into the ground. 'There, the fourth corner. 'Tis a square, each wall's to be three perches long. We'll place the gateway so it faces the stream.'

His companion scratched an ear. 'How high d'ye want it?'

'Ten feet. We'll need slits for the bow, four huts, a store-house, granary and a look-out platform in that oak over there.'

'Anything else?'

'Yes. I want a sod hut on the edge of the wood. I've plague powders and intend using them. All those who find us must spend two days in the vapours 'afore joining us.'

'Anything else?' repeated his companion glumly.

'Aye, but I've yet to think of it.' Sampson grinned and slapped the cartwright across the shoulders. 'Don't look so worried, Mouse. We've ample time and no shortage of timber. Thomas an' I once wintered in a hole in the ground. T'was no jest. This time I intend lodging in comfort.' He turned as Thomas came striding towards him across the clearing.

'I've set a line of snares. The mast's ankle deep in places, there'll be no lack of boar an' game. I saw some fallow and the rides are thick with roe, good bucks amongst 'em. I reckon we could feed five score mouths without venturing more than a mile. All we need now is wine.'

'We must find some. An ambush'd do us no harm. T'would bind us together an' tell you an' I which of the men can use a bow.' Sampson indicated a lean-to hut in one corner of the clearing. 'I've set 'em to work cutting broadcloth for hosen and jerkins. Once sewn we must burn what we're wearing. They may be infected. I want nothing left to chance. For now we're nine, but others may join us and by Candlemas we could be four score strong. God forbid, but if the Death broke out amongst us then we'd be needing a burial pit – if any of us was alive to dig it.' He smiled. 'Look, I've marked out the stockade. Mouse has axes, we'll start fellin' timber as soon as we've eaten.'

Thomas glanced up at the trees: the clouds were low overhead, heavy with snow. He trembled slightly. 'You're sure it wouldn't be safer to keep moving?'

'Aye. 'Tis best we stay put for the winter. We're an hour's ride from Joshuah an' the highway, two from Cranborne. Few enter this part of the Chase. Audley's in Tewkesbury and the sheriff won't leave Sarum Castle until the contagion's over. Come spring it may be time to break camp and move on. But for now our survival depends on keeping apart from pilgrims an' pedlars, anyone who may have come from a shire where the Death's still raging.

Thomas nodded agreement. Today, he reflected, was Old Twelfth Night, the seventeenth day of the new year. A month ago he had been lying delirious in Joshuah's hut; an invalid wracked by bed-sores and tortured by the images of fire and Audley that were the sum of his madness. Though still weak and haunted by doubts, he could now run, joke, stalk deer. At times he felt as if he had been reborn; but at others, confused by his debt to Sampson and the cause of Matilda's absence, he thought of himself as something only temporarily patched and mended. Noticing the men leave the lean-to, he pushed his thoughts to one side and said: 'What d'ye think of 'em?'

Sampson studied them. All seven had found them within days of leaving Joshuah's hut and setting up camp in the clearing. First to join had been Ned. A wrestler, broad-shouldered and heavy with the flattened face of a weather-worn gargoyle, he had been a bishop's champion prior to the Death, and the contraband prayers and incantations provided by his master were still sewn into the lining of his jerkin. Next to him stood Mouse, the cartwright on whose talent as a carpenter much now depended. Beside him stood Stutter, the soap-seller, grey-headed and scarred by the pox, a chatterer not cursed by the impediment that had provided his grandfather with the family name. Nearby, on a fallen tree, sat Ebenezer Cooke and Gilbert the minstrel. Of the former he knew nothing but his trade – every meal they ate was proof of his skill – but in the latter, capable only of plucking at his pyre and lamenting the death of his wife and babes in ill-matched verse, he detected something of the anger and sorrow that were the residue of his own feelings for Matilda. Behind Gilbert stood Yule and Hugh the fuller. Though born at Christmastide, Yule shared none of its traditional characteristics. Dour, taciturn, as lean as a hop-pole, he alone had refused to discuss his past. Like Gilbert, the fuller was still suffering from shock. Unable to pay the scutage on his mill, its doors had been barred even though his wife and children lay dead inside it. Before fleeing he had killed his bailiff with a mill slat. But these were facts, and Sampson knew little about their character. Of the seven he most trusted Ned. Even-tempered, as strong as an ox, a veteran of Crécy where he had served under Sir Robert Knollys, Sampson sensed in him the resilience and quickness of wit that all would need if they were to survive the uncertainties ahead.

*   *   *

The stockade took two weeks to complete. By then snow covered the ground and they had felled much of the surrounding coppice, reducing the risk of attack and making the clearing much easier to defend. The band numbered seventeen, its newest recruit being a solemn-faced Franciscan who had revoked his vows because of the behaviour of his brother clergy during the plague. Two days later they mounted their first ambush, acquiring wine and horses from a vintner who had elected to cross the Chase without benefit of a guard. That evening Joshuah visited the encampment. After they had eaten he took Sampson and Thomas aside. Leaving the stockade, where the others were celebrating the success of the ambush by downing the wine, they walked across the clearing to where it merged with the woods.

'I've news of Matilda,' said Joshuah. 'She's living in a byre on the edge of the village. She'll speak to no one, but has found employment as a swineherd.' He turned to Sampson. 'You still love her, don't you?' he added softly.

'Aye, I love her.' Sampson sighed and perched on an oak stump. 'And curse myself for it whenever I think of her.'

'Be patient, lad. Time grinds stone to sand, an' 'tis time she needs.' Joshuah paused and glanced at Thomas. 'And you, my friend. How did you feel as you rode homeward on a merchant's sumpter?'

'Relieved he had no guard. I too need time 'afore having to fight again, and so do the men.'

Joshuah nodded. 'You've saved 'em from the Death, Sampson; now you must train an' keep 'em busy. Let 'em brood and they'll grow restless and start quarrelling. Think ahead, make plans, talk to Ned and heed what he says. Rumours of your return are already being gossiped about. 'Afore winter's end others will join you. Use 'em well, for when Audley returns it'll be with the sheriff for company. You're his bastard, and his conscience, and he'll not feel safe until both you and Thomas are in the grave. Oh yes, he'll be back. And when he does blood'll be spilled, an' t'will keep on spilling until either you or he are no more.'

Thomas pressed a cheek to the shaft of his bow as high overhead the moon swum palely against the blackness. It was worn and thin as an old coin. Lifting his eyes to its face he felt as if he was staring right through it into the emptiness beyond.

Part Four

THE JUDGEMENT

CHAPTER SEVENTEEN

'Git up! C'mon, boy!' Encouraged by yet another slap on its rump, the ox gave a final low of complaint, lumbered down the bank and trampled its way into the reeds that bordered the track. Its drover cried 'Woah!' and tugged at the traces as behind him in the cart he heard a stack of bread-crocks being smashed into shards. The marsh was deeper than anticipated, the stagnant water reeked of decay. It rose round his knees, bubbled up in his wake as he hurriedly cut the surrounding sledge with a bill-hook. After gathering it into piles and heaping it over his pots, he climbed onto the cart and gazed southward along the track. He could hear hooves and the rumble of wheels, see the plume of dust that marked the column's progress. Grinning, he uncorked a flagon of ale, emptied it over his face and jerkin, lay down amongst the reeds, and waited.

*   *   *

Sir John Swayne lifted a hand towards the marsh. 'How much more o' this mire is there?' he snapped. 'My men are foot-sore. We ride, but they march – and have been since daybreak.'

His companion smiled. 'We'll be in Cranborne by noon. The route may be longer, but there's less likelihood of the rebels being warned of your coming. Boots can be replaced, a sheriff's levy cannot.'

Swayne grunted. The May sun was uncommonly hot and he felt as if he was being baked alive in his armour. It was new and stiff and in need of rocking, and the joint gussets still chaffed at his skin. He had only worn it once before, a month earlier, on the day he had been knighted and created Sheriff of Salisbury as a reward for all he had done as its mayor during the plague. He had then thought the knighthood an honour, now he was not so sure.

Hearing an officer bellow orders, he turned in the saddle. Behind his retinue rode a squad of mounted archers and the ten score foot-archers and pikesmen that constituted his levy. To their rear, through the dust, he could see the massive outline of his two siege engines. But it was at the baggage waggons bringing up the rear that he peered longest, for amongst them was one containing his most precious cargo – the two bombards loaned by the king for the attack on the rebels. He frowned, shifting his gaze to the sallow faced monk astride a palfrey alongside him.

'I've told you 'afore, Audley. I've no taste for this business. Hooke was a skilled physician. He served Sarum well.'

'Yet he chose to flee when you needed him most.'

'And so, sir, did you I believe. I doubt Saint Benedict would have approved of a shepherd abandoning his flock for fear of the Death.' Swayne sneered contemptuously. He had no time for pious cant: even less for beginning his year as sheriff by destroying a band of outlaws and watching its leaders be hung.

Prior Audley ignored his scorn. 'They sowed the wind, they must now reap the whirlwind. His majesty's orders were clear. They're traitors, common cut-throats. Since the Holy Feast of Epiphany they've killed a dozen men, ambushed with impunity and mounted two armed attacks, one on an earl of England, the other on the royal chancery clerks.'

And your appointment as Abbot of Salisbury is dependent on my getting rid of them for you, thought Swayne angrily. He'd do it – it was his duty and he had no choice, but the prospect of hunting down the one physician he had ever trusted in order to win Audley his abbotcy had soured his appetite for the task ahead. Glancing at his companion, he said: 'We'll break camp after dark, mounting the attack at dawn. Will you be joining us?'

'I fear not. I must offer prayers for those who gave their lives to God when the contagion struck the priory. Anyway, I am a man of peace, not war.'

Detecting the quaver in Audley's voice, Swayne looked at him more closely. He had wound his reins round his fists, but his fingers were trembling, his face was pale and his small green eyes were fixed firmly on the road ahead. Swayne scowled. During

234

the Death he had seen too much fear on too many faces to be blind to its causes. Something was troubling Audley; and it was not a dislike of bloodshed.

Noticing a soldier wade from the marsh, he called out: 'What is it?'

'A reed-cutter, sire.' The soldier grinned. 'He'll not bother us. I doan' reckon he'll wake till the morrow or ken what day it is when he do. You could put to sea in his belly, sire, he's that full o' ale.'

'Good.' Swayne turned to the captain of his retinue. 'Keep a close watch for travellers. All those bound for the Chase are to be delayed until morning. No word must reach Hooke of our intent.'

The march continued: the soldiers cursing at the dust in their throats, the siege engines swaying as their wheels jammed in the ruts and the armourers lashed out at the oxen yoked to their carriages. As the column passed, the dust settled and silence returned to the marsh.

Deep in the reeds the coots had already started feeding again when Will the potter finally opened his eyes. Jumping from the cart, he led his ox back on to the road. Shortly afterwards he turned off on to a narrow bridle-way that skirted the marsh, climbed the moorland beyond it and then looped northward towards the heart of the Chase.

*   *   *

Swayne watched in disgust as the girl, her face smeared with dung and her pelisse torn and black with filth, was dragged through the watching crowd now gathered under guard in the market place. Despising himself for allowing Audley to humiliate her, he turned and looked round; at the derelict cottages on the far bank of the river, the women in widow's weeds, the bewildered faces of the men-folk and children – the debris left behind now that the flood-waters of pestilence had finally receded. Appalled by the poverty of those who had survived, he turned again as Audley dismounted and the girl was flung forward on to her knees. She winced, clutched her belly and climbed unsteadily to her feet as the prior began speaking.

'So we meet again, goose-girl,' he said. 'And now I see why

you chose to hide instead of welcoming me home. Your kin may be dead, your brother an outlaw, but you at least dress in your true colours: those of the village slut whose field has been ploughed and seeded.' Audley glanced round at the crowd. 'And which of these oafs is the father? No, of course, I forget – no strumpet knows whose bastard she bears.'

Matilda pressed her hands against the rounded shape of her belly as she stared at Audley. For a moment she debated telling him that it was his grandchild she carried. She felt herself redden, from anger not shame, as the soldiers began grinning and the mounted knight behind Audley shifted uncomfortably in the saddle. Still horrified by what the soldiers had told her as they dragged her from her cowstall, still dazed by the suddenness of Audley's return, she tried to adopt the cowed timid expression of the servile peasant woman greeting her overlord. Instead she sneered and said: ''Tis not only whores who sire bastards, your worship.'

Even as she spoke she regretted it. Aware of the insinuation in her voice, and enraged by her contempt, Audley paled, his fists tightened. 'For that I could have the tongue cut from your mouth and fed as swill to swine.'

'Leave her be,' growled Swayne. 'We've not come to Cranborne to settle old scores, but to bring the King's Peace to the Chase.'

'And she can help us,' replied Audley, eyes still fixed on Matilda. 'She's Woodward's sister. Aren't you, whore? When did you last see him?'

'I'm not his keeper,' said Matilda. 'We've not spoken or met for months an' I know no more of him than anyone else in the village. 'Tis you who made him an outlaw, an' I'd wish you in Hell 'afore serving your cause.'

'I seem to recall you saying that once before – and the whip persuading you to change your mind.' Audley smiled. 'But for once it isn't necessary. We know where he is.' He paused, glancing at the group of armourers busy nailing together the timbers that were to act as gallows. 'A fitting music for our meeting,' he added. 'For it knells the noose for Woodward and all those foolish enough to spurn the law.'

Matilda frowned, tilting her head. 'Including Hooke, your worship?'

Audley took a pace toward her as the blood surged into his head and began pounding against his temple. 'Why do you ask?'

They stared at one another. In his eyes Matilda saw a look that seemed to dare her to reply. She ran her hands across her belly, Sampson's unborn child. Suddenly her fear fled. She smiled. 'But Hooke's your bastard, isn't he, your worship? Surely no father could watch his own son hang?'

Silence. Then Audley stepped forward and struck her face with the back of his hand. The second blow drew blood. He raised his fist to strike her again, then, aware of the eyes of the watching soldiers, slowly unclenched it and forced an ashen smile. 'Say that again, whore,' he whispered.

Matilda wiped the scarlet from her mouth. ''Tis said that the outlaw Sampson Hooke is your son.'

For an instant she saw his madness. Aware of the risk she had run, terrified of what might happen, she watched as he struggled to master his emotions. Finally, his head trembling with rage, he said: 'I am God's servant and sworn to the blessed state of chastity. Would I have returned here, with soldiers, siege engines and two cannon, if Hooke was my son?'

Matilda smiled. 'That, your worship, is a question you must put to yourself, not me.' She curtsied, reached forward and kissed the ring on his hand with blood-stained lips, then moved backwards without adding to what she had said.

Audley allowed her three paces. 'Sergeant!' he cried. 'Heat an iron and place her under arrest!'

Another, sterner voice interrupted him. 'Sergeant! Dismount an' I'll see you swabbin' dungeons!'

Choking on his rage, Audley pivoted on his heels as Swayne added: 'You forget yourself, sir. These men are under my command, not yours, an' I'll thank 'ee to remember it. Anyway, surely a man of God can find the charity to ignore Chase tattle?'

'But the girl is a whore!'

'What proof have you?'

'Her belly suffices. And as she has no licence to peddle herself she must be punished by being branded on the lower lip. That is the king's law, Sir John, and not even you can revoke it.'

As Audley spoke, Matilda cried out and slumped to the ground. For a moment she had believed herself immune to anything he could do to her: now she knew better. She lifted her head towards Swayne in a wordless plea for help. His sympathies stirred by her courage and his own dislike of Audley, Swayne met her gaze as he sought for a solution that would appease the prior.

'The creature is with child,' he said finally. 'In her condition the iron could prove fatal. You say Woodward is her brother: surely justice would be better served by insisting she accompany us when we attack the stockade?'

Audley reflected for a moment, then nodded, smiling. 'Aye, t'would be robbing to excess if both were to die. For by this time tomorrow Woodward will be a carcass.' He paused, glancing at Swayne. 'I've decided to ride with you myself.' He turned to Matilda. 'You and I, my dear, will watch together as Hooke and your brother are bound and shackled like curs to their leash. Then you will learn whether Hooke is my son.'

Swayne had observed the gradual shifts in Audley's expression over the last few minutes – shock and panic turning to anger, ruthlessness, and now cunning and delight. During the Death he had grown used to the conflicts between conscience and instinct that pulled his fellow men first this way then that – indeed, he had known them himself. Yet Audley seemed to combine a man both pitiless and in need of pity. It seemed unlikely, he thought, that the prior had ever given love or been its recipient. There was something strangely stunted and imperfect about him. Surely no woman would have willingly carried his child? Turning away to watch his men water their horses, he decided that the girl's accusation lacked foundation; that if anything it hinted at a need unfulfilled, not satisfied.

Later that day, as Swayne's scouts returned with a few villagers found hiding in the woods and his men prepared for the attack, Audley went alone to the priory. So many of the monks had died during the plague it had been evacuated. Empty and silent, its cloisters echoing his footsteps, he felt as if islanded in the one place that linked both his past and future. It was here he had once come, young and dedicated, determined to serve his Order: here too he had met Sampson for the first time. He entered the orchard. The trees were in blossom. Pinks and creams tipped their branches and the air droned to the murmur of bees. He breathed it in, hoping its scents might soothe or help him find the peace he craved. But instead, glancing through the

238

trees, he found himself face to face with a mound of rubble: his dovecote. In too embittered a mood for anger and staring at it as it was now – looted, no two stones left standing, those who had once nested in it food for the villagers during the winter – he began to fear that everything he had striven for might one day end up in ruins at his feet. He climbed through the rubble, pausing briefly to pick up a dead pigeon and cradle it in his hands before gazing out over the valley toward the downland beyond.

'So you know, and now seek vengeance,' he whispered, gently stroking the lifeless bundle of feathers with long delicate fingers. 'You're doomed, Sampson. I cannot save you now. There'll be no pardon, no mercy shown. And as God be my witness, my son, the whole world will see my smile when the hangman cuts you down and begins his butchering.'

*   *   *

'Stand back, friend.'

'Next!'

A moment later, as the outlaw who had found Will wandering lost in the woods pulled him clear, a horseman, lance levelled, galloped past him towards the quintain in the middle of the clearing.

'He's a dead 'un,' grinned the outlaw. He was right. The rider was holding his lance too tightly. It struck the shield mounted on one arm of the quintain and a second later the bag of earth hanging from the other arm swung round and slammed into his back, sending him flying from the saddle.

'God's tooth man!' bellowed the massive figure standing beside the quintain as the rider climbed sheepishly to his feet. 'Are you blind or brainless or both? Mounted on a mule an' aimed at a hayrick an' you'd miss it! Next!'

'Ned the wrestler,' explained the outlaw. 'Should 'a been gentle born, for he's a way with the lance that'd not shame a princess's favours. Up with the lark, bed when 'tis dark. Some of his men are as true with the lance as any knight in the lists.'

Will gazed round in disbelief.

'Takes the breath away at first, doan' it?' said the outlaw. 'Did I. Look over there. Woodward's bowmen.' He pointed at a group of archers lined across the far end of the clearing. As they watched, one lifted his bow at a straw filled sack hanging from a branch and being swung on a wide arc. 'He'll hit it at each end o' the swing. Two arrows in less time than you'd fit a quarrel to a crossbow. You'll not get better than that. There's near two score of 'em, an' all can do it.' The outlaw slapped Will across the shoulders. 'They may call us wastrels, but damme, we can sting fiercer than any bumble. Over there – swordplay. There – quarterstaffs an' grapplin'. Above us –' He pointed into the trees, 'men on sentry go. We've someone overlookin' every track in the forest. I clapped eyes on 'ee an hour back.'

Will shook his head in astonishment. There were perhaps fifty men in the clearing and it echoed to the clash of staffs and steel. A cart trundled by laden with buck, another appeared out of the forest filled with bags of flour. A line of well-fed horses stood tethered to a rail; whilst a smith shoed one, the armourer sharing his forge sat hammering the dents from a set of back and breast-plates.

'Raise us a cloth o' gold pavilion an' I reckon King Ned himself 'd think he were a campaigning if he came here. But instead,' added the outlaw proudly, 'we've that.' He pointed to the far side of the clearing.

Ahead of them stood the stockade. Its timber walls rose sheer from the stream. Lines of sharpened stakes angled outwards from its base and summit and a squat, battlemented tower protruded above each of its corners. They crossed the drawbridge and entered the encampment, passing down a straw strewn avenue lined with huts. At the far end, in the lee of the wall, Will saw a granary, storehouse and loose stabling for the horses. Men moved busily in all directions: a group of women were kneading dough and shaping it into loaves.

'We've every trade in the guild roll. Fletchers, coopers, tanners, wheelwrights, even a brewer,' said Will's companion, indicating a stocky figure pouring the wort into a vast butt of ale.

The potter grinned. 'I need a bumper o' that, and soon.'

The outlaw laughed. 'You'll get it. No man gets turned away without first eating his fill. You hopin' to join us?'

'Aye. Sampson, Thomas an' I served together at Crécy and Calais.'

'They're legends now, friend, fit for the ballad and the scribe's chronicles. 'Tis Hooke who's made us. Lord knows what it be that courses through 'im, but t'ain't blood, that's for sure. But for 'im we'd all be at the end of a noose or dead of the plague. He doan' sleep for more 'an two hours a day, an' 'tween times he drives himself harder than spate water a mill-wheel.'

The outlaw continued chattering as he led Will towards a thatched hut in the corner of the stockade. Suddenly the potter smiled and halted in mid-stride: he had seen Sampson. Bearded, his face burned by wind and sun, dressed in knee-length boots and a chain-mail doublet, he sat perched on a trestle table talking to two members of the band. The years had brought changes, for he looked older than Will remembered. His face had filled out and lost its gawkishness, and there was a sense of self-assurance about him where once had been impetuosity. Then Will noticed that though his eyes still sparkled, the skin beneath them was lined and drawn. As he stood there, waiting for Sampson to look up, he heard one of the outlaws tell him that the flour had arrived and that a potter had been found in the forest.

Sampson nodded. 'Good. Take a sack to Tollard, there's folks there that have lacked flour since Lenten. We've no need of a potter, but I'd best see him. According to Cooke we're short of herring. I've bullion here. Take Jeb and his cart to the Exeter highway. Stop a fish-pedlar. Pay his price but check they've been well salted.' He paused, turning to the other outlaw. 'Ned's in need of better lances and more armour. Tell Thomas, he'll know where to get 'em. But warn him to be wary and to take plenty of men with him. That's all for now. Bring me the potter when's he eaten.'

'He's already here, lad,' murmured Will.

Sampson looked up. Suddenly recognition dawned, and his face broke into a smile as he rounded the table and embraced the potter. Still clasping each other's arms they drew apart. 'Of course,' said Sampson, 'I should 'a guessed.'

Will chuckled as he scanned the familiar face he had last seen when Horton's retinue had been disbanded. 'You're famous, lad. An' now I know why.'

'Infamous, you mean.'

'God-ha-mercy! They're singing of you an' Thomas in every tavern from here to the sea.'

Sampson frowned. 'Aye, I've heard. Yet I'd happily take a glue-pot to their mouths. The more they sing of us, the quicker

Swayne 'll take up arms and come 'a questing.'

'He already has, lad.' Will hurriedly told him what he had seen when acting the sot in the reeds.

Sampson stared blindly into the distance as Will spoke, the lines beneath his eyes gradually deepened. 'So they've come,' he muttered finally. 'I'm almost glad, for it had to happen. We're ninety strong now and as ready as we'll ever be. Have you spoken of this to anyone else?'

'No.'

''Tis best that you don't. The men might panic. I must find Thomas, there's much to be done if we're to outwit Swayne and his engines.'

Astonished by Sampson's calmness, Will asked for news of Thomas.

'Let him answer for himself, for here he is.'

Will turned as a lean figure dressed in Lincoln-green broadcloth, a brace of bows over one shoulder, came striding towards them. Suddenly his eyes lit up and his mouth gaped open in amazement. 'Will!' he cried, as the potter ran forward and locked him in his arms. Their greetings and questions over, the two men joined Sampson.

'I hope you weren't seen entering the woods,' said Thomas. 'T'would go hard with Nellie and the children. We're outlaws, every one o' us. Condemned to wear the wolf's hood and be a butt for any who find us.'

Will's face clouded with sorrow. 'Nellie's dead, Thomas, and so are the bairns. The Death snatched 'em all.' He smiled, forcing their memory from his thoughts. 'And now I've come to join you.'

Thomas closed his eyes. 'Aye,' he sighed. 'We've all of us suffered. Sampson lost his dam. I my brother, sisters and those who gave me issue. There's not a man among us who's not heaped clod o'er a loved one. Sometimes I think 'tis the dead who bind us.'

Will glanced anxiously at Sampson. There was a loneliness, a despair, an acceptance of his fate, in Thomas's voice that he had never heard before. Aware of what he had noticed, Sampson slapped him across the shoulders.

'No man,' he said, 'could be more welcome or have come at a better moment. Near Cranborne he saw Swayne and a column of

242

archers and pikesmen.'

'Aye, an' there was a monk riding with him,' added the potter.

'Audley!' Thomas paled. 'So he's returned. There've been times these last few months when I thought he'd forgotten us.' He paused, trembling slightly as he whispered: 'What'll happen to Matilda?'

For the last few minutes her face had haunted Sampson's thoughts. But now, fearful of betraying his concern and adding to Thomas's misgivings, he made a final effort to forget her. 'We've heard no news of her for weeks,' he said. 'She may have fled the village or had time to hide. 'Tis Swayne that matters now.' He sighed. 'Half a year ago he and I shared a common foe. He was a good mayor, a man I'd not willingly cross swords with.'

''Tis you he's hunting, lad,' growled Will.

Sampson nodded. 'I know.'

'He'll water the horses, eat and move on,' said Thomas, 'attacking us at dawn.'

'But for Will we'd 'a been slaughtered as we slept.'

'That's why he avoided the Chase.' As he spoke Thomas realized that he and Sampson were thinking as one again for the first time since his return from France, that each was helping the other to work out Swayne's intentions and agree a plan of defence – a plan which, even now, had begun to form in Sampson's brain.

*   *   *

Daybreak. A herd of deer moving silent and hesitant beneath the budding oaks on the edge of the clearing, the encircling bluebells making them seem to be knee-deep in a lake of mauve. Thomas high above them, nervously fingering his bow. Glimpsing a face hidden in a neighbouring tree, he peered round; now alert and clear-headed as he meticulously reviewed every detail of the plan to make certain nothing had been overlooked. Surrounding him, perched on wooden platforms bound to branches, his archers lay waiting. Looking down he could just see the line of men crouched on the walk that ran the length of the stockade. Somewhere away to his left Ned and his lancers would be standing beside their horses. Nearby, in the cover of the forest, Sampson would be giving the final instructions to his men. And there was nothing any one could do but wait . . .

The waiting went on. The sun lifted. The deer browsed. Some of the outlaws grew restless, fidgety, impatient. A first shaft of sunlight struck Thomas's face. Suddenly he stiffened. A twig had snapped. The sound repeated itself. One of the roe sniffed air: then they were gone, the entire herd bounding as one into the forest. Silence again. Then the distant whinny of a horse, the tramp of boots. Thomas unslung his bow as that same sense of unreality he had known before the Crécy Fight scattered his concentration. This was the moment he feared most: the dry throat, the hollowness in the pit of the belly, the waiting. He glanced at the two outlaws beside him on the platform. Both were grim-faced. One held the prepared arrows and a lighted tallow, the other a hunting horn. He peered down into the clearing, heart racing as he drew a mental bead on the open barrel standing hidden in the bracken. His eyes lifted, raking the undergrowth. Then he saw them, and smiled.

They were doing as Sampson had forecast, advancing line abreast, the archers flanked by small groups of foot-soldiers carrying pikes and swords. They had divided into two, and he could see a troop of horsemen moving round toward the rear of the stockade. The main force continued its advance, sunlight glinting against their helmets as they left the cover of the forest and entered the clearing. Then, unaware that they were now within range of the outlaws hidden high overhead, they fanned out. Suddenly Thomas's smile vanished. Two teams of oxen had halted on the rim of the clearing. Behind each of them, mounted on a sledge, was the long rounded shape of a cannon.

Too stunned to react, he watched in horror as the sledges were turned, the oxen unhitched and a cart carrying powder and shot drew up alongside them. Then he shook his head. He was wasting time. Few of the outlaws had seen cannon in action and once they began firing their din alone was capable of unnerving the band. Beneath him small groups of soldiers moved silently into position. He lifted his bow, took one of the arrows from the outlaw beside him and slowly drew back on the string. He nodded. The outlaw touched the tallow to the pitch-soaked cloth wound round the arrow. It sputtered and began smoking. Thomas took aim at the barrel's lip, waiting until the cloth had ignited before firing. He had spent much of the previous evening perfecting this one shot: there was no reason why he should miss – and he didn't. He grinned as he followed the trail of fire that was his arrow's flight. Suddenly a sheet of flame shot high into the air. 'Sound the horn!' he cried. Even as he spoke there was a shrill blast in his ears and within seconds the first volley of arrows had begun falling on the soldiers below. By now the flames had spread and started running along the gridded lines of pitch, brimstone and dry bracken so carefully laid by Sampson. Soon the entire clearing resembled a neat fiery tartan, each plaid boxing in and cutting off one group of soldiers from the next. Some, their hosen or leggings alight, screamed as they threw themselves into the dewy grass; others, still panic-stricken, turned and fled, only halting when they had reached the safety of the forest. Those who were spared the flames and held firm could do little to stem the attack. For much of the time they were firing blind at an all but invisible enemy; an enemy trained by Thomas to maintain a firing rate so withering that the sky turned grey above them as the endless enfilade rained down from the trees. Suddenly a puff of smoke obscured one of the cannons. There was a roar, a rumble of thunder. A moment later part of the stockade wall splintered and collapsed. The outlaw beside Thomas lowered his bow, his face pale.

'We've sinned!' he cried. ''Tis the Lord o' Hosts speaking!'

''Tis a bombard! Made by man to kill man. Now get back to your post and keep firing!' Shouldering his bow, Thomas gripped the rope that trailed from the platform and launched himself into the air. The ground rose up to meet him. He let go of the rope, covering his face with his hands as he fell through a dense thicket of bramble. Then he was on his feet again, dodging and stumbling as arrows sped past his head.

'Thomas!'

He turned to see Sampson crouching with his men in the undergrowth. 'They've cannon, two of 'em!' he gasped.

'But the brimstone?'

'It fired well. They've fallen back into the forest.'

'We'll use the mantlets and try an' out-flank 'em,' shouted Sampson, pointing at a line of large wooden shields mounted on runners.

Thomas tried to reply but his words were drowned by the roar of the other cannon. He ran on, only halting when he heard Ned bellow 'Charge!' and a troop of horsemen cantered passed him. Lowering their lances as they entered the clearing, spurs flailing, hooves tossing up earth, they wheeled towards the cannons and quickened pace. Those working them turned too late. Horse and men slammed into one another, finally parting when Ned ordered his men to regroup in the wood.

By now the defence of the stockade had been joined by the entire band. Episodic and confused, punctuated by brief pauses, Thomas knew that its outcome would only be clear when the field lay silent. For despite the success of their initial attack, the outlaws were outnumbered and unable to prevent the two siege engines being hauled into position. Beside the soaring central tower of the trebuchet the smaller mangonel looked almost ineffective; but Thomas had seen both in action outside Calais and knew that in well-trained hands each was as deadly as the other. The trebuchet was a giant see-saw, its tower a fulcrum balancing two arms – one of them weighted, the other supporting a sling: its cousin, the mangonel, could catapult a hundredweight boulder for four hundred yards. Both were within range of the stockade. The men firing them were protected by a timber clad shelter roofed with shingles, and Thomas watched helpless as each was armed and prepared for action. Suddenly a drum rolled. A moment later two boulders hurtled high over the clearing, describing a perfect arc before landing. One splashed harmlessly into the stream, but the other cleared the stockade and punched into one of the huts. Thomas began trembling as he thought of the havoc they would cause once the range had been balanced. There was no one he could call on for help: Ned's lancers had vanished, Sampson's archers were harrying the armourers crouched round the cannons in an attempt to prevent them reloading. Reaching a decision, he sprinted for the cover of a stack of cut cord-wood on the rim of the clearing. Of the two engines, the trebuchet was the closest. A second boulder had been placed in the sling and the men behind the shelter had already begun cranking the cogged lever that winched the arm into the firing position. Placing a bundle of arrows beside him, he took aim at the rope linking the arm with the pulley-drum. His first five shots went wide, but gradually, as his concentration returned, they started skimming the rope. Certain of his skill, his confidence reinforced by igniting the brimstone, he took

246

another arrow from the pile beside him and adjusted his stance before freezing into a motionless extension of the bow in his hands. The rope filled his vision, became the only object he could see or was aware of. He fired. His arrow sailed the air, its steel head slicing through the rope. The arm jerked upwards. The boulder rolled from the sling and fell heavily to the ground, leaving behind it an engine now useless until someone risked certain death by climbing the tower and feeding a new rope through the blocks.

Though Sampson noticed the rope break, he paid it scant attention. Kneeling on the far side of the clearing, his men lined either side of him, his defence of the stockade had developed into a hard-fought struggle to prevent the cannons refiring. The armourers working them were flanked by archers, but though they had managed to spoon powder into both breeches, their attempts to ram it home and lift the balls into the barrels had all failed. But now reinforcements were emerging from the wood. Sampson quartered the undergrowth behind them. A moment later he saw Swayne, helm raised, directing the attack from the saddle of his charger. The sheriff's retinue surrounded him, and it was only when one galloped off to deliver orders to an isolated pocket of pikesmen that Sampson realized that he was now face to face with the father he had sworn to destroy, and that beside him, her hands lashed round the neck of a mule, sat Matilda.

For a second his mind went blank. Audley had not seen him. Matilda, white-faced and expressionless, sat rigid on the mule staring blindly ahead of her. Suddenly Audley joined Swayne and began shouting and gesturing towards Matilda. Sampson felt the prickle of sweat against his skin. Instinctively certain he was suggesting she be used as a weapon to panic Thomas, he raised his bow and took deliberate aim at his father's throat. A hundred paces separated them. There was no chance of his missing, and a quick thrill – part pleasure, part dismay at the extent of his hate – pulsed through him as he took his fingers from the bowstring.

He had left it too late. Even as the arrow flashed silver in the sunlight, a mounted archer blocked its target. It struck him high on the chest. As he spun and fell, Audley finally looked up, his eyes fixing on Sampson's. The father smiled, the son lowered his head as if unable to acknowledge the moment. Then it passed

247

and the smile vanished as Audley cried out and pointed at his son. Sampson began trembling as he saw Matilda shudder and shift her gaze towards him. Both his father and the woman he loved were now staring at him. Reading pain in one and forgiveness in the other, but too confused to apportion either emotion, he turned away, switching his gaze to the shadows behind them. A moment later he heard a horn shrill, saw steel glint and faces turn. Suddenly Ned's lancers swept from the undergrowth and charged into the rear of Swayne's retinue. Grinning his delight at their timing, his thoughts still obsessed by Matilda, Sampson rose and bellowed her name. She hesitated, then kicked her mule into a trot as those guarding her turned to face their attackers. Still smiling, Sampson lifted his bow as Audley gave chase, arrows whistling past him. Eventually, his face showing both fear and rage, the prior seemed to realize his folly; for after once snatching at the mule's reins and letting them slip from his fingers, he spurred his palfrey to the canter and vanished into the forest. As if dazed Sampson started running towards Matilda. A moment later Thomas dashed from cover, forced the mule to a halt and cut the thongs that bound her. Within seconds she was in his arms and being carried to safety. Sampson fell to his knees, too overcome by shock and bewilderment and the noise of battle, to let what he had seen take root. Behind him he heard the drawbridge splash over the stream, and the outlaws inside the stockade pour through the gateway, pausing only to fire at the trapped soldiers before continuing their advance across the smouldering clearing. Swayne galloped forward and tried to rally his men. Now under attack from three sides and above, they began to fall back in disarray, leaving both siege engines and the cannons behind them as retreat turned to flight and they fled headlong into the forest. Sampson glimpsed the band begin dropping from the surrounding trees to give chase. Some cheered, others tossed their bows high into the air. Laughing, the tears drenching his cheeks, he rose to his feet as he realized that the battle had been won and that what he had seen, as Matilda slid from the mule into her brother's arms, had been the swollen belly of a woman with child – his child.

CHAPTER EIGHTEEN

'Aye, 'tis yours. I've lain with no other, nor will I.'

'So why can't you love he who made it?'

As Sampson turned towards her, Matilda parried his question by gazing back to where the walls of the stockade rose above the undergrowth. The once bare trees were a miscellany of greens, and here and there, on the rim of the clearing or in the glades beyond, she could see the pink of campions and the delicate purple pyramids of the first orchids trembling in the breeze. All was so peaceful, so perfect, and yet inside her was a melancholy not even the advent of summer seemed able to assuage.

'I don't know,' she said finally.

''Tis now ten days since we rescued you and repulsed Swayne. But not until now have we spent an hour alone. For most of the time you ignore or avoid me. Is that what you want, this distance that divides us?'

'You can't fashion love like boots out of leather.'

'In three months, Matilda, you will bear my child.'

'Can no woman enter childbed without loving the man who put her there? When I gave myself to you, t'was done freely. Would you now chain me like a cur to its master's leash?'

''Tis my child!'

'No!' retorted Matilda angrily. ''Tis an outlaw's child. The half-fashioned babe of a man who has chosen to forget that his days have number, and will end when he's cut down from the noose an' drawn an' diced by a hangman's hatchet. This child will know none of that. Nor will I be left a widow with no grave to weep beside. I've said my gratitude for all you've done for Thomas, and for saving me. Ask for more and you may hazard

249

what you have.'

Sampson rolled on to his side, bruising and flattening the bluebells beneath him. 'What I am or will become is subject to Our Lord and the stars that guide our fates. If I'm to die as you say, so be it. But 'tween now and then can we not share what we've made, the babe in your belly?'

Matilda let her head rest against the tree behind her. Overhead the afteroon sun blazed gold in a cloudless sky. During the months she had been carrying the child she had begun to perceive an instinct in herself she had not thought existed. Its slow, almost imperceptible growth had made her cautious, protective, wary of anything that might cause it harm. But was it really her belief in Sampson's fate that made her hold back? Or was it some flaw within that made her as incapable of sharing the child as she was of admitting love? Or was it Audley, the father, all he had caused her to suffer?

'Sampson!'

She turned. A moment later Will the potter loomed out of the undergrowth, leading a horse by its reins. He blushed. 'Thomas told I you were here. I've just ridden from Joshuah's. I've news, 'tis important.'

Seeing his flushed face and excitement, Sampson rose. 'What is it?' he demanded.

'Thomas must hear it, and Ned.'

Torn between Matilda and the band's welfare, Sampson hesitated. Finally he looked down at Matilda. 'I must leave you.'

She smiled. 'A woman's place . . .'

Aware of her taunt, he lifted her to her feet and the three of them walked back across the clearing, joining Thomas and Ned where the two cannons sat on their baulks near the entrance to the stockade. The remaining outlaws were matching quarterstaffs or practising with their bows in the butts, and Sampson smiled to himself as he realized how much had been achieved since rebuffing Swayne. Success had given them the self-confidence they lacked. They were a true band now, well-disciplined and ninety strong, not a random collection of outcasts flung together by the effects of the plauge. During the past ten days they had rebuilt the trebuchet and, under the guidance of a smith who had worked bombards in France, taken turns at arming and firing the cannons.

Will slapped the barrel of one of them as he sat on the grass. 'We've trespassers to the Chase,' he said, 'or will have within two days.' He paused and uncorked his ale-skin before continuing. 'Five days back a line of pack-horses left Corfe Castle for London town. Accordin' to the gossip reachin' Joshuah, there's nigh on two dozen of 'em. They're carrying panniers. Joshuah's spoken to a pedlar who was passing 'em when one o' the horses lamed and the panniers had to be removed. Guess what's in 'em? A brass-bound chest so heavy it took two men to lift.'

Sampson frowned. 'So what? A wealthy merchant might easily stay overnight at Corfe as the governor's guest. He could be trading in silks, spices – anything.'

Will grinned. 'An' what would a merchant be doing with exchequer clerks, a dozen knights in the king's colours and an armed escort of near ten score soldiers?'

'Bullion,' whispered Ned.

'No one knows. The chests are padlocked and sealed, and those guarding 'em have been promised a year an' a day in a dungeon if they e'en lay a finger on the locks.'

'Where are they now?' asked Sampson.

'Blandford Forum. They leave tomorrow. In fear o' falling foul of us the king's loaned 'em some hobilars to serve as scouts. The knights are to strengthen the escort when crossin' the Chase. They're not travellin' the main highway, but intend keepin' to sheep-walks and tracks to avoid the chance of attack.' The potter paused, downing the last of his ale before raising a triumphant finger. 'Now 'ere's the beauty of it. They're in need of a guide, someone who knows the Chase better than his own kin. I doan' have to tell 'ee who Joshuah thought might provide it.'

No one spoke. The implications of all that Will said were so immense that each needed time to organize his thoughts. 'It could be a trap,' said Ned finally.

Sampson disagreed. ''Tis too complicated, too unlikely. 'Tis Swayne's task to put us on the gallows, not the king's clerks.'

'And what if the chests are baited with pebbles?' countered Thomas.

'No. Once nipped, twice shy. 'Tis gold, jewels, something worth the trouble being taken to make certain they reach London.' Sampson snapped a blade of grass and placed it

251

between his teeth. 'There's one mystery: can we trick whoever's commanding the escort into hiring any of us as a guide?'

'And if he did, which way should we lead him?' added Thomas.

'Through the forest,' suggested Ned.

'No.' Sampson patted a cannon. 'We've these and the engines now. It must be a coombe or valley, but one close enough to give us time to position the bombards without being seen.'

Beside him, Thomas pondered a moment, suddenly snapping his fingers and crying: 'I've got it! Long Coombe. The track narrows. 'Tis wood on one side, down on t'other. We can attack from both flanks. There's no finer site for an ambush anywhere on the Chase.'

'You'll not fool 'em that easy,' growled Ned. 'Even mice let cheese alone when scenting a trap.'

'No, Thomas is right,' insisted Sampson. 'The coombe shelves. You don't know you're in it till you're there. By then it'll be too late.'

'And how will this help our babe or you outwit Audley?' said Matilda quietly.

Sampson turned towards her. 'It must be done,' he said gravely. 'Since letting it be known that I'm Audley's bastard, the gossip's spread. Another successful ambush and news of it may reach the king. Warwick will hear of it. He's a powerful friend, and one who'd serve our cause if he could. There's a chance, no more, that he'll demand Audley be brought 'afore the king and examined.'

'Why not ride to Clarendon and beg clemency? More corpses won't win you a pardon.'

'We're outlaws, Matilda. 'Tis no longer just Thomas an' I. We've ninety souls in our keeping.'

Matilda looked down at her belly. 'And I suppose the ninety-first don't matter?' She raised her eyes to Sampson. 'Your own tongue condemns you.'

Stung to anger, determined to evoke some other response from her but reproach, Sampson met her gaze and said: 'I must go. No commander should have to wait for his guide.'

'No!' cried Matilda.

There was a silence. She reddened and lowered her head. Aware of a sudden happiness inside him, Sampson lifted her chin.

He smiled. 'So you do care?' Her eyes filled with tears, then she turned away, evading his gaze.

Later that evening, as darkness washed over the clearing, a mule and rider slipped unnoticed across the drawbridge. Only Matilda witnessed their departure, and as they vanished into the night she touched the rounded curve of her child and began crying.

*　　　*　　　*

Morning in Blandford market place: the air thick with dust and the stench of dung and horse harness, soldiers shouting, hawkers chanting the praise of their wares, the endless cacophonous clatter of hooves, wheels and clogs. Though it was market day, the crowds swarming through the square were for once less curious at the price being paid for the wool clip than they were at the presence of so many soldiers. Only the serving-maids in the taverns had grown indifferent to their bustle, and one grinned wearily as she refilled the ale-pots on a table whilst the archers sitting round it peered over her bodice and boasted of the pleasures to be found in their company. Casually brushing a hand from her rump, she turned toward the grubby figure squatting on the cobbles outside the tavern doorway.

'No 'ogs permitted in the parlour,' she said. 'Ale's a ha'penny the pint. There's scrag, pease an' gruel.'

But the man seemed not to hear her, and she snorted and clapped her hands to her hips when he rose and walked out into the sunshine. He walked slowly, limping slightly, but his eyes missed nothing: the pages busy polishing their masters' armour with sand and vinegar; the horse lines, where many of the soldiers sat dicing and drinking as they awaited the order to mount; the exchequer clerks in their travelling cloaks and galligashkins gazing hawk-like at the stack of heavily guarded panniers lying heaped round the market cross; the short-tempered sergeants whose job it was to keep the peace between the townsfolk and the escort and make certain that none of those under their command deserted or became too drunk to stand.

The man pushed purposefully through the crowd. It was the sergeants he had been watching most closely, for only a few had

253

dared enter the small circular pavilion that screened the knight commanding the escort from the stares of the costers and their patrons. The selection of sergeant was vital. It needed to be someone whose advice the commander respected, someone to whom he would listen. And Sampson had made his choice.

'Your honour!' he cried, limping towards a scarred red-bearded figure standing near the horse lines.

The sergeant turned, glanced at him, and as quickly dismissed him as another peasant who filled his belly by begging.

Sampson limped closer to him, chomping on blackened teeth before spitting a pellet of dough into the kennel. ''Tis said you're in need of someone willun' to see you safe o'er the Chase,' he mumbled finally.

'So?' The sergeant scrutinized the shabby wretch standing in front of him. His jerkin was torn, a spade hung from his back and at his bare mud-splashed feet, linked to its owner by a length of twine, stood a foul-smelling spotted pig with a ring through its nose.

Sampson plunged on. 'Well, your honour, No Name Hog's the man you're wantin'; and that's I. There ain't a patch o' briar big enough to hide a hare in from 'ere to Sarum that I ain't acquainted with. Truffle-hunter see.' He lifted the cloth covering the basket under his arm and indicated the black wart-like tubers sitting inside it. 'Doan' look much do 'ey?' he added, 'but each is worth its own weight in shilluns.'

The sergeant seemed unimpressed. 'What manor are you from? Are you villein or free-born? Who's your master?' he demanded.

Sampson scratched an ear, tittered, spat a second pellet into the gutter and said: 'Doan' rightly now. Ain't got no kin but Hannah 'ere.' He paused, patting the pig. 'She's as old as I. Weaned on 'er too, some say. As to who owns I, there ain't no record of that. Been roving the Chase an' spadin' for truffles since I was a pup. Yes, your honour. No Name Hog know's Chase better than a palmist the lines on 'er own hand.'

The sergeant continued his scrutiny. Sampson felt his eyes bore into his own. Suddenly he ordered Sampson to follow him and turned towards the pavilion. Reaching it, he bade him wait and ducked beneath its awning. Listening, Sampson heard voices. Suddenly the awning lifted and the sergeant beckoned him inside.

The air was close, and the dozen knights lounging on the saddle blankets strewn over the cobbles looked ill-humoured and impatient in the yellow light coming through the ceiling of the pavilion. Every now and then one looked up and glanced at the knight sitting at a folding writing-bench near the entrance. Sampson studied him carefully: the hard suspicious face, the flat twisted nose so obviously broken and badly reset, the voice that still held traces of Norman blood when he finally spoke.

'Out!' He pointed at the pig.

'Oh no, can't allow that, your honour,' huffed Sampson angrily. 'Where I go, so do Hannah. Best truffler a man could want. Can sniff out a half-pounder in Hinton Bushes quicker than a French terrier. She's a snout worth a silver sovereign, an' that's the fact of it.'

Ignoring Sampson's reply, the knight lowered his quill. 'You claim to know the Chase,' he said.

'That's right, your honour. Got the wot of it see.' Sampson tapped his brow.

'And could you guide us from here to Sarum in four days?'

'Four! Be harkin' to Bow bells by then!' Sampson straightened his back. 'Do it in two, an' there's an end to it.'

'Take the oaf and his hog on, Fitzwalter,' growled one of the other knights.

'Aye,' added another. 'We've spent long enough in this sewer. There's no wench without the pox worth bedding and the wine's worse than wormwood.'

Fitzwalter turned to Sampson. 'Do you know who we are?'

'King's men, they say, an' with a royal ransom in valuables for company. But that's gossip mind, gossip,' said Sampson hurriedly.

'Twelve days ago,' said Fitzwalter, 'Sir John Swayne left Sarum intending to destroy the outlaws in hiding on the Chase. His men were routed, his cannons and siege engines captured. I've no wish to share his fate.'

'You won't, your honour, not if No Name Hog be your guide.' Sampson rolled up his hosen and pointed to the blood-stained bandage bound round one knee. 'See this? Flesh wound, arrow, an' the price paid for venturin' too near them rebels. For years I been digging for truffles in the forest. But not now. Woodward

says t'ain't to be done. Not with words, mind, but with the bow.'
He shook a fist. 'I've no time for 'em. Hang 'em high, I say; 'tis no
more than their due. Nay, your honour, they'll not sniff us.
They've straw for brains an' mud for blood, mix 'em together an'
you could build Babel's tower. Why, there's tracks o'er Chase
that not even the coneys know.'

Fitzwalter rose and sauntered idly towards the truffle-hunter.
A knife flashed, an instant later he had cut the bandage from
Sampson's knee. Sampson flinched at the pain. Fitzwalter
glanced at the gangrenous open sore that capped his knee,
turning away as the stench of rotting flesh reached his nostrils.

'You've employment,' he said finally. 'Threepence a day and
an extra shilling when we reach Sarum. You seem harmless. But
I warn you, play me false and the hog 'll end up spitted with a
pippin in its snout and you'll not lift a spade again.' He turned to
the sergeant. 'Order the men to mount. We leave within the
hour.'

*　　　*　　　*

Sampson shifted in the saddle and stared up at the kestrel hover-
ing high overhead. Its presence, he thought, seemed an omen.
For it too lay in ambush, if only for a vole or shrew panicked into
movement by the sound of the advancing column. He tried to
smile at the irony, but couldn't. Ahead, shimmering in the noon
heat, lay the outline of the woods above the entrance to the
coombe. Two miles divided them, and each step brought them
closer.

'You certain where we're bound?' asked the scout riding
alongside him.

'Course I am. Ain't we, Hannah?' he replied, only remembering to pantomime his part at the last moment. Glancing at the pig
trotting obediently beside his mule, he added: ''Tis loam here-
abouts, an' easy diggin'. Why, I've . . .' He fell silent as the
scout, who had long ago lost interest in the nonsensical chatter of
their guide, cursed and galloped on ahead. Sampson watched
him rejoin his companions. It was the scouts who concerned him
most. Active, inquisitive, constantly on the move, he was beginning to fear that one might stumble on the outlaws before the
coombe was reached. Yet so far all had gone to plan. He had

bought Hannah from a swineherd driving his pigs to market, the truffles from a stall in the town. Though that part of his disguise had proved straightforward, the wound – itself a last minute thought – had been harder to fake, and he had prepared the mixture of blood and offal and bonded it to his knee with lute after deciding that Fitzwalter's suspicions could best be countered by offering proof of having suffered at the hands of the outlaws. And now, after a night spent camped on the downs, Long Coombe was finally in sight. He turned in the saddle.

All was as it should be. The archers in the van were about fifty paces behind him. A further twenty paces separated them from Fitzwalter and his knights. Behind them, moving in single-file and flanked on both sides by a column of archers, were the pack-horses. The exchequer clerks and a troop of swordsmen rode in the rear. Satisfied that no premonition of danger had caused Fitzwalter to change the formation of the column, he again began following the movements of the scouts. They were about half-a-mile ahead, methodically criss-crossing the scrub that bordered the track. Long Coombe lay ahead of them. It was no more than an extended dip in the road, down on one side, wood on the other, and beyond it, already visible as a white smudge of chalk that cleft the furze, the track veered sharply eastwards. Its sudden change of course lodged like a wind-blown seed in Sampson's mind. It germinated, became a plan, and when the scout next reported to Fitzwalter he turned his mule and joined them.

'See there,' he said, pointing east of the coombe. ''Tis there you'll find trouble 'a lurkin'.'

'Explain yourself,' snapped the knight.

'There's a dry dyke that runs close to the track. 'Tis deep, and as snug a bolt-hole for a rogue to skulk in as any on the Chase.'

'Very well.' Fitzwalter turned to the scout. 'Order your men to search the dyke. Report back when they've cleared it.' Sampson smiled as he took his place at the head of the column, and his smile broadened when the scouts skirted the coombe and galloped eastwards.

The ride continued, the sun beginning its descent before the track started shelving and Sampson led the column through the narrow entrance into the coombe. Its sides steepened, turning swiftly into vertical chalk cliffs that rose high over the track.

257

Sampson squinted against the sun as he scanned the lip of the cliff. Suddenly he saw movement, a bow stave, a flicker of sunlight on a cannon's muzzle. He pressed his knees to his mule, silently urging it on in an attempt to widen the gap between those behind him. Now trembling, he suddenly heard Fitzwalter bellow his name. He rode on. Ahead lay sky, the far end of the coombe. The blue periwinkle and yellow gorse that climbed its slopes merged in his eyes, becoming a brilliant, blinding green. Sweat dampened his hands. The clatter of hooves and harness bounced back off the cliffs as a deep boom that pounded at his head . . .

'Halt!'

Sampson kicked his feet from the stirrups and prepared to dive from the saddle. Above the din he could hear Fitzwalter calling his name. This time he turned. The knight was peering up at the top of the cliff. Suddenly he drew his sword and waved it at Sampson. 'Take him!' he screamed. ''Tis a trap . . .!' His next words were wasted. A second later the entire coombe re-echoed to a cannon's roar.

* * *

Thomas's nervousness had vanished at the same moment as the cannon discharged. Throughout the morning, whilst watching the column approach, his doubts at Sampson's ability to trick its commander into employing him as its guide had gradually evolved into something far worse: a belief that his disguise would prove inadequate and that he would be forced into betraying the position of the band. Thus, as if the firing of the cannon signalled a release from his own loss of nerve, his first thoughts, as the stones packed into its barrel raked the column, were of Sampson, the voice of calm, last seen riding unfettered on a mule in the van.

But now smoke was rolling across the roof of the coombe and he could see no sign of either the mule or its rider. Still lying prone on the edge of the cliff, outlaws on either side of him, he pushed himself to its brink and peered downwards as the first volley of arrows streamed into the smoke. Waiting for it to disperse, he began to fear that they had left it too late, that the delay in igniting the powder might have cost Sampson his life. Then he glimpsed a hand trying to attract his attention. He waved, re-membering all they had planned as he watched Sampson take cover behind a dead horse. Other horses milled round him; many were riderless, others terror-stricken, and their constant shies added to the chaos. But the column was moving forward again. There was no chance of their being able to withstand an attack from above, survival depended on being able to break out of the coombe. The second cannon thundered, its ball slamming into the opposite cliff and causing a small landslip which par-tially blocked the track and slowed the pace of the advance. As Fitzwalter's men began picking their way through the rubble, there was a hum overhead. A moment later a boulder crashed amongst them. Thomas grinned contentedly: all that had hap-pened had been planned and precisely timed, and he saw it, not as the cause of suffering, but as final proof of his recovery, an as-sertion of his status as an outlaw. Another boulder dropped into the coombe. By now Ned and his horsemen would be waiting beside the mangonel in the woods to his rear, ready to ride round to the far end of the gorge and cut the escort in two. Thomas studied the column, quickly fixing its progress in his mind before ordering the outlaw beside him to sound the horn.

As it trumpeted, the line of outlaws on the far side of the coombe broke the skyline and loosed their arrows towards the track below. But the escort kept moving, and the outlaws had to crawl along the summit of the ridge in order to maintain range. The soldiers' discipline was superb. Never once did any break rank, and the knights, their visors protected by their shields but unable to retaliate, rode as if immune to the arrows that kept glancing off their armour. Thomas peered towards the far end of the coombe, measuring the distance between its exit and the leading horsemen.

'Cease fire!' he shouted. The outlaws' fire gradually slack-ened. Temporarily reprieved from the constant hail of arrows that had dogged their every step, the column hurried on towards safety. Eventually instinct prevailed. Without warning the archers in the vanguard suddenly spurred their horses into a canter. The gap between them and the pack-horses lengthened. Thomas smiled: the bait had been taken. The leading archers cleared the exit to the coombe. He looked round at the outlaws lined alongside him. As ordered, each had taken aim at one of the soldiers flanking the pack-horses. He lifted his bow, waiting until Fitzwalter and his knights had reached safety before shouting: 'Fire!'

Few survived that first bombardment, and those that did jostled their way through the dead and wounded without a thought for the panniers in their charge. A moment later Ned and his men emerged from the cover of the woods and lined up back to back across the track, dividing the pack-horses and clerks from the rest of the column and preventing Fitzwalter from mounting a counter-attack.

Thomas turned to those beside him. 'Cover Sampson!' he cried. ''Tis time he joined us.' Picking the weighted end of a coil of rope from the grass, he swung it in a succession of circles round his head before letting go. It snaked high into the air, falling within a few paces of the horse beyond which Sampson was hiding, a shield covering his head. His face rose above its withers. Thomas glanced the length of the coombe, then lowered his arm. Sampson vaulted the horse and sprinted to the foot of the cliff. He gripped the rope, it tightened, lifting him into the air. An arrow struck the chalk above him as he began walking up its face like a spider whilst Thomas and another outlaw hauled in on the rope. Soon he was level with the summit and helping hands were dragging him to safety. Rolling on to his back, he fell exhausted to the grass and stared up at the sky, breathing deeply.

'The day's ours!' cried Thomas.

Sampson smiled, then the beginnings of shock welled through his body as the tension that had built up inside him since leaving the stockade finally snapped. He turned and looked out over the coombe. Thomas was right, victory was certain. For though Fitzwalter had charged Ned's horsemen, the attack had been beaten off and those trapped in the coombe were slowly retreating, leaving the pack-horses where they stood. The track bore the scars of battle: dead horses lying on their backs like upturned tables, blood-red chalk, the cries of the wounded, the motionless misshapen corpses of the fallen. It was an awesome sight, and, as Sampson waited for the last soldier to flee the field, he felt for the first time a sense of horror at the endless killings that trailed in the wake of the band and had become its signature – a signature no prayer or plea for forgiveness could blot or erase.

How many men had he, a healer of men, sent to their deaths? How heavy would the burden of sin be when he finally joined them? Suddenly he saw himself as the sailor being swept towards the lip of the whirlpool carved on the chancel screen in Cranborne Priory. He felt a hand on his brow, one which soothed him from his thoughts before tracing the curve of his skull. He looked up. Matilda was kneeling beside him, a sad smile edging her lips.

'Aye, I care,' she said, 'but only because until now I was foolish enough to believe that the child might be the making of the man. Now I know better. For what you have done this day is put a rope round each of our necks, mine as well as your own.'

Sampson closed his eyes. 'If you cannot love me, at least grant me peace.'

She laughed slightly. 'You live, Sampson: 'tis only the dead who know peace. Come, see what your folly has won you.'

Shrugging her aside, Sampson rose and looked down into the coombe. Apart from a handful of outlaws guarding its entrances, the entire band had gathered round a square chest being lifted by Ned and Will from one of the panniers. Sampson watched as Thomas shook the lock and inserted an iron bar between it and the catch. Suddenly the lock snapped and the lid flew open. Inside the chest lay a pile of long leather rolls, each shaped like a sausage. Picking one one out at random, Thomas cut the knot at one end and shook it. The coins inside it fell to the ground. He opened another. The same shower of gold tinkled to the dust. Those round him began cheering and gathering up the coins.

'Here, we've found one of 'em playing dead in the gorse.' He turned as a knock-kneed and wide-eyed clerk, his skull-cap askew, was pushed towards him through the crowd.

Thomas lifted one of the coins. 'What are these?' he demanded. 'P'rhaps 'tis only peasants an' paupers who needs' must ask, but never have I seen one 'afore.'

The clerk nodded. 'That's right, sir. They're solid gold and newly minted.'

Thomas placed the coin flat in one hand and looked down at the sailing-ship stamped into the gold. 'What are they worth?'

'Half-a-mark. They're to be called the *noble*.'

Thomas smiled. 'Six shillings and eightpence! 'Tis a fortune in one coin.'

'That's right enough,' said the clerk gloomily. 'But 'tis true. Every pannier is as full of 'em as the next. We carried them from the mint for safe-keeping in the vaults of Corfe Castle when the Death broke out in London. We were taking them back to the city.'

'Outlaws we may be, but 'tis the king's mint we've robbed!' cried Thomas as all round him men began cutting open panniers and forcing the chests. Seeing Sampson and Matilda standing on the edge of the cliff, he grinned, scooped a handful of coins from the ground and shouted: 'Look!'

'All that glitters . . .' murmured Matilda.

'You're wrong, Matilda. Watch,' said Sampson.

Thomas threw the coins high into the air. They rose through the shadows. Suddenly the sun struck them and they spun and glittered in its light before tumbling downward into his cupped waiting hands.

CHAPTER NINETEEN

Thomas hesitated as he scanned the glowing grinning faces lit up by the torches scattered round the stockade. With them he felt a kinship he had never known before, a sense of belonging and shared purpose that had been absent during his childhood and youth. There were some whose names he still did not know, others who bore the bandages and scars of the attack on Fitzwalter's soldiers three days earlier. In build, character and history no two were alike. Only one fact united them: the sovereign offered jointly by the king and Swayne as reward for each of their heads. Gratitude and anxiety now mingling, he lifted his gaze to the sky; but it offered no comfort. Clouds hid the moon, veiled the stars in their perfect blackness. He stood, waiting for a hush to descend over the encampment before turning to Will.

The potter lifted a coin into the light.

'See this?' he cried, grinning happily. ''Tis a noble. Well, friends, 'tis what we are now – every man Jack of us. It may have taken me two whole days to count 'em, but t'was better than tallying sheep for they gave me the sweetest dreams a man could wish for. The sums are these: two dozen chests with three hundred coins in each. Total 'em up an' what do you get? I'll tell 'ee. Two an' a half thousand pounds worth of freshly minted coin o' the realm!' He paused, letting the cheers and laugher that followed subside before continuing. 'That's the ken of it, my friends! 'Tis a king's ransom! With land at a groat the acre and no manor steward earnin' more than forty shilluns' 'tween Michaelmas's it makes each of us as wealthy as Edward of England. Question is – what's to be done with it?'

'Spend it!' shouted someone.

Thomas ignored his cue. Tongue-tied, unable to give voice to the seethe of thoughts that were his unformed plan for the future, he sat mute as other members of the band took up the cry. Suddenly the pieces clicked into place. He rose to his feet.

'On what? he cried. The outlaws fell silent 'Most of you have been here since the year was new born,' he went on, gaining confidence as what he wanted to say finally took shape. 'You came to us as strangers, joining Sampson an' I because you had lost hope and all that was dear to you during the Death. But the sexton tolls no more. The Death is over: and we must move on. We've robbed, ambushed, drubbed those sent to destroy us and snatched enough gold to last each of us a lifetime. The fates have stood by us. But luck, my friends, is like a well – bottomless till dry. Even now Swayne is recruiting men to his colours an' preparing to pay us a second visit. There'll not be a third. They'll fall for no gins nor turn tail an' flee. They'll surround the stockade, staying firm until the skin hangs loose from our bones and we've not muscle enough to even lift a bow. At day's end no man or dam amongst 'ee will leave the forest alive.' He paused. Sober, puzzled faces stared back at him. He had their attention now, and as he watched what he had said take root he felt a sudden self-disgust for first holding out a straw to their hopes and then snatching it away. He went on.

'Since robbin' the mint Sampson an' I have done naught but argue. We cannot agree what's next to be done. He believes we should divide the gold and disband, each of us returning to our homes or going where we will. I think otherwise. We are a band of outlaws five score strong. Divided we are like links in a chain, but together we are the chain itself. To me it seems t'would be best if we remained as one, using the king's gold to add to our numbers. There are men cast in our mould in every shire in the land. Let us find them. Let the band become an army. And then, my friends, let us march to London's gates and petition the king to listen to our grievances and right the wrongs that have fitted us for the noose!'

Beside him, Sampson shook his head in despair as Thomas warmed to his theme. For two days they had argued over the band and its future, but Thomas's views had so shifted over the winter months that it had been impossible to make him see sense. Once cautious, circumspect and myopic, the band's success had encouraged him to see it not merely as a vehicle for robbery but as an instrument capable of forcing change, of ridding England of men like Audley and the laws that kept them in power. It was an extraordinary ambition, not least because Thomas's mind moved with the plodding, unhurried deliberation of an ox. But it was also treason, and Sampson had known him too long to imagine him as mastering the role of visionary peasant leading an outlaw army. It was, he had decided, a result of his sickness; a need to prove something to himself that the weeks of near madness had distorted and made credible. He himself was certain that the entire plan was doomed to failure. No monarch, least of all Edward of England and victor of Crécy, would allow himself to be dictated to by a rag, tag and bobtail horde of serfs and self-confessed felons. And yet Thomas's call-to-arms was obviously as appealing to the band as any preaching friar's sermonizing, for as he finished they rose as one and began cheering and waving their bows.

'Who are these outlaws you speak of?' asked one as the noise faded.

'I'll tell 'ee,' replied Thomas. 'We're surrounded by men such as we, those who've been forced to flee their homes and seek refuge in the woods. They'll find us. We'll seek 'em out. 'Afore long we'll be as many as the coins we took from the panniers.' He halted, deliberately lowering his voice to a whisper. 'Which outlaw do the minstrels most sing of? Which has a royal forest for a kingdom and a ballad for every deed? One man and one only: Robin Hood! An' 'tis to him we must go!'

Sampson stood and tried to make himself heard. But no one heeded him. Thomas refused to be silenced and with barely a pause to draw breath he continued on; cajoling and moulding the mood of those listening with the skill of a travelling player.

'We are serfs, fit only for the plough-tail!' he cried. 'Men formed in the likeness of Christ but kept like beasts! What can we call our own? Nothing but our empty bellies. All round us we see others wax fat on our labours; our lords, priests, monks like Audley. They say 'tis the Devil that steals men's souls. Maybe, but 'tis Holy Church that cuts their purses ! All our lives we work; work an' pay. Pay to wed or be laid to rest! Pay to grind corn in our lord's mill! Pay to take a wrongdoer to court, pay to attend it! Pay to cross a bridge, travel the highway, enter a town

265

with goods for market! Only birth is free. But we make up for it, my friends; we make up for it. For life is long and there are more ways to milk a mortal than any cow in our master's byre.'

As he listened, Sampson glanced at Ned. His mouth hung open in a wrapt smile, his eyes gleamed and his expression was of someone almost in a state of trance. The rest of the band were now shaking their bows and singing Thomas's words back to him as though words alone might lift the yoke. And yet, observed Sampson, there was a bland and vacuous look on many of their faces. As in Sarum during the plague, he felt that each was being swept headlong by a tide none could comprehend, by its ignorance and hope. Only Will and Matilda, both grim-faced and solemn, seemed to share his fears. The potter caught his glance.

'He's as mazed as a Lenten hare,' he cried as Thomas's voice rose into the night. 'We've funds enough not to work again till the worms begin theirs.'

Sampson smiled. 'But you'll come with us?'

'To meet Robin Hood? Aye, I'll come. The man's either a saint or the biggest trickster alive an' I've long had a hankerin' to know which: that's if he lives at all, which I doubt.' Will shook his head. 'So we're leaving the Chase an' heading north for Nottingham?'

Sampson shrugged, only now accepting the reality ahead. 'If that's as the men want. I promised Thomas I'd abide by their decision.'

'Pah! So 'tis to be Thomas Woodward, the peasant's champion. I reckon t'won't be long 'afore we all of us rue the day. Hark at 'em,' growled Will as the outlaws surged round Thomas and lifted him high on to their shoulders. 'Anyone 'ed think he'd won 'em the keys to Heaven itself.'

'Give him time, Will. Hood may live; his men may join us.'

'Aye, an' fish might fly.'

When the meeting broke-up and new sentries had been posted, the band dispersed – some to their huts, others gathering round a bonfire. They were in bombastic and ebullient mood, and though not drunk it seemed to Sampson that Thomas's eloquence had done the work of wine, made them reckless and hotheaded. Apart from Will – Matilda had been terse and evasive since returning from Long Coombe – no one had asked him why he thought it wiser that they disband; and their obvious impatience to begin the ride north made him feel that they were moving blinkered towards a vision so elusive it would actually recede the nearer their destination became. He too had heard the ballads of Robin Hood and his Men, but more than one minstrel he'd met had admitted to inventing what he sang. Hood's deeds were legendary. Even the most ignorant knew of his feud with Nottingham's sheriff. But legends, he had argued when Thomas first proposed they combine, were facts embroidered by fiction and certainly not substantial enough to warrant a two hundred mile ride into a world so unknown that none of them knew where Sherwood Forest was. But Thomas had brushed aside his fears, and was to do so again when they met inside his hut to discuss the journey after the meeting.

Thomas remained silent at first. But even in the dim light from a tallow Sampson sensed that the effects of the band's acclamation still lingered in his thoughts. His eyes glowed like fire coals, his movements were fussy and hurried, and there was a conceit to his silence that suggested someone possessed by his own myth – a myth still to be created. But in this Sampson had misjudged him, and when he finally spoke he knew at once that all the frailties and doubts that shaped him had yet to be laid.

'Matilda may spurn you,' he said suddenly, 'but at least you share the babe. I lack even that. A man alone has time to brood on his future. P'rhaps I've brooded to excess, but 'tis fact that the laws that made me a serf bound to soil are those of men who are afraid. What do they fear? How can a peasant tilling his strip or scratchin' for gleanings harm his lord?' A smile passed across his face. 'Strange how we've changed. T'was you who once picked me to my feet, you who taught me what the Death would bring, you who mended me an' made me draw a bow again. Now hark at you.'

''Tis not the wrongs I doubt, but the methods you've chosen to right them: armed uprising, a march on London. 'Tis treason.'

'We've no other choice. Most of the men would be caught an' hung if they left the forest. To send 'em packing with a purse full of gold would be to send 'em to the gallows.'

Sampson sneered and rose angrily to his feet. Reaching the door, he turned and said: 'I pray God you know what you're doing. I don't, an' I don't think Ned or the men do either. They'll follow you, not because they understand your preaching but because they're trapped and frightened and what you said has given 'em hope. You're not capable of miracles, Thomas. You an' I know that. An' I'll not rest easy until we've put this folly behind us. And may the Lord watch o'er an' keep us; for if there's one thing I'm certain of, 'tis that we'll be needing Him 'fore 'tis done.'

*   *   *

Still tooo angry to sleep, Sampson began walking round the perimeter of the stockade. Above him, shapes in shadow, the sentries paced its walls. Near the gateway an orange glow discoloured the darkness, picking out the faces of the small group of outlaws still gathered round the bonfire's embers. He could hear the strumming of a lute, the gruff deep-toned voices of the outlaws as they joined the minstrel on the chorus of one of the Robin Hood ballads. The music made his temper worsen. As a child, he too had sung the ballads – and believed them. Only later, with a cynicism that at times left him isolated and confused, had he begun to doubt their veracity and Hood's existence. But he knew that to the band, to Thomas, and to most countryfolk, the Nottinghamshire outlaw was flesh and blood whose deeds none doubted. His victories, they shared. For in him they saw proof that it was possible to resist those who oppressed them. As if by proxy, what they dare not do, he did for them; and in their imaginations they replaced the barons and clerics made to beg for their lives by Hood and his men with their own landlords – humbled, robbed of their wealth, as poor as they.

But all this was supposition – the man might match the minstrels claims – and Sampson put the outlaw from his thoughts as he returned to the hut. For it was not only Robin Hood that troubled him. Since gazing down on the dead in Long Coombe, he had begun to realize that death's shadow haunted the world of the outlaw, making it dark and unnatural, one in which Matilda's coldness towards him could not warm and blossom into love. The distance between them was widening; it would widen still further if Hood existed and joined them and they turned south to march on London. During the last few days he had found himself longing to forget Audley and the band and take Matilda to a town where none knew them, where he could practice as a physician and she could look forward to childbed without fear of what lay ahead. Yet he knew he could not share the dream with her. She would deny any chance of love, accuse him of deserting Thomas, of revoking his vow to kill Audley.

He glanced up. She was standing in front of him, eyes creased into a quizzical frown and cloak wrapped tightly round her breasts.

'I couldn't sleep,' she explained.

'Nor I.' Sensing the lack of hostility in her mood, he smiled. 'Come, let's walk 'afore going to bed.' Without thinking she linked an arm through his. 'Do you promise not to argue?' he added.

She grinned. 'I'll try.'

They wandered slowly through the encampment, passing the horses at their tethers and the two siege engines standing side by side near the entrance. Glancing round, Sampson said: 'In a week from now all this t'will be a memory. In a month we'll be in the Forest of Sherwood. In three, God help us, we'll as like as nay be resting our heads on the spikes above Moorgate.'

'Thomas believes otherwise.'

'Thomas be damned. What of our babe? Ride with us, Matilda, and it'll end up being cut from your belly 'afore time and drowned like the unwanted runt in a litter of pups.' Sampson turned towards her. 'Stay here. Go back to Cranborne till the babe's been born.'

She trembled slightly, then stiffened. 'No. I must follow Thomas. I sought peace by leaving you once before; look what happened to me then.'

'I thought t'was me you fled from?'

'Aye, you an' my own true self.' She paused, smiling sadly. 'You're afraid, aren't you?'

'Yes, and so would any man with sense. But 'tis Thomas who calls the tune now. Why? Because he's an archer the equal of Hood and I'm only the fool who risked death by guarding each of 'em against breaking out in the buboes, who built this stockade, who mounted its defence and led Fitzwalter to the slaughter.'

'You sound bitter, as if you can't abide Thomas leading the

269

band.'

'You're wrong. The cap fits me no longer, nor would I wish to wear it.'

'Why not take your share of the money and leave?'

'How little you know me.' Sampson sighed. 'I once swore to you that I'd take care of Thomas. If I went back on my word when he most needs me t'would give you further cause to scorn me.'

'But Thomas is mended.'

'Is he? Would I could be so certain.'

Matilda turned from his gaze. Suddenly she smiled and said: 'I think you use Thomas as an excuse, a bluff behind which you've chosen to hide your true reasons for remaining with the band. 'Tis me an' the babe that are keeping you, isn't it?'

Sampson ignored the question. Turning her head towards his, he said: 'Only the guilty can see the guile in others. And what of you, Matilda? Are you not doing the same? If I left you, would you still ride with him?'

'I don't know.'

'You do. ''Tis just that you're scared of admitting it to yourself. Love blinds. Your words, not mine. 'Tis not Robin Hood you an' I are questing for, but each other.'

*   *   *

To Sampson that same air of chasing illusion persisted when, two days later, the outlaws rode from the stockade for the final time; first surrounding it, then loosing a salvo of fire-arrows at its walls. Flames quickly engulfed it and they watched in silence, shading their faces against the heat, as the massive trebuchet turned into a fiery beacon and finally broke open like a budding flower and collapsed on to the cannons beneath it. Ned had packed them with powder and blocked their muzzles with daub. They were too cumbersome to take, too valuable to leave, and when the first finally exploded chunks of iron burst high into the air. An instant later the barrel of the second rose in their wake, only exploding and dissolving into fragments at the apex of its climb. No farewell could have been more awesome. The ground trembled, the horses whinnied and the leaves on the surrounding trees trembled and wilted as if blown by a fervid wind.

270

The heat could still be felt when the outlaws turned their backs on the burning corner posts that defined the shape of the stockade. No one spoke much, each kept his thoughts to himself, but, as they rode across the clearing, there were few who did not turn in the saddle and take a final look at the pall of black smoke that hung over its charred remains.

Once clear of the forest they headed across the downs towards Joshuah, briefly pausing to receive his blessing for the journey ahead. After their departure the hermit climbed on to the roof of his cell and watched them; a long caravan of horses, panniers packed with gold and provisions, threading its way up the slopes of a valley before turning northwards and vanishing over the sky-line.

★   ★   ★

The journey took nearly a month and by its end their numbers had doubled. The first to join were two shepherds on Salisbury Plain, the second a small group of outlaws in hiding on the Cotswold Hills, and from then each day saw the column's ranks swell with wayfarers, fugitives and peasants in flight from the Death – still raging in the northern shires. Some wore rags, others were armed with pitchforks and scythes, but under Sampson's unwilling tutelage the column gradually assumed the character of an army; and an army on campaign. In the evenings Thomas trained them as archers, mendicant friars preached angry rhetorical sermons listing the grievances they wanted redressed. By day they rode on, occasionally skirmishing with this sheriff or that baron as they crossed his lands. Some fell by the way; the sick and the maimed, the dead. One of the women gave birth to a son. The landscape changed. The Cotswolds gave way to the Midland vales; flat open country picked out in cider orchards, lime-washed hamlets, fat cattle. North of the Avon the vales became a patchwork of open-field strips. Day by day, as horizons changed, they passed lines of stooped peasants cutting hay or their heavy wains rumbling homeward. And now, with July half over and after skirting Nottingham and crossing the Trent, they were at last within the bounds of Sherwood Forest.

It rose round them, a world of giant oaks that shaded the afternoon sunlight. Sampson, Thomas and Matilda were riding at the head of the column, and Matilda peered anxiously into the gloaming as they moved deeper into the forest.

'Are you alright?' asked Sampson.

'Yes.' She smiled. Her belly had become swollen and heavy during the weeks spent in the saddle. The constant motion had fatigued and exhausted her. Saddle-sores had formed on her thighs, dust filled her eyes. But despite her discomfort she felt a curious sense of elation. During the past month circumstances had forced her and Sampson to spend much of their time together. Only they doubted Robin Hood's existence and Thomas's ability to work the miracle he sought; and in sharing that uncertainty she had come to understand how much else they shared. Their arguments had been few, and Sampson's presence had both reassured her and made her realize how much she depended on him. And yet he was still blind to the obvious and she had yet to admit it to him. Love blinds. She shivered excitedly as Thomas said:

'I reckon we're an hour's ride from his camp.' He glanced the length of the column, grinned and added: 'In six weeks we'll be at London's gates with a thousand men at our backs.'

'That last inn-keeper didn't seem to have much liking for the man,' replied Sampson. 'Some have laughed at us, others called him a sham.'

'Perhaps he's robbed 'em?'

'Taverners, peasants? Hardly the Robin Hood who takes from the rich to give to the poor.'

Thomas laughed at his fears. 'Nonsense! There's no outlaw who's done more for our cause. By tnis time tomorrow he'll be riding with us.'

'God forbid that you're right,' growled Sampson, staring unhappily ahead of him. A moment later the undergrowth parted and a small boy stepped from the shadows.

Puzzled by something strangely disproportionate about him, Sampson shielded his eyes and studied him more closely. Suddenly he cried out and reached for his bow: the figure now approaching was not a boy, but a grown man, a dwarf.

The dwarf lifted his arms as Thomas's bow rose beside Sampson's. 'No, Little John ain't pretty, that I'll grant 'ee,' he said. 'But there's no cause to make a bow butt out o' him.'

'You're Little John?' cried Thomas in disbelief as the column

272

came slowly to a halt.

The dwarf laughed. 'John I was dubbed in a Lincoln town font, an' little I is. What other name would fit so snug on a wretch such as I?'

He was as much like a hobgoblin or wood-elf as any creature Matilda had seen. He stood as high as her stirrup irons, had rings through both ears and a plump friendly face that made his stunted body seem even smaller than it really was.

He laughed again and said: 'So here we is, squandering time on our hail-fellow-well-met's in the Forest o' Sherwood. I'm Little John an' you're strangers from damme know where. Do you still intend using me for a butt or may I lower my arms?'

'We're looking for Robin Hood,' explained Thomas.

'Is that so? Take me for a fool for not a' guessin'.' Little John began chuckling, his eyes twinkled. 'And in the absence of Will Scarlet an' Friar Tuck it must be I who you hope'll take you to his lair. That's right, ain't it?'

'No,' snapped Sampson, his voice sharp with contempt. 'You don't expect to trick us into mistaking a dwarf for one of Hood's merry men?'

'Well, 'tis your error, friend,' retorted Little John. 'For I'm an outlaw alright, with no more rights than a beast of warren.' His chuckle grew louder. 'Stay in Sherwood long enough an' you'll learn that even a month of May has forgotten how to be merry.' He turned to Thomas. 'You want Robin, an' you shall have him.'

Swallowing his bewilderment, Thomas shouldered his bow and held out a hand in greeting. 'I'm Thomas Woodward an' this is Sampson Hooke. We too are outlaws, ten score strong and a month on the highway,' he said, indicating the column behind him.

Little John's chuckle turned to laughter. 'Do you mean to tell me you've spent a month in the saddle for the sake of a meeting with Robin?'

'Aye,' said Thomas gravely.

The dwarf shook his head. 'Then I'd best delay you no longer,' he said finally. 'Come, follow me.'

The outlaws began chattering amongst themselves as they moved on. Though few had reconciled Little John the dwarf with the Little John thought to have toppled Robin Hood into a

273

stream with one blow of a quarterstaff at their first encounter, they were in an expectant mood. But conversation ceased as the shadows lengthened. Occasionally they saw a small herd of red deer moving silently across a glade, the fawns gambolling awkwardly behind the hinds on long spindly legs. But such sights offered scant comfort. The forest was damp and gloomy, and their guide, his size often causing him to vanish as he lolloped through the undergrowth, maintained a shrill eerie cackle that grew louder whenever he turned to look back at the solemn faces behind him. Once they passed a corpse dangling from a noose.

'One of the sheriff's men,' explained Little John. 'We keep a few strung up as a warning to the others. Dead men's bunting we call 'em. Makes the living think twice 'afore venturing any further.'

Matilda shuddered as she stared at the faceless corpse. She turned to Sampson. 'I'm frightened,' she whispered. 'We were wrong. Hood exists. Come Sabbath we'll be marching on London.'

'Aye, an' if Little John's a dwarf an' cut-throat what manner of man must his master be?'

'He seems to be mocking us.'

'That's because we're fools, an' he knows it.'

'What'll happen to us?'

Sampson tightened the grip on his reins. 'I don't know. An' I'm not sure that I wish to.'

It was nearly dusk when Little John blew the hunting horn hanging from his waist and led the column into a large open clearing filled with makeshift hovels. Outwardly it seemed more like a village than the hiding-place of fugitives. Swine, goats and poultry wandered untended through the mud. Women, many of them with child and dressed in rags, rose from their cooking fires to watch their arrival. A horde of unwashed children appeared from nowhere. The men emerged from their hovels. Few carried bows or seemed concerned at the presence of the column. Most were scarred by the pox or a wound that had festered before healing. Some had been branded, all wore an ill-fitting mixture of rags, armour, skins and the blood-stained livery of those they had killed.

Still cackling, Little John ran across to the far side of the clearing and vanished into a small hut roofed with leaves. When he reappeared, a stranger stood framed in the doorway beside him, gazing at the column. Followed by the dwarf, he began walking across the clearing: a tall, wiry figure with close-cropped hair and a short grey beard flecked with gobbets of fat. As he drew closer, Sampson noticed that a livid red weal circled his neck. Reaching the outlaws, he touched it.

'Thrice they've put a rope round my neck,' he said, 'an three times they've cut me down when they thought me dead. Yet I live. They say those who thrice cheat the hangman will do so for ever.' He smiled, but it was the sad troubled smile of someone too weary to find pleasure in the promise of eternal life.

'My master,' announced Little John, giving an exaggerated bow.

Thomas paled and turned to the stranger. 'You? Robin Hood?' he cried.

The smile became a sigh. 'So, like every fool who comes questing for Robin you also expected a gallant in Lincoln green with a haunch of poached venison in one hand, a distressed maid in t'other and an arrow 'tween his teeth. Instead you find this; a man of two score years with feet a' rotting in their boots, marked by the noose and pained by the stone. No, my friend; none of us is what we seem.' He paused, suddenly a tired and broken caricature of his own self-portrait. He lifted his eyes toward Thomas. 'Is it Hood you're looking for?'

'Yes.'

'Then let I be he.' Robin raised his arms at the surrounding trees. 'For this,' he cried, 'is Sherwood Forest, the greenwood, the outlaw's refuge, the domain of thieves where the poor get fed and the rich get robbed. Pah! Let the Devil take it! I'm a brigand not a Goose Fair peep-show. A common murderer, not the fantastical prodigy that keeps the minstrels in song. Look! What do you see?' He paused, indicating the watching fugitives gathered in a circle behind him. 'Hardly the stuff of legend, are they? They sleep by day an' debauch by night. That's if none of 'em is too drunk to rut! Now p'rhaps you'll go and leave us in peace!' He spun and began walking towards his hut.

The bitterness and contempt in his voice were self-evident. Even Thomas sensed them. Stunned, still clinging to the image of the outlaw leader that had inspired and supported him during the past month, he dismounted and hurried after him.

'Sir!' he begged. 'At least listen to the reason for our coming.'

Robin turned, snapped: ''Tis the going I wait on,' then strode the few paces to his hut. Turning his back on Thomas's pleas he sat and began whittling shavings from a piece of wood.

Watching him, Matilda suddenly knew that there would be no march on London. But instead of feeling relieved, the numb and distant look on Sampson's face made her tremble with fear. 'You're going to leave us, aren't you?' she said. 'Thomas, the men – even the babe an' I.' She glanced at her brother. 'He may sicken, become demented again . . .'

'T'was his madness that brought you here, let it guide you home,' said Sampson. 'I'm a free man, Matilda. I'll do an' go where I please.'

'I thought you loved me?'

'You're wrong.'

Matilda slumped forward in the saddle and began crying. 'You bastard,' she murmured.

'Aye, 'tis exactly what I am.' He paused and nodded toward Thomas. 'We'd best join him. He'll see the truth soon enough, and when he does he'll need comforting.'

Matilda stifled her tears as she dismounted and followed Sampson across the clearing. For an instant she felt only hate: for Sampson, her brother, even the babe in her womb. Then the moment passed and she knew that even without Sampson beside her she would bring forth his child, have it as a memory of what she had shunned and only now understood how much she needed. Catching him up, she said: 'Is it only Thomas who matters to you?'

Sampson halted. 'No,' he snapped. 'For I'm done with all of you an' 'tis only I, Sampson Hooke, who concerns me now.'

'You're lying.' She turned her face to his. 'Please, say you love me.'

Sampson stared at her for a moment, then said: 'No. T'would make you think you still owned me even when I'm no longer beside you, an' I'll not give you that pleasure.'

'You're wrong, Sampson.' She closed her eyes and whispered: 'I love you . . .' But left it too late. For Sampson had stopped listening to her and had hurried on to where Thomas was explaining the reasons for their journey to Robin Hood.

'The money we stole from the mint,' he was saying, 'is enough to buy us food, horses and arms. For we came here to ask you to leave the forest and ride south with us on London. Your name is known. With you at our side men would flock to our cause.'

The whittling ceased. 'Our cause . . . ?'

'You're an outlaw, so are we,' cried Thomas. 'Our cause is the same. For though Christ and his saints be abed we will rise up and force the king to quash the laws that made us what we are, serfs who starve and . . .'

'Enough!' bellowed Robin, stabbing his knife at Thomas. 'Starvation makes men desperate, and if they were that they'd a' done your task for you years ago. Keep 'em hungry an' they'll keep working. That's one trick those who own 'em know well. Anyway, Edward of England's a king, not a reed to be blown this way an' that by an outlaw afeared o' the noose. No, friend, march on London and you and those who ride with you'll end their days putting leaves on Tyburn tree. You've bullion an' five score men. Spend it, send the men home, but don't come begging to me. You say you want to serve the poor? Do so. Become a slum friar, a healer, a tumbler who makes 'em laugh – anything but a prophet; for in the wake of prophets walk widows an' fatherless babes.'

Matilda lifted her eyes to Sampson's. She held his gaze for no more than a second, but during that time a look passed between them that she recognized as proof of love and he mistook for accusation.

'It won't work, lad,' added Robin, still talking to Thomas. 'Does Little John seem the "young giant, brisk and bold" that the minstrels sing of? As to the rest, all they want is a full belly, a hogshead o' ale and no reeve with a whip at their backs.'

'And you?' said Sampson quietly.

'Aye, an' then there's me.' Robin's shoulders sagged and his face took on the creased, crumpled look of something old and unwanted. There was a silence, then he smiled and turned to the dwarf. 'For God's sake tell 'em John. I've done with words.'

Little John laughed slightly and again bowed towards his master. 'Meet Robin o' the Moor, dubbed Hood by himself not ten years back when still a footpad an' sheep thief.'

Thomas's eyes widened. He glanced at the dwarf, then at Robin. Suddenly he cried out and fell to his knees.

'There, lad,' murmured Robin. 'An' let's hope the truth puts some sense into 'ee 'afore 'tis too late. There's no such creature as Robin Hood, nor has there ever been. He's a fable, a will-o'-the-wisp, a man of my making and of minstrels an' bards in need of a song. I warned 'ee that none of us is what we seem. How could Hood exist? The ballads alone span the reign of six monarchs. I was born Robin alright, but to a maker of clogs. By nine I was an outlaw, having first avenged my own's dam's rape by teaching myself the longbow an' killing the tipstaff who'd bedded her. T'was then I met John here, the fool in a travelling fair. For a while we roamed the Dales with a pair of performing bears, adding to our takings by doing tricks with the bow. We stole eggs, fowl, what mutton we needed. I too believed in Hood. So we came south and began searching for him. We killed a soldier. I was taken but survived the noose. After two years hunting for Hood we realized he didn't exist. T'was then I decided to invent him. John here had been called Little since first he ceased growing. I began calling myself Hood. At first it was done in jest. But folk believed me. So I became him, setting up camp in this clearing and giving shelter to those who found us. As to the ballads, some I penned myself to put flesh on the fable and make the sheriff hesitate 'afore entering the forest.' He smiled. 'An' now hark at me. I'm the people's dupe, sixteen verses and a rousing chorus, a peg to hang hope on when you've no hope left. For 'tis the ballads that brought you here and make the poor believe someone cares for 'em. And do they speak the truth? No, nor will they. We're what others want us to be, you an' I, not what we are.' He paused, shrugging his shoulders in the detached manner of a man who had long ago come to terms with the events he was describing. 'The rest is chalk an' cut cloth. And though I don't doubt it'll outlive us it won't be the truth. As to you, lad; stay the night and return home on the morrow. You say a prior wronged you? Kill him if it'll make you feel better, but don't start preaching or trying to right wrongs, for it won't work. There, and if what I've said makes you see reason it'll have been worth my words and your weeks on the road.'

Thomas said nothing when Robin finished speaking. The outlaw's confession had drained him, cleansed him of the dream that had inspired this meeting. His mind inched cautiously towards new ideas, and to convince himself that serfdom was not immune to change nor the creation of divine will he had first had

278

to ride roughshod over a structured, ordered world which forbade dissent and in which every bird, beast and mortal had its place. It had been a perilous journey, and more than once, terrified of damnation and God's wrath, he had tried to retrace his steps. And now it was too late. Now he sat stunned by all Robin had said, rudderless, adrift without purpose or plan, a phantom who sat hunched and staring into the fire as darkness slowly descended.

Later, before retiring into his hut, Robin turned to his visitors and said: 'Don't you go telling anyone what I told 'ee tonight. Folk may be singing of me a thousand years from now an' I wouldn't want some sanctimonious poetmaster rewriting the ballads and spoiling their pleasures. Men need the likes o' I, be we fact or fiction, an' I've a notion that the names Robin Hood and Little John may still be remembered when many a king's been forgotten.'

Sampson smiled at his boast. And yet . . . ? No, it was impossible. Robin was a fraud, when he died so would the ballads. After all, he was an outlaw. And when outlaws died they were cut down and buried and quickly forgotten.

*   *   *

Drizzle was falling from a leaden sky when the band retraced its steps through the forest on the following morning. The change of weather matched its mood, for the outcome of their meeting still haunted their thoughts. Only Sampson, riding alone at the head of the column, rain splashing against his cape, knew where they were bound and what lay ahead. During the previous night, unable to sleep, he had rolled on to his back and stared up into the darkness, holding and then dismissing the faces of those he loved after mapping their futures for them. Ned and Will could take care of themselves. To Thomas he saw himself as a crutch that must now be discarded. Matilda as someone he would always love but had failed to win.

These same thoughts, now tempered by anger, returned to him as the sprawling dispirited column splashed through a brook and turned on to a track near the edge of the forest. Suddenly he lowered his head against the rain and rode to the rear of the column, reining in alongside Thomas and Matilda.

'I'm going to call a halt,' he shouted, evading Matilda, 'divide out the gold into shares fair to all and advise the men to return to their villages.'

Thomas nodded blankly.

'I've leaving you an' Matilda, Thomas. Going west to take ship for Ireland. I've finished with Audley, the killings, the falling asleep not knowing if dawn'll find you pinned to your pallet by a soldier's blade.'

Matilda began sobbing. Thomas looked up and murmured: 'As you wish.'

'As I wish! If I'd had my way we'd never have left the Chase. That's right, Thomas. Close your eyes, pretend we're not here, that it's a mistake, a dream that'll cease when you wake.'

Unable to look at Matilda, he turned and cantered the length of the column, calling it to a halt. The band gathered round him. Finally he dismounted and cried: 'This venture has failed an' now 'tis over! There'll be no march on London, no Robin Hood riding at our head! The gold will be divided amongst all. There is sufficient to allow each of us to go where he pleases. But be wary. We are condemned criminals who will pay for our deeds on the gallows if caught. Tell no one where you've been when you reach your villages. If 'tis to a city you're bound, remember that you'll be free men after a year and a day in its walls. Those who joined us most recently should be safe enough. The rest of you, those who were with us on the Chase, I can only wish well. I know 'tis sparse thanks for all you've done, but try not to forget this last half year. Not one of us will know such times again. We were strangers who became brothers, brothers who for a brief moment fought for a cause common to all. We survived the Death, being hunted, the ride that brought us here. Now we must cheat the hangman.' He paused, sadness and regret turning the words to a whisper as the first tears filled his eyes. 'Farewell, my friends, and may God bless an' keep you in his care . . .'

Silence. Rain in runnels on capes, the squelch of hooves in the mud, eyes darting bewildered from Sampson to Thomas and back again. Will the first to find voice.

'You may be a prior's bastard! But where you go, so do I!'

Others took up the cry. Sampson looked at them through his tears. Ned, plain-spoken and dependable; Stutter and Mouse, the long and the short, made one by a mutual dislike that nourished and bonded them together; and Will. How could he abandon a man who had once saved all their lives and whose grumbles and jests were as much part of the Crécy campaign as the fight itself? He strode angrily towards Thomas.

'You tell 'em!' he shouted. 'T'was you who brought 'em here!' But Thomas turned away. Once again he tried to convince them of the need to disperse. With repetition, reality gradually dawned. Aimless and confused, they sat together on the verge whilst the panniers were unpacked, the money counted into heaps, and each filed passed Sampson to fill his purse.

That afternoon the first to leave saddled and mounted their horses. By early evening small groups of horsemen could be seen moving along the tracks and bridleways that skirted the Forest. Some turned north, intending to go on pilgrimage to Fountains Abbey or the shrine of Saint Cuthbert at Durham; others went east toward the Fens and Walsingham; still more headed south into the Midlands. Watching them go, Sampson began to understand that though some would settle and some keep moving, they would carry Thomas's vision of a new England into every corner of the land. He smiled to himself. One day, like a weed tossed casually aside, it might burst forth as a tree strong and tall enough to shelter the heirs of those who had been part of the band.

Suddenly he knew that the time had come to follow in their wake. All afternoon he had delayed his departure. He could do so no longer. Leading his horse with a trembling hand, he walked to where Thomas and Matilda sat beside the track.

'Farewell, Thomas,' he said. The outlaw lfted his head. His face was wan, bereft of expression. Sampson smiled. 'You've nothing to say to me, no word of farewell after all we've shared . . .? Thomas turned and lowered his head. Sampson stood staring at him for a moment, then dropped a purse at Matilda's purse. 'For the babe. I've more than I need.'

'So you think payment suffices?' she whispered.

He closed his eyes. 'I've done with fighting, Matilda. Please, don't let's part on a quarrel.' He paused. 'Take care of the babe.'

Tears and rain mingled on her cheeks as she gazed up at him. 'Aye, I'll look after it; and tell it that's its father loved it so much he couldn't even wait till it had left the womb 'afore deserting it. Why can't you look at me, Sampson? Do you so hate the woman who carries your seed that you can't even face her when parting?'

'Please, Matilda.'

'Look at me.'

'No!'

'So you'd leave without knowing what Ned, Will – any fool – saw days ago an' thought you'd soon see for yourself? Or must I force open your eyes with my own two hands and keep them open till you wake from a blind man's slumbers? Look at me, Sampson.'

He slowly raised his head and lifted his gaze to hers.

She smiled. 'Now do you understand? Take horse now and you'd be departing from a woman who loves you so much she fears her heart might crack an' break open 'afore you finally see sense.'

Sampson stared at her without speaking.

She rose and moved towards him. 'No, 'tis not because you're going and I'm afraid what'll happen to me. Nor will I change my mind or leave your side when next you're being hunted.' She smiled again, brushed her hair from her face. 'I love you, Sampson,' she whispered. 'Or would you have me make every crier in the land proclaim it from village green an' market cross 'afore believing me?' She reached forward and drew him into her embrace, lifting her lips to his as a sudden flurry of wind made the rain squall against the locked shape of their bodies.

★   ★   ★

By nightfall few of the band remained, but amongst them were both Ned and Will. Indifferent to Sampson's pleas that they leave, their eyes tracked his every move, as if defying him to elude their gaze and depart unnoticed. A stag was slaughtered and spitted, a barrel of ale bought from the nearest tavern. Soon the band's dissolution began to seem like a wake.

Will got drunk. 'What else can a man do when his friends slip a knife 'tween his ribs?' he jeered, heckling the still silent Thomas.

Sampson tried to calm him. 'Go with Ned. Join the army. We'll be at war with France again 'afore long.'

'An' file the soles from me feet tramping the countryside at the whim of a king? No. I'd rather nail 'em to English clay than put to sea again.' Suddenly a brawny arm reached out and plucked the potter from the ground.

'You bide with me. I'll take care of 'ee,' growled Ned.

The wrestler's grip left no room for argument. Will relented and stalked off into the night. As the remnants of the band prepared for sleep, the rain stopped, leaving behind it a cloudless sky. The men fell silent. Sampson and Matilda lay side by side and gazed up into the blackness.

'Why didn't you tell me 'afore?' asked Sampson.

'Pride, fear you'd scorn me, the hope that you'd see it for yourself – I don't know, nor does it matter.'

'Hearts don't crack. I'm a physician, remember?'

'This one would if you'd left me.'

'I nearly did.' Low in the southern sky Sampson could see the outline of the Eagle traced in its six stars. Beneath them lay the Chase, Sarum, the world he knew and could now share with Matilda. 'We'll head south,' he said. 'Enter Sarum in disguise and lodge in a tavern till your confinement. We've gold enough.'

'No, not Sarum; somewhere where none know us.' Matilda placed his hands against her belly. 'Feel, 'tis restless now. Let's go to Avalon, to Glastonbury. We'd be safe there. We could wed, an' I'd like to touch the Holy Thorn and drink from Chalice Well for the sake of the child.'

It was a simple suggestion, a hint of peace and an end to travelling. Sampson smiled. 'That's where we'll go. You, Thomas an' I. The rest must fend for themselves.'

'Thomas?'

'He needs help. 'Tis only you an' I who can give it.' Suddenly Sampson whispered: 'Pack the panniers and wake him now.'

'Why?'

'We'll leave now. 'Tis best. I'll saddle the horses. Not even Ned 'll find us come morning.'

Matilda rose, hurriedly packing before waking her brother. Sampson untethered the horses and led them through the grass as Matilda and Thomas crept silently from the fire.

*   *   *

Ned watched them disappear into the darkness before lifting his blanket. Crawling across to Will, he clamped a hand over the

283

potter's mouth and growled: 'They've gone. Trouble 'll find 'em soon enough, an' I reckon they'll be glad of the company when it do.'

Will grinned, glanced round at the sleeping shapes of the other outlaws, then reached for his bow. 'Let's go, my friend.'

Minutes later they had vanished into the night.

CHAPTER TWENTY

Dust, sun and a sky the pellucid blue of a mid-August morning. A clump of willows, like stooped old men in conversation, hunched over a wayside well and drenching those sheltering from the heat in their shade. Men, women and a handful of children; the young dressed like their elders in the broad-brimmed hat and sun-bleached dun-coloured gown of the pilgrim. Some sleeping or breaking fast on bread and cheese, others filling their flagons and washing their feet in the stone trough beside the well.

Few trees broke the monotony of the flat marshlands that bordered the road and this one stand of willows seemed the focus of a world within a world, a magnet which few passed without first pausing in their journeys. Another traveller turned off the track, glancing round at his new companions as he slumped in the shade. Most were like him – foot-sore pilgrims resting for a moment before continuing on towards the holy shrines ahead. But one group of four men and a woman, though dressed as pilgrims, seemed out of place. It was the woman who made them conspicuous. Striking rather than beautiful, she emanated the serenity that betokens the final stages of pregnancy, and her blue eyes, windburned skin and black, braided hair seemed incongruous amongst the dumpy pink-cheeked matrons gathered round her. One other fact made the group stand out, the men were carrying longbows instead of staffs.

After splashing his face with water from the trough, the pilgrim sat down beside them. 'Bound for yonder?' he asked.

'Aye, if we make it,' replied one of the men. 'My mistress will soon be in childbed. The babe may not wait.'

The traveller grinned at the woman. 'You've picked a fine spot to whelp, ma'am. Like every other inn-keeper on the pilgrim-ways those in Glastonbury 'll dilute your ale and double your board if you give 'em the chance. Pilgrims?'

The man nodded. 'Since the Feast of the Nativity we've journeyed to seven holy places to give thanks for being spared the Death. This'll be the last.'

The pilgrim pointed through the trees to where a small chapel bestrode the summit of a conical mound that rose high over the surrounding levels. 'You've two leagues left. For that 'tis the Tor and Saint Michael's church, a beacon for palmers since Saint Joseph himself buried the Holy Grail on Chalice Hill.'

'Is that where you're bound?'

'No, lad. I'm for Corunna and the shrine of Saint James.'

'Lord help 'ee,' growled another of the pilgrims sitting near the well, tapping the scalloped pewter badge on his gown. 'I sailed to Compostella three summers back. Fourteen days at sea. Two score an' ten of us packed in rows below decks like so many herring. Could neither piss nor pray. Might have been Moorish slaves, not God-fearing travellers in search of Our Lord.'

Another pilgrim joined them, proudly indicating the vernicle brooch pinned to his hat brim. 'Damme, man. When I went to Rome we near died . . .'

Sampson smiled as he listened to the pilgrim's account of his journey. As a child he had been happiest sitting unnoticed in the tavern parlour whilst the pilgrims round him exchanged information on routes, shrines and inns. In their company he had been shipwrecked, miraculously healed, a witness to visions, scorched by desert suns. And now, in appearance a pilgrim himself and a month after leaving Sherwood Forest, he was within sight of their destination and sitting beside a Somerset well surrounded by marsh and peat bogs. He turned to Matilda, waiting for her face to betray some sign of the pain that had made them leave the highway.

'Are you ready to go on?'

She nodded, grinning bravely. 'Aye. The sooner we reach the town, the quicker we'll find lodgings.'

Sampson turned to Ned and asked him to saddle the horses. The wrestler chuckled as he did so. 'Now did you regret us tracking 'ee down when we did? 'Tis Ned do this, Will that. You'll be a

286

father soon, and in need of more than a pair of unpaid ostlers.'

'Aye, I'm glad you found us. But I'd a' willingly pole-axed the both of you when you first came a' cantering in our wake.' Sampson frowned as he glanced at Thomas. Yes, he was glad; without them Thomas's silence and self-pity would have driven him mad by now.

Thomas's silence continued as he mounted his horse. During the long ride south he had withdrawn into his shell. Though yet to display any symptoms of having broken-down again, he now inhabited a world whose only outward signs were an expressionless face and the return of both the twitch in his feet and the tic in one eye. Throughout the journey he had ridden in the rear, leaving Sampson to make all decisions and doing only what was asked of him.

After leaving the shade, the five of them joined the peasants, merchants, pilgrims and clerics hurrying to and fro along the raised causeway that cut across the levels towards Glastonbury. It was a desolate and windswept landscape. Behind them lay the limestone folds of the Mendip Hills. Ahead, a whale breaking surface, the Polden Hills shimmered in the haze. Between the two lines of hills the ground lay flat, and the only things to break its emptiness were the Tor, the rooftops of the town huddled beneath it and the square outline of the abbey tower.

'The Isle of Avalon,' murmured Matilda in awe. 'T'was here that King Arthur and his queen died and were buried. Here too that Joseph of Arimathea planted his staff. Now 'tis the Holy Thorn, putting out leaves at Christ-tide when no other tree is in leaf.'

'Would that they'd chosen somewhere else,' complained Ned. 'Every divine an' knight in the land seems to be heading this way.'

'After Crécy the king founded a new order of chivalry in memory of Arthur,' explained Sampson. 'They call it that of the Garter. Now there's not a knight alive who doesn't come here to be blest 'afore lifting his lance.'

'That's as may be,' continued Ned as yet another knight and his page clattered by. 'But I've seen two that I served under during the Fight. The next to pass may have ridden with Fitzwalter or be a monk you robbed.'

Sampson laughed at his fears as they rode on. Occasionally

they passed a field of teazles, their tall flowering heads a brilliant purple in the sun, or withy beds through which lines of women moved waist deep in stagnant, peat-stained water as they slashed at their stems with sickles. Dykes chequered the levels. Once they glimpsed a canopied barge being rowed through the reeds, pennons, bunting and heraldic flags fluttering from its mast. Behind it, its bows level with the bank, a lighter laden with lead was being hauled toward Glastonbury by a string of oxen.

'Mined on Mendip,' said the packman riding beside Sampson. 'Like reddle,' he added, patting the sacks slung across his mule and holding up hands stained red by the ochre which gave the rind of the local Cheddar cheeses its colour. ''Tis the abbot's private waterway. T'was he who ordered it cut and dredged. Makes the church plumper an' us packmen poorer.'

As he spoke the two boats vanished behind another withy-bed. Shortly afterwards they entered the outer bounds of the town, passing a colony of lepers selling basket-ware by the road-side before joining the crowds waiting to squeeze through a toll-gate. 'Remember,' whispered Sampson, 'we carry bows because we're journeymen fletchers on pilgrimage and have brought the staves as a thank-offering.'

His caution was wasted. The porters snatched their pennies without glancing at any of them. Moments later they were being pushed along a narrow, cobbled street lined with inns and lodging-houses. Pilgrims boasting every accent in the land swarmed round them. Brash knights in silk doublets and tight-fitting hosen sauntered by, followed by courtesans in litters or long barrel-shaped carriages arched with painted canvas and pulled by matching horses. Monks peddling relics and badges competed with cheapjacks selling eels from basins. Above their cries friars could be heard chanting their sermons whilst pardon-ers offered indulgences from sins. Beggars and cripples hobbled through the crowd. Wherever he looked Sampson saw those who had come to Glastonbury in hope of a miracle – of having a limb straightened, the sight restored to an eye, the palsy cured. The noise was deafening, and even after leading Matilda into a side-street Sampson had to bellow to be heard.

'We'd best find lodgings.'

'Leave that to me,' cried Ned, joining them. ''Tis worse than Gommorah. I've a notion a little persuasion may be needed 'afore we find a bed. I'll meet you outside the abbey.' He grinned, balled his fists and forced his way towards the nearest inn-yard.

Sampson turned to Matilda. 'We can be wed here.'

'Aye, an' see our first-born baptized on the same day.'

'You sure you're alright?'

She laughed excitedly, clapping her hands together and roguishly kissing his lips. ''Tis magic. I want to go everywhere, do all that's to be done.'

Sampson smiled at her naivety; even now he occasionally forgot that until riding north to Nottingham she had never left the Chase or entered a town. They set off, Will pausing to down a mug of ale in every tavern they passed whilst Thomas brought up the rear. They were soon lost. Streets became alleys festooned with laundry. Alleys turned into courts where back-street hawkers sat filling flasks with a murky water that Sampson knew would later be peddled to the ignorant as having come from the Jordan.

Suddenly they found themselves in a large open space crowded with pilgrims. In its centre was a well, round which a mule slowly circled. As it plodded, a chain of leather buckets rose from the well and tipped a reddish water into a drinking trough. Here the crowd was thickest; for after sipping the water many prostrated themselves in prayer or began intoning psalms. Sampson halted as he heard the shouts of the monk standing on the lip of the well.

'Friends, fellow sinners in Christ!' he was shouting. ''Tis here Saint Joseph buried the Saint Grail! From that time to this a blood-red spring, the blood of Our Saviour himself, has poured forth from the ground! Come! Drink of it! A ha'penny is charged, but which of you would place value on a taste of Our Lord's blood? Here lies the Grail, the platter used by Our Saviour at the Last Supper and into which the blessed Saint Joseph received His life-blood at the Cross . . .!'

Matilda turned to Sampson. 'Can I? For our child.'

'Of course.' Sampson helped her from the saddle and led her to the front of the crowd. The water was chill and brackish, but sipping it Matilda felt more at one with her faith than at any time in her life, of having somehow been strengthened and replenished by Christ himself. As she knelt on the worn cobbles and

289

began reciting the Ave, she suddenly saw Thomas kneeling beside her. Unsure of his mood, she hesitated before reaching out and touching him. He turned towards her, healed, reborn, the very faintest of smiles crinkling his cheeks. Then Sampson knelt on her other side. Content, no longer embittered or haunted by the need to conceal her emotions, she closed her eyes and concentrated on her prayers, praying first for Sampson and her brother and then the child now stirring in her womb. The hour of confinement was close; she knew it, could feel it as surely as she could feel the sun's warmth or the tickle of hair on her brow. Rising to her feet, a sudden tremor of pain stabbed deep in her belly.

Leaving Chalice Well behind them they made their way downhill towards the abbey. Pilgrims thronged round them. The town was steeped in the divine mysteries and despite its noise and bustle, all of them felt humbled by the knowledge that Matilda was to bear her child here, in Glastonbury, the cradle of English christianity. Their awe increased when they first had a clear view of the abbey. For after hurrying past a market cross and entering its grounds through a gate-house it suddenly rose full square in front of them, straddling the surrounding meadows like a stone collosus, its ribbed nave, tapered transepts and soaring tower dwarfing the hordes of pilgrims gathered in its shadow. From high above them bells boomed out over the levels, calling the faithful to prayer.

'T'was here that a wattle church, the first in all England and dedicated to the Virgin Mother, was raised by Saint Joseph and Christ's disciples after the death of Our Saviour,' explained Matilda as they moved closer to the abbey. ''Tis said that no part of the building is free of the bones of the saints. For 'tis here that Saint Patrick, Saint Bridget and Saint Joseph himself were all buried.'

Tethering their horses, they joined the long line of supplicants waiting to enter the Saint Mary Chapel and pray before its shrines. Monks, pardoners and licensed hawkers jostled past them with their wares: votive candles sold by the inch, lead badges stamped with the great seal of the abbey, flasks of consecrated water and wine. Listening to their cries, Will grew angry. ''Tis worse than a market,' he growled. 'Pardoners! Hark at that one.' He indicated a corpulent tonsured cleric weighed down by the string of indulgences hanging round his neck. 'Jus' listen to him! The man's a charlatan!'

'. . . I will, as a special favour,' the pardoner was shouting, 'show you a very holy and goodly relic, which I myself brought wrapped in silks from the Holy Land.' He held up a feather. 'This, friends, is one of the Angel Gabriel's very own wing quills, left behind in the Virgin's chamber after visiting her in Nazareth!'

'Pah! 'Tis a goose feather!' cried Will. 'He'll next be showing us the comb of the cock that crowed at Pilate's or a plank from Noah's ark,' he added as a small crowd gathered round the pardoner to touch, for a fee, the feather and win remission from sin or protection from harm.

Sampson turned away, but wherever he looked he kept glimpsing those who eked out a living by trading on the ignorance of pilgrims: chaplains peddling what were obviously fake relics – a nail from the cross, a twig from the bush in which God spoke to Moses; the bedesmen whose income came from praying for the souls of others; the guides who carried the crippled into the chapel and helped them place broken limbs in the worn holes cut into the sides of the shrines. Even some of the pilgrims had found a way of turning the fear of divine retribution into a source of profit; for a few were professional palmers, hired by the wealthy to win them penance by proxy. Sampson shuffled forward, his eyes still sweeping the crowd . . .

'Oh God!' Suddenly he halted in mid-stride. His face paled, but his eyes stayed fixed on the cleric standing with his retinue of soldiers and monks on the edge of the crowd.

The cleric glanced up. Their eyes locked. For a split-second father and son shared a gaze that denied the existence of those round them. Audley's sallow face and tight, thin lips tensed into a shocked smile. For a moment Sampson thought he might turn away and ignore what he'd seen. Suddenly his smile distorted to rage and Sampson knew he had lost. Reaching for his bow, he moved back through the crowd towards Thomas and Will.

'Audley!' he whispered. 'He's seen me.'

Matilda frowned as she rose on to tip-toe and looked round in search of Sampson. Suddenly she heard someone shout: 'Arrest them! Dead or alive!' and turned in time to see Audley point at Sampson and his bodyguard draw their swords. An instant later a longbow and arrow appeared in Sampson's hands. Matilda screamed. Others joined in. The line of pilgrims dissolved round her. Holding her swollen belly she ran after them, taking cover as Audley's bodyguard surrounded the three fugitives. No one moved: the prior, his men and the outlaws stood frozen like a tableau cut from ice – a tableau which finally melted when Sampson, a grim, set look on his face, lifted his bow at his father and simultaneously tilted his head towards the crowd. Matilda followed his gesture. Ned, his capuchon low over his eyes to avoid being recognized, was pushing his way towards her.

The wrestler wrapped an arm round her as she started crying and Audley shouted: 'Lay down your bow, Hooke. You've no hope of escape.'

Sampson drew back on the string. 'If we die, so will you. I missed you once, but I won't do so again.'

Audley sneered. 'So, after first fleeing the Chase like curs with their tails 'tween their legs you would now stand an' snap. Where's the girl?'

'Beyond harm.'

'But you are not. Nor is Woodward.' Audley smiled. His guard had been reinforced and the three outlaws stood circled by soldiers.

There was a sudden commotion behind them. A moment later a monk wearing the robes of a prior emerged from the front of the crowd. Waving his hands, he shouted: 'In the name of God! Stop!'

Audley turned. 'What do you mean?' he cried angrily.

'As you know, this is hallowed ground, my lord abbot,' explained the prior. 'And all those within its bounds have right of holy sanctuary. No fugitive can be slain or taken from here. To do so would be sacrilege.'

So Audley was now an abbot. Matilda felt her legs weaken and begin trembling beneath her. She could hardly believe what had been said. Nor could Audley. Striding towards his brother monk, he screamed: 'They're outlaws! Common felons who've murdered and robbed and whose right to live has been forfeit by their crimes!'

The prior refused to be silenced. 'As long, my lord, as they remain here they are under the protection of Holy Church and have the right to abjure the realm without let or hindrance from you or anyone else. Order your men to lay down their arms.' He paused, turning to Audley's bodyguard. 'Do as I say. If not you will depart this town having first been excommunicated for sinning against the word of God.' The soldiers, faced with choosing between Audley's anger and being cast out from the church, did not hesitate: one by one they sheathed their swords and shouldered their bows. Ignoring Audley, the prior turned towards the outlaws.

'By command of Walter, Abbot of the Holy Abbey of Glastonbury, I order you to lay down your arms and confess your crimes in God's house before the hour of Vespers. You may remain here for forty days. At the end of that time you will stand at the door of this abbey, bare-headed, bare-foot and wearing only your shirts and publicly proclaim your repentance before the king's coroner. You will then be assigned to a port, to which you will walk, carrying a cross in your hands and going neither to the left nor right of the highway until you reach the seas. There you will take passage, going daily into the tide to your knees until a vessel can be found willing to carry you from this realm. Where you land, you will remain; not setting foot in England without the special grace and pardon of our lord the king.'

For a moment Sampson stood where he was, eyes and arrow both fixed on Audley. Finally he lowered his bow and knelt in front of the prior. Thomas and Will followed his example, leaving Audley to grow hoarse as he continued bellowing at his bodyguard and brother monk. But the soldiers ignored his orders, the prior seemed impervious to his curses, and eventually, as the chattering pilgrims formed into line again and the pedlars picked up their wares, he gathered his robes round his chest and stormed from the abbey precincts. Shortly afterwards, without glancing at Ned and Matilda or even acknowledging their presence, the three outlaws were led away by an escort of unarmed monks.

Ned growled as he watched them go. 'So miracles still happen,' he said, frowning. 'Trouble is, lass, I doan' reckon it'll take Audley forty days to undo that one. Time 'll teach him a way of breaking in and snatching 'em. 'Tis up to us to get to 'em first.'

'But how?' blurted Matilda, fighting against the constant waves of pain that kept flooding through her body. 'Don't you understand, Ned? I'm in childbed, the babe's being born!'

Ned comforted her as he tried to decide what Sampson would have done in his place. 'I've found us lodgings,' he said finally. 'I'll take you there, then return for the horses. There's a fortune in gold on 'em. Like moths to a candle, the clink o' coin should attract some rogue willing to help us.'

★   ★   ★

As if in a dream Sampson stared up at the shadowy, wraith-like face that had loomed out of the darkness a moment earlier. 'But . . .?' A hand stifled his words.

'Ssh. This is Daniel, a local wildfowler.'

'Aye, an' this is a den o' beasts. The guards doan' stand on ceremony. We must move, an' quickly.' Another voice, another face: swarthy, tense, toothless.

The hand lifted from his mouth. Still speechless, he glanced at Ned and the stranger before turning towards the half-open shutters through which they'd appeared. Disbelief muddled his thoughts, leaving him uncertain what to do. Ned told him. 'Rouse Thomas an' Will an' follow us. We've a boat hidden in the marshes.'

Sampson rose from the straw and crept through the darkness, passing the other fugitives sprawled asleep in the sanctuary chamber. Since sitting in the abbey freedstool and confessing his crimes a few hours earlier, his thoughts and mood had been in permanent flux. At first, the enforced separation from Matilda had lowered his spirits: the birth of her child was imminent, she might panic, Audley might order a search for her. But gradually, as his faith in her ability to take care of herself returned, his thoughts shifted to Audley. For the suddenness of the encounter with his father had served to remind him of the promise he had once made Thomas and Matilda. He now knew that the ride north had merely postponed the inevitable; that until Audley lay dead he could make no plans nor be anything but an outlaw. A month of indecision had ended as he lifted his bow. At that moment he had returned to the world he knew best, had become someone whose survival depended on patience, cunning, adapting to change.

After rousing Thomas and Will the four outlaws climbed through the window and stole silently through the shadows, led by Daniel. Creeping through the graveyard to the rear of the chapter house, Sampson heard the distant chanting of monks: Lauds, he decided, and after midnight. Ahead of him the domed outline of the kitchens rose sheer into the night. Its doors were open, and the light from the ovens glinted crimson on the rows of copper pans hanging from its walls. Beyond the kitchens, so high that at first he mistook them for stars, he saw the flicker of torches and heard the faint cries of the pilgrims camped on Weary-all Hill beside the Holy Thorn. He hurried on after the others, scaling a wall and following them through a maze of back-streets and passages before floundering through open fields, sedge and bog to where moonlight glittered on water.

'Ned?' Matilda's voice.

'Aye, 'tis us,' answered Daniel. 'Climb aboard.'

'I need help. I'm in pain. Have you found them?'

'Aye, there 'ere right enough.'

Matilda began crying as Sampson splashed through the water and clambered into the long punt lying amongst the reeds. She was lying in the bottom wrapped in Ned's cloak. He embraced her, felt her belly pulse gently against the flat of his hand. 'We're safe,' he whispered. 'Now relax and try and breathe as evenly as you can.'

She smiled, moon and stars mirrored in the whites' of her eyes. 'Thank God you've come. I'm not sure I could 'a done it without you. I was frightened . . .'

'There's no need to speak.' He turned to Ned as Daniel pushed the punt clear of the reeds and began poling it through the water. 'Where's he taking us?'

'Deep into the marsh where none 'll find us. 'Tis a lost village. Few know of it. According to Daniel some say t'was Camelot, others the holy place of the Druid tribes.'

'Is he to be trusted?' Sampson glanced at the silent figure of the wildfowler as he punted them through the reeds.

'Lord help him if he ain't. So far he's proved his worth. We've no choice but to take the chance. If not . . .' Ned reached for the knife at his waist.

'Where did you find him?'

'He found us. He was taking some fowl to the cellarer in the abbey kitchens when Audley spotted 'ee. He noticed you move away from Matilda. He followed us to our lodgings.'

'Why's he helping us?'

'For the score of gold nobles I've promised him for taking us to safety. This boat's his home. He snares an' nets fowl for a living and makes what extra he can helping fugitives flee sanctuary.'

The outlaws lapsed into silence. Sampson crouched in the bottom of the punt and comforted Matilda, leaving the others to take turns with a pole. They slid on through the night along a broad dyke that ran straight and still into the darkness. Peat bogs rose above them. Once they heard the splash of an otter. Occasionally a bittern boomed from amongst the reeds or they glimpsed cattle with gleaming nostrils and faces made monstrous by the angle staring down at them from the levels. The punt made hardly a sound. Its long pitch-daubed hull skimmed the stagnant water and only the monotonous splash of the pole marked its passage through the night. Matilda began whimpering as the pause between contractions lessened and the pain increased. Daniel remained silent. Standing in the stern, arms rising and falling in perfect rhythm as he lifted his pole from the water and thrust it deep into the mud, it was impossible to see more than his silhouette. Watching him, Thomas felt that they owed their rescue to a phantom, a ghost who would vanish from their lives as abruptly as he had entered them.

Eventually he guided the punt into a warren of narrow channels that cut through the marsh. At times the water grew so shallow that all but Matilda had to jump overboard and push it over bog or clear a path through the lush skeins of reed that blocked their route. At others they found themselves gliding across open lakes where great flocks of duck and greylag rose honking into the sky. Finally, after half-carrying the punt up a creek humped with mud banks, the channel tapered to a halt. The ground shelved upward. Giant sedge, its roots deep in the peat, rustled round them as they lifted Matilda from the punt.

Daniel explained where they were. 'There's a timber trackway that leads back through the reeds to an isle. 'Tis mud an' silt, but firm enough. Some winters it floods and you wouldn't know it was here. You'll find the bones of some hovels. One's still standing. I'll be back come daybreak with food.'

'Don't you want payment?' asked Thomas as he and Will lifted the panniers out of the punt.

'Aye, but later. What can a man do with gold when he's nettin'' goose? I doan' need to trust 'ee. There's no way off here but boat, and that's leaving with me, now.' And then he was gone, vanishing into the darkness.

They watched him go, each aware of their isolation and dependence on him. 'He'll be back, if only for these,' muttered Ned, slinging a set of panniers over his shoulders and setting off through the reed. The others followed him, Matilda at the rear with an arm round Sampson and Thomas. They found the track-way. It had been built on piles and raised above the marsh, water lapped at its sides. After fifty paces it gave way to an open expanse of knee-deep grass smothered with sedge and weed. Ned stumbled over a post, then, through the darkness, he glimpsed the round shape of a small hut thatched with loose bundles of reed standing out against the sky.

The hut was dry and weatherproof. After carrying Matilda through its entrance Thomas and Sampson carefully lowered her to the floor. Suddenly she cried out and began drumming her arms against the mud. Sampson turned to Thomas. 'I want hot water, blankets and firewood. Hurry! Another hour an' she'd 'a had the babe in the boat.'

Ned appeared in the doorway. 'I've done some quick scoutin'. 'Tis marsh for miles. Let's hope Daniel knows where we are.'

'I've an inkling that not even the Almighty knows that,' grumbled Will, his face scratched and torn by the reeds.

'Morning 'll tell us,' said Sampson.

Matilda gripped his hands. 'By then you'll be a father.'

*   *   *

Sampson's son was born shortly after dawn. When he finally allowed the others to enter the hut it lay silent in Matilda's arms with a pensive, almost inquisitive expression on its face and with its blue eyes wide open. She lifted it up to the light.

'This,' she whispered, 'is Hereward.'

Will approved. 'A good name, an' fittin' for an outlaw's bairn. The Wake himself, the greatest of all of us, was called Hereward.'

'Aye, an' he spent his days in fens such as these,' added Ned.

Thomas said nothing as he stooped to kiss the child. His eyes met Matilda's, and he knew at once that it bore the name, not of an outlaw, but of their father: the father they had both loved and both watched die. He smiled and wiped the tears from his face. Will slapped his back.

'Come on, lad. Let's leave 'em be and take a look at this isle o' ours. I reckon all three of 'em need a nap.'

They began exploring their hiding-place. It was small, no more than an acre, but wherever they walked they kept stumbling across circles of broken post ends protruding from the silt. Flood water had scoured the floor of one hovel, leaving a compacted clay base in which the rim of a bowl lay embedded. Thomas prised it loose with his knife, finally lifting out a shallow bowl hammered out of bronze. Elsewhere they found shards of pottery, shaped pieces of flint, a weaving comb carved from an antler and the corroded remains of what had once been a brooch.

'What in Hell made anyone want to settle here?' said Will, gazing round at an unbroken horizon of reed.

''Tis a village on a lake,' said Will.

'Perhaps it really was King Arthur's Camelot,' suggested Thomas.

Will grunted. 'I always thought them knights were fools. Now I'm sure. None but the demented would 'a dwelt here.'

'Nay, t'aint't Camelot,' said Will. 'I reckon 'tis the place of the Druids and sprites.'

'In which case I'll not rest happy till we're safe on dry land an' I've a fistful o' ale to hold . . . Lord alive! Here comes one of 'em now!' Will's mouth gaped open as he spotted Daniel trampling through the reeds.

Having only seen him by night, none but Ned were prepared for the creature that finally emerged. His features were unremarkable; squat and bow-legged, a carbuncled nose and a ringed ear were the only eccentricities that gave character to his face. But his dress was extraordinary. His jerkin was made entirely from goose skins, sewn together and then reversed, and his boots consisted of a pair of their necks, turned inside out, stitched up at one end and then stretched. Will gawped at him in amazement.

'Paste a pair o' wings an' webbed feet on 'ee an' I reckon you'd be fit for the pot.'

'Scorn if you must,' said the wildfowler, dropping a goose and a brace of teal at their feet, 'but you'll not find better cloth than this on a tailor's shelves.' He patted the hard blubber of his

298

jerkin. 'Waterproof, see. An' with a lining of down.' He grinned. 'The babe been born?'

Thomas told him.

'A man-child, eh. An' the first to 'a been hatched on here for many a season.' Daniel frowned as he saw smoke rising from the fire outside the hut. 'Best damp that down as soon as we've eaten. Makes folk curious. There's others like I, fisher folk as well as fowlers. There's a small hamlet not a mile across the flats.'

Sampson joined them by the fire as they spitted and cooked the duck. As they ate Daniel told them that after lifting his snares he'd paid a brief visit to Glastonbury. 'There's more soldiers than pilgrims in town this morning. Audley's been joined by Lord Fitzwalter. They've ordered every lodging-house and hospice to be searched an' set-up road blocks on the tracks leading out of town.'

'Are we safe here?' asked Sampson.

'For a week or so, no longer. Others know of this place. Someone 'll land here given time.'

Sampson glanced at Thomas. 'In a week Matilda will be strong enough to travel. We'll leave then.'

'Where shall we go? We've no horses.'

'We've the money to buy more.'

'I'll do that for 'ee,' offered Daniel. 'I know a dealer in nags who doan' ask questions.'

'Good.' Sampson paused. 'We'll go to Sarum. If Audley's now an abbot it must be of Sarum. 'Tis the last place they'll think of looking for us. Until then we're in your hands, Daniel.'

'I'll not let 'ee down.'

Thomas frowned. 'Why are you helping us? Until yesterday we were strangers to you.'

The wildfowler shook his head. 'Not so. You're outlaws. I've done the same for others 'afore 'ee and, like it or not, you've all been branded by the same iron. Anyway, twenty nobles is a fortune to the likes of I.' Needing time to match his answer to the words he wanted, he paused for a moment. 'I'm a hunter. I know what it means to be hunted.' He lifted the dead goose lying beside him. 'See this? To you 'tis jus' a bird. But to me 'tis all I've got. I loves 'em like the maid her babe. I can talk to 'em, I wear 'em, eat 'em, sell 'em an' share the flats with 'em. I know how they feel, see: me being the hunter an' them the hunted. There, that's the best I can say. Words doan' come easy to I.'

Unknown to Sampson, Matilda was awake and had heard him mention Audley. Tears brimmed in her eyes as she hugged her son to her breast. Audley, always Audley. Wherever they went and whatever they did, that one word followed in their wake like a shadow that could be ignored and forgotten but seemed incapable of exorcism.

When they left the island a week later those same thoughts returned to her. The horses were waiting for them in a tumble-down grange on the edge of the levels. As she climbed into the saddle and wrapped Hereward in her cloak, she heard Sampson say: 'And now for Audley. 'Tis our turn to play the huntsman.' She glanced back at Daniel: the innocent who understood what it meant to be stalked. She turned: a woman in a man's world who had spent the last week nurturing one whilst its father plotted the death of another. Suddenly she sensed that the end was close and began trembling. One question remained unanswered: were those who rode beside her the hunters, or were they the hunted?

CHAPTER TWENTY-ONE

The chamberlain opened another door and slapped the dust from his fingers. 'It seems certain she died in the Death,' he went on. 'She's not listed in the burial rolls, but they're incomplete. Many threw themselves into the pits or fled the city before dying. Dark and fearful days. But now, thanks to God's mercy, behind us. By her will the tavern was left to her sole heir, her son Sampson. However, I regret to say – for such men bring no credit to Sarum – that Sampson Hooke is a notorious outlaw with a price on his head. Under the king's law the goods and property of all fugitives are forfeit to the crown. In this instance the mayor's office is acting as vendor . . .'

'But can we purchase it, your honour?' Will glanced at Ned as he spoke; a Ned almost unrecognizable with his beard neatly trimmed and dressed in new hosen and a broadcloth doublet.

'Of course.' As if creating the chance to retract his words with only a gesture, the chamberlain lifted a finger and added: 'There's one final detail to be settled . . .'

'You said four hundred marks. We've got it,' replied Will.

The offer was acknowledged by raised eyebrows and a suspicious stare. ''Tis a lot of money for a potter and wrestler . . .'

Will had anticipated the question. 'We're both freemen, your honour. ''Tis a lifetime's savings. I've long had a hankerin' to live in Sarum. Ned here was given bounty money when he stopped fisticuffin' for my lord Bishop of Winchester.'

The mention of someone as influential as Bishop Edendon seemed to placate the chamberlain. The wariness left his face to be replaced by an agreeable smile. 'Excellent. Sarum needs new blood to replace those who fell in the plague. You must forgive my caution; rogues abound. As to this tavern, the fabric is sound enough, but the cellars are empty and, as we observed downstairs in the parlour, many of the rooms have been looted.'

'With so much to be done, can we lodge here and make a start on the work?' asked Ned as they climbed another flight of stairs and peered into the garrets.

'Indeed you may, sir. I've the keys on me. The license to trade is still binding and the sale should be sealed within the week.' The chamberlain took a parchment roll from under his arm, spread it open on a table and dipped a quill into the ink-well hanging from his scrip. 'Now, if you'd oblige by signing or making your marks here . . . and here. Excellent.' He patted the wet ink with his kerchief, rolled up the parchment and began the descent to the kitchens – his business concluded. Minutes later, a portly figure in the ermine robes of his office, he waddled under the courtyard arch and vanished into the market day crowds.

Will grinned. 'Excellent,' he said, mimicking the chamberlain.

'An' thank the Lord for it. Come on.' Ned hurried across the yard and entered the stables. He whistled. A moment later three heads emerged from the hay piled high at one end. 'Recognize this?' he shouted, holding up a large bronze key as Sampson, Matilda and Thomas brushed hay from their hair and climbed down from the rick.

Sampson took the key and placed it flat in one hand. 'Aye, the parlour door.' He gave a wistful smile as memory flooded back. 'An' 'tis yours now.'

'No, Sampson,' replied Ned. ''Tis yours by rights, an' we'll not part with a penny unless you consent.'

Sampson's eyes skated the empty stalls, Mervyn's sword, the spear-head that had blinded him at Bannockburn. He placed an arm round Matilda. 'Even as a child I never wanted to play the taverner. Nor do I now. I'm an outlaw. One day I hope to practice as a physician again.' He tossed the key to Ned. 'No, 'tis yours. And there's no two men in the land I'd rather owned it than you.'

But when he entered the kitchens nostalgia caught up with him. He sat where he had always sat – in front of the fireplace with its now rusted spits and broken dog-wheel. Yet the sense of distance between the present and his last memories of the room seemed immeasurable. The kitchens, once loud with female voices, the smells of burnt fat and damp washing, symbolized more than anywhere else in the tavern the apron-strings he had cut when becoming apprenticed to Buckle. Buckle; even he had receded so far into the past that his name had the sound of a stranger's. He looked round to where he had sat working on his preventive for the plague when last in the tavern. The faces of his mother and Beatrix rose before his eyes. He smiled gratefully when Matilda, sensing his melancholy, distracted him from his thoughts by asking what they should do next.

'Hunt Audley,' replied Thomas. It was as simple as that. He was an outlaw, Audley had made him one; no revenge could be sweeter.

'And what of me an' Hereward?' retorted Matilda sharply. 'What'll happen to us when you're being hounded for his murder?'

Sampson quickly calmed her. 'We'll leave him be for the moment. He may not have left Glastonbury yet. But if he has, he'll be well guarded. He's Abbot Roger of Sarum now, remember. A man of consequence with a mansion in the Close and a seat on the chapter. God, to think I'm an abbot's bastard!'

'But he doesn't know we're here,' persisted Thomas. 'And now Ned an' Will own the tavern we can leave our lodgings and hide in the attics.'

'Is that safe?' asked Matilda.

Sampson shrugged. 'Why not? To everyone in Sarum Will's a potter and Ned a wrestler. 'Tis only me they'll recognize. We'll be safe enough here until after . . .' He stopped, silenced by uncertainty. 'We must get word to Joshuah, let him know we've returned.'

Thomas tightened his leggings, then rose to his feet. 'I intend finding Audley.'

*　　　*　　　*

He did so on the following day. It was late afternoon, and the wind blowing across the market place flattened the smoke as it rose from the louvres and chimney-tops on the surrounding tenements. The women's whimpels and the market stall awnings flapped in the gusts. A hog scavenged through the refuse, cats stalked starlings, the nut-sellers at the bottom of Oatmeal Row sat huddled beneath sacks as the wind rounded the end of the row and tugged at the baskets of filberts and walnuts hanging from their nut-hooks. The final hours of a September day: one during which Thomas had entered the Close and found Audley's mansion. Two armed guards had stood at the gate, he had seen others patrolling the garden that ran down to the Avon at its rear. But of its master there had been no sign. Only one man had approached the house as he watched it: a stooped, white-haired ancient dressed in mendicant rags. Thomas had not spared him a second glance. But now, wandering idly across the market place, the beggar began to nag at his thoughts. His manner, gait, the arrogance with which he had brushed aside the guards but stroked not struck the door knocker – all were familiar. A chord had been struck, but with a lightness of touch so delicate he barely noticed it. And then the thought left him as he suddenly heard a voice cry: 'Oyez! Oyez! Clear the street for Abbot Roger of Sarum! Make way!'

Pulling his hood low over his brow he joined the small crowd that gathered whenever any of the cathedral dignitaries moved in procession with his retinue through the streets. But the crowd watched in silence: little love was lost between the townsfolk and their spiritual shepherds. Thomas peered over the heads of those in front of him. A beadle carrying a mace strode by followed by a monk swinging a censer, and then he saw him: the snake-like green eyes, the long ashen face enclosed by a gris-lined cowl, the simple gown of the Benedictines replaced by robes embroidered with cloth of gold crosses on a background of weld. He was lying propped against a bolster on a canopied litter flanked by soldiers, chaplains, monks and his household servants. A steward carrying wine and a dish of sweetmeats hovered beside him, whilst a monk read aloud from a Book of Hours. Staring at him, Thomas was reminded of a pampered cat. As he passed he lifted a bejewelled hand and smiled at the crowd. It was a disdainful smile; unnatural, measured, a subtle reminder of the rewards of success and of the gulf between an abbot and the rest of humanity. Thomas followed the procession for a while, only hurrying back to the tavern, heart pounding against his chest, when it reached the North Gate of the Close.

Sampson and Matilda had spent the afternoon alone with Hereward in their attic room in the tavern, making love for the first time since before his birth with a languor and gentleness so perfect that only the cries of the carpenters at work on the floor below finally returned them to the present. They drew apart, lying silent and side by side on their pallet. Sunlight filled the room, brindling Matilda's skin when she rose and picked Hereward from his cradle. Sampson watched her. Her breasts were heavy with milk, but the rest of her body felt lean and supple when she lay down again, lifted her head on to his chest and locked a leg round his. Her hair streamed black across his belly. Suddenly she said: 'You and Thomas won't leave Sarum till he's dead, will you?'

'No.'

'He's your father, your own kin.'

'That makes no difference.'

'And afterwards . . .?'

'We've gold a plenty. We'll go to London, somewhere where no one knows who we are. Become as other people.'

'And be wed?'

'Aye, and that.' Sampson paused. He could feel a tiny finger trying to grasp a toe. 'By the time Hereward's a man those who've hunted us – Audley, Swayne, Fitzwalter, even the king – will all be dead.'

'But they're alive now. And searching for us. Have you forgotten what Joshuah told Will yesterday?'

'So Fitzwalter's convinced we're in Sarum because we were spotted crossing the Plain. It means nothing. We could have returned to the Chase, travelled east or taken ship for Flanders.'

Matilda rose to her haunches and flicked her hair over one shoulder. 'But we didn't. We came here. And this morning were woken by a column of soldiers entering the city.'

'Stop it!'

'Why? Are you afraid of hearing the truth?'

Sampson stood, angrily pulling on his doublet. 'We'll get him. And soon. After that we'll have peace.'

'Aye, the peace of the grave,' retorted Matilda scathingly.

The sudden shouting woke Hereward. Sampson ignored his

cries. 'You're a woman. You'll do as I say and go where I order.'

'You're scared, Sampson; so scared you won't even admit it. Threatening me won't make you a valiant.'

'Get dressed, woman! You're a shard-born sorcerer's daughter, a country serf. I'm your lord and you'll speak when ordered.'

Matilda smiled palely. 'Sometimes you sound like Audley.'

'I'm his son, aren't I?'

'Aye, you're his bastard alright. An' try not to forget it when he lies dead at your feet. We're not wed yet, and may never be. You don't own me, nor will you when we're wed.'

'I thought you loved me?'

'I do. But I hate what Audley is doing to you. You're changing, Sampson, and soon you may cease being the man I fell in love with. Here, this afternoon, I gave you my body. Demand my soul as well and you may lose what you have . . .!'

*　　　*　　　*

Such arguments were rare and ended, as this one did, in tears and protestations of love. Matilda had lost her temper; partly out of frustration, partly because anger was the only weapon she could use to make Sampson realize what was happening to him. But Sampson's anger ran deeper, for it defined a change that had come over him since returning to Salisbury. His father had become an obsession, and without knowing it Matilda had touched on the riddle that vexed him the most. Audley was evil, but had he, his son, inherited some part of his character? Would killing him be proof that he had, or could he honestly justify it before God as an act of reprisal for the suffering he had caused?

Such were the questions that troubled his thoughts when the four outlaws and Matilda gathered in the kitchens later that evening. A fire was blazing, a leg of pork spat fat from the spit. Ned and Will were in a jovial mood; the deed of sale had been sealed, the tavern was theirs. But Thomas's initial excitement at seeing Audley had turned to rage.

'If I'd had my bow he'd be dead,' he said suddenly.

'An' so would you,' added Ned.

Sampson rapped a fist against the table, forcing himself to regard Audley with a surgeon's detachment. 'We now know where he lives. How do we reach him?'

'Attack the house at night,' suggested Thomas.

'The Close is walled, the gates close at curfew.'

'Ambush him.'

'In a city? No . . .' Sampson paused. 'He's well guarded. We must think of a means of destroying him that doesn't depend on the bow.' He rose and began pacing the flags. Suddenly he snapped his fingers. 'I've the answer. Do you remember Robin telling us he'd once written a ballad intended to dissuade the sheriff and his men from entering Sherwood Forest? We'll do likewise. But instead of scribing it about ourselves we'll write it about Audley, beginning with my birth and his attempt to poison Buckle. We'll dress as troubadors and sing it in the taverns. Other minstrels may hear it. They'll start singing it. The story will spread. It'll reach Audley. It may panic him, perhaps even lead to his dismissal from office.' He hurried over to the dresser, returning with quills and paper. 'We'll call it . . . the Ballad of the Infamous Prior.'

Matilda had been watching him whilst he spoke. His eyes had brightened. He seemed oblivious to her concern, to have become someone to whom plotting ruin was part jest, part cunning and part sport. Suddenly frightened, she turned away and lifted Hereward to her face.

*   *   *

Plucking at the lyre on his lap, Sampson gazed down from the gallery of the Old George at the crowds in the parlour below. Boisterous and rowdy, most were tossing bones to their dogs or sloshing ale over one another. Above the noise he could hear Thomas shuffling nervously beside him. 'Do you think they'll hear us?' he shouted.

'God help 'em if they do, you've the croak of a frog. As for this . . .' Thomas stared glumly at his harp. 'The strings might make snares, but I'll be damned if they'll make music.'

Sampson smiled. ''Tis the words that matter, not how we shape 'em.' Distracted by laughter, he looked down at the antics of the jester entertaining the crowd. He was running along the tops of the tables, bells jangling, grinning inanely and rolling his eyes as he poked his wand at the breasts of the parlour maids. Eventually he lost his balance and tumbled headlong to the rushes. Climbing to his feet, he waved his wand at the gallery and announced the presence of two minstrels.

Sampson blushed, Thomas's feet began twitching as the crowd turned towards them and waited for them to strike up a tune. 'Remember,' whispered Sampson, 'we play it fast and flee as soon as 'tis done.' Thomas nodded and placed his fingers against the harp strings as beside him he heard Sampson cry: 'Ladies, revellers, men of Sarum! The Ballad of the Infamous Prior!' An instant later, their feet tapping, their voices raucous but loud, they began singing:

> There once was a monk named Audley, Brother Roger was his name.
> And though he wore a habit, lechery was his game.
> He lay with wenches, one, two, three, come a' tumblin' in the hay.
> Slip your gown my pretty lass, please lass now don't delay.
>
> No, don't go away, keep your pence, there's much more tale to tell.
> For the prior may be an abbot now, but he'll end his days in Hell!
>
> Many years ago in Sarum, the dust from his feet he shook.
> Taking for his lodgings in the tavern of the Widow Hooke.
> There he courted her with flattery, with the Book, God's word and prayer.
> Oh, widow woman in your mourning robes, 'tis you he would ensnare.'
>
> No, don't go away, keep your pence, for there's much more tale to tell.
> For the prior may be an abbot now, but he'll end his days in Hell!
>
> Aye, he wooed, begged and pleaded, though the widow was full of woe.
> And friends must we needs tell 'ee, her belly it did grow.
> The months went by as months they do, from numbers one to nine.
> An' the widow bore a bastard boy when finally t'was her time.

And so they went on as the crowd began stamping in time to the tune. Some started jeering whenever Audley was mentioned, others banged their mugs against the tables and joined in on the chorus. Thomas and Sampson soon gave up any pretence of playing their instruments, but their gruff voices found pitch as verse followed verse and the story gradually unfolded. They sung of the meeting between Audley and Sampson, the attempt to poison Buckle and Sampson's flight to the Chase, their early ambushes, the whipping of Matilda, the deaths of Alice, Hereward and Widow Hooke and the growth of the outlaw band; concluding by singing:

And must sinners go unpunished, and the innocent be wronged?
Aye, that's what we would ask of thee at the ending of our song.
For Audley he walks free an' bold but the outlawed can only hope,
That they won't hang from the gallows high and the Devil be spared the rope!
Drink deep, my friends, an' toss us your pence for there's no more tale to tell.
For the prior may be an abbot now, but he'll end his days in Hell!

As they finished both minstrels were bombarded with pennies. They bowed, fumbled for some of the coins, lifted their instruments and descended into the parlour. From all sides they could hear cheers and the banging of mugs and trenchers. The crowd's response, mingled with demands that they repeat the ballad, delighted but worried Sampson. He could see two soldiers sitting staring at him from the corner. 'There's trouble astir,' he said to Thomas as they jostled towards the door. 'We'd best be out o' here 'afore anyone starts questioning us.'

Reaching the door, they found the landlord barring their exit. 'Come now,' he cried. 'They're callin' for more.'

Sampson shifted uneasily, his eyes still fixed on the soldiers. 'We've a night's journey ahead. We're due in Winchester on the morrow,' he lied.

The landlord glanced at Thomas's fingers. Though bruised

and swollen by his attempt to master the harp, they lacked the calluses and stubby squared off nails of the travelling minstrel. 'T'was a fine ballad, an' true I'm thinkin',' he growled finally. 'But Abbot Roger won't take too kindly to it. I doan' suppose either Woodward or Hooke could 'a had a hand in the making of it?'

Sampson laughed. 'No. 'Tis said they've disappeared. Anyway, they're too busy plunderin' the Chase to have time for scribing ballads.'

The landlord tilted his head toward the soldiers. 'Swayne's men. Did you know that a reward's been posted for Woodward and Hooke, dead or alive? Some say they're here in the city.' He paused and stepped aside. 'If I was who I think you is I'd be twenty leagues from Sarum come dawn.'

The two outlaws thanked him for his advice and hurried into the street. It was dark outside. Crossing New Canal they turned towards the tavern. Suddenly they heard footsteps behind them. They stopped, melting into the shadows as Thomas lifted his knife from its sheath and a hooded minstrel carrying a harp over his shoulder loomed out of the darkness.

Seeing the glint of steel, he halted and murmured: 'Put it away, friend. I mean no harm.'

'What do you want?' demanded Thomas.

''Tis strange troubadors who can neither sing nor pluck a string.'

'Meaning?'

The stranger smiled. 'I'd like the words to your ballad. I'll sing it, have no fear of that. But I'll sing it where the men who matter will hear it. What's more I'll do it justice.'

Sampson hesitated, then drew a sheet of parchment from his scrip and handed it to the stranger.

The minstrel took it. 'Thank 'ee. I'll get a scrivener to make copies for others. Give me a week an' I'll have every songster in Sarum chanting it.'

'Why are you doing this?'

'Afore the Death I used to travel the fairs with a minstrel called Gilbert. A kindly man, and one who fell into good company after his missus an' littl'uns passed on.'

'Gilbert's dead, he died on the ride north,' said Sampson without thinking.

310

The minstrel grinned. 'I know. God keep you Master Hooke, and you Thomas Woodward.' He turned and vanished into the night.

*　　*　　*

Two days later Ned returned to the tavern with the news that all had been waiting for: he had seen a large crowd gathered round a minstrel singing the ballad outside the Guildhall.

That evening he and Will visited every pothouse in the city: in over a score the resident minstrels had added it to their repertoire. By the end of the week the number had doubled. On the following day Matilda heard it being sung outside the North Gate of the Close. 'I saw Audley as well,' she announced. 'Folk started jeering as he passed. Surely he realizes 'tis because of the ballad? What do you think he'll do?'

'Ignore it. He's no other choice,' replied Sampson.

Thomas was not so certain. 'If mud's thrown, some sticks. It might easily cause him to panic.'

'No, not Audley.'

'If only something would happen,' said Thomas impatiently.

As if in answer to his request Swayne ordered a search for the two minstrels who had first sung the ballad, a search that quickly assumed the character of an organized man-hunt. Squads of soldiers replaced the porters at every bridge, gate and exit from the city. Faces were scrutinized, questions asked, licences to trade were carefully examined. Many of those staying in taverns and lodging houses were roused from bed and questioned. One morning Audley was pelted with refuse when on his way to celebrate Mass in one of the city churches. His body guard was strengthened, the ballad was banned and a half-hearted attempt was made to expel all minstrels caught singing it from the city. These precautions added to Thomas's impatience. As September continued and the first grain carts trundled through the streets towards the corn market, Matilda became irritable, Sampson tense – a coiled spring as likely to snap as function when the need arose. Ned and Will re-opened the tavern, and, after a nocturnal visit by the watch, it was agreed that it was now too hazardous for all five of them to remain in the building. Thomas disguised himself as a journeyman fletcher and took a room in a slum alehouse less likely to be searched. Sampson and Matilda dressed as pilgrims and moved into a small hospice near the Avon. To Matilda it seemed that they were no nearer their goal than on arrival, and when the five of them met all attempts to plan ahead were frustrated by their ignorance of Audley's reaction to the ballad. But it was still being sung, and their spirits lifted when late one afternoon Thomas joined his sister and Sampson in the tavern stables and announced that the Prince of Wales, accompanied by the Earl of Warwick, had arrived in the city.

'They've heard it. Both of them. By Poultry Cross. I was there,' he blurted, momentarily too excited to marshal his thoughts. 'Have you been into the market place today?' he added. ''Tis said some fool intends flying from the roof of the cathedral. Half the city's headed for the Close.'

'Let's go and watch,' begged Matilda. 'I'm sick of sitting cooped up in that hospice like a broody on clay eggs. No one'll spare us a glance. They'll be too busy watching.'

Sampson gave in to her pleas. Leaving the stables they joined the crowds pouring through the East Gate of the Close. To their left, jutting high over a line of houses, the cathedral nave and its still uncompleted spire soared upward into the evening sky. In front of them, beyond the belfry and those gathered on the grass, lay a walk bordered by elms and the stone mansions of the dean and chapter. Amongst them was Audley's. Sampson stared at it. Two soldiers lolled against the gate, the shutters were drawn. Matilda tugged at his wrist.

'Look!' she cried.

He followed her outstretched finger. Far above him and etched in silhouette against a mackerel sky, he could see a lone figure standing on the parapet that overlooked the west front of the cathedral. The last of the sunlight refracted into gold as it struck the stained glass windows beneath him. Inside the cathedral the choristers were chanting Vespers. They were singing unaccompanied and their unbroken voices could be heard above the shouts of the hawkers. The grip on Sampson's wrist tightened.

'He's got his wings on!' cried Matilda.

He had strapped them to his arms. They had been made out of canvas stretched over wooden struts and even from below

312

Sampson could see that their under-surfaces had been primed with a painting depicting ruby-cheeked cherubims playing shawms and trumpets. Suddenly Thomas pointed towards the parapet and cried:

'I've seen him 'afore!'

'When?' snapped Sampson.

'On the day I first came to the Close. He entered Audley's house.'

'Are you sure?'

'Aye. He was wearing the same rags. I thought t'was a beggar. But even then I could 'a sworn he an' I had met!'

Both men shielded their eyes against the sun and peered upward. A moment later the miniature figure stepped forward to the edge of the parapet and raised his wings.

'Oh God!' Sampson reeled from Matilda's grip as if struck by a blow. For an instant the one word stayed stuck in his throat like a bone. 'Buckle!' he finally whispered.

Even as he spoke a sudden hush fell over the crowd. Some crossed themselves, others muttered the Paternoster. But Sampson ignored their prayers as he struggled to clear his brain and comprehend what was happening. Buckle's flight was doomed. But what was he doing here? What reason had he for plunging to his own death? Then it was too late for questions.

Buckle's gown billowed round his head as he jumped and began falling. For a split-second he was flying. Then his arms rose parallel above his head and his wings crumpled, the canvas shredding as the struts snapped. Women and children screamed. He cartwheeled in mid-air, bounced into a buttress and hit the ground with a dull thump. At this moment the choir, unaware that he had jumped, broke into plainsong, filling both cathedral and Close with an overlapping flow of descants and harmonies conceived in praise of God. Then all was pandemonium and screaming as the crowd surged forward. Horror-struck and confused, Sampson hesitated before ordering Matilda to return to the tavern. Her eyes widened with fear. Then she turned as, followed by Thomas, Sampson pushed his way through the crowd to the spot where Buckle had fallen.

The battered, lifeless body lay face up, eyes open, motionless save for the tiny trickle of blood dripping from his chin into the green of the grass. The crowd circled him. A monk was rummaging through his clothes for some clue to his identity whilst the surrounding priests prayed for the salvation of his soul. Sampson turned to Thomas and whispered hoarsely:

'Why? Why did he do it?'

'He was mad. Capable of anything.'

'Flight? No, everything he did had a reason.' Sampson buried his face in his hands. He stood there for a moment, eyes closed, before lowering his hands and lifting his head. Audley's mansion. The guards had abandoned it. It stood deserted, deep in shadow; raised by the dead, home to the living – thick, cold stone. He shivered, suddenly knowing it contained the answers he was searching for.

'Audley,' he murmured. ''Tis because of Audley he jumped.'

Turning his back on his master's corpse, he forced his way through the crowd. He began running. Thomas caught up with him as he reached the house. The front door was bolted. They slipped along the drive leading to the stables at the rear, trying each door as they went. The third opened. Seconds later they were safely inside a small buttery listening to the giggles of a maid in the neighbouring room. Leaving their refuge, they crept along a passage into a large, open, empty hall that stretched the height of the house and ended in a vaulted ceiling. A fire was burning in the central grate. Thomas felt the dry prickle of sweat against his skin as Sampson placed a foot on the staircase that swept upward to the gallery. To steady his nerves, he unslung his bow and fitted a string to the stave notches before fumbling for an arrow and following Sampson. Laughter, then a whistle. The two outlaws ducked behind the balustrade as a scullion entered the hall and tossed more logs on to the fire. A woman's voice, coy but teasing, called out to him. Chuckling, he started loosening his jerkin before disappearing again. Sampson rose and tip-toed across the gallery to the line of doors on its far side. Heart racing, every muscle tight and taut and ready to uncoil, he raised the latch on the first: a small chapel, musty, empty, the alter candles burning bright in the gloom. The second and third opened into deserted bedchambers. Two doors left; one of them studded oak inlaid with a crucifix. He pressed himself flat against the wall. Thomas raised his bow. He nodded and kicked open the door. Thomas dived through it, rolling sideways before springing to the crouch and circling the emptiness with his bow.

Silence. The loud buzz of a fly beating against closed shutters. A tapestry on one wall. A chest, rosary beads, a tester bed, the hairless, naked foot hanging twisted over the rim of the bed . . .

The door clicked shut behind him. He turned. The blood had drained from Sampson's face and he was shuffling towards the bed with the expressionless eyes and outstretched arms of a somnambulist returning to his slumbers. Thomas turned again, his eyes following the line of the foot to where it vanished beneath a quilt and reappeared as the blanched, bloodless face lying motionless at the head of the bed.

'Audley!' he cried.

Sampson seemed not to hear him. He was staring at the two lines of verse scrawled in scarlet ink across the far wall. Beneath them, in a rough and spidery scribble, someone had written his own signature and drawn a large cross followed by the words, 'Thomas Woodward, his mark.' His voice faltering, he read out the couplet: 'Drink deep, my friends, and suck him dry, for there's no more tale to tell. The prior may be an abbot now, but he'll end his days in Hell,' and then, with a chilling premonition of what he was to find, he approached the bed and pulled the quilt from his father. He cried out, collapsing to the floor as the vomit welled from his throat and vertigo filled his head.

Thomas rushed forward. 'What is it? Oh my God . . .'

Someone had tied Audley to the bed. He was naked. Scores of bloated leeches teemed across his albino body. Some lay in clusters round the open wounds on his chest and arms, their jaws moving as they sucked the blood from his body. One wriggled slightly, then shifted position and clamped its mouth to the broken skin tissue that linked its crimson abdomen to a vein.

Appalled and speechless, Thomas stood spellbound for a moment, then took the quilt from Sampson and placed it over Audley's corpse.

'He hated him,' said Sampson finally in a bland, almost dream-like voice.

'Who did?'

'Buckle. He was mad. The method matches the man. T'was he who did it.'

'But he's dead! How could he have killed Audley? And why?'

'He must have come here 'afore he jumped. Don't you understand? Warwick and the Prince of Wales had heard the ballad.

315

Buckle knew that. He despised us, both of us, father an' son. Audley would have been questioned. We might have been pardoned. But not now. Not with Audley dead and those words on the wall. That's why Buckle killed himself. 'Tis he who's the victor, Thomas. Even in death he's won. They'll think we did it.'

'Unless we wash them off and flee 'afore Audley's found.' Thomas snatched the quilt and turned towards the wall.

'We're too late, Thomas. Listen.'

Suddenly Thomas heard footsteps on the stairs and the rattle of swords. Dropping the quilt, he picked up his bow and took aim at the door, waiting until it burst open before firing. He saw a soldier fall backwards into those behind him, then the door slammed shut. Reaching for a second arrow, he heard a voice shout:

'Surround the house! Tell Swayne they're here!'

Thomas glanced round the room. 'The window!' he cried. 'Quickly!'

Sampson remained motionless, eyes fixed on his father. Thomas shouted at him again. His whole body began shaking. Suddenly, in a moment of uncontrolled violence, he picked up a chair and hurled it at the leaded glass, viciously clearing away the splinters with a chair leg before throwing open the shutters. It was a full thirty feet to the ground. 'Tis too far!' he cried.

Thomas pointed to the bed. 'The rope round Audley. Quickly!' Firing an arrow into the door as a deterrent against entry, he waited impatiently whilst Sampson untied the rope that bound his father. 'You go first,' he ordered. Leaving one end fixed to the bed, Sampson tossed the other through the window, climbed on to the ledge and began sliding towards the ground, gritting his teeth against the pain as the rope seared his fingers. Thomas followed, launching himself into the air as the door was flung open behind him and a quarrel sped past his head. Reaching the ground, he shouted: 'Make for the river! 'Tis our only hope!' He turned, sprinted past the stables, through a knot garden, down a bank and dived head first into the Avon. Surfacing, he heard Sampson splash into the water beside him; and then he heard more splashes as the first arrows and quarrels sliced deep into the water. He began swimming, threshing out wildly as the current carried him downstream and out of the line of fire of the pursuing soldiers. The elms and willows overhanging the bank rose round him, exaggerating the gloom. He glanced up at the darkening sky and edged closer to the bank. Ahead he could hear the distant roar of a weir. Feeling the current quicken, he hurriedly swam into the shadows, finally touching bottom in water that lapped his neck. Sampson joined him. They stood rigid for a moment, eyes peering into the gloom.

'They'll post guards 'tween house and bridge,' whispered Thomas.

Sampson nodded, wiping the water from his eyes. They were hidden behind a curtain of willow whose branches trailed heavy with weed in the river. A moorhen drifted by, its chicks line abreast behind it like a string of grubby barges in the tow of a hoy. 'We'll stay here till dark,' he said finally. ''Tis safe enough. They may think we were hit or drowned in the weir.'

'And then?'

'Return to the tavern. But we must leave Sarum tonight. Matilda, Hereward, you and I.' Sampson fell silent as he noticed the flicker of approaching torches. They heard voices:

'They must 'a moved on.'

'Aye, an' some other bugger 'll pocket Swayne's two hundred marks . . .' The two soldiers tramped past their lair, their voices fading.

'So that's what we're worth,' whispered Sampson.

'They'll not claim it though.' Since reaching Sherwood Forest Thomas had felt as if he was living a nightmare, a nightmare that had worsened when Audley recognized them in Glastonbury and had done so again when Sampson lifted the quilt from his father's corpse. But at that same moment it had also ended. For Audley lay dead; not by his hand or Sampson's, but by those of a deranged physician whose few appearances in his life had always redirected its course. To Buckle he owed his first meeting with Sampson, the knowledge that Audley was his father and his own return to Cranborne during the plague. And now, with both Buckle and Audley dead, what change of direction would result? What future lay ahead? He smiled to himself. Though shivering and sodden and neck deep in water, he felt certain of not merely eluding those hunting him tonight, but the hangman as well.

Sampson did not share his confidence. The reality of his father's death had left him shocked and stunned. He could see no reason why Swayne should link Buckle's suicide with Audley's murder. Sampson was a physician, Swayne knew that; the leeches and misquote from the ballad pointed indisputably towards his involvement in the abbot's death. It was a heinous crime, one which no sheriff could ignore or king pardon. He had once thought his father's death would mark a liberation, a new beginning: he now feared otherwise. Feeling trapped and frightened by events beyond his control, he suddenly thought of Matilda waiting anxiously with Hereward in the tavern. He tried to shut them from his mind. But whenever he did so the waxen face of his father filled the void.

The cathedral clock tolled eight, the curfew hour. The two outlaws rose dripping from the river and crept slowly through the darkness, pausing at the first sign of torches and returning to the river to by-pass the guards on the bank. Reaching the Close wall, they slipped across Saint Thomas's Street and hurried homeward through the silent chequers that mapped the city. They twice had to hide from the foot patrols still searching for them and the clock had struck ten before they finally fell through the kitchen door of the tavern.

*   *   *

Midnight, and the argument still unresolved. It had begun on their return and continued unabated when they eventually left the tavern and began moving through the darkness towards the earth ramparts that enclosed the east side of the city. Sampson and Will were its leading protagonists.

'For the last time, Will,' whispered Sampson angrily. 'You an' Ned are to bide in the tavern. 'Tis yours now. Audley meant nothing to you. 'Tis our affair.'

'I'm coming with 'ee,' growled the potter, glancing up at the dim outline of the ramparts.

'You're not! An' that's an end to it.'

'An' who'll take care of Matilda an' the babe if you finish your days on the gallows?'

Matilda reached out and placed a hand on his arm. 'I once promised Sampson that I'd never leave him. If the gallows claim him, then you can help me. But until then Hereward, he an' I belong together. Where one goes, so must the others. I'm not

318

staying, Will. But you must. One day I may need comforting, and it'll be you an' Ned that I'll turn to.'

Hereward was strapped on a blanket bundle on Sampson's back and he could feel the warmth of his breath on his neck. Matilda was kneeling beside him, one hand resting lightly in his. He squeezed it. 'We'll take no risks an' travel only by night. At Poole we'll take ship for Flanders. We've ample money. Exile's better than the noose. Two years hence Audley, us and what we did will have all been forgotten. We'll return, and get word to you as soon as we land.'

As if to end the argument, he stood and turned towards both Will and Ned. 'We must part,' he said softly, 'an' 'tis folly to do so bickering. We've a three day tramp to the coast. Farewell, my friends, and may God keep you.' He shouldered his bow, lifted Matilda to her feet and began climbing the ramparts.

'Hey!' Will gave chase.

Sampson stopped. 'Go back. 'Tis better that we meet as free men than die side by side on the gallows. Now go, an' return to the tavern 'afore the watch find you.' He walked on, Matilda beside him, Thomas in their wake. Reaching the summit, he strode downhill into the vegetable plots that surrounded the city before glancing back. Ned and Will stood high on the ramparts, their cloaks billowing out behind them in the wind. Will moved forward as if to follow them; Ned pulled him back. Sampson smiled contentedly and turned his face to the wind.

CHAPTER TWENTY-TWO

Matilda glanced at her brother and asked him if he could see any sign of the soldiers. Her voice sounded forced. Her fingers played nervously in her hair as she waited for his reply, twisting it into knots that spun loose when she suddenly pressed her knuckles into her eyes, stifling tears.

Thomas scanned the horizon, shading his face with his hat against the glare of the morning sun. 'There's a horseman coming from Sarum way,' he said finally. 'But no soldiers, yet.' Jumping from the roof of the hut, he sat cross-legged on the grass and began fitting new flights to a bundle of arrows.

'Is that all you can think of, more killings?' said Matilda.

Thomas looked up, frowned, and started to comfort her. She turned, glanced briefly at Sampson and Joshuah and walked over to the well. Leaning against its stonework, she stared out over the Chase.

Joshuah watched her. 'She's a brave woman.'

'Yes.' Sampson was cradling Hereward in his arms. He rocked him again, making himself smile as two fat fingers tugged at his beard.

'Hold firm, my friend. If only till you've gone.'

Sampson closed his eyes and bit deep into his lower lip. ''Tis hard, Joshuah. 'Tis a pain unlike any I've known. He paused, burying his face in his son's. 'Why? Why with Audley dead and the band broken do they have to keep hunting us? 'Tis almost as if we were vermin.'

'Calm yourself, lad,' said Joshuah gently. 'What made Swayne realize you'd left Sarum? Were Ned an' Will caught returning to the tavern?'

'No, I don't think so. I'm sure Swayne had no notion where we were till yesterday. We were dressed, as now, as pilgrims. T'was just chance our being recognized and having to fight. And now they're everywhere. At every bridge, cross-roads an' toll-gate. There must be nigh on a thousand men-at-arms questing for the four o' us.'

'Aye, that's right. 'Tis said Fitzwalter's joined Swayne and brought knights and archers loaned by the king,' admitted Joshuah before suggesting they head east towards London.

Sampson shook his head. 'We must reach the sea. 'Tis our only chance.' He could feel his son's eyes staring into his. There was a knowing look to their gaze that made him tremble and falter. He turned towards the hermit. 'You'll take care of them, won't you, Joshuah?'

'I'm an old man, but I'll do what I can. An anchorite's cell is no place for a woman.'

'Matilda's a strong woman, stronger than either Thomas or I. She can fend for herself. 'Tis this one I fear for.' Sampson kissed his son. ''Tis wrong for a babe to spend his first months on God's earth being hunted for the sins of his father.'

'You're no sinner,' chided Joshuah. 'I've lived long enough to know which have strayed from the ways of the Lord and which haven't.'

'But I've done wrong. Yet 'tis Matilda an' the babe who must suffer. We've no choice but to part. They're looking for two men with a woman and child. Without them, Thomas and I may yet reach Flanders.'

'Which way will you go?'

'South.'

'Do you know it?'

'No.'

Joshuah picked up a twig and drew a line through the ashes of his fire. ''Tis nigh thirty miles to the coast. Here's the Stour. The river marks the Chase boundary, after that 'tis marsh an' moor to Wareham. 'Tis a riverside town – small, but with a castle and well-fortified against the Breton pirates who used to sail up the Frome to sack it. Beyond it lies the Isle of Purbeck. 'Tis only an isle in name. For most of it's high, open country like the Chase. In the middle of it, here, is Corfe. Keep your distance. The castle's well garrisoned an' they'll not have forgotten that t'was you an' Thomas who snatched the mint money they'd guarded during the Death. Beyond it lies Swanage and the sea. There'll be fishing smacks a' plenty there, Flemish galliots, cogs heading up Channel with Purbeck marble. Someone 'll take pity on you if you pay 'em enough.'

Sampson examined the map, mentally implanting its picture in his mind. 'We ought to go,' he said finally. 'The longer we delay, the greater the risk.'

'Say farewell to her alone.'

Sampson turned towards Matilda. Her raven hair lapped her shoulders and her face was tilted towards the distant woods. He handed his son to Joshuah and walked towards her. He whispered her name and said: 'We must go.' She lowered her head. ''Tis not the end, Matilda. We're not doomed yet.'

'And nor is an oak when it comes into bud. Look at them now.' She pointed to where the forest straddled the horizon, an immense golden dome whose dying leaves glittered umber and orange as they streamed eastward in the wind.

'To every thing there is a season, and a time to every purpose under the heaven. They'll bud again.'

'Don't quote the Holy Book at me, Sampson; for I know it as well as you. This is the time to weep, to mourn, to pluck up that which is planted.'

'You're wrong. For the seed we planted is the son who suckles you. Would you risk having him torn from your breast by remaining with me when so many are hunting us?' Sampson slid an arm round her waist, drawing her towards him. Her body pressed tight against his; not supple and yielding, but tense, taut, every muscle rigidly under control. Suddenly her eyes flooded with tears and he felt her hair turn damp against his skin.

'You make it sound so final,' she whispered.

'I don't mean to, nor will it be. One day we'll be wed. Until then Joshuah, Will and Ned 'll take care of you. Without Thomas an' I you'll have peace. That's what you always wanted, isn't it?'

Matilda said nothing as he ran her hands over his face. Even with her eyes closed she knew every inch of it: contours, bones, two chipped teeth, the way his hair flopped low over his brow, its ends turning darker where they joined his beard. 'I love you, Sampson. I'd not have changed anything we've done,' she mur-

322

mured.

'Ssh. Don't mourn my going. We'll be back.'

Matilda glanced at the gaunt face of her brother. He sat silent
and pensive, knife flashing as he pared his flights and trimmed
his arrows.

Sampson followed her glance. 'There's few with conscience
enough to do as he. He failed, but the trying will live on. None of
those who heard him speak 'afore we left the Chase will forget
what he said.'

'It was you who saved their lives, who kept them from the
Death.'

'He may have helped them save their souls. Life's short, eternity endless.' Sampson paused, smoothing the hair from her
cheeks. 'We must go. I'll send word to the tavern as soon as we're
safe.' They kissed, clinging on to one another even after their lips
had parted. Sampson lowered his arms; his face set firm, his
manner now brisk and swept clean of emotion.

Thomas rose and embraced his sister. 'I'll take care of him.'

Matilda smiled, hiding her grief. 'Don't let him blame himself
for what's happened. 'Tis the fates. No one's at fault.'

They stood together and watched Sampson as he picked up his
son and lifted him into his arms. Suddenly Matilda turned away
and said: 'Go.' Thomas nodded, gathered up his arrows and
bow, slung his pack over his shoulder and walked over to
Joshuah.

'Will you bless us?'

'Aye.' The four of them knelt in a circle round the fire whilst
the old hermit repeated the Blessing. They said the Lord's
Prayer together, turning the familiar words into a gentle hum
that matched the wind's moan as it trawled through the grass.

Suddenly Sampson and Thomas rose and crossed the track,
waving once before heading southward towards the forest.

Matilda stood and started to follow them. She halted beside
the well, shedding no tears nor ceasing to smile until the distant
trees had finally engulfed them.

CHAPTER TWENTY-THREE

Sampson broke down as he stepped into the forest, only lifting his head from the bole of an oak when he could weep no longer. Thomas sat beside him in the shadows, but said nothing. With the parting from Matilda behind them, only the will to live now mattered, and he knew that no one burdened by tears had a chance of outwitting those trying to track him down. So he waited, alert, clear-headed, as fine an archer as any in the land, his mind focused on the journey ahead.

And as that journey began Sampson's spirits lifted. They were moving through a familiar world, through glades and thickets where they had once set snares and stalked stag. The deep enduring silence of the woods gradually dispelled his sadness. They supped that night on fresh venison. Morning found them refreshed. That day they skirted Cranborne and headed south through stubble and landlocked marsh towards the Stour. They reached the river in late afternoon, first fording it and then making camp on the far bank for the night. They remained there throughout the following day, breaking camp at dusk, setting a course by the stars and hurrying south across windswept scrubland that rolled endless and desolate into the darkness beneath the light of a waning moon. They halted shortly before dawn, exhausted, hungry, their clothes still wet after a sudden squall in the night. They woke to see a long line of mounted men-at-arms and knights advancing towards them through the scrub.

''Tis us they're hunting,' said Thomas, sinking to the gorse.

Sampson turned his head towards the roofs and steeple that rose above the heath behind them. 'Wareham,' he said. 'Once there we'll be safe.' Undoing his pack, he quickly removed the begging-bowl, hand-bell and two wide-brimmed hats that completed their disguise. 'If you're questioned say we're bound for Swanage to take ship for Compostella.'

'Armed with bows an' bundles of arrows?'

'Put the arrows in the pack, unstring the staves and hide them 'neath your cloak. Hurry.'

Whilst Thomas acted on his suggestion, Sampson planned their next move. 'We mustn't be seen here. 'Tis an unlikely place for pilgrims to camp an' they'll not be fooled 'afore searching us.'

They began crawling through the scrub, reaching a narrow bridle-way without being challenged. They crept along its verge, finally straightening when it entered a copse. Leaving cover, they followed the bridle-way past a group of cottages to where it merged with the main highway. Ahead of them, at the far end of a raised causeway, lay Wareham. Surrounded by ramparts and marsh, the town sprawled round a slight rise crowned by a stone keep. After a brief pause the two outlaws walked on to the causeway and joined the few peasants driving their livestock to market. Behind them, the first of the soldiers had reached the highway and started forming into a column. Ahead, porters and sentries stood beside a toll-gate.

'Slow the pace,' murmured Sampson. 'Let 'em pass us. They may distract the guards.'

Thomas nodded and began limping. Hearing hooves, he held out his begging-bowl and cried: 'A mite, friends, for the infirm! 'Tis pilgrim's fare we're wanting,' as the knights in the van suddenly cantered by.

'Devil take 'ee! Out of the way, oaf!' bellowed one of them, hitting out with his whip.

'Gently, gently,' whispered Sampson as Thomas's hand turned into a fist. Grinning sheepishly, he quickly shouted: 'God bless 'ee, sir. He didn't mean no harm,' as the knight suddenly spun in the saddle and gave both of them a supercilious but inquisitorial stare.

Once the last of the men-at-arms had ridden by they shuffled on towards the gate. A few had halted to gossip with the guards. Thomas lowered his hat brim and handed a porter his toll.

'Welcome to Wareham. Where are 'ee bound?'

'Swanage. We travel in the care of the Lord,' replied Thomas, giving the traditional response of pilgrims entering a town.

'Let him be your shepherd.' The porter waved him on. Behind him he heard one of the soldiers say:

'Any sign of 'em?'

'Nay,' growled the porter. 'They ain't been through 'ere 'an that's a fact.'

The soldier laughed. 'You'd best be right. Swayne's in no mood for mistakes. He wants 'em dead. An' soon.'

Forcing himself to remain calm, Thomas limped on and entered the small way-chapel beyond the toll-gate. The handful of pilgrims praying inside it ignored him as he knelt on the flags and waited for Sampson to join him.

'Swayne's here. So's Fitzwalter,' whispered Sampson when he finally did so.

'They seem to know which way we're bound.'

'Swayne's guessing, blocking every highway. He'll have men in every town in the shire. We're safe enough for the moment.'

'We ought to avoid the streets though.'

'There'll be a wayfarer's hospice somewhere in town. We'd best find it and stay there till morning.'

*   *   *

'Where are 'ee bound, friend?'

Sampson lifted his staff towards the early morning haze still shrouding the hills ahead. 'Swanage.'

'Been staying here?'

'Aye, one night. In the Bell Lane Hospice.'

'An' what awaits a pilgrim in Swanage? Surely not Saint Adhelm's Chapel? 'Tis a sailor's chantry.'

'No. I've booked passage for Compostella and the shrine of Saint James.'

Thomas, his pilgrim's disguise replaced by the boiled leather jerkin of an itinerant bow-maker, was standing well back in the line of peasants and pedlars waiting to go through the bridge toll-gate on the south side of the town. But he stood close enough to Sampson to sense that something he had said had aroused the porter's suspicions. He glanced round, carelessly easing his bow from his shoulder and fitting a string to the shaft. To his left, below the bridge, raw clay was being barrowed up a ramp and tipped into the hold of the barge drawn up against the town wharf. The four archers and three pikesmen guarding the bridge were watching a second barge hoist sail and slip its moorings. Their horses were cropping the withered grass at the far end of the bridge, beyond which a causeway, bordered by saltings and marsh, ran level towards the hills. Apprehensive, he edged closer to Sampson as the porter returned with a bluff churlish sergeant. It was the sergeant who spoke:

'So you're bound for Spain, eh?'

'Aye, that's right,' replied Sampson.

The sergeant shook his head. 'You're not, my friend. No ship afloat would sail for Corunna from Swanage. A port must have the king's licence to ship pilgrims. Swanage don't. No pilgrim in Christendom would tramp this way if bound for Compostella.' He drew his sword, turned to the soldiers leaning over the bridge and shouted: 'Arrest this man!'

Too dazed to resist, Sampson stood motionless as the soldiers started running towards him and the sergeant's sword pinned him to the parapet.

Thomas lifted his bow. Keeping it waist high, he angled an arrow through a gap in the crowd. It sped forward: sapling birch, steel tipped, unseen and silent, death for the sergeant. Without waiting to watch him fall, he snatched another arrow from his quiver and pushed through the crowd towards Sampson. A woman screamed. Behind him he heard a trumpet sound the alarm. Now face to face with the guards lining the bridge, he fired again. One grunted, clutched his stomach and slowly collapsed to his knees. A second lunged at him with a pike. He crouched, an arrow gripped in both hands, waiting until the guard was almost on top of him before suddenly side-stepping and plunging the arrows into each of his thighs. At this, his companions dropped their weapons, climbed on to the parapet of the bridge and jumped feet-first into the water below.

'Let's be gone!' cried Thomas, sprinting to the nearest horse and throwing himself into the saddle. A moment later he glimpsed Sampson mount the grey beside him and snatch at its reins. He turned, kicking his own horse into a trot. It whinnied and lowered its head, quickly lengthening stride. Sampson had drawn level with him before it reached the gallop. He glanced back. The first knights had broken through the crowd and crested the bridge. The chase had begun.

At the far end of the causeway the track divided. Without

pausing to rein-in Thomas took the right hand fork. Cottages
sped by, a kelp laden cart, children, a summoner on a palfrey, a
ploughman leading his oxen into the fields; and then only the
fields themselves were left to flash by as they galloped on toward
the hills ahead. Thomas rose in the saddle and leant low over the
mane of his horse. It picked up speed, hooves biting deep into
the loose sand that rutted the track. He looked back again. The
gap between themselves and the heavily armoured knights had
increased. 'Where are we bound?' he cried.

'God knows,' bellowed Sampson. 'We might be able to shake
'em off in the hills. 'Tis about an hour to the sea . . .'

'Swayne'll send for more men and cut off the isle from the rest
of the shire.'

'We'll find a boat. Steal an' sail it ourselves if we have to . . .'

Gradually the fields gave way to the open heath that merged
with the foot-hills. The haze dispersed, revealing rounded
clouds that sailed cream over the tops of the hills and duplicated
themselves as shadows on the slopes below. A buzzard hung lifeless against the sky. The track beneath it twisted and turned as it
cut an upward route between the purple of heather and the white
humps of grazing sheep. The outlaws slowed the pace as they
began the climb. Below them they could see the knights fan out
into a line. Further back they glimpsed dust rising round a
column of mounted archers. The track steepened. Dismounting, they hurriedly led their horses across the turf towards the
ridge ahead, scattering the sheep as they went. Reaching its
summit they paused to draw breath. In front of them the ground
dropped steeply into a narrow valley that lay parallel to the hills
and then sloped upwards again. Beyond it, a boundless waste
that sparkled in the sunlight, lay the sea.

Slumped against their horses, they both gazed out to where
white crested waves rolled one into the next as wind and tide
drove them up-Channel. 'I once vowed I'd never put to sea
again,' growled Thomas finally.

Sampson smiled grimly. 'You may not have to. For though
we're caught 'twixt the Devil an' the deep blue brine we've one
advantage – height.

Thomas tossed him a bow and broke open another bundle of
arrows. They turned and crawled back to the summit of the
ridge. The archers had dismounted, continuing the advance on

328

foot. Thomas fired a single arrow high over their heads, correcting the range and angle of fire with successive shots until certain of straddling the line. Two men fell before the knight leading the assault realized his blunder and ordered the retreat. The archers divided; some staying where they were, the remainder spreading out and extending the length of the line until it stretched across the hill.

'Swayne intends encircling us,' explained Sampson. 'He'll send men round to our rear and hold firm until we run out of arrows.' As he spoke a detachment of knights wheeled west and cantered out of sight.

Thomas lowered his bow. 'We'll next see 'em in the vale behind us.' Suddenly aware how exhausted he was, he sighed and added: ''Tis a grave prospect. As bleak as any we've faced.'

Sampson's face clouded with despair. 'We're trapped,' he whispered. 'Thank God Matilda and Hereward are safe.'

Thomas frowned. Sampson's mood was changing. The will to live had left him, his head had bowed, his shoulders slumped. Sensing that he had all but admitted defeat to himself, Thomas turned, mounted his horse and began the descent into the valley. Glancing back, he saw Sampson lean against the saddle of his grey. His hands were trembling, his cheeks glistened with tears.

Reaching the valley, they headed east along its base. The sun vanished behind cloud. The sky darkened and the wind grew chill with the threat of rain. Thomas became uneasy: their bows would be useless if wet. Riding through a hamlet whose occupants offered no wave of greeting, he began to feel that they had strayed into a world that would not hinder their passage, but would not shelter or assist them either. The horses tired and they were forced to halt in the lee of a sheep pen.

The halt was to be brief. Peering over the wall, he suddenly saw a troop of archers riding towards them. Hearing shouts, he turned: the first of the knights had rounded the hill. Momentarily panic-stricken, he stared at them open-mouthed before mounting his horse and ordering Sampson to follow. They were spotted leaving the pen. A horn sounded, the archers quickened pace as they galloped up a rough track that climbed the southern flank of the valley. Their lead had shortened by the time they reached its crest. Below them, beyond the cottages nestling against the hill-side, lay a curved bay backed by shale cliffs which rose high and sheer at either end.

'They'll be boats on the beach!' cried Thomas as they sped past the cottages. 'We'll take one, fire the sails of the rest.' They reined-in at the edge of the cliff as the leading archers swept over the sky-line behind them. Thomas scanned the shingle. The tide was low. Flat tables of black rock ran level to where the breakers crashed against them. Gulls skimmed the cliff-face, others stood perched on the roof of a fisherman's hovel built above the tide-line. The line of nets stretched over racks outside it lifted as a sudden gust of wind squalled across the bay.

'We'll leave the horses here!' shrieked Sampson. 'Take the biggest of the boats!'

Thomas turned towards him, face pale, his eyes drawn. 'We won't,' he whispered. 'There are none to take.'

'There must be!' Sampson fell silent as he stared at the deserted beach. ''Tis all over, isn't it?' he murmured, suddenly glimpsing the nets and seeing in their mesh the image of his own trapped and entangled body.

Thomas gripped his arms and began shaking him. 'No, Sampson. 'Tis only now it's begun. We'll try an' hold 'em off till nightfall, then double back under cover of dark.'

'To what purpose? We're as good as dead.'

'You may be. I'm not. And I intend fighting.' Without waiting for a reply, Thomas rode along the rim of the cliff to where it soared high over the bay, finally turning his horse loose and completing the climb on foot. Looking back, he smiled as he watched Sampson plod uphill behind him surrounded by gulls that rose from the ledges along the cliff in flocks so vast it seemed as if part of the cliff-face was peeling away.

Their eyes met. Sampson shrugged and said: 'We're doomed, Thomas. But 'tis better that we die together.'

Thomas grinned and knelt behind the low dry-stone wall that ran along the edge of the cliff. 'We'll fight from here.' He gazed round, planning their defence. A wide bridle-path separated them from the cliff. Beyond the wall the land sloped gently downhill to where the archers had halted just out of range and formed a half-circle that made escape impossible. The knights had joined them, a second column of archers had reached the cottages.

'How many arrows have you left?' he asked.

'A score, no more.'

'We must make each of 'em count.' Thomas paused. He could feel the worn shaft of his bow resting warm and light in his hands. He held it up. 'Since first lifting it,' he said, 'I've lived my life by the bow. I've mastered it, used it to kill my foes an' fill my belly. 'Tis right that I should die by it an' not the rope.'

Sampson lay his head against the wall. 'Just you an' I,' he murmured. 'Sea on one side, those hunting us on the other. Strange how blind we can be. It needed no seer to warn us it might end like this. Yet I never believed it would happen. Not to us. When we left Matilda I felt certain we'd meet again, be wed...' Though speaking aloud, he was talking to himself; seeking to justify and explain.

'You've loved an' been loved,' said Thomas gently. ''Tis worth the dying to have known that.' He glanced over the wall. Suddenly a quick, cold shiver pulsed the length of his spine. 'They're coming.'

He watched in silence as the line of archers stepped within range and raised their bows. A lance lifted, dipped. The sky filled with the greyness of arrows and the soft purr of their flight. He ducked, pressing his face to the wall as the noise grew louder and the first of the arrows clattered against its stones and slapped into the turf behind him. He looked at them, unsure whether he wanted to prolong what lay ahead. 'So we're to be fed fuel,' he said finally, plucking the nearest from the grass and rising to his feet. He fired, missed, fired again. But though his third shot struck its target the gap in the line was soon filled.

As it began, so it went on. The archers would fire, the outlaws duck behind the wall then quickly stand and retaliate as best they could. The surrounding turf was soon pin-pricked with arrows. By mid-afternoon hunger and fatigue had begun to take their toll. Thomas's arms grew leaden and heavy. Sampson found himself struggling to retain concentration. Every now and then it slipped, momentarily stranding him in a margin of consciousness where all was remote, irrational, the stuff of dreams. Towards dusk an attempt was made to overrun them, and though they beat it off they were unable to prevent Swayne and a squadron of knights reaching the cliff path. But the sheriff's casualties were immense. The side of the hill was strewn with the dead and wounded. Listening to their cries, Sampson gradually realized that they were turning from a dull echo inside his head into a protracted and hideous scream that could still be heard when he clamped his hands to his ears. Suddenly something snapped inside him and he knew he could listen no longer. He turned to Thomas.

'Let's throw down our arms!' he cried.

Thomas looked at him in disbelief. 'They'll hang us, Sampson. 'Tis kill or be killed.'

'Swayne won't go! We'll leave here dead or not leave at all.'

'It'll soon be dark.'

Sampson closed his eyes. 'I'm tired, Thomas. Tired of running an' hiding an' trying to convince myself that the Lord's on our side wherever we go and whatever we do.'

'No! We fight!'

'In which case you must do so alone.'

Sampson dropped his bow and climbed on to the wall, both arms raised above his head. An instant later he cried out and toppled backwards, an arrow hanging from his shoulder.

Thomas stared down at him. 'You fool!' he shouted. ''Tis a miracle you're not a corpse. We're outlaws. They'll show us no pity. Dead or alive it doesn't matter . . .'

'Watch out!'

Thomas spun. Swayne was charging towards him at full gallop. He lifted his bow, hurriedly fumbling for an arrow as the sheriff levelled his lance. He fired. Swayne's charger faltered, whinnied, collapsed to its knees and began sliding towards him with its legs splayed out on either side of its belly. As it came to a standstill, Swayne rolled from the saddle and struggled to his feet. He drew his sword. Thomas lifted his bow again, taking aim at the unprotected face advancing towards him. Suddenly, as if from nowhere, he saw Sampson stagger into his line of fire and deliberately block his aim. 'Move!' he cried.

'No!' screamed Sampson. 'He's a good man. There'll be no more killings!'

Thomas side-stepped, only turning when he heard someone clamber over the wall behind him. But it was too late. His bow was torn from his grasp. Within seconds a line of pikes had pinned him to the wall. Ignoring the soldiers, he turned to where Sampson lay clutching his shoulder. 'Why?' he whispered.

'I had to, Thomas. We've spilled enough blood you an' I.'

Sampson closed his eyes, only opening them when he felt a sword at his throat. Swayne was standing above him.

'You saved my life, master physician,' he said gently. 'I won't spare yours. You know that, don't you?'

'Yes.'

'Kill us now an' be done with it!' shouted Thomas as his arms were pinnioned behind his back and bound with rope.

Swayne smiled at him. 'As you would have done to me? No, you'll not cheat the hangman. 'Tis the gallows for you. Take 'em away! Both of them!'

CHAPTER TWENTY-FOUR

'T'would be wrong of me to promise salvation, only the Heavenly Father can do that. You have erred and strayed from His ways and must wait on His judgement.' The priest paused and looked again at each of the outlaws before making the sign of the cross. 'Christ's words to Martha after her brother's death may comfort you when . . .' He stopped; embarrassed, ill-at-ease, uncertain how to say it.

Sampson glanced up at him, smiling. '. . . they lower the rope round our necks?'

'Yes. Then.' The priest took shelter behind his cowl and rapped on the door. It opened. He turned and vanished and it slammed behind him again. An abrupt, harsh echo exploded the silence. A key turned.

Thomas listened to the flap of his sandals as they receded along the passage linking the cells. As one noise faded, others were born: the hammering, the rasp of a saw, a carpenter bellowing at his apprentices. He turned to Sampson.

'What did our Lord say to Martha?'

Sampson sat hunched on the flags, his head lolling against the damp stone wall behind him. 'He that believeth in me, though he were dead, yet shall he live.'

Thomas nodded, completing the verse. 'And whosoever liveth and believeth in me shall never die. Father taught me that when I was a child.' A half-smile played briefly on his lips. 'Strange, isn't it? I've waited so long for this moment that I'm no longer afraid of it.' He ran his hands down the grey full-length gown issued to the condemned. They were sticky, wet with sweat. 'I wonder who else has worn these?' On the wall above

Sampson previous occupants of the cell had scratched messages and fragments of prayer. The hammering ceased. His mouth grew dry. ''Tis done,' he muttered. Some of the messages were obscene, others blasphemous, but most were pleas for forgiveness: 'Forgive us our trespasses', 'Lord have mercy', 'John's son, found guilty of sheep theft on Ascension Eve, the Year of Our Lord, 1322, do beseech his Saviour's pardon'. A name, a date, that final walk to the Wareham gallows . . .

He crossed the cell and peered through the slit window, clamping a hand round its single bar. The gallows had been built in the centre of the market place beside a solitary yew tree. Dense, crimson with berries, it towered bulbously upward, dwarfing the two pairs of timber posts that stood side by side in its shadow. The cross-pieces had been nailed into place, the two carts drawn up beneath them. Suddenly he saw a thick-set figure with a shaven head and docked beard toss a coil of rope over one of the cross-pieces and thread one end through a slip-knot. He pulled it tight, tied a second knot and began shaping a noose with his fingers. Thomas let go of the bar and pressed his brow to the window ledge. Behind him he heard Sampson adjust the bandage round his shoulder.

'The hangman's begun his work,' he said emptily. 'Does it hurt?'

'No. T'was only a flesh wound.'

'It seemed odd being given cloth to patch a wound that'll never have time to mend.'

Sampson looked up at Thomas. 'What I did on the cliffs was done for both of us. Not for now, but later. Do you understand that?'

'T'was two days ago. In an hour none of it will matter.'

'One hour. That's all that's left us.' Sampson sighed. 'I'd give much to see Matilda and Hereward again. Just once. Alone.'

'You may yet. Didn't our jailer tell us that folk are flocking from all over the shire to watch us die?' Thomas turned to the window. Though it was still early morning, the twilight hour between dawn and sunrise, a small crowd had begun to encircle the gallows. He forced a thin smile. 'Let 'em come,' he murmured. 'I'm frightened,' he said suddenly. 'Last night, lying awake in the straw, I tried to remember how it was when I was a child, where I went wrong. Yet it seemed that the fates had

335

guided me, led me by the arm like a lover his lass. If I was to begin life again it would happen as it has. I'd be here, now, Thomas Woodward, outlaw, waiting to be hung.'

'It'll be quick.'

'No, 'tis not that which scares me. 'Tis what comes after, when we're dead.'

'Don't be.' Sampson rose and joined Thomas by the window.

' 'Tis hard not to.' As he watched, Thomas saw a line of soldiers march through the crowd and surround the gallows. ' 'Tis time.'

Suddenly the door creaked open behind them. It was Swayne. He stood there for a moment, nervously slapping his gauntlets together before entering the cell.

'Are you ready?' he said.

Sampson lifted his hands. 'What man is?'

'Aye, we both must have found that out in Sarum during the plague.' Swayne paused, a sad and distant look on his face. Then he added: 'I've spoken to the king.'

'And . . .?' Sampson moved towards him, eyes bright with hope.

Swayne turned away. 'He didn't believe a word of what you told me to tell him. The notion that Abbot Roger was your father and murdered by Buckle was, he said, a fiction, even a tale worthy of turning into a ballad, but not a true account of your lives.'

'So there's to be no stay of sentence?'

'No, I'm sorry . . . But because you saved my life he agreed to revoke the order that you both be drawn and quartered. It'll be a hanging, no more.' The sheriff crossed to the window. 'The crowd is growing. I've had to call in more men to keep them back. My own bodyguard has been jeered at and pelted with dung. Death may make you martyrs.'

Thomas stared at the two ropes hanging from the gallows. 'Better a living dog than a dead lion.'

Swayne turned. 'We must go. The time is near.'

As the two outlaws embraced each felt the other's heart beating against his own. They drew apart.

'Farewell, my friend,' whispered Thomas.

Sampson smiled. ' 'Tis no farewell. We'll meet again 'afore long.'

'But where?'

'We'll know soon enough. Come . . .'

Sampson walked calmly through the door. A squad of soldiers took up position on either side of him. Thomas looked round their cell for a moment, then followed him along the passage and out into the market place.

As they emerged into the square fists were raised amongst the crowd. Someone started heckling the soldiers. Others joined in his taunts as the two outlaws were led towards the gallows. The noise grew steadily louder when Thomas climbed on to one of the carts and stood, head raised, beside the rope.

'Up you go,' growled the sergeant behind Sampson.

Sampson lifted himself on to the neighbouring cart and walked across its boards to where the noose hung dangling from the cross-piece above his head. He turned and glanced at Thomas, now curiously anxious and concerned as he stared into the crowd. Sampson followed his gaze. Suddenly the blood left his face and his legs buckled beneath him. 'Matilda!' he whispered hoarsely. Hereward in her arms, she was standing beside Joshuah towards the front of the crowd with her face frozen into an expressionless mask and her eyes fixed on his.

Sampson trembled, then straightened. For a moment he stood suspended on the brink of tears, the grief that filled his thoughts. He took an involuntary pace towards her, then halted. He forced himself to lift his gaze, knowing that if he stared at her too long there was a chance she might be recognized and arrested. Away to the south a thick mist pressed gently against the windswept marshes beyond the town, veiling their greenness with a glaze of grey. The sun had not yet risen above the distant hills and the morning air was keen and sharp in his throat. The noise of the crowd became amplified in his ears, gradually evolving into a curious silence that left him detached from what was going on round him, disembodied from the nearness of his own death. As if through a haze he felt his arms being roped behind his back, the roughness of the noose as it was lowered over his head, the squeak of the knot as it was pulled tight against the side of his jaw. Suddenly the cart jerked beneath him. For a split second he thought death had come. And then he swallowed, gulping air as he realized that a horse had been reversed on to the cart and hitched to the shafts. He could hear a priest intoning the penitential psalms, feel the onion breath of the hangman against his cheeks as he asked him if he wanted the hood. He shook his head, glancing at Thomas when he also declined it. The hangman turned and nodded at Swayne, now mounted and surrounded by his retinue on the rim of the crowd. The sheriff slowly eased a gauntlet from his fingers and lifted an arm. Sampson felt the blood begin pumping into his head, his muscles slacken, his body turn cold. Thomas turned towards him; teeth chattering, every sinew in his face taut and tight against the skin. Sampson switched his gaze to Matilda. The crowd's jeers grew louder. A stone struck one of the soldiers standing in front of the cart. She tried to smile. The hands of the son he would never see again nor watch grow to manhood were buried in the black of her hair. His head started reeling. The noise grew distant, a muffled boom of sound. A sudden dazzle of light made him close his eyes . . .

'Now . . . !'

He snapped them open again. Swayne's hand had dropped. Suddenly he saw Matilda smile. She side-stepped. Ned stood behind her, the bow in his hand aimed straight at the horse hitched to the cart. He scanned the crowd, eyes widening in disbelief as he watched bows being lifted and the familiar faces of the outlaw band emerging from beneath their hoods. Then all was confusion and blur as he heard women scream, Swayne bellow orders and the panic-stricken cries of the soldiers as that first volley of arrows slammed into their ranks. In those few seconds the whole of his life passed through his thoughts. Forgotten memories surfaced again, bearing him back to childhood and a small grubby boy with scarred knees and pockets laden with conkers whose days were spent angling for trout in the shadowy backwaters of the Avon. And then he heard Will's voice beside him and felt a knife slash at the noose and the rope binding his arms. The blood ran warm to his fingers as he was helped from the cart and led to a waiting horse. He climbed into the saddle and moved forward, forcing his way through the crowd. Behind him he heard Ned, Will and the remaining outlaws take to their horses. Houses, faces, an open toll-gate flashed by. Trees rose above him. Suddenly he glimpsed both Thomas and Matilda riding alongside him.

'Where are we bound?' he shouted.

338

Matilda began laughing. 'Home to the Chase!'

'When?' he cried as the outlaw band closed up round him and the tears streaked wet against his cheeks.

'Now . . . !'

A sudden movement he could neither recognize nor comprehend made him raise his head. Sunlight blazed gold inside it. It rose further, lifting his eyes to where clouds coursed the sky, borne by a wavering wind.